"What happened?" Ray asked, turning to Buck and Hobnob.

"Saw men loading a girl into a boxcar," Hobnob explained. "Didn't get a close look, but she must be your siren. And that train. I've seen it once before, and heard rumors aplenty about it. They call it *The Pitch Dark Train*."

"Is it—?" Ray began.

"Yes," Buck growled. "The Gog."

Terror struck at Ray's heart. "We're going after her, right?"

The Clockwork Dark

The Nine Pound Hammer
The Wolf Tree
The White City

To Emily
& Ashley

Keep reading
& using
your imaginations!

THE CLOCKWORK DARK

—THE—
NINE POUND HAMMER

—JOHN—
CLAUDE BEMIS

A YEARLING BOOK

Text copyright © 2009 by John Claude Bemis
Cover art copyright © 2009 by Alexander Jansson

All rights reserved. Published in the United States by Yearling, an imprint of Random House Children's Books, a division of Penguin Random House LLC, New York. Originally published in hardcover in the United States by Random House Children's Books, New York, in 2009.

Yearling and the jumping horse design are registered trademarks of Penguin Random House LLC.

Visit us on the Web!
randomhousekids.com

Educators and librarians, for a variety of teaching tools, visit us at
RHTeachersLibrarians.com

The Library of Congress has cataloged the hardcover edition of this work as follows:
Bemis, John Claude.
The nine pound hammer / John Claude Bemis. — 1st ed.
p. cm.—(Clockwork dark ; bk. 1)
Summary: Drawn by the lodestone his father gave him years before,
twelve-year-old orphan Ray travels south, meeting along the way various characters
from folklore who are battling against an evil industry baron known as the Gog.
ISBN 978-0-375-85564-1 (trade) — ISBN 978-0-375-95564-8 (lib. bdg.) —
ISBN 978-0-375-85386-9 (ebook)
[1. Fantasy—Fiction.   2. Orphans—Fiction.
3. Brothers and sisters—Fiction.   4. Folklore—Fiction.]   I. Title.
PZ7.B4237Nin 2009   [Fic]—dc22   2008022503

ISBN 978-0-375-85565-8 (pbk.)

Printed in the United States of America

14 13 12 11 10 9 8 7 6 5

For Amy—my love, my lodestone

CONTENTS

—THE—
NINE
POUND
HAMMER

HE WAS BEING HUNTED.

The man sank to his knees in black water. The night air pulsed with the reverberations of a multitude of insects, punctuated by bullfrog croaks and the occasional splash of something leaving the muddy banks for the safety of the swamp water.

Before him, two others struggled through the marsh.

"Go!" he cried. Dragging his legs through the muck, he pulled himself up on cypress knees to the slippery embankment. Free of the mire, he ran. The palmettos and spiny bracken tore his trousers as he ripped away low-hanging limbs and spirals of Spanish moss.

Some distance behind, a hound bayed.

The other two stopped before a large pond. One was a girl with wide eyes as fierce as lightning flashes. Scratches crisscrossed her pale arms, and a gash on her cheek bled freely. Her lips trembled. By her side stood a man with long dark hair streaked with silver; it fell about his face and covered his eyes. He held the girl's arm with one hand.

In the other he held a sparkling silver pistol.

The girl pulled toward the pond.

"No," the gunman said. "We need another way."

"But . . . the hound!" she cried.

As if in answer, a roar erupted from the dark, shaking the trees around them and silencing the buzzing chorus of insects and frogs. An icy breeze pushed back their hair as their damp clothes grew crisp.

"Go around," the first man said. "Follow the pond's edge to the north and there's a crossing."

The gunman nodded and urged the girl forward. As the two disappeared into the brush, another roar tore through the trees, felling limbs and flattening shrubs. The moisture in the marshy earth froze, pushing to the surface in splinters of ice. At his back, the man heard the cracking of ice forming at the edge of the pond. He removed his straw hat and dropped it to the ground.

With a snort of cold air, an enormous muzzle broke through the trees. Slowly the hound stepped out. More massive than a bull, it was seven feet at the shoulder. Its jaws were huge. Each tooth was as long as a hunting knife. Its dark metallic eyes were set deep into bone-white fur, tufted and spiked with frost. The groaning and whining of gears churned from beneath its flesh.

The man faced the monstrous hound as it snarled and leaped forward.

Ray jerked awake. The voices of the other orphans chirped over the rattle of the train. He was in the passenger car, Mister Grevol's exquisite passenger car, with his sister, Sally, napping at his side.

Ray settled back onto the soft velvet bench and opened his hand. On his sweaty palm lay the lodestone. He hadn't meant to nod off with it in his hand. He knew better.

Pushing the lodestone into his pocket, Ray craned his neck to scan the passenger car for Miss Corey. She was still not back.

Miss Corey had given the orphans an extensive list of rules, instructions, and threats the morning before Ray and Sally and the other seventeen children boarded the beautiful, dark train with its powerful ten-wheeler locomotive:

"Mister G. Octavius Grevol is a highly respected industrialist," Miss Corey had warbled. "He has generously allowed us passage on his personal train. I expect you"— she had looked directly at Ray, who at twelve was the oldest of the orphans—"to be well-behaved, well-mannered, and to remain at all times in the passenger car designated for our use."

But Ray had never been very good at listening to rules, instructions, or threats. He had decisions to make and needed someplace quiet to think. As he stood, he glanced down at Sally. With her hands pillowing her dirty cheek on the upholstered bench and her tattered boots kicked up against the lacquered black paneling, Sally—all the orphans, really—looked out of place in Mister Grevol's princely train.

Ray started down the aisle toward the back of the passenger car. He stumbled a moment with the sway of the train but steadied himself against the back of the next bench before continuing. Some of the orphans were taking naps, but most were talking boisterously or playing with jackstraws or corn-husk dolls on the ornately quilted seats. They were excited, and they had good reason. They were traveling on a marvelous train away from the horrible city. Soon they would reach the South, where Miss Corey had arranged for them to be adopted. Wishing he could share their enthusiasm, Ray reached for the vestibule door's polished brass handle.

As he stepped out onto the vestibule, a coal-smoke wind met him, accompanied by the noisy clatter of the train's wheels. He quickly shut the door. Finally, he was alone.

The vestibule was a short open-air passage between the train cars. Ray settled his elbows on the railing and looked out at the green and gold fields speckled with clusters of trees and white clapboard farmhouses. The wind batted his brown curls across his brow. Ray pushed them back as he took the lodestone from his pocket.

The lodestone began moving at once, tugging against

his grip. Ray clutched it tighter and wondered, as he had again and again over the last month: What was it pulling toward and why did it keep showing him the monstrous hound?

His father had given him the dark stone eight years ago—before Sally was born, before his father had left. Ray had only been four at the time, but he still remembered it vividly.

"I'm heading down south for a job of work, Ray," his father had said that morning on the banks of Lake Wesserunsett in rural Maine. His father had grown up in the Blue Ridge Mountains of eastern Tennessee, and his words sometimes sounded funny compared to the way New Englanders spoke. "Might be a spell before I'm back."

Then his father had taken out the flannel pouch he always carried in his pocket. He opened the drawstring and slowly removed a rock.

"What is it?" Ray asked.

"That's a lodestone," his father said, placing the stone in Ray's hand. "They're magnetic. Folks use them to make compasses. But this ain't no ordinary lodestone. I want you to keep it safe while I'm gone. It'll guide you when you have a need." Then he added with his lopsided smile, "It'll help me get back home, too."

But it hadn't. Ray's father had never returned. Eight years had passed. Eight terrible years.

Ray looked down at his hand, feeling the lodestone pressing against his fingers as if the little stone was struggling to escape.

The door to the next car opened. Ray jumped and backed against the far side of the vestibule. Miss Corey would be furious!

Out stepped a tall, elegantly dressed gentleman. He held a gloved hand to support his silk stovepipe hat against the wind. With his fine striped suit of black and reptilian green and a curling silver mustache sprouting from his angular face, Ray had no doubt who this gentleman was: Mister G. Octavius Grevol.

This was worse than Miss Corey! Miss Corey might take a belt to Ray's leg, but this man could have him thrown off the train.

Mister Grevol gave a slight "a-hum." Ray took his woolen apple cap from his pocket and adjusted it tightly over his brow as he headed toward the door.

Mister Grevol clanked his ebony walking stick against the metal floor. "What do you think of my train?" he asked. His voice was smooth and refined like the purring of a cat, or possibly more like a lion, as there was an undertone of strength in that soft growl.

"It's okay. I never cared much for trains," Ray lied, hoping to put off the gentleman without causing offense.

Mister Grevol smirked and removed his stovepipe hat. He propped his gloved hands together on the silver cap of his walking stick, letting his gaze settle on the ribbon of black smoke that was drifting off from the locomotive into the clear summer sky.

Ray eyed the gold chain dangling between Mister Grevol's vest pockets. If Ray had encountered this gentleman a few months earlier on the streets of Manhattan, he might have excused himself, squeezed past the gentleman with a polite apology, and walked away with the gentleman's gold watch. But this was not Manhattan. And he no longer needed to steal in order to keep Sally warm and fed.

"See, my parents were killed by a train," Ray told Mister Grevol. He flicked his eyes toward the towering gentleman. A curious expression showed in Mister Grevol's crooked black eyebrows.

"How terrible," Mister Grevol replied, his eyes wandering to the lodestone in Ray's hand, then following the several feet of twine attaching it to Ray's belt. "Growing up alone can be a challenging prospect. Dangerous, I'm certain. But a boy like you is full of resources. I deduced right away that you are clever and, might I add, daring. I bet you've done all manner of doughty deeds. For example, may I ask, have you ever jumped from a moving train?"

Ray frowned. He had tried to rattle the old gentleman with his lie about how he had become an orphan, and now Mister Grevol was turning the trick on him.

"Lots of times, dozens of times," Ray answered, which was in fact true. "Back in the city, I could get on a moving train and off again better than any of the other kids. They called me Spark 'cause I could jump on and off trains and streetcars like a spark jumps from flint."

Mister Grevol chuckled. "Isn't that impressive!" He brushed at his sleeves with his black leather gloves. "And refreshing."

"Refreshing?" Puzzlement flickered on Ray's brow.

"Your honesty," Mister Grevol said. "At last."

Ray felt like a deflated balloon. Somehow Mister Grevol had seen through his lies. "I'm sorry. I didn't mean to . . . I know I shouldn't have left the passenger car. . . ."

Mister Grevol cocked his head, narrowing his black eyes.

Ray looked down, running his thumb across the knot in the twine that was wrapped over and over the lodestone's surface. "I just needed a place to think, and I thought I could come out here and—"

"And then I so rudely interrupted you." Before Ray could argue, Mister Grevol shook his head in polite disagreement. "No, I did. What's worrying you, if I may ask?"

"It's my sister," Ray said. "We've had such a hard life, you see? And now we're supposed to get adopted . . . by someone. A nice farm family, I'm sure. But families almost adopted us lots of times in the city, and they always changed their minds. Because of me . . . I'm just too old, I guess. I'm not so sure if she's to get a good family that I should stay with her." Ray gave a deep sigh, feeling the tightness in his throat.

Mister Grevol nodded sympathetically. "You're a considerate and wise young man. And you're right to be concerned for your sister. But I'm wondering about you. I'm wondering what *you* will do."

"What do you mean?" Ray asked.

Mister Grevol brought his hand to his cravat. "Look at me. I've built a career in locomotives and engineering. And how? By disdaining the easy, comfortable life. I've avoided attachments, do you see?"

Ray began to mumble, but Mister Grevol pointed a finger at him and continued. "Attachments are vicious betrayers. They lead to all sorts of unsettling feelings: jealousy, loneliness, dependence, the need for acceptance. The sooner you unchain yourself from others, the sooner you'll find your true strength. And the sooner you do that, the sooner you'll find your true destiny."

He looked down at Ray, drawing his eyes across him and then the lodestone, before a smile returned to his wide mouth. "You most clearly have street smarts, as they like to say. You have gumption. Let me ask you: Is this train really going to bring you to your destiny? Are you going to leave your fate to"—Mister Grevol waved his hand toward the car with the orphans—"that Corey woman?" He shook his head and lowered his voice. "No. Find your own way in this world."

The door from the next car opened, and a man wearing a dark, plain-cut suit and a round bowler hat leaned out. He grinned sourly at Ray, flashing a gold tooth, before turning to Mister Grevol. "Excuse me, sir. Mister Horne wanted to see you."

"Thank you, Mister McDevitt." Grevol looked back at Ray. "I've enjoyed meeting you . . ." He paused, gesturing with his walking stick.

"Oh! Uh, Ray. Ray Fleming," he said.

"Yes, Ray Fleming." Mister Grevol tipped his head at Ray before following the man with the gold tooth.

Ray watched them depart through the coupe door, wondered if the gentleman had realized that Ray had once again lied when he gave his last name.

The lie about his last name had come too quickly for Ray to stop. He had been Ray Fleming for so long now, it had become habit.

After his father left—the same year Sally was born—his mother had insisted they no longer use their last name, Cobb, and began moving them from city to city. She would never explain why. Ray kept expecting his father to return, but the years passed and he never did.

While the lodestone hadn't helped his father return, it had helped Ray and Sally. Even before their mother had died of scarlet fever, the lodestone had begun giving Ray dreams—sometimes of a cascading waterfall or a campfire crackling—but the dreams were more vivid than ordinary dreams. Others were fantastical. A man leaping from a high bluff, only to become a great hawk, then flash and disappear. A moonlit beach where silver-skinned women rose from the surf.

The dreams were interesting, but they weren't what helped Ray and Sally. After their mother died and the two were forced to live in the squalor of lower Manhattan, Ray did what he had to to take care of Sally. Sometimes he stole food or people's purses, whichever was easier.

But more often the lodestone would help. Ray would feel a sudden shudder from his pocket. He would take out the lodestone and follow the jerking movements until it led him to a dropped coin or a forgotten bag of apples in the back of a livery or a bunch of old boxes in an alley they could use for shelter.

Then a month ago, just after Sally had met Miss Corey and convinced Ray to move into the orphanage, the lodestone began pulling urgently to the south. Ray had snuck out from St. Anthony's Home to see what it was pulling toward. It always led him to the southern end of Manhattan Island. Wherever it was leading Ray was much farther south.

The nightmare had begun at the same time. The terrible vision of the hound pursuing him—although Ray somehow knew it wasn't him—through the swamp.

Ray had always wondered if his father had known what the lodestone could do. Had he meant it to help Ray? Were the dreams showing him something his father had wanted Ray to know?

Ray looked back through the window into the passenger car. Sally was peering up and down the aisle, looking for him. He put the lodestone back in his pocket and reached for the door.

Sally was stringing a cat's cradle when Ray returned to the seat beside her.

"Miss Corey said we're not supposed to leave the car," she said, spreading her small fingers wide as Ray moved the string through the tangled design.

"Just stepped out for some air."

She frowned at him. "Something's bothering you."

Ray continued threading the cat's cradle with her. "No, there's not."

She slipped her hands from the web of string and pressed her finger against his furrowed brow.

Ray laughed. "What would I be fretting about?" He pushed her finger away. "You're going to get a wonderful family, just like you've always wanted."

"*We're* going to get a wonderful family," Sally corrected. She untangled the grimy muslin dress from her knees before nestling herself into Ray's arms. "Our family will take care of us and we'll be together, just like you promised. So stop fretting and read me some of my book."

Ray picked up the small, blue-linen-bound book from the seat and opened it.

"Ray," Sally asked, her head leaning against his

shoulder, "do you think our new family will mind if we read Papa's book?"

"No," Ray said, opening *The Incunabula of Wandering* to a chapter on rabbit warrens. "I'm sure they won't."

Their mother had never liked them reading the *Incunabula,* though Ray had not known why. His father had scribbled notes in the margins, covering any blank space. Ray had tried over the years to understand the book, to learn something more about his father from the notes. But he could barely decipher his father's cursive script, and the bits he could read were too bizarre to gather their meaning. He wasn't even sure what the book was about; it seemed to be composed of random and unrelated chapters. It was full of poems and articles on animals, wild herbs, topography, and more complicated subjects.

It wasn't just the book that had caused their mother to act secretive. She had never wanted to discuss anything to do with their father. After eight years, after all they had gone through, Ray had to assume that his father was dead. Why else wouldn't he have come back?

But what had happened to him?

In the night, the only sounds on the train were the rumbling of the metal wheels on the track and the soft breathing of the children. The lights had been dimmed, but Ray couldn't sleep. He watched the moon race behind the trees as he tried to quiet his thoughts.

He squeezed the lodestone, feeling its heavy pull. Would Sally be better off without him?

Ray's thoughts were interrupted by the sound of the door opening behind him. Footsteps thumped down the aisle, and Ray quickly feigned sleep. A figure passed him, the crisp knocks of leather boots alternating with the clunk of a walking stick on the wooden floor. Ray peered up in time to see the black and reptilian-green suit disappear out the door. Through the window, the vestibule was dark but for an orange glow that illuminated Mister Grevol's face as he lit a cigarillo.

Mister Grevol had left his car at the back of the train. Sally and Miss Corey and the orphans were all asleep. If Ray wanted to leave, he would never have a better opportunity.

Ray's heart felt mashed; his throat constricted. He reached for Sally's coat and bundled it. Sliding to the edge of the seat, he tucked the coat under Sally's head and stood up. Her nose twitched, but she did not wake. He glanced out at the vestibule. Mister Grevol was drawing on his cigarillo, causing a red glow like a phantom eye to form at the tip.

Ray turned away from Sally and Mister Grevol and headed down the aisle. He opened the door onto the vestibule and went into the next car. Ray was momently stunned by the luxury of Mister Grevol's parlor, with its silk-upholstered furnishings, thickly carpeted floor, and crystal decanters of wine secured on an ebony hutch. The man with the gold tooth was sleeping in a chair, his head propped on one cupped hand.

Ray tiptoed through to the next door, crossed the vestibule, and went down the hallway of a sleeper car; the walls were paneled with detailed marquetry, and brass lamps cast warm yellow light down the expanse. When he reached the caboose, Ray peered through the beveled glass of the door and spied the brakemen up in the cupola, watching out the high windows above the train.

Ray entered quietly, backing against the caboose's wall, out of the brakemen's line of sight. The two were idly chatting above, smoking cigars and sipping coffee. Moving carefully, as close to the walls as possible, Ray made his way out the open door to the balcony at the end of the train. He stepped into the rushing night air, hoping that the wind would blow away the tears in his eyes—if he was going to jump from the train, he needed to be able to see clearly.

Ray tried to steady his shaking hands by clamping them to the railing. The caboose's balcony was dimly illuminated by a single electric bulb. Beyond the rail was little more than the swirl of moving darkness. At what point had the train entered a forest? Towering trees curled over the tracks, blocking any moonlight that would have helped him see where he was going to leap.

Ray removed his wool cap, folded it, and stuck it into the pocket of his tattered coat. He had jumped off a moving train before, but those had only been streetcars and omnibuses. They were never going this fast.

Ray swung a leg over the railing to the side of the train. The wind intensified as he eased his other leg across and tightened his hand on a beam overhead. He tried to gauge what lay to the side of the tracks—bushes or boulders, grass or tree trunks? He wiped a hand across his eyes, but it was no use. There was no telling what was out there.

Ray touched his hand to the lodestone in his pocket. The lodestone would guide him—to what, he did not know. But Ray was certain his father had meant for it to help him.

He leaped into the dark.

Ray's mind went blank. By the time he reached the ground, he had spun completely around. The heels of his brogans touched for a moment on the loose earth and then he tumbled, somersaulting over and over until he landed on his stomach with a gasp.

For a brief moment, he was conscious enough to look up and watch the sooty orange glow of the train as it disappeared into the night.

RAY OPENED HIS EYES. RAISING HIS HEAD FROM THE HARD earth, he saw a faint pinkish color beyond the treetops; it was nearly daybreak. He tried to lift himself but was so sore and bruised, it was easier just to roll over onto his back first. He gingerly poked a finger along his chest. There were plenty of spots that caused him to flinch, but nothing seemed broken. He touched his palm to his forehead but found no blood.

Ray slowly sat up. His first thought was to check his pocket for the lodestone. It was still there, securely tied to his belt with the length of twine, but a painful bruise had formed where the stone had hammered into his thigh. He felt lucky that this was the worst of his injuries.

He got to his feet, stiff, sore, and thirsty. As he spat dirt from his mouth, Ray looked around at the vast woods surrounding him. Leaning his head back, he listened. All he heard were birdsongs and the wind swishing through the trees overhead.

Ray took out the lodestone. As he held the cold, dark stone in his hand, it began to move across his palm, inching toward his thumb. Closing his fingers to catch it, he turned until he faced that direction. He wondered if it was still pulling south. The sun was rising to his left, so he decided it had to be.

The lodestone tugged toward the shadowy wall of trees. Ray looked once down the train tracks in the direction Mister Grevol's train had gone. He turned back to face the forest. Taking his cap from his pocket and squaring it on his head, Ray set off into the trees.

Ray walked on and on throughout the morning. What began as a rolling hill country set beneath a canopy of oaks and maples soon grew more dense and dark. He could not imagine any stretch of forest going on so long. But this was the South, and to his mind, that meant a wilder, greener, and more mysterious place than the cities up north. The forest was brimming with an eerie solitude, punctuated only occasionally by a rustling squirrel or flittering birds.

By noon the wilderness grew so dark that Ray could barely tell if it was night or day, and a spell of dizziness struck him as he considered the vastness of the wild that surrounded him. He cursed himself for being so ridiculously impulsive. Did he think he could jump into the middle of nowhere without any thought to what he'd eat? It wasn't Seventeenth Street, where he could swipe a cold sausage from a street vendor's pushcart. This was quite possibly seventeen miles to anywhere.

Ray was not sure what he had imagined the lodestone would lead him to, but it had not been this looming, desolate wilderness.

He rested in the afternoon at a creek bubbling from a mossy boulder. Ray cupped his hands in the cold water and drank, hoping it would stop the complaints growing in his stomach. He would be out before dark, he assured himself. Maybe he'd find a farm with a warm meal and comfortable bed. Even sleeping in the straw of a stable would be fine.

Emboldened to get out of the woods, Ray stood and checked the lodestone. It was still pulling in the same direction, so he continued. But as night fell and he was still in the vast forest, Ray curled up at the roots of a big black locust tree, hungry, footsore, and more than a little frightened. Eventually he slept.

Things went no better the following day. He was alone, in a place both alien and potentially dangerous. Late in the afternoon, Ray found some berries and, painfully hungry, he ate them. Fifteen minutes later, he got sick. No more berries, he decided.

He slept that night in an abandoned logging camp. The walls of the lean-to shelters were riddled with bullet holes.

He hoped as he searched the jumble of buildings that he wouldn't find a dead body. He didn't. But he did find a couple of water skins and a moth-eaten blanket. All the food had long since rotted into black puddles in boxes.

He filled the water skins the following morning in a stream. He had never been this hungry in his life—even at the worst moments when he and Sally were living on the streets.

After about half an hour of walking, a buzzing of bees brought his attention to a hollow log partway up a rise in the forest. Bees, he thought. That meant honey! Faint with hunger, Ray decided a few bee stings might be worth it. After shooing away the hovering bees with his cap, Ray crouched on his blanket to dig out the honeycomb.

Reaching up to his shoulder into the log, he touched something soft, instead of a sticky honeycomb. Working it close enough to grab, he pulled out a yellow hat. The color was striking against the dark greens and grays of the forest, but what surprised Ray most was not the color itself but the reason for it: the hat was formed completely of dandelions, as fresh and bright as if they were growing on a spring lawn.

Ray turned the hat over in his hands, thinking how strange it was to find a hat in a log—especially a hat made of flowers. Ray wondered if fatigue and hunger were driving him to hallucinations. Then he heard a faint voice over the rise.

Ducking behind the log, Ray's first thought was of men

with guns who had shot up the logging camp. What if they were bandits and he had stumbled onto their camp? Was it too much to hope that they would feed him?

Ray crept to the top of the hill and found himself on a rim overlooking a wide depression in the ground that was encircled by close-growing trees. At the bottom, a small man was sitting alone at the roots of a single massive oak.

The man had a jagged explosion of golden-yellow hair and was whining and whispering to himself piteously. The man's clothes were tattered and patched in a hundred places with a different square of fabric for every hole. On his ankle he wore a leather fetter with an iron lock, the chain curling around to the oak at his back.

As Ray leaned forward to get a better look, the root under his hands gave way with a crack, sending him splayed forward on his belly partway down the slope. The wild man looked up with surprise. Ray snatched the dandelion hat from where it had fallen and scrambled back up to hide again behind the tree.

"Is that my hat?" the wild man called in a peculiar high-pitched voice.

Ray's heart thumped in his throat as he tried to decide whether to speak to the man or simply run away.

"Where did you find it?" the man called again, waiting a few silent moments for an answer. "What you hiding for? En't going to hurt you." Ray heard him rattle the chain. "Here I'm tied to the tree and can't get away. Can you help me?"

Ray called from around the tree. "Have you got any food?"

"No, en't got nothing for you to eat. Sorry. Can you give me my hat?"

Ray fidgeted behind the tree. The lodestone had pulled him this direction, hadn't it? Ray took a deep breath and came around the tree, looking down cautiously at the strange man at the bottom of the depression. "Who are you?"

"Peter Hobnob," the man said.

"How long have you been here?" Ray asked.

"Not too sure. Few weeks I guess." Peter Hobnob was standing now, and Ray could see he was not very tall— maybe a little more than five feet. His features were thorny, all points and angles at his nose, chin, and eyes. He didn't look as dangerous as he had when he was talking to himself like a crazy man, and Ray supposed that as long as he was chained to the tree, he couldn't attack him.

"How could you be out here that long and not eat? You've got to have some food."

Hobnob smiled, his expression youthful and puckish. "I eat whatever blows my way, if you see my meaning."

"No, I don't," Ray said.

"None's the difference. So can you toss me my hat?"

Ray decided there was no harm in it; he started down.

"Stop there!" Hobnob yelled with agitation as Ray reached the bottom of the slope. "Mind the acorns!"

"The what?" Ray noticed for the first time that there

were acorns all over the bottom of the depression, surrounding the giant oak and the wild man.

"Don't take another step. Them acorns. They's dangerous."

"What do you mean?"

Hobnob tapped the hard trunk of the oak and said, "Devil's oak. Wicked tree it is. Them acorns is poisonous, along with the leaves and bark and near everything else it's got. Step on one and you let out the poison. Be dead before you realized you breathed it in. Come a little closer and toss the hat over to me." He motioned with his hands for Ray to throw the hat.

"I've never heard of a tree like that," Ray said, looking up at the branches doubtfully.

"Heard of it or not, none's the difference," Hobnob said, waving his hands impatiently.

Ray ran his fingers curiously over the soft yellow petals covering the dandelion hat. "How did you get out here?" he asked.

Hobnob sighed and answered. "Locked me out here as punishment."

"Who?"

"The Pirate Queen."

"The wh-what?" Ray stammered.

"Pirate Queen. She's my boss—the captain of the *Snapdragon*. Terrible woman she is." He shivered. "Don't much like working for her. None of us do, but who's going to tell her you're quits? Recall old Joshua trying that once.

Sewed his lips shut, she did. Or did she cut out his tongue? Don't recollect exactly as I weren't there at the time, but he never complained much after. No, none of us did."

His voice dropped to a whisper. "You know, she wears a necklace with a bullet on it. Cursed charm it is. The very one that pierced the skull of Abraham the Emancipator. You know him?"

"No." Ray was wondering how sane this man really was.

"Don't know the president? One from the War of the Rebellion?"

"Abraham Lincoln?"

"That's the one," he said, firing his finger like a pistol.

"She wears a necklace with the bullet that killed Abraham Lincoln?"

"Just for spite." Hobnob smiled grimly.

Ray scratched his head and asked, "So are you a pirate?"

"Not rightly a pirate. Just your common thief. Who are you anyway?"

"Ray, Ray Fleming. So why did the Pirate Queen chain you up out here?"

"See, she says I stole her silver dagger." Hobnob made a slicing pantomime with his finger. "The one she uses to cut the tips off her cigars."

"Did you steal it?" Ray asked.

Hobnob scratched at his thicket of hair. "Well, yes. But she wants it back, and I en't got it no more."

"Where is it?"

"Lost her cursed ripper. This here's the Lost Wood."

Hobnob threw his hands out in a wide arc. "All manner of things, people, and such get lost in this wild'ness. You, friend, for example, and that silver dagger. Dropped it over these here woods when I was flying along—"

"Flying! What were you flying in? A balloon or something?"

"No, nothing like that. Just flying. With my hat, see?"

Ray shook his head and screwed up his brow. "So she's locking you up until you find the dagger, but you can't find the dagger if you're tied up?"

"Something like that. But she don't think I lost it. Wants me to confess where I've hid it. Sends one of the pirates from the *Snapdragon* out here every few days to get me to fess up."

Ray glanced around, wondering if some pirate was walking up at that moment. "But you're a thief. Can't you pick the lock?"

"Can't. But the key's out there somewhere." Hobnob gestured to the field of acorns surrounding him. "Hidden in one of them acorns."

"Not much of a thief if you can't pick a lock," Ray said.

Hobnob seemed to wilt—his shoulders, head, and hands drooping loosely with exhaustion. "If you could just . . ."

Ray looked down at the dandelion hat. "Sure," he said, taking a step closer.

"Careful!" Hobnob squeaked.

Ray took the hat in a firm grip, gauged the distance to Hobnob, and flicked the yellow hat out. For a few yards the hat was on course, but then it curved away, landing softly in the acorns several yards from the thief. Hobnob put his face in his hands and shook his head.

"Sorry," Ray said.

"Not much of a thrower, are you?" Hobnob sank back to the ground.

"Look, I'll try to get the hat." Ray began to tiptoe toward the hat.

"No!" Hobnob barked. "Don't go walking any closer. You'll step on an acorn and murder us both."

"Let me see what I can do." Ray pulled the lodestone from his pocket. He untied the end of the twine that connected the lodestone to his belt loop. "I think I can fish it out."

Hobnob rolled his eyes.

The lodestone would give him enough weight to swing the makeshift fishing line out to the hat. But Ray still needed a way to snag the hat. He needed a hook. Ray looked around. There was not much, except sticks. That would have to do.

Ray wedged a broken twig through the twine on the lodestone. He had his hook. Ray eyed the dandelion hat. He walked around, careful not to tread on any acorns, until the hat was about ten feet away. The twine was only a little more than three feet—too short to reach the hat.

"Just a moment," Ray said, but Hobnob seemed to have given up hope.

Ray ran back up the hill to the log where he'd left his blanket. He pulled off some loose wool threads from the edge and began tying them together to lengthen his "fishing line." As he returned to the edge of the acorns, he swung the lodestone around on the string. With the right toss, he might hook the hat and be able to pull it back. But if the lodestone struck one of the acorns too hard . . .

Hobnob lifted an eye to watch and scratched at the golden clutter topping his head. "What you doing?"

"Just watch," Ray said. He began swinging the stone around in a circle above his head, building momentum. Then he extended the line farther, swinging it closer and closer to the hat. The hook hit the hat several times but never snagged.

Ray needed to try a different approach. This time, he swung the stone to land on the hat, hoping to catch it that way. It hit the far side with a thump.

"Careful!" Hobnob hissed. Ray inched the stone along until it met the hat. Continuing to pull slowly, he felt the broken twig catch the hat.

"You got it," Hobnob whispered. "Keep pulling."

Not wanting to lose the hold, he gingerly slid the hat across the acorn tops. Just as it was a few feet away, the twig came out.

"Tarnal!" Hobnob cursed. "Can you reach it?"

Ray pulled the lodestone back and saw that something was stuck to its side. It was a brown acorn. That was odd. All the other acorns surrounding the Devil's oak were a distinctive cinder color.

"It's right there. Can't you get it?" Hobnob complained.

"Hold on," Ray said. "Look."

He pulled the acorn off the lodestone and felt the magnetic tug that had held them together.

"Put it down," Hobnob urged.

"Didn't you say the key was in one of the acorns? This acorn's magnetic." He tapped it a few times to the lodestone, each time feeling the connection. Then he gave the acorn a little shake. "There's something inside it."

"How do you know?"

Ray began squeezing the acorn in his palm.

Hobnob leaped to his feet in alarm. "No, you tarnal idiot!"

Ray felt the acorn crack.

Hobnob winced. "Once you open your palms you got about two seconds. I give myself three."

Ray held his breath as he unfolded his fingers. Lying in his palm, along with the broken shell of the acorn, was a tiny iron key. He held it up for Hobnob to see. Hobnob's face broke into an amazed smile.

"Can't believe it! That's luck."

Ray palmed the key and swiveled his arm back. "I'll throw it to you."

"No!" Hobnob pleaded. "No. You en't going to make it. Just . . . just put it on the stone and swing it over on the rope."

Sticking the key to the lodestone and tucking the tiny handle beneath the knot for good measure, Ray swung the key across the acorns to Hobnob. Hobnob grabbed it and took the key from the lodestone.

"Don't much like iron," he muttered as he put the key in the lock at his ankle. "Got a bit of an allergy, you see." With a click, Hobnob pulled the lock off the leather fetter encircling his leg, while Ray pulled back the lode-stone.

"Oh, that feels good," Hobnob groaned with pleasure. "Yes, sweet freedom. Ha, ha!" He hopped up quickly, and they both heard the sharp crack under his heel.

Ray froze. Hobnob turned to look at Ray, the mirth melting from his face. As soon as Hobnob lifted his foot, the poisonous fumes would be set free.

"You'll want to hold your breath," Hobnob whimpered. "And of course . . . run!"

Ray took great galloping leaps as he propelled himself up the hill. He looked back for a moment to see Hobnob running, one hand tightly clamped over his nose and mouth, the other snatching the dandelion hat, and all the way crushing and smashing the poisonous acorns as he escaped. The two didn't stop until they put a vast distance between them and the Devil's oak.

* * *

"Can't thank you enough, lad. Really I can't," Peter Hob-nob said as he led Ray through the woods. Ray had to jog to keep up with the tiny thief's brisk pace.

"Where are we going?" he panted.

"Bit further, see. En't going to forget this. No, sir. Peter Hobnob never forgets . . . what did you say your name was again?"

"Ray."

"En't going to forget this, Ray."

"Are you going back to the Pirate Queen?"

"Gracious, no," Hobnob said, ducking under a fallen tree. "She'd have my nose."

Ray pulled aside branches as he followed. "Will you look for her silver dagger, then?"

"And incriminate myself further?" Hobnob clicked his tongue and then said, "You should seriously consider the larcenous arts as an occupation, by the way. Good business in thieving. Especially these days with the Ramblers all but gone."

"Ramblers?" Ray asked, his pants snagged on a bramble. He heard a little tear as he pulled them loose. "Who are they?"

Hobnob looked over his shoulder. "Can't be more than a handful scattered about. They's protectors. Heroes of the Wild. No, en't seen none of them around since the day John Henry fought the Machine. They was all killed after that, by the Gog. Heard tell that the Gog is building a new Machine. Hope it en't true of course, but you never know. No, thieving's never been so good. Booming. Ah, here we are."

Ray stopped short and nearly stumbled into Hobnob standing before a thicket. A tangle of wild shrubs spread out before him, covered in dark fruit.

"Gooseberries." Hobnob smiled. "Said you was hungry. Here you go."

"They're not . . . poisonous?" His mouth watered.

"Gracious, no!"

Ray rushed forward and pulled handfuls of the currant-like berries from the vines. With one hand he stuffed the gooseberries into his mouth. With the other he filled the pockets of his coat. He had never tasted anything so delicious, and for a moment he forgot that the thief was standing with him.

"Well, best be off," Hobnob called.

Ray turned, his lips stained with the juice. "You're leaving?"

"Don't worry. Just keep going that way"—Hobnob waved his hand—"and you'll find your way out before nightfall." Then he added, "But be careful. Lost Wood is full of bandits and the like."

Ray frowned. "I haven't seen another person besides you for days."

"Well, you never know. Bound to be someone from the *Snapdragon* along to check on me any day now. Don't want to get caught by one of them, unless it's Big Jimmie. He's a nice sort. You'd get along fine with him, unless he's tired. Gets right cranky when he en't had a nap. Good luck."

Hobnob gave him a wave and stuck the dandelion hat on his wild jumble of hair—the yellow of the dandelions matching hue for hue with his yellow hair. The golden color began to drain away instantly, wilting to a gray-white. "Won't forget that good turn you done me, Jay."

"It's Ray," he said.

As the dandelions turned to puffy wisps, Hobnob's body grew misty and began to scatter slowly like smoke. His fading face gave one last merry smile before he disappeared into a million tiny white seedpods, drifting away in the breeze.

RAY STARED WITH BEWILDERMENT AS THE LAST DANDELION pods disappeared up into the canopy of leaves. Had that really happened? Hobnob had flown away, just as he said he could!

Ray took the lodestone from his pocket. As his fingers wrapped around the stone, he felt its pull return. He screwed up his brow and then looked at the shadowy forest. Putting the lodestone back, Ray took out a handful of gooseberries and set off again.

As he journeyed, he took out the lodestone from time to time to check his direction. His thoughts drifted back to what Hobnob had said about John Henry and some wicked machine and Ramblers. He certainly knew about John Henry—everybody had heard that legend. But a wicked machine? In the story Ray remembered, John

Henry had beaten a steam drill before dying at the end of the competition. Nothing about—what was it?—a Gog!

After another hour, the forest began to change again, decorated now more frequently with wildflowers. The trees were not so close together or as menacing. Ray felt emboldened that he might at last be coming to the edge of the Lost Wood.

Voices echoed through the trees. Ray froze. The pirates from the *Snapdragon*! They were coming for Hobnob. Or had they heard Ray and begun following him?

Ray spun around and saw an enormous tree. Long ago, it must have been a titan among the other oaks and hickories, but at some point the tree had broken about twelve feet from the ground. It reminded Ray of a severed column from a picture book on the ancient empires. If he could get up there, it might be the best hiding spot.

Ray pulled himself up on the pegs of old limbs. As he reached the place where the tree had broken off, he saw an opening in the trunk where the tree's interior had become hollow with rot and age. It seemed almost like a giant well.

Something sparkled from the shadows just inside the opening. Reaching in, his finger touched something metal and sharp. He flinched back and then leaned down to peer closer.

A few feet into the opening, there was a small ledge of rotten wood, before the opening descended deep into the trunk. The silver handle of a stiletto protruded from the rotten ledge, its blade sunk several inches straight in. Ray threw his legs over the opening. Reaching down once more, he gave the handle a jerk, releasing it. It was the Pirate Queen's dagger. It had to be! What were the odds of discovering it?

A voice drifted, close enough now for Ray to make out the words. "Just a little farther."

Not wanting to risk being spied, Ray lowered himself into the opening, squatting with his heels on the ledge where he had removed the silver dagger. He was there only a moment before the rotten wood of the ledge broke, plunging him headfirst into the dark belly of the tree.

He was surprised to find that his shoulders didn't land on rotten wood, and he was more surprised that he was lying on warm, coarse fur, which gave a squeal and began moving from under him.

Ray pushed and pulled his way around, backing as far against the interior wall of the trunk as he could. He inhaled sharply on the acidic stench that filled the dark. Something—or some things—were moving about the interior of the tree. A wet nose pressed into his cheek, sniffing. He touched a finger to the muzzle and felt something akin to a dog snout. He may have lived in the city nearly his whole life but he knew this wasn't a dog. And it was too big to be a raccoon.

It was a bear. Probably just a cub, but a cub has a mother and she would come home sometime.

The bear cub mewed and was answered by another, which sniffed at Ray's hands. He tightened his grip on the dagger and said, "It's all right. Not going to hurt you." One answered with a lick at his forearm. "Yeah, nice bear. We're friends, right? Thanks for the licks. When's mama coming home?"

He squeezed himself around the cubs and felt the sides of the trunk, trying to find a handhold to climb out. A gruff snort from outside stilled Ray's scrambling. It felt as if a cold stone slipped down his throat. The tree then shook down to the roots with the clambering weight of the she-bear climbing up. Ray fell back into the two cubs, which were snorting with anticipation at the return of their mother. The circle of bright sunlight at the top of the tree darkened into shadow. The she-bear sniffed at her den.

What was he going to do? Ray's mind raced. He could think of only one way out. But it was going to be a rough ride.

The great she-bear turned around atop the tree and backed into the hole. All the light was sucked from overhead as the bear inched into her den. She slid down toward the bottom, her claws scraping the sides to slow her descent. As she backed up nearly onto Ray, he gave the she-bear a quick jab in her rear with the dagger, not enough to harm her but enough to give her alarm. She gave a howl that rattled Ray through his bones. Like a cannonball she launched out of the top of the tree and dropped onto the ground below—with Ray clinging to her back.

* * *

Not far away from Ray, two figures passed into the Lost Wood, searching. The first was small—a Chinese girl with a long braid of sleek black hair extending from the crown of her head to the small of her back. The other was enormous—a young black man who stood a full eight feet.

The girl held out her hand, which, unlike the rest of her pale skin, was solid midnight black but for tiny luminous markings moving slowly to and fro. "Just a little farther," she said after examining the markings. She returned her hand to rest on the hilt of her knife. The girl wore a mandarin-orange silk tunic and loose black pants. On her feet were tattered slippers in need of restitching at the toes.

"You been saying that all day," the giant said, wiping his hand across his head of short black curls. He wore denim overalls, plain and sun-faded, over a simple cotton shirt. Burlap sacks in various states from empty to bulging dangled from a thick leather belt cinched about his waist.

The girl looked once more at the markings on the back of her tattooed hand and then scowled. "Should be here . . ."

The giant gave a wild smile. "Ah, I spy them."

He strode forward into a sun-speckled glade thick with colorful wildflowers. The giant took a wistful sniff as he gathered handfuls of Solomon's seal and monkshood, rolled them in damp cloth, and placed them in one of the sacks tied to his wide belt.

The girl followed him into the glade and settled against the trunk of a willow. "Why are you picking those yellow ones?" she asked. "Nel didn't say anything about any yellow flowers."

"They're pretty," the giant said.

The girl rolled her eyes and placed her hands behind her head.

"You remember what that root was Nel told us to get?" the giant called after a moment of contemplation.

"Of course not, he told you what to get, not me. I don't know why I keep going with you on these expeditions."

The giant caught her teasing smile from the corner of his eye. "Because I'd never find the train again."

"Why don't you write down what herbs Nel wants gathered?" the girl asked.

"I hate making lists. Puts too much pressure on me. I don't like being anxious."

"But see, you get to have the satisfaction of checking off your progress as—Hey! What's that?"

There was a roar and a snapping of underbrush and shrubs. The girl leaped to her feet, whipping the bowie knife from her belt as the she-bear burst into the clearing. The enormity of the beast alone would have given them pause, but what shocked them most was the boy riding on her back like a rodeo cowboy. The bear-rider was straddling her tightly with his knees and held thick folds of loose fur with both his hands.

The giant toppled out of the way. The bear turned and charged again, but the girl jumped between it and her friend, raising her knife. The she-bear reared back on her hind legs, her claws ready to rake into the small girl.

The giant lunged, bracing his head low and plowing into the bear's stomach with his massive shoulders. The bear tumbled over several times, quickly clambered back to her feet. The rider was thrown into the air, his head striking the trunk of the willow where the girl had been sitting moments before. He collapsed.

The she-bear hesitated before the giant. She sidled around in an arc, baring her teeth and growling. The giant reached up and broke a stout limb from a tree, taking a few swings to measure the weight of his club. The girl eased around to the side of the bear, ready to leap, ready with her knife. The she-bear turned her head back and forth between the two.

From the roots of the willow, the rider lifted his head and extended an arm. "Don't . . . she's just protecting her cubs."

The girl and the giant looked at one another and then at the strange rider.

"Is she yours?" the girl called. "Are you one of those gypsy bear-tamers?"

The rider's eyes were drifting as he fought to stay conscious. "Just . . . protecting her cubs. . . ." Blood trickled from below his cap across his brow.

The giant lowered the club and backed up a few steps. The girl looked less comfortable with lowering her defenses, but when the giant waved her back, she did so. The she-bear snorted a few times, watching the three. Then she turned and loped toward the rider. She stopped above him and gave his forehead a lick before galloping off into the thickets.

Ray drifted in and out of consciousness. His skull felt inches too thick and pulsed painfully. The world seemed muted and hazy. He forced an eyelid open and saw the forest floor bouncing below him. He closed his eye and tried not to be sick.

". . . and I don't think we should be taking him with us," someone said.

"He's hurt. We have to." Ray could feel the rumble of the voice reverberate through his body. He was being carried over someone's shoulder, and whoever it was must have been huge because the ground looked a long ways down. The other voice sounded like a girl, but Ray felt too nauseated to turn his head and check.

"But Nel sent us to collect herbs. He didn't say anything—"

"He'd say the same as me. The boy's hurt. He needs help."

"Pirates?" Ray whispered.

"What did he say?" the girl asked.

"Not sure."

Ray mumbled, "Are you . . . Big Jimmie? You taking me . . . to the *Snapdragon*?"

"I think he's knocked squirrelly," the giant said.

Ray's vision swirled, and he passed out.

* * *

When Ray next came to, he was lying on the grass. He squinted at the rosy halo of a sunset. The trees were gone from overhead; he was out of the woods. The giant was wiping Ray's forehead with a wet handkerchief.

"I think he's got a fever," the giant said in a voice so low that it rumbled and vibrated more out from his body than from his mouth.

The girl snorted. Ray turned to look at her. She was sitting in the grass looking away from him, down a stretch of railroad track.

In certain neighborhoods of the cities where Ray had grown up, there had been Chinese immigrants, many running groceries or employed as laborers. It seemed strange to Ray that he should find someone Chinese out here in the middle of nowhere, and without the slightest tinge of an accent.

Ray looked up at the giant's earthy brown face. His jaw was wide and his features chiseled, but his curly eyelashes and friendly dark eyes eased Ray's worries.

"Where are you taking me?" Ray asked.

"To our train," the giant said. He spoke in a slow, calculating drawl, as if his mouth were full of sticky sweet molasses.

Ray listened for the sound of a train, a whistle or a rattling of the track. But the world was quiet except for a chorus of katydids. There was no train coming, and they must have been miles from a depot.

"Where is it?" He was growing dizzy again. He struggled to keep his attention on the giant and the girl.

The giant chuckled and looked at the girl.

Ray followed his gaze. The girl gave a scowl either to Ray or to the giant or to both and tucked her hand into the fold of her tunic.

For a moment, Ray thought her hand had been black. Or was it a tattoo? He thought he saw on the dark skin of her hand an unearthly glittering, a shimmering and swirling cosmos of faint sparkles. But Ray decided—before he slipped into unconsciousness again—that he must have been addled from the fall.

Ray woke with the gauzy morning sunlight on his face. The straw-tick mattress beneath him was soft, but the threadbare sheets were wet with perspiration. A woman leaned over him. She was pleasantly plump with small, pinched features. Her misty-brown hair was pulled into a knot at her nape, with loose strands dangling about her face.

Gently she slid an arm under Ray's neck and lifted his head. Something cool and wet touched his lips. "Take a bit more, dear," she said. "Fever's near broke, but you need rest. Drink and sleep."

Ray swallowed. It was spicy on his tongue, causing a little tingling as it went down.

"Where am I?" Ray whispered. The room felt as if it was moving, swaying and jolting beneath him.

"Safe, now shhh," she said, lowering his head back to the damp pillow. Ray's eyes fluttered, and he fell back to sleep.

Morning light filtered in again, but the quality was different enough to make Ray believe it was not the same morning as the one he last remembered. Ray felt under the sheets and realized he was wearing only his underclothes. He rolled over and noticed a bundle on the floor next to the tick mattress: his cap, belt, and jacket stacked neatly on top of his tattered leather brogans. He reached a weak hand to lift his cap. Under it, he was relieved to discover the lodestone lying next to the silver dagger.

He ran his fingers to the back of his head and felt a scabbed wound. Standing brought a brief wave of dizziness, and he steadied himself against the walls of the curiously skinny room. It was little more than a bed and the floor beside the bed. At the foot of the bed was a window showing a sunny green field of corn. Turning, Ray saw a door with a curtained window.

Beside the door was a tin plate draped with a red cotton napkin. Ray lifted the napkin from the plate, revealing biscuits, greasy pieces of chicken, and cold potatoes. He set the food aside. First he wanted to figure out where he was and where his clothes were. Ray picked up his wool cap and noticed that the top was torn open from his accident. His brogans were in no better shape. The toes were worn nearly to little oval holes and the leather soles were swollen and cracked. Were they really that abused from the trek through the Lost Wood? Ray slid them on his feet, took a cold biscuit from the plate, and went in search of the woman.

Opening the door, Ray looked right and then left down a narrow hallway lined with windows on one side, more doors on the other, and a vestibule at each end. This was a train, he realized. The train was no longer moving, but out the window he did not see a depot or a station, only a sun-dappled clearing, bordered by a forest. People were walking around outside. Maybe one of them would know where the woman was with his clothes.

Ray began down the hallway toward the vestibule. Although he had never slept in one, he had wandered enough trains to recognize this car as a sleeper—much messier, however, than any sleeper car he had ever seen. To reach the vestibule, Ray had to maneuver across a jumble of crates and trunks scattered about the hallway. Strings of blue, red, and green bottles, rusty hardware, and bundles of drying herbs hung from the ceiling. Ray kept banging his head against the bottles, causing a clanking chorus that sounded like a gypsy tinker wagon.

Through the windows, he saw people erecting a long canvas tent and carrying boxes around a clearing. Where had they stopped the train? Surely not on a main line. He decided that this must be some sort of secondary rail, the sort that breaks off around towns to connect with mills and factories. He had lived in enough neighborhoods around smaller rail lines to know.

Where was the plump woman? He couldn't go wandering around in his underwear.

As he reached for the vestibule door, somebody beyond opened it first. A girl looked up and gasped, *"Caramba!"* touching her hand to her throat with a start.

Ray was startled, too, but not for the same reason.

The girl was quite possibly the most beautiful he had ever seen. She had large black eyes, long fluttering lashes, and honey-colored skin. Her hair fell in thick black ringlets over her shoulders. She wore a fluted layered dress of exotic reds and purples, stitched with shiny spangles.

He was equally surprised by the rattlesnake draped about her neck. The serpent swayed out from her shoulder, poking its tongue to inspect Ray and shaking its rattles. Ray jerked back.

The girl's eyes went from Ray's face down to his attire, and then she erupted into laughter. Ray looked down at his gray woolen underclothes and bare chest, his pale, skinny legs protruding from the unlaced boots. He did his best to cover himself, more from embarrassment than modesty, but she had already looked away, giggles rippling out from the vestibule.

"Está despierto," she called. "He's awake." She gave him one last look up and down, snorted, and closed the door.

A moment later the door opened again and this time it

was the warm brown face of the giant who had carried Ray from the woods that looked in. As he saw the giant now, Ray realized he was a boy not much older than himself.

"You're up. You feeling all right?" he said.

"Yeah, where am I?"

"Welcome to the *Ballyhoo*. It's our train." He blinked several times and chuckled. "Where's your clothes?"

"That's what I was going to ask you!"

A pained expression crossed the giant's face, and he slapped a hand to his forehead. "Forgot . . . I'll be right back."

Ray's appetite had returned with a sudden complaining growl. He went back to his room and sat on the edge of his bed, devouring the plate of food. As he was licking the remnants from his fingers, the giant squeezed into Ray's room.

Tossing the shirt, trousers, and socks into Ray's lap, he said, "Still a little damp. Ma Everett decided to wash them for you, and I was supposed to hang them up. I forgot. My mind seems to wander sometimes. Sorry they ain't dry. Meet me outside when you change." He squeezed back into the hallway, and Ray heard him curse as he stumbled on the wreck of crates and clattering bottles.

After dressing and lacing up his brogans, Ray picked up the lodestone, retied the twine to his belt, and began slipping the stone in his pocket. He stopped and then slowly took the lodestone back out. He stared down at the dark rock. It wasn't moving.

"You ready?" the giant called.

Ray went out into the hallway, narrowing his eyes at the odd assortment of people busily working outside. He tossed the lodestone a few times in his hands, waiting to see if it would begin moving again. It didn't.

With a frown, Ray dropped the lodestone in his pocket and stepped out onto the vestibule.

"Never seen anything like it. That bear was bucking, and you were flopping all around like a catfish," the giant laughed.

He was leading Ray past the busy people—nearly a dozen—carrying rolls of canvas, dragging platforms, and hoisting banners above the clearing. As Ray had suspected, the train had stopped on a weed-tangled secondary rail line. Fields, ripe with high summer, extended on the back side of the *Ballyhoo*. On the side of the train where the tent was erected was a clearing of grass, bordered halfway by trees, then a burned-out factory. Beyond were the first clapboard houses on the edge of a town.

The *Ballyhoo* had none of the elegance or beauty of Mister Grevol's train. This was a working train—a squat old eight-wheeler locomotive, rusty in places, with only six cars behind the tender. Ray doubted it could pull much more than that.

"You had a good ride on that old bear before she threw you," the giant continued. "But what I can't figure is why that bear didn't maul you! All she did was sidle up and lick you like you was her baby."

Ray narrowed his eyes with confusion. "I don't really remember much after I hit my head."

"Well, she did. Beats all, don't it? What's your name anyhow?"

"Ray. What's yours?"

"They call me Conker. That girl you met in your drawers—that's Marisol." Conker pointed toward a tent several yards away. The black-haired girl was laughing as she talked to two boys putting up a makeshift fence of ribbon and pine poles.

"She has a snake on her shoulder," Ray said.

As if it somehow answered Ray's question, Conker replied, "She comes from the desert, out in Sonora, if I recollect." Then, almost as an afterthought, he added, "She's a snake dancer."

"A what?" Ray said.

Conker kept walking, and Ray had to hurry to catch up to the giant. Conker nodded to his right, not slowing his pace. "There's Si. You remember her?"

The Chinese girl who had been in the forest with Conker was unwinding a heavy coil of rope with the help of a soot-faced young man. As she spied Ray, she turned away quickly, snapping the long ebony braid on her head like a whip.

"She?" Ray asked.

"Yeah, Si."

"Her name's *She*?"

"Not like 'she.' Just Si, spelled *s-i*. Sounds the same, I reckon. You'll have time to meet her properly soon, but our pitchman wants to see you first."

Ray was somewhat surprised at the strange people working. They were an exotic group. Not even in the cities up north, even among the sailors and dockworkers, had he seen so many different kinds of people working together.

"What's a pitchman?" Ray began, but they had reached an area where a number of crates were stacked in various states of being opened and sorted.

"Nel," Conker called.

An elderly black man popped up from behind a crate. He had bright manic eyes shining from his exceptionally dark face. His wide plume of silver hair was capped with a burgundy fez and a long tassel.

"Yes, yes," he chuckled, clapping his hands together as he stood and stomped toward Ray. "Here he is, alive and well. Welcome to Cornelius T. Carter's Mystifying Medicine Show and Tabernacle of Tachycardial Talent!"

Ray's eyes hurt momentarily from the man's screaming orange and red plaid suit. On one foot, the man wore a tall leather riding boot. The other leg was a polished mahogany peg extending from below the knee.

"Tabernacle of Tacky-what?" Ray mumbled.

"Tachycardial. Means *heart-pounding*!" he explained.

"Son, I found the surest way to establishing credibility with the yokels—i.e., our customers—is to be flamboyantly verbose."

Ray looked at Conker.

"He likes to talk fancy," Conker said.

"And are you Mister Cornelius T. Carter?" Ray asked.

Waving his hands from his head down toward his foot, he said, "I am. I can see that despite your reticence to fully embrace the more ornamental aspects of speaking that you are no simpleton. They call me Nel. Peg Leg Nel. And what is your . . . er, moniker? What name do you go by, son?"

"Ray Fleming."

Peg Leg Nel shook Ray's hand heartily and clasped his shoulder.

"Not a provocative name for an entertainer, but a durable name I'm sure. I did hear however that you gave quite a performance to Conker and Si in the forest. Bearriding! How . . . uncustomary! You may yet grow to overtake your name, dear Ray."

Nel tilted Ray's chin up with a finger and inspected his face. "I trust that you are recuperating from your injury?"

"Yes," Ray said. "I'm feeling better."

Nel nodded his head vigorously, saying, "Well, we are quite busy as you can see. Much to be done to be ready by two in the afternoon."

"What's the show? Is it a circus or something?" Ray asked.

"Circus?" Nel's wooly brows nearly covered his eyes

as he frowned. "No, son. You must have drifted during my introduction. We are a medicine show, Ray. Tonics. Salves. Nostrums. The like. Not the proprietary medicines of a common pharmacologist, mind you. I'm a root worker. But it takes more than a quality product and mere hawking to draw in the customers. People like a show. That's how the masses are enticed, and we have the talent here to provide first-rate entertainment on par with the finest revues and rigmarole around. What we lack in splendor, we make up for in sheer audacity. I trust that you'll do us the honor of viewing a performance?"

"Sure," Ray said.

"Blunt, a little taciturn, but certainly not curt, are you?" Peg Leg Nel smiled down at Ray with a vast mouthful of glistening teeth.

"Come on, Ray," Conker said. "You can help me get things set up."

Nel wagged a finger. "Well, don't forget, you've been indisposed with an injury, young Ray. So restrain from overexerting yourself. Now, if you'll excuse me . . ." Stomping away on his peg leg, he added with an ear-jarring laugh, "Bear-rider. Ha! My goodness."

Ray learned that the medicine show was set up just outside the textile town of Hillsboro. The timing had been selected to coincide with the cotton market, which was to close in a few days. Nel had paid some travelers a week earlier to post pasteboard signs on trees and telegraph poles around Hillsboro to announce the show. Farmers from the surrounding community were in town to auction their bales. If the season had been good, they'd have money to spend, and Peg Leg Nel was happy to relieve them of a few bits.

Nel's crew was busy rushing about the performance space, getting the show ready. Nel was directing two men as they carried supplies from the train. Marisol and some others Ray didn't know yet were setting up gasoline torches. Curious glances were cast toward Ray, but everyone was too busy to be interrupted.

Conker introduced Ray to Eddie Everett, the grimy young man Ray had seen earlier with Si. His face, neck, and hands were blackened and smudged with soot, which contrasted oddly with his clean outfit and the crisp derby cocked on his head.

Ray helped Conker and Eddie carry pieces of the stages to the open-sided tent, which was erected in full above the clearing and against the side of the train. The tent was partially fenced off, as Ray had noted earlier, with long bands of satin ribbon. They set up the three stages against the side of the train and hung a moth-eaten velvet curtain from the sleeper car as a backdrop. From the center stage Peg Leg Nel would pitch his tonics.

"See how this middle stage is set closer to the ground," Conker explained to Ray as they worked. "Nel says it's more persuasive if the tip—that's what we call the crowd—is closer to him. Builds trust with the customers, he reckons. Other two platforms on either side are taller. They're for the performers. Better that they're higher. Makes the show more exciting."

Conker waved his hand around the shaded interior of the tent after setting down a pair of tables on the center stage. "No chairs either, see. Nel used to put out chairs for folks. But he figures it's best they ain't too comfortable. Keeps them paying better attention. Also makes the tip seem bigger than it is. Audience gets more excited if it's harder to see and a little too crowded."

Ray nodded, taking it all in. "Sounds like he's trying to trick them," he said, and Eddie laughed.

"No." Conker smiled. "Ain't trickery exactly. People like to be entertained. And for Nel to entertain, he's got to use a little gimmicking. That's what I believe they come here for."

"They want to be tricked?" Ray asked.

"No. They want something unbelievable. And we give it to them. Nel'd like to think it's the tonics, which are really good, mind you. You ought to know! Cured your concussion, didn't he? No, it ain't why they come. Not really."

"And all without the usual ploys," Eddie added.

"Like what?" Ray asked.

"Like geeks."

Ray raised an eyebrow. "What's a geek?"

"Performers who bite the heads off live snakes and such." Eddie smiled, relishing the look of disgust on Ray's face. "Ha! Marisol, she'd hate that, wouldn't she?"

"Yeah." Conker nodded. "No. We got no geeks, no hootchy, no blackface. We got talent enough without all those . . . Hey, there's Buck. Buck!"

Ray turned to see a cowboy passing beside the stage, staggering slightly with slow steps. The man was hard-faced and ragged as a cedar tree. His eyes had a sunken quality, the heavy lids barely cracked. He wore a fringed doeskin coat and tall, decoratively stitched cowboy boots—each deeply oiled and rubbed smooth but discolored in patches from wear and weather. Between the crisscross of gun belts slung across his waist and the tall, flat-brimmed hat, he was the very image of the Wild West gunslinger Ray read about in penny Westerns.

The cowboy cocked his head at the sound of his name, his gaze passing back and forth across the three of them. It struck Ray as strange the way his head swiveled so loosely on his neck. His eyes seemed shut, and after giving a sniff he strode on, not stopping for introductions.

"That's Eustace Buckthorn. Don't mind Buck," Conker whispered. "He's just a bit crotchety sometimes."

"What's wrong with him? He seemed . . . drunk."

"Drunk!" Conker laughed. "He ain't drunk. He looks that way on account of he's blind."

"He is!" Ray looked back at the cowboy. "What's he do?"

"I reckon you'd have telled from his outfit. He's our sharpshooter. Good one, too."

"How's he shoot when he's blind?"

"Got me," Conker said, and began walking back toward the entrance to the tent.

Eddie took Ray's elbow as he added, "I've heard that he murdered his own brother."

"He wh-what?" Ray stammered.

"And didn't he take up once with a band of pirates, Conker?"

Conker nodded. "Say he was in love with one of the pirates, too. Their queen, way I heard it."

The Pirate Queen! Hobnob's boss and tormentor. Ray looked once more with curiosity at the sharpshooter. Buck was just reaching a car—the third from the end. As he started up the steps, Ray noticed long silver and black hair falling from his cowboy hat.

"Ray!" Eddie called. "Lend a hand?"

Shaking the thoughts away, Ray ran over to where Eddie was pulling a canvas roll across the lawn. As he took a corner of the canvas roll, Ray asked, "Do you perform, Eddie?"

"Not me, I'm what they call the bakehead. That's the name for the fireman on the trains." Eddie nodded toward the low, flat car just behind the locomotive. "See the tender? It's where the coal is stored. I shovel it into the tenderbox up in the locomotive—keep the engine running. I hate my stinking job! Always getting burned. I wish Redfeather would let me borrow his copper."

"You ought just to ask him," Conker said.

"He won't." Eddie sighed.

"What's the copper?" Ray asked.

"Oh, just some Indian charm Redfeather wears on a necklace. Keeps you from getting burned. He doesn't even need it! I'm the one that needs it. And this stinking filth! I can't ever get clean of all this coal grease." He frowned as he continued, "Pa says I've got to work my way up. Maybe to brakeman next if my brother ever moves on. Then one day . . . engineer, like Pa."

"Your father drives the *Ballyhoo*?"

"Ox Everett," Conker interrupted as he dropped an armload of blue painted poles. "That's him over there." Ray followed Conker's nod toward a tall, portly man with a long walrus mustache. Mister Everett wore a shiny engineer's cap and blue striped denim suit. He was talking to Peg Leg Nel and a young man a few years older than Eddie who was nearly a twin of the bakehead, if you scrubbed Eddie down in a bucket of hot water and dressed him in more suitable work clothes.

Eddie and Ray put down the canvas roll at the entrance of the tent and began helping Conker put together the poles. Eddie explained, "That's my brother, Shacks, and you met my ma, didn't you?"

"Not properly," Ray said.

"Well, she already's taken a liking to you, but watch out for Pa," Eddie said meekly.

"Don't listen to him, Ray," Conker chuckled. "A little hard sometimes, but Ox Everett's a fine engineer and an old-time friend of Nel's. Fought in the war together. He and Nel love playing music. You'll hear come showtime. Eddie and Shacks are hot shots, too. But couldn't have the show without Mister Everett. He does all the arranging. Talks to the local officials, persuades or pays them. Whatever it takes to get things set proper."

"One day, the *Ballyhoo* will be mine," Eddie added with a wistful expression as he started driving the metal poles in the ground. "She's the greatest train around!"

Ray looked again at the flaking paint and rust, the leaking oil from the axles, and the weathered wood paneling the cars. "Is she fast?" Ray asked, assuming her better qualities lay beyond appearances.

The proud look faded slightly from Eddie's soot-covered face. "Well, no. Not particularly."

Securing the framework of poles to the ground with guidewires, Conker smirked. "She breaks down all the time."

"So by greatest train around," Ray said, "you mean the greatest train here . . . sitting right in front of us."

Conker roared with laughter as Eddie made a face.

Then Conker added, "She may not look like much, Ray, but she's home."

Steering the conversation away from the *Ballyhoo* so as not to offend Eddie further, Ray asked, "What do you do, Conker? Are you a performer or do you help on the train?"

The giant turned around, dwarfing Ray in the shadow of his height and scowling face. "Can't you tell? I'm the strongman."

"Oh," Ray said, cowering a moment. But Conker broke again into his easy laugh and clapped a coal-shovel-sized hand on Ray's shoulder.

"Come on, I'll show you my handiwork. Grab ahold of the other side of this roll and we'll get it hung up at the front gate. Painted the sign myself."

After attaching the corners of the canvas roll to the framework of poles, Conker let it unfurl. Ray stood back with Eddie to admire the ten-by-twelve-foot sign introducing CORNELIUS T. CARTER'S MYSTIFYING MEDICINE SHOW AND TABERNACLE OF TACHYCARDIAL TALENT. If Conker hadn't already found his calling as a performer, he could have been an artist.

The spitting image of Peg Leg Nel, although with a few less wrinkles and not quite so wild-eyed to Ray's mind, peered down from the center. Below the oval-framed portrait, a scrolling banner announced CORNELIUS T. CARTER along with the title ROOT WORKER.

"That's me." Conker pointed to a bare-chested likeness of himself lifting a globe, like Atlas from the old myths. If anything, Ray thought Conker had been too humble in his self-portrait. The real Conker was much more imposing.

Ray scanned the other images. He found the SNAKE DANCER, Marisol, her torso and arms covered in slithering pythons. Buck was there, too, sporting an outstretched pistol above the label BLIND SHARPSHOOTER. Below him was a young man in a turban swallowing a sword. SWORD SWALLOWER. There was an Indian with a feathered headdress. Flames encircled him. FIRE-EATER. A Chinese girl, who must have been Conker's friend Si, was twisted in a knot and encased in a ridiculous number of locks and chains. She was listed as the ESCAPE ARTIST.

"Think you'll stick around, Ray?" Eddie asked.

"I'm not sure," Ray said.

"Well, you ought to stay here with us," Conker said. "We can use a hawker out front and help setting up and breaking down. Always plenty of work."

Ray looked around at the medicine show's tent and the rickety train. Conker put his hand to Ray's back, directing him toward the train. "Come on. Nearly lunchtime."

* * *

Ray was greeted warmly. First by the rich smells coming from the makeshift dining room erected in the grass on the backside of the *Ballyhoo*. In the shade of a wide oak, a table was created from old doors and sawhorses. It took four mismatched floral tablecloths to cover the length. An assortment of chairs and benches from the train were set about, most of the medicine show already seated and scooping heavy servings onto their tin plates. Enormous cast-iron pots and pans were heaped with different steaming dishes: a buttery, yellow cornmeal cake, hissing pieces of fried chicken, dark oily greens flecked with cut potatoes and bits of fatback, gooey mounds of yams, and ears of corn, the husks blackened from roasting. Ray had no doubt the last had been stolen from the field that stretched out behind them.

The next greeting came from Ma Everett's warm arms enfolding Ray. "Glad you're out and about, young one. Spent so much time with you in there, I feel I already know you."

Ray smiled at the small, pinched face he recalled from the brief windows of wakening from his feverish sleep.

"I'm Ma Everett," she chirped.

"Yes, I know," he said. "I'm Ray."

"You feeling better, dear?"

"Yes. Much. Thank you for all you did."

"Nothing, nothing," she said. "Take a seat, anywhere.

Fix a plate. You still look a fair bit peaked. They haven't been working you too much, I hope."

"He insisted," Conker said, mashing Ray into a chair at his side. He began shoveling heaps on his plate. Ray imagined that Ma Everett could have cooked all day just to keep Conker alone fed, but serving himself from the enormous pans, Ray realized that there would be more than enough to feed the entire medicine show and half the town of Hillsboro.

Ray noticed a strange object beyond the shade of the oak, toward the caboose of the *Ballyhoo*. It was a cedar pole stuck into the ground. The branches were stripped, and upturned bottles of ocean blues, ripe greens, fire reds, and golden yellows were fastened with wire to where the broken limbs had been. Looking around, he saw another one farther away, on the edge of the cornfield near the tent.

"What are those poles?" Ray asked Conker over the clank of silverware and loud conversation swimming about the table.

"Hmm? Oh, bottletrees," he murmured.

"Salutations to our bear-rider," Peg Leg Nel called from down the table.

Conker whispered, "Think Nel's got you in mind for performing. What do you think of that?"

"I think he's mistaken," Ray said, noticing that Si was listening discreetly. "I'm no showman."

Si glared at Ray from the opposite side of the table, sitting between Ox and Ma Everett. She sneered and looked away when their eyes met, returning to a book she was reading by her plate. Ray felt distinctly that she had something against him, but he wasn't sure why. His eyes shifted to her hands, which he noticed were covered with red silk gloves.

With a quick scan, Ray realized that the blind cowboy, Buck, was not there.

A straw-haired boy sat down in the empty seat next to Ray, followed by an Indian boy with two sleek braids draped over his shoulders. Both wore dusty wool trousers and loose cotton shirts not much different than Ray's, although theirs were less threadbare.

"Heard you were practicing a hootchy-kootchy routine for Marisol," the straw-haired boy said, drawing snorts from the Indian boy at his side. "I should warn you we don't have a burlesque act in this show. We're wholesome entertainment."

"Leave the boy alone," Ma Everett said sharply.

"Just ribbing him, Ma," he said. He gave Ray such a big smile that Ray decided it was best to laugh along. The boy snapped his fingers. "You're all right. Ray, right? I'm Seth."

Ray nodded, reaching to shake the boy's hand and then leaning over to the Indian, who said in a soft voice, "My name's U'melth Hamatsa-Xalmala, but it's too hard for most to pronounce, so everyone just calls me Redfeather."

"Where are you from, Redfeather?" Ray asked, taken aback by the incomprehensibly long name.

"The northwest coast of Canada—a village off Vancouver Island," Redfeather said, drooping his head so that his braids nearly fell in his food. "I'm Kwakiutl, although here I'm just the Fire-Eater."

"Yeah, I saw your picture on Conker's sign. Are you the sword swallower?" Ray asked Seth.

Seth snapped his fingers again and pointed at Ray. "That's right. The star performer," he added with a smug smile.

"More like star imbecile," Si muttered.

Seth opened his mouth to reply, but Ray quickly asked, "How did you all learn to do these things?"

While Seth glared at Si, Redfeather answered in his soft voice, "Some things you're just born with."

Then Seth added, smiling churlishly at Si, "And some of us work hard to be this amazing."

Ray knew he was going to have a hard time remembering everybody—all these new names and strange faces. It seemed that the medicine show was made up of two groups. There were the performers: The pitchman and root doctor, Peg Leg Nel. The blind sharpshooter, Buck. Conker, the strongman, and Si, the escape artist. The snake dancer, Marisol. The two boys—Seth, the sword swallower, and Redfeather, the fire-eater.

And then there was the Everett family: Ox Everett, the engineer. His wife, Ma Everett. Eddie, the fireman, and his older brother, Shacks, the brakeman. They operated the *Ballyhoo,* fixed meals, and helped to assemble the show, as well as providing music.

The meal was unlike any that Ray had ever shared. In the breeze under the oak, Ray could scarcely finish his plate for simply enjoying the sense of being a part of something he could not quite name. What was it when people laughed and ate and shouted across the table to one another?

"Where are you from, Ray?" Ma Everett called across the din. "Not from around here, I can hear."

The meal was slowly coming to an end and many of the faces around the table turned to listen, which made Ray self-conscious. Peg Leg Nel had removed his orange plaid coat and relaxed with his shirtsleeves rolled up his wiry, dark arms and his silk cravat loosened below his collar. He removed a small briarwood pipe from his shirt pocket. Across the table, the engineer, Ox Everett, was chewing something noxious-smelling that, when spit, looked like oily molasses.

"From all over up north, I suppose. We moved around to a lot of cities."

"Your parents still living up there, Ray?" Ma Everett asked.

"No, ma'am. Both my parents are gone. I have a sister somewhere down here. Hopefully she's been adopted and has found a wonderful family."

Ma Everett wasn't the only one whose face winced with sympathy at the understanding that Ray's parents were dead. She gave him a gentle smile. "What are you going to do, dear? Are you looking for your sister?"

"No. Well, I'd love to see her again, but she's . . . better off for now. I'm not sure where I'm going."

Ma Everett cast a pitying look at Nel, who was eyeing Ray thoughtfully.

Ray said to the pitchman, "I did think that—if you would, sir—you could give me some work to do today. Not for money or anything. Just to help repay you all for taking care of me."

"Well, certainly, son. Always appreciative of an extra set of hands. You'll work the hawking stage with me. Two shows today. Should be bustling! I'll situate you at the charge of collecting money—with me supervising, of course. Give Everett here a much-deserved respite so he can enjoy playing his devil's box. See me at the stage in— let's say half hour's time."

At that, the table began to clear in a rustle of movement.

"Thank you, sir," Ray said. "Thank you all." He nodded to Ma Everett and the others.

As Ray dropped his plate with the others in the soapy bucket, Peg Leg Nel stood from the table and called out to him. He waved Ray over and leaned close as he spoke. "Ray. If you decide not to embark on other employment, you got work—something more long term—right here if you want it. I'm of the mind that, in time, you might want to take up the calling of . . . divertissement, i.e., entertaining. Never been one to badger the reluctant, but just thought I'd mention. My point is . . . we'll have you if you'll stay."

Ray's hand brushed against the lodestone in his pocket. "Thank you, sir. I'll think about it." And as he looked once more at the empty table, Ray came upon the word that described Nel's medicine show.

Family. They were a family.

Sitting on the edge of the stage stitching the hole in his cap, Ray counted the days since he had last seen Sally. It might as well have been years ago, for all the time he could gauge. The hungry days wandering in the strange wood and the fever left abysmal holes in his memory. A wave of longing crushed down upon Ray and briefly his eyes burned.

Had she found a good home? And if so, where was it? Maybe the family would let him visit her, explain why he had left. But how could he possibly find her? She could be anywhere. There were hundreds of towns, thousands and thousands of houses across the South.

Ray tied off the last stitch and bit the end of the thread off. Plopping his cap on his head, he took out the lodestone. It was still not moving. He wondered if it had led him here, to the medicine show. And if so, why? He put the lodestone back and kicked his heels against the stage as he looked around the tent.

The performers were away, most likely cleaning up and getting dressed before the show. Ray noticed a few townspeople gathering beyond the entrance, reading the sign or at least looking at the pictures and casting curious glances toward the stage. He overheard a man say to another, "Won't catch my God-fearing soul around no darkie hoodoo." But as he stormed off, Ray saw the other man count the coins from his pocket while he waited for the show to start.

Where was Peg Leg Nel? Hadn't it been half an hour? Ray walked around, but saw nobody but Ma Everett, washing the plates with a long-handled brush. "Missus Everett, have you seen Mister Nel?"

"No, dear. Probably getting ready in his car."

"Which one is that?" Ray asked.

"You'll get oriented to the train soon." She pointed to the first car after the locomotive and tender. "That's the sleeping car, where you'll stay. Next is the mess car—the kitchen, dining room on the go, and storage. I leave out snacks there, in case you're hungry before supper. After that one's Buck and Nel's car. Head on down there. You'll find him."

Ray nodded a thank-you and walked down the gravel right-of-way beside the train. When he reached the mess car, he hopped up the steps on the vestibule and went in. On a normal passenger train, the car would have had tables for riders to sit and eat. This one had been modified for the *Ballyhoo*. The stationary tables were removed to make room for the show's supplies. There was a cast-iron potbelly stove mounted to one wall and a simple wooden table, with biscuits and leftovers from lunch laid out on tin plates. Shelves were covered in jars of pickled vegetables and various preserved fruits. Several salted hams and strings of sausages swayed from the ceiling. The room smelled sweet and sticky with wood smoke and grease.

Nobody was there, and Ray passed across the vestibule to the next car—Nel's car. His was another sleeping car that had also been altered. There was a short hallway with two doors and then an open area where the rest of the carriage rooms had been removed.

This was obviously Nel's workshop as well. In cabinets and shelves, filling crates, and hanging from pegs in the ceiling were the supplies for the medicine show's tonics. Coils of dried snakeskins. Wide-mouthed bottles filled with earthy-brown roots. Tins holding various claws and teeth. Strings of fragrant herbs. Jars of bleached bones. Powders and liquids in a rainbow of colors. A table sat in the middle of the room, covered in all manner of bottles from tiny droppers to gallon-sized flagons.

Ray knocked at the doors—calling out Mister Nel's name—but got no reply. He crossed the vestibule to the next car and found the door locked. As he walked down the steps and continued around the side of the train, he reached a boxcar. The side was open and most of its contents emptied—apparently already set up for the show.

Voices came from the opposite side of the boxcar. Nel was speaking to someone. Ray climbed up onto the vestibule connecting the locked car and the boxcar. As he came down the other side, what he heard gave him pause.

"How's our new arrival?" Nel asked.

"Needs more time," a hoarse low voice replied.

Peeking around the side of the train, Ray saw that Nel was talking to Buck. Buck's head nodded and turned in small loose motions. His eyelids were parted slightly, and Ray saw the ghostly white encompassing the iris, the pupil nothing more than a pinhole spot.

Nel's voice cracked with worry. "What if he finds . . . ?"

"He won't. He has no idea I was there or where we went. He's still searching the Terrebonne wilderness, I'm sure. Why would he look on a train—and with a medicine show? He'd never suspect it. We're safe for now. I'm certain."

"I'm not exactly comfortable with this, Buck."

"What would make you comfortable?" Buck's voice was brisk and gravelly. "To let the Enemy have—?"

"No, but I'm . . . we're entertainers! Businessmen. Not . . ."

"Not what?" Buck snapped. "Ramblers? When are you going to accept that he's still out there and growing more powerful every day?"

"Look, Buck. I've purchased the car just as you asked. It's protected as best we can manage. If I'd known that's where you were traipsing off to all those times . . . What will you have me do?"

"Just the medicines for now and stop being so nervous. By the way," Buck added in a louder voice, taking his hat from his bobbing head and gesturing across Nel's shoulder. "The kid's here."

"The kid?" Nel turned around, his eyes momentarily

wide with apprehension. Before Ray could duck back behind the boxcar, Nel called out. "Oh, my bear-rider. Ferreted me out," he laughed awkwardly. "We were just discussing . . . some issues with the tonics. Nothing to concern yourself over. My, time's escaping me and our shows are imminently approaching. We've got one in the afternoon and another in the evening."

Nel smiled, striding toward Ray in his bandy-legged walk. Clasping a hand to Ray's shoulder, the pitchman said, "If we arrest the first crowd properly with our heart-pounding performance, they'll spread the word for a bigger evening arrival. Come, let's discuss the nitty-gritty of the money collection."

Ray looked back. Buck's blind eyes could not have seen him, but he had somehow known that Ray was there. At that moment, the midday shadows cast Buck's face in a strange light. With his hat removed and his long silver-streaked hair falling about his face, Ray realized he had seen Buck before.

Ray's eyes fell to the silver pistols at Buck's belts. The nightmare. Buck had been there, with the girl and the other man, running from the monstrous hound.

AS THE EVERETT MEN BEGAN PLAYING MUSIC, A CROWD
gathered in the muggy shade beneath the worn old canvas
tent. A bench was set at the back of the lower, center stage,
where the three Everetts ripped through tune after tune.
Mister Everett played a blond violin and Eddie a dark mahogany parlor guitar. Shacks rapped his fingers across a
gut-string banjo.

At the front of the stage, Peg Leg Nel danced about,
tapping his pegged leg in time with the beat and leading
the melody on a harmonica. At times he'd release his
hands from the harmonica, suck it entirely into his mouth
as he continued to play it, and then spit it back out, never
missing a note from the song. He would occasionally—and
seemingly on a whim—jerk the harmonica from his lips
and begin singing in a warbling tenor voice. Ray wondered

if these were the intended lyrics or if Nel just generated lines on the spot.

The side stages were empty for the moment, but as Ray had noticed earlier, they were strategically set up against the *Ballyhoo*'s sleeping car so that the performers could wait inside and come out the door at either end onto the two performance stages. Several displays of Nel's various tonics were set up on the center stage.

Ray sat behind one display next to Shacks, his thoughts whirling. Buck had been in his dream! Ray shuddered. Did that mean that the nightmare was real?

"You ever worked a show before?" Shacks asked.

Shacks was older than Eddie, maybe nineteen or twenty, Ray guessed, judging from the scrap of hair sprouting from his chin and atop his lip. Like Eddie, he had Ma Everett's small features but wore his father's serious expression.

"No, never. Seen plenty in the city but never this . . . fancy," Ray said. "You like working for the medicine show?"

Nel switched from a minstrel song about golden slippers to a rollicking version of "Arkansas Traveler." Shacks looked over to note the key from the position of Eddie's fingers and then turned back to Ray.

"Show life's all right," Shacks said, knocking his thumb rhythmically along his banjo strings. "Like picking music. But the train life, that's for me."

Ray turned his attention to the crowd. Men and boys,

both black and white, in dirty farm clothes were clearly visitors in town for the cotton market. He saw families, most likely the citizenry of Hillsboro, who were out for the entertainment and the hope of buying something that would cure their varying ailments, both real and imagined. Men in ascot-stuffed vests and ulster coats and women in bustle dresses and bonnets seemed to be of more affluent means, while others—barefoot or in little more than rags—couldn't have come with a penny in their pockets or to their names.

Nel ended the breakdown with a wild flourish of his hand, pointing to the three musicians on the stage. "The Everett Family String Band!" he announced as the audience applauded. Mister Everett alone stood, bowed as the representative of the band, and then gestured to Nel.

"Our illustrious pitchman, Mister Carter. Take it away," Mister Everett announced.

Having been introduced to the crowd as the pitchman, Nel began. Ray recognized that, although ceremonial, this gesture by Mister Everett was intended to legitimize Nel to an audience that might not otherwise accept the Negro pitchman. The effects and sentiments of the War—although it had been twenty-five years since Appomattox—still lingered strongly in these rural towns.

"Ladies and gentlemen, boys and girls, welcome to Cornelius T. Carter's Mystifying Medicine Show and Tabernacle of Tachycardial Talent. Today you will be astounded, amazed, abased, and abducted by our arousing acts. I hope you enjoy our perplexing and prodigious performances, but we are here today not only to delight the senses but also to bolster the body and soothe the soul.

"How many of you felicitous folks have come here today on sore feet? Are you suffering from corns, blisters, busted toenails? Shoes squeezing your toes together like too many sardines in a can?"

As Peg Leg Nel went into his spiel about various foot and knee ailments, Ray felt he immediately understood a large portion of the logic underlying the medicine show. Ray saw various people toward the front of the stage, from hobble-backed old men to small pink-cheeked girls, twisting and squirming in their shoes. Ray felt even his own feet become particularly sore and swollen with each sentence of Nel's pitch.

"Apply amply before going to bed each night and you are guaranteed to be remedied within a week," Nel concluded before striking the band back into a song. "Allow me to introduce our first performance of the afternoon. Kidnapped by Bedouin slave traders as his family crossed the Sahara . . . he was sold to a Turkish sultan, who passed on his people's ancient art of combat and swordplay. . . ." The pitchman directed the audience's attention to the stage on the left, where a pair of tall candles were sitting in golden candelabras. "The dexterous, the dynamic, the deadly . . . Prince Ottmon of Arabia."

Dressed in a Turkish caftan and turban, Seth strode out

onto the side stage with a rectangular case about the size of a guitar. He set the case down on a stool between the candelabras and opened it, allowing each latch to click dramatically. First he took out a wide scimitar, turning it back and forth to sparkle in the candlelight. Then he removed a smaller cutlass, the blade intricately etched with Arabian designs.

With a shout, Seth flipped forward, over his sword case on the stool, to the front of the stage, startling the audience. Then he leaped away, swinging the scimitar over and over at the thick burning candles. The sword went through the candles each time, but left them seemingly intact. Then stopping between the candelabras, he swung the swords out wide and tapped the candles with the blades. The candles toppled and rolled to the floor of the stage like diced sausages.

Seth speared the stage floor with his cutlass and, making a flip, landed with his hands on the hilt of the sword, balancing himself upside down as the crowd roared with applause. Somersaulting off, he kicked the sword into a whirl. Catching the tip on his upturned finger, Seth suspended the cutlass as if it were held up by a string. Ray looked closely, but the sparkling blade did not draw a single drop of blood.

For his finale he slid a long, slender sword from his belt into his mouth, nearly to the hilt. His head tilted back and his arms outstretched so that he no longer held the sword.

The audience burst into a frenzy of cheers, shrieks, and whistles.

As Seth bowed over and over and over, Nel tried to draw the audience's attention back to the center stage. "Thank you, thank you, ladies and gentlemen. Does your stomach hurt? Feel like knives are poking your esophagus? Gastric discomfort got your bowels speared with distress? Then try *Baron Bayonet's Bonbons. . . .*"

Ray sold out of the tablets in less than a minute.

"Friends, you've heard of the great gunslingers of Deadwood and Dodge City," Nel continued after pitching various other stomach and bowel tonics. "The cold steel of Billy the Kid, John Wesley Hardin, and Wyatt Earp bloodied many a Wild West street. You've heard of the amazing Annie Oakley and Wild Bill Hickok. They were all dead-on shots with a six-shooter. But, friends, they all had two things that our next performer did not."

Peg Leg Nel paused, then slowly pointed to each of his eyes in turn. He gave a hard stomp to the wooden stage.

"Yes, friends, the gift of sight," the pitchman said. "From the high-plain sagebrush prairies of the Wild West. Don't be alarmed, folks. He may be an eagle-eye shot, but he's completely blind. May I present: Montana Hodder."

Eustace Buckthorn walked out on the right stage, tapping his way with a worn oak cane that Ray could only assume was to play up Buck's blindness to the audience.

Buck's outfit was no different than the one he had been wearing an hour earlier when Ray had been caught listening to his conversation with Nel. His slate-gray, wide-brimmed hat contained Buck's rowdy hair, but long silver-streaked locks fell over his eyes.

Buck dropped the cane to the floor of the stage. His hands went to the twin holsters slung low across his hips. Ray could hear the whispers from the crowd.

"Is he really blind?"

"Sure, look—he ain't got no eyes."

"He's got eyes. I see them under his hair, but they's white as milk."

Ray felt a rush of awkwardness and irritation at the way the crowd discussed Buck's blindness with no regard to whether the cowboy could hear them. But to watch Buck's raised chin and firm stance, he was either used to the treatment or keeping his own anger stoically hidden.

Nel hopped up to the opposite stage, where a stack of cheap porcelain plates had been placed. "Ready!" he cried, and tossed two of the plates up toward the top of the tent. A pair of sandalwood-handled pistols flashed from Buck's holsters and fired in rapid succession. The plates splintered into tiny shards raining down on the stage. Several people in the vicinity tucked their hands over their hats and went scurrying for the thick of the crowd.

Cheers burst out, but Buck's expression remained placid. Nel began throwing more of the plates, sometimes a high one, sometimes a quick series of plates. Each of Buck's bullets met its mark.

"Can we have a volunteer from the crowd?" Nel called.

There was general murmur but nobody came forward.

"Come now, brave people," he cajoled. "Let my assistant demonstrate."

Nel waved Ray up to the front of the stage. Peg Leg Nel hadn't said anything about being a part of the performance! As the eyes of the audience shifted to Ray squatting at the back of the stage, he had little time to let his fear stop him. Ray walked hesitantly to the spot where Nel situated him.

"Take off your cap," Nel whispered. "Keep a straight back. Don't move and you'll be fine."

The pitchman gave him a wink and placed an apple on his curly head. As Nel backed away, Ray kept his shoulders back and stood motionless. He felt certain that Buck had done this hundreds of times. Nel wouldn't have brought Ray up if there was any danger.

But a sudden image came to his mind—a flash of Buck's face when Ray had been caught listening to his conversation with Nel. Although Buck had been trying to assure Nel, the pitchman had seemed scared. They were in some sort of danger. What if the secret of what they were hiding in the locked car was something terribly important, important enough to want to keep Ray quiet . . . permanently?

This was irrational, at least Ray hoped, but as Buck drew his pistols, all the worst possibilities erupted in his mind.

Buck never turned to face Ray. He just gave a quick sniff. Buck drew back the hammer on the pistol, extended his arm out to the side, and fired. The apple exploded into sticky confetti.

Ray sputtered a few pieces off of his lips and brushed the apple bits from his shoulders. The crowd applauded, and Ray smiled gingerly, feeling proud that he hadn't flinched in the face of fear. He wished Conker could have seen it. As he reached the spot at the back of the stage, Ray saw that someone had noticed. Buck's face was turned slightly toward Ray, a curious expression flickering on the cowboy's brow.

"I'll do it!" a man shouted from the front. Nel smiled and motioned for the man to come onto the stage. The man had a stringy beard that extended under his chin, more on his neck than on his face. He was laughing and showing off a gap-toothed grin to the men who were with him.

"You're nuts, Lenny," his friends laughed and goaded from the crowd.

"Not as batty as him." Lenny pointed at Buck and sniggered. "Get it? Batty."

His friends contorted their faces in confusion.

"Bats is blind," Lenny explained.

His friends howled.

When Lenny came up on the stage, he strolled right up

to Buck, pointing in his face and waving his hands in front of the cowboy's nose. "Sure you can't see?" he laughed.

"Put the apple on your head," Buck said in his unexpressive gravel voice.

Lenny danced over to the table and took a pair of apples. Rather than removing the ratty porkpie hat from his head, he placed one of the apples on the top of his hat and slipped the second into his coat pocket as a snack for later.

"Alrighty, Mister. Don't miss." He chuckled. "You sure you don't want my granny's spectacles?"

Buck slowly stepped around, facing the guffawing man. His boots thumped with each step. "You might want to take that hat off," he said.

"You betcha, buddy." Lenny grinned. "I got it off." He touched a hand to the porkpie but didn't remove it.

Buck held the pistols hip level. The audience took a collective breath. All was quiet but the snorts coming from Lenny's nose. Then the pistols discharged in three ear-shattering blasts. The apple disappeared into a white cloud of particles. Lenny's face clamped with visible fear as the second bullet formed a smoking hole in his porkpie hat. What were once chuckles now became whimpers when he reached his fingers down to his hip, where a hole was smoking from his coat pocket. Lenny pulled out the other apple, blown into a gooey cream by the third bullet.

Lenny scuttled from the stage to the heckling of his friends.

* * *

The afternoon continued with another pitch from Peg Leg Nel and a lilting version of "Bonaparte's Retreat" from the band. Ray watched Conker emerge on the left-side stage carrying a black lacquered trunk. For a moment he thought this was going to be the giant's performance, but Conker left the stage after placing the trunk before the wondering audience.

Ray helped Nel with the tonics and tinctures. As the pitchman heard people's ailments, he'd call out a name such as *Simpleton's Memory Salve* or *Gold Brick's Lassitude Livener,* and Ray looked through the crates to deliver the tonic. As he went back and forth, he kept an eye on the stage, watching the performance and wondering which performer was going to use the trunk.

The black lacquered trunk was no bigger than an ordinary footlocker and had a gold Oriental dragon encircling the four sides until it met its own tail. The crowd restlessly scratched their heads and whispered to one another, waiting for what would happen.

The trunk rumbled and shifted; then it was still again. A sharp crack rang out as the lid popped open. Two bare feet could be seen sticking up from the interior. The feet pulled back into the trunk, and then a figure emerged, standing up slowly. At first Ray could not make sense of what he was seeing. It looked like a jumble of chains wrapped around a potato sack, no taller than three feet.

Something was erupting from beneath the small bundle of chains. It reminded Ray of a butterfly emerging from a metal chrysalis. Then in one moment the chains went from taut to loose and rattled down into the box. What remained was a pretzel of a figure. Ray couldn't believe anybody could get so tangled up. It looked like somebody had gotten twisted up in some horrible piece of machinery. He had to look carefully to distinguish a leg from an arm, a shoulder blade from an ankle.

Si was tied up with her arms wrapped around her back until they emerged from either side of her waist. But her torso was also tied to her legs, which were wrapped over her shoulders. How had she gotten those chains off? Ray wondered. How had she opened the box? Come to think of it, how did she fit in that tiny box in the first place?

Si rolled forward out of the lacquered trunk, careful not to tip it as she exited. With her feet firmly planted on the stage, Si rose and began slowly winding around like a miniature carousel. It seemed that at any minute she would reach the point where her waist could twist no further and she would pop in half. The ropes began loosening from her torso. Twisting back the other direction, Si worked the ropes off her back until they collapsed at her feet. In a bizarre spiral, her shoulders surfaced from between her knees, and she rose upright to the whistles and applause of the audience.

Nel called out to the audience, "Does anyone have a handkerchief we might borrow?"

A man wearing a gold badge on his collar extended a

handkerchief up to Nel. "Thank you, sir," Nel said, inspecting the square of blue cloth. " 'H.M.' Your initials here in the corner?"

The man nodded and mumbled, "Henry Mulvey."

"Thank you, Sheriff Mulvey." Nel then showed the handkerchief to Si. She gazed at it and then turned her back to the audience.

"Sheriff Mulvey, I'm going to hand back your handkerchief, and if you would, give it to someone in the audience." Mulvey nodded and then walked through the crowd. "Is someone else in possession of the napkin, sir?" Nel asked. Mulvey came back to the front of the stage and nodded.

Si turned and walked to the edge of the stage. The audience watched her curiously, and as she jumped from the stage, the crowd backed a few steps from the exotic-looking girl. Si wandered through the audience until she reached an elderly lady in a cottage cloak. Si nodded at the woman's sleeve.

Nel called to the lady, "Dear woman, do you have Sheriff Mulvey's square?"

A smile broke out on the woman's face as she produced the handkerchief from the cuff of her dress. Cheers and applause followed Si as she returned to the stage.

Ray's eyes were drawn to Si's dark hand. It swirled with slight sparkles, like lightning bugs in twilight.

* * *

Ray laughed as Conker lifted a fat woman up in a chair one-handed.

"Ray," Nel hissed for the third time, batting Ray's head with his fez. "We've nearly reached the denouement and I need you to go retrieve more tonics. There's a boxcar toward the back of the *Ballyhoo*. You'll find the extra supplies of tonics. We're dispossessed of the *Johnny Chapman's Apple-flavored Arthritis Anodyne*. Can you remember that? Get a dozen bottles and some tins of the *Chief Joseph's Nasal Naphtha*. They're all labeled. Hurry! After Marisol and Redfeather, we'll be bustling with customers. Run!"

Ray looked once over at Conker as the giant lifted four people effortlessly, each pair clinging together to a bench ten feet above the stage. Sorry to miss the rest of Conker's performance, Ray dashed off the back of the stage. The noise of the crowd dissipated until all Ray could hear was the lone melody of Mister Everett's fiddle. He reached the side of the boxcar and climbed up through the open doors. Ray pulled the Pirate Queen's silver dagger from his coat pocket and used it to pry the lids off several boxes. Jangling bottles and tins in their crates, he read the labels until he found the *Arthritis Anodyne* and the *Nasal Naphtha*.

A sound jerked his head from the task. He cocked an ear and listened. It was faint at first, but as he focused, he could detect a soft singing. Ray dropped the bottles into an empty crate and slipped out the door of the boxcar. He tilted his head about until he discovered the source of the song. It was coming from the locked car next to the boxcar.

The singing was low and melancholy, and Ray placed his ear to the door to listen better. There was something about the voice, something about the song that made him want to listen, made him want to get inside the car. Ray was suddenly overwhelmed with a desire to pick the lock, to break down the door, to tear the side off the train if only it would allow him to hear the singing better.

"What do you think you're doing?" A sharp voice startled Ray. The spell was broken and Ray turned shamefully to face the Chinese escape artist. Si's eyes flickered as she saw the dagger in Ray's hand.

"Using it to pry the lids off," Ray explained as he slid it back into his belt.

Si scowled. "I assumed you were a half-wit, but that's not a lid. That's what we like to call a door. Nel sent me to find you. Now, get back to the show with those tonics!"

As Ray followed Si, he glanced back once more at the locked car.

The musicians were playing a slow, sinuous song in some exotic scale that accentuated Marisol's serpentine dance. She wore tinkling bangles on her wrists and ankles. A pair of rattlesnakes coiled down each of her arms, shaking their tails in time with the dance. A black viper, exposing its long fangs at the audience, was wrapped around Marisol from her waist to her neck, but Ray could not pay attention.

His heart was still pounding. His throat felt hollow and dry. What had just happened to him?

After Marisol finished and Ray helped Nel sell the next batch of tonics, he was starting to feel less shaky.

"You all right?" Shacks asked as Ray settled back to the floor next to him. Ray nodded and turned to Nel at the front of the stage.

"Allow me to introduce our final performance of the afternoon . . . from the land of Cochise and Geronimo, grandson of the only warrior to escape the Salt Canyon Massacre in the Arizona Territory . . ." The pitchman pointed to his right. "The bloodthirsty Chiricahua Apache scout . . . our fire-eater . . . Ember Joe!"

Stepping out from behind the curtain on the left-hand stage, Redfeather wore his pin-striped brown pants and a newly donned crimson shirt over which he had layered dozens of necklaces of beads, shells, polished bones, and copper. His long braids were crowned with a pepper-red silk sash. A stream of fire burst from his mouth over the heads of the ducking crowd. Squeals jumped from those at the front of the stage.

In the middle of the stage, Redfeather placed a copper bowl filled with burning coals onto a stool. He took two flaming batons from the bowl and began spinning them through his fingers and throwing them high in the air. He danced and somersaulted, all the time creating twin circles of flames with the batons. After returning them to the copper bowl, Redfeather poured a vessel of oil onto the hot embers, shooting tall flames up from the bowl.

Redfeather rolled up one of his sleeves past the elbow. He pulled a penny from his pocket, showed it to the audience, and then stuck the penny and his hand into the center of the flames. The audience shouted. Dumbfounded, Ray leaned forward to get a closer look and saw that although the fire lapped Redfeather's arms, his flesh had not the slightest indication of being burned.

Redfeather pulled his hand from the flame and held up the glowing molten penny for all to see. The fire-eater then pinched down on the penny, mashing the coin into a lumpy shape, which he then rolled in his hand into a string of copper. Putting the melted coin back into the flames, Ray watched as Redfeather fashioned the copper that had once been a penny into a ring. Redfeather dropped the copper ring into a bucket of water on the edge of the stage. As the audience applauded, Redfeather took the cooled ring from the water and tossed it to a young boy standing at the front of the stage.

"Give him a hand," Peg Leg Nel urged the crowd. Redfeather took a bow. Nel then asked, "Would you like to see our fire-eater bob for an apple?"

Nel took an apple from a bowl by his tonics and tossed it up to Redfeather. Redfeather placed the apple into the flaming copper bowl. Ray could see the apple burning, its skin quickly turning a papery black.

Standing before the bowl of fire, Redfeather pushed his

braids back over his shoulders and readied himself. To Ray's astonishment, Redfeather plunged his head into the heart of the flames. Then Redfeather stood upright, the charred apple locked between his teeth. His face did not seem to have even broken a sweat, much less been burned.

The audience erupted in whistles and cheers.

As the performers poured out onto the stage to take a final bow, Nel beckoned Ray to the front of the stage. Several customers gathered around with outstretched hands full of coins, bills, even some barter items. "Get these people some of the *Molly Pied Salve*. Yes, sir. Burning belly? Ray, hand that man a *B. Zell Bub Tincture*." Ray snapped to work, taking money and handing out the medicines.

As he did, he thought about the performers. Conker was unusually strong and Seth skillful, but Si's tattoo was something more. And what he had just seen Redfeather do was . . . impossible! Ray realized now what Seth and Redfeather had meant at lunch when they said some performers were born with skills but others had to work for their talent. No amount of work and training could have taught Si or Redfeather to do the things they had done.

Nearly an hour later, Ray and Nel finished with the last customers.

"We'll have more tonight. Sorry, folks," Nel said over and over. "Come back at seven o'clock this evening and we'll have more—more miraculous tonics and more astounding acts! Tell your friends."

As the last people exited the tent, Nel turned to Ray,

drawing his sleeve across his sweaty forehead. "I take it you enjoyed the performance?"

"Yes," Ray said.

"Well, we're heading off tomorrow. I could certainly use your help."

"Where are you going next?" Ray asked.

"Winston," Nel said. "And then vagabonding south to—"

"South?" Ray asked. "You're going south?"

Nel spread his hands and gave a wide grin. "Unless the cardinal points have shifted, I do believe we'll venture south."

"Then I'm coming with you," Ray said, unable to contain his relief as he smiled. The lodestone had been leading him south before it inexplicably stopped . . . before it had brought him to the medicine show.

"Of course you are." Nel nodded. "Abide as much time as you wish with us. The job is yours. Come. Let's get more tonics unloaded from the boxcar."

RAY HAD BEEN UP LATE WITH THE OTHERS, DISASSEMBLING the medicine show's tent and stage and packing everything into the *Ballyhoo*. He woke the following morning to find the train already traveling.

Ray stepped out into the cluttered hallway, rubbed his eyes, and walked to the vestibule to get some air. On the other side of the low-topped tender car, Eddie was working with his father up in the locomotive. Eddie gave a friendly wave before lifting another shovelful of coal from the tender.

"You're awake," Conker said from behind him.

Ray turned and then looked up at the giant crouching in the doorway to the vestibule. "Is it late?" Ray asked. "I was exhausted."

"Midmorning, I reckon," Conker said. "You missed breakfast. Ma Everett left out some food for you."

Ray followed Conker down the hallway. He had trouble getting the hang of how to sway with the movement of the jostling train. As he fell against the wall when the train took a turn, Ray imagined that it was like being on a ship. Soon he'd forget about the nauseating back-and-forth motion, and by the time they stopped, it would probably feel strange to walk on solid, motionless ground. But for now he felt a little sick and had to keep looking out the windows to keep steady.

Conker pointed to a door as they passed. Ray could barely see where he was pointing, as the entire hallway was filled with Conker's enormous frame.

"You know that's the washroom there? You're close to it, so that's good." Conker then pointed to a door up ahead as they crawled over the boxes and debris in the hallway. "Here's my room, but I most never sleep there at night. Too tight. Can't fit on the bed. I rather sleep in the boxcar or outdoors or sometimes in Nel's car when the weather turns cold."

As Conker opened the door to show Ray his room, he lurched back with a yelp, nearly crushing Ray in his panic. A copper and black viper as thick as a man's forearm slithered across the quilt on his bed. Conker fell to the floor as he scrambled away from the snake.

Seth and Redfeather burst from the room next door— Seth howling with laughter and Redfeather tentatively chuckling behind him.

"Get—get it—away from me!" Conker stammered.

Ray wasn't keen on touching the snake but felt he had to help the terrified giant. "You heard Conker. Get that snake out of his room!" Ray snapped at Seth.

Seth waved his hands. "Easy there, rube. It's just a little joke. No need to get crabby." Glaring at Ray, he cupped a hand around his mouth and shouted, "Marisol! Javier's out again."

Marisol emerged from her room, farther down the hall. "¿Qué está pasando? What's he doing down there?" She pushed playfully at Seth as she came down. "You teasing Conker again?" She whispered something, and the viper slid from the bed, coming out into the hallway past the terrified Conker, and to Marisol's hand.

Ray raised an eyebrow. "Did you just speak to your snake?"

"So?" Marisol lifted the fat viper, caressing him like a pet Pomeranian.

"How . . . can you do that?" Ray asked.

Marisol's eyes darkened and then she hissed, "Déjame solo."

"Come on," Seth said, knocking his shoulder into Ray as he followed Marisol back to her room. Slouching with his braids dangling against his shoulders, Redfeather glanced briefly at Conker and then Ray. He seemed about to say something but then turned to catch up to Seth and Marisol.

Ray helped Conker to his feet. "I hate them things," Conker mumbled. "Anything with scales." He shivered.

"Why don't you stand up to them?" Ray asked. "I grew up in the city. Bullies like Seth, you just have to act tough. You don't usually have to fight them. Just stand up for yourself, and they'll leave you alone."

"Oh, they're just fooling is all, Ray," Conker said good-naturedly but looking a little embarrassed. "Besides, this ain't the city. And they ain't bullies. Seth just likes to kid around, and Redfeather . . . well, he just goes along with Seth."

Ray shook his head.

Conker stopped at the last room before the vestibule and knocked. "Si. You in there?"

Si opened the door, but her smile faded as she saw Ray.

"Hey, we're going to the mess car," Conker said. "You want to come?"

"No. Not now. I'm busy."

"Doing what?"

Si looked again from Conker to Ray. "I'm just busy, that's all!"

Ray said, "That was a great performance, by the way. Really amazing."

"Thanks," she said reluctantly.

"I guess that's how you found the *Ballyhoo*."

Si's eyes narrowed.

"You know?" Ray added. "Back when you and Conker rescued me in the forest. You found your way to the train with . . . your hand, right?"

Si slipped her tattooed hand into her loose sleeve and

scowled. "I guess you think that makes you some kind of genius?" She slammed her door before Ray could say any more.

"Did I say something wrong?" Ray asked Conker.

"Aw, don't let her get to you. Si acts tough, but she's a kitten. You'll see."

They left the sleeping car, crossed the windy vestibule, and went through the door to the mess car. Conker went to the cabinet and took out a plate piled with cold flapjacks, a square of grits, and several pieces of curly bacon.

After sitting down at the table, Ray began eating. "I'm glad you're staying on with the show," Conker said, taking a big bite from an apple.

"Yeah, me too," Ray replied through a mouthful. "Conker, how can you all do these things?"

"What do you mean?"

"Marisol speaks to snakes," Ray said. "And Si has that tattoo. Redfeather can hold fire. I mean . . . it all seems so impossible. Doesn't it?"

Conker shrugged, shifting his eyes uncomfortably as he munched on the apple. "I don't know for certain," he said. "I reckon none of us do, 'cause Nel don't like talking about our parents. But I can figure it."

"Figure what?" Ray asked.

Conker stopped chewing and leaned closer. "That our parents were Ramblers."

Ray's brow twisted. Hadn't Buck mentioned something to Nel about Ramblers? And Hobnob. He had been babbling on about the Ramblers and John Henry and some Gog machine thing.

"Who are the . . . ?" Ray began to ask, but at that moment the door to the mess car opened, ushering in the wind and noise of the train. Ray and Conker turned to see Buck step in. He wasn't wearing his gun belts or his cowboy hat, and Ray was struck again by the image of Buck in the swamp.

Buck paused, sniffed, and said, "Little late for breakfast, boys."

Conker stood. "Ray overslept. I'm just . . . showing him around. Come on, Ray. Let's go see Shacks."

Ray quickly shoveled down a few more bites and placed the plate in a bucket on the floor. As Conker looked at Ray and cocked his head toward the back of the train, he said, "Where's Nel, Buck?"

Buck poured a cup of coffee from a tin kettle. "Taking a rest."

"Oh. Okay. See you later." Conker quickly led Ray to the door.

Ray looked back at the grim cowboy once more before stepping onto the vestibule. Buck's pale eyes seemed to be staring right at him as the cowboy sipped from his cup of coffee. Ray looked away quickly before realizing that Buck couldn't be looking at him. Or was he—in the cowboy's own mysterious way?

Ray followed Conker onto the vestibule and through the car that Buck and Nel shared with Nel's workshop.

When they reached the next vestibule, Ray realized they were standing before the locked car. Conker put a hand to a ladder next to the car's door. "Can't go through."

"How come?" Ray asked.

"Off-limits," Conker said. "Buck's orders."

"Why?" Ray asked.

"Got me." Conker shrugged. "Nel just bought this car a few weeks ago from some circus in Richmond, but none of us know what for."

"Have you heard anything . . . any singing coming from it?"

Conker furled his brow. "Singing? No. Why? You heard that?"

Ray nodded. "It wasn't like any music I've ever heard before. It sounded . . . eerie. And it did something to me. I'm not sure what, but it was strange."

Conker said, "I guess that's why Nel and Buck said for us to stay away from it. No telling what's in there. Let's get. You okay climbing up on top?"

Ray looked at the ladder. "Up on top of the train?"

"Yeah."

"Is it safe?"

"If you don't fall off. I never have."

Ray took a deep breath. "Okay," he said. "I guess I've already jumped off a moving train."

"You have?" Conker asked with admiration.

"I'll tell you all about it," Ray said. "Lead the way."

Ray followed Conker up the ladder to the top of the

car. He was relieved to see a metal railing around the sides of the car, in case the *Ballyhoo* took a sharp turn and Ray slid to the edge. Fortunately, that didn't happen. With the gale-force wind whipping around them, they crawled to the other side and came down the ladder.

On the next vestibule there was a door to the boxcar. As they went in, they had to scramble over the piles of crates, rolls of canvas, and assorted supplies stored for the performances.

"Not so bad, huh?" Conker asked as they came out the other side and went into the caboose. "Hey, Shacks."

Shacks nodded from up in the cupola. As the brakeman, his job required him to watch the train and the tracks ahead and be ready in case his father signaled to stop.

They went out to the platform at the back of the caboose. Conker sat on the metal grating, dangling his feet over the railing. Ray settled down next to him. "So who are they?" he asked. "The Ramblers?"

Conker cast one glance back at Shacks in the caboose's cupola. "I ain't for sure," he said. "Nel don't like talking about them, but I heard a little from Buck. You know in the old stories, Ray, where there's knights adventuring around, protecting the weak, standing up against the wicked? Ramblers are kind of like that. You ask the regular old person and they'd never have heard of them. But they knew what they did. Some goodness that came to pass, some terrible event that was averted: the Ramblers were usually behind it. They didn't take credit, didn't ask for no money or parades or recognition. They just did what they was suppose to do and slipped away again into the wilderness."

"And you think your parents and Si's and the others' were Ramblers?" Ray asked.

"My daddy was." Conker nodded. "And I think some of the others' were. There's things I've heard Buck or Nel mention that made me put it together. Things about how they all died way back around the same time. And besides, how come else we could do these things?"

"So how did you wind up with Mister Nel?"

Conker said, "My mama, she was a good friend of Nel's."

"Do you remember her?"

"Not really. Just little snippets and such."

"But how did she die?" Ray asked.

Conker sighed. "That I don't know."

Ray wondered over it all for a moment before saying, "I met this man when I was lost in the woods—before you and Si found me—named Hobnob. He worked for this Pirate Queen."

"There's pirates still around?"

"I guess so," Ray said. "He told me the Ramblers were killed by the Gog."

Conker frowned. "Never heard of no Gog."

"Hobnob also said John Henry destroyed the Gog's machine. I've heard of John Henry, but not about a machine. I didn't even know John Henry was real."

"I don't know nothing about that machine," Conker

said, a fierce look forming on his face. "But John Henry . . . he was real."

"Really?" Ray asked.

"Sure," Conker said. "He was my daddy."

Ray's eyes widened. "He was?"

Conker nodded. "I hear so many stories about him, I don't know half of what's true. But I know he was a hero." He squeezed his fists tightly. "And, well, look at me, Ray. I'm big. I'm strong. But I ain't a hero, not like my daddy."

"You fought that bear," Ray reminded him.

"And I was scared, too. Only did it 'cause I was worried about Si."

Ray sat next to Conker in silence for a while, watching the shadows of clouds racing over the land. Ray's hand clutched the lodestone through the fabric of his britches, and finally he said, "Conker, I think there's some reason I wound up meeting you."

"Why's that?" Conker asked, turning his head to look down at Ray.

Ray took the lodestone from his pocket and began telling Conker about his parents and why he had left his sister to follow the lodestone's strange pull and the mysterious dream with Buck. "But now it's not moving anymore," Ray said at last.

"So you reckon it led you here?" Conker asked. "Why you think it did that?"

"I don't know," Ray said. "My father told me it would guide me when I had a need."

Conker clutched his knees with his huge hands, drumming his fingers as he thought. "But what need did you have?"

"That's what I haven't figured out yet," Ray said.

Late in the afternoon, the *Ballyhoo* stopped outside the town of Winston. The show was not scheduled until the following afternoon, and Nel decided the stage could be set up in the morning. Seth, Redfeather, and Marisol headed into the town to get a soda at a drugstore. The rest lounged around to listen to the Everett men practicing songs in the shade of a grove of trees.

"Si," Peg Leg Nel called from the window of his car. "I need to hasten you and Conker on an errand."

"More supplies?" she asked, approaching his car. Conker and Ray followed.

Nel ran quickly through a list of herbs and roots, ". . . bindweed root, maybe some boneset or sumac, just a few leaves of fern, Devil's shoestrings if you can find them. I suppose that's it."

"Can Ray come?" Conker asked.

Nel blinked several times, as if just noticing Ray standing there. "Why, of course. Educate the lad on the task of woodland pilfering. We'll add it to his professional duties. Hurry, before night falls."

Conker turned to smile at Ray, who returned the smile eagerly. When he smiled at Si, she only glowered.

"Come on, you grinning idiots," she said.

Si led them from the lot next to town, where the medicine show would be held, across a field of tobacco, and into a forest of beech and elms and cedars. Long shadows crisscrossed the muggy forest, and soon they reached a creek bed bursting with full summer foliage.

"So what should I look for?" Ray asked.

Si was already kneeling to cut a small brown root from the earth with her knife. "What's that one?" Ray asked, screwing his nose up at what seemed to be a mass of tentacles trailing from the bottom.

"A root," Si replied dryly, placing the cluster in a sack.

"I know that," Ray said. "What kind?"

"That's the bindweed," Conker explained. He then pointed to a number of sprouts pushing their way from the leaves and bracken. "Look over there. See them, with the little green leaves. Those are Indian cucumbers. Dig up some of them."

Ray pulled out the silver dagger. "No, don't mess that up," Conker said. "Here you go." He handed Ray a brown-handled barlow knife. Ray unfolded it, got down on his knees, and began to dig the plants from the ground.

"I don't remember Mister Nel mentioning these," Ray said.

"No, they ain't for Nel," Conker said. "They're for Ma Everett. She likes these for pickling. Awful good, too."

"I wouldn't know," Si said. "You usually eat the whole jar before anyone else gets a taste."

Conker chuckled as he looked for more plants. While

they worked, Conker explained how to look at the leaf configuration and what nuts the squirrels were collecting and the fleshiness of fruit to determine what was edible. Ray caught on quickly how to spot curly dock and cattail stands, wild plums and black walnuts.

After an hour, they had found all the roots and herbs Nel needed, along with many greens, fruits, nuts, and tubers for Ma Everett's kitchen. By the time they returned to the *Ballyhoo* with the berry-red sun setting in the west, Ray's head was swimming with all Conker had shown him.

Si took the sack for Nel to his car, while Conker and Ray headed for Ma Everett's mess car. She wouldn't use their findings tonight, as the table was already set for supper. As they approached her car, Conker stopped Ray.

"I been thinking on that lodestone of yours and how come it led you to us."

"Oh, yeah?" Ray asked, pulling his thoughts from the lists of wild plants he had learned.

"What about the dreams?" Conker asked in a low voice. "Maybe another one of them dreams will tell you how come the lodestone stopped moving when you got here."

Ray nodded slowly, remembering the horrible hound. The idea of seeing it again frightened him. He would have to muster all his courage. "I'll let you know what happens."

"Do that." Conker smiled. "Come on. Let's eat. I'm starving."

* * *

That night, after a long, raucous meal followed by a concert in the moonlight by the Everetts and Nel, Ray made his way to his room. He untied the twine knotted around the lodestone. As he undressed and pulled the quilt up over his waist, Ray took a deep breath and clutched the lodestone, holding it to his chest.

Soon he fell asleep.

He dreamed of the Hound.

Ray again found his vantage point in the dream to be that of the man who was helping Buck and the girl escape.

The man ran faster than before, fueled by something stronger than fear. He had to lead the Hound away from the trail the other two had taken through the swamp. He gauged his speed, not wanting to go so quickly that the Hound caught the others' path. The frosty beast was slowed by its sheer size. Small trees toppled as it passed, but also hampered its pursuit.

Reaching the edge of a pond, the man rushed into the black water, wading at first with great steps and eventually having to swim. At the far side, he pulled himself up, heavy with mud and rank water as he turned to wait.

A howling wind had risen. The trees all around croaked and groaned with the force. He planted his feet at the edge of the water and touched his hand to the flannel bag at his belt. His wet clothes began to harden with ice. Shivering, he stomped his feet and shook his arms as he fought to keep the deadly cold from slowing his movements.

Caught in the roar of the wind were a thousand smaller horrible sounds; whines and moans—like the rusty gears of a long-fallen machine suddenly coming to life—pierced his ears. Plants that had barely felt a frost, rarely seen a snow, never had a hard freeze, suddenly all constricted at once with the plummeting cold. There were snaps and screeches like taut wires breaking apart. And under all the noise came a low, guttural growl. The man shifted his feet and opened the red flannel pouch tied to his belt.

Across the pond, a snout emerged six feet above the frozen bracken. White teeth bared. Clouds of frost puffed from its white nose. The snout pushed forward, revealing steel-colored eyes. The hungry rumble from its chest shook the earth. Squeezing out from the trees, the Hound toppled full-grown cypresses at their roots until it stood opposite the man at the other bank of the pond. The beast pulled back and unleashed a hurricane-force roar.

The man's clothes tightened across his chest, rippling at the back. He had to take a step to brace his stance. Bitter cold encased him, stiffening his muscles into knots. The trees behind him exploded into a thousand shards. A white wave of solid ice swept out across the pond, encasing one of the man's tall boots where he stood. He pulled a yellow stub of tallow candle from his flannel pouch and held it at his hip.

"Come to me, Hoarhound!" he cried. The beast responded with another roar. The man's shirt and pants became a heavy plate of ice. The man raised the candle and it burst into flame. An enormous orange light surrounded him. The Hoarhound stepped out onto the ice, cracks extending from its heavy paws with each step.

"Come, you clockwork devil, so I can drive you back into the Gloaming, where you were forged!" the man shouted.

The Hoarhound continued forward slowly. Its fur was bone white, as were its curling gums and claws. It lowered its face until its nose was nearly touching the frozen pond.

With his other hand, the man removed a small, wrapped parcel of ground herbs. He squeezed it until the paper crumbled in his palm. The Hoarhound reared back on its haunches, its muscles tightening like the coils of a spring.

As it leaped forward, the man cast the powder into the air in a great arc. It caught fire and swept out to meet the Hoarhound in an explosive collision. For a moment the spot, midway across the pond, burned in a blinding flash. The man rushed onto the ice, running toward the wall of flame. Out of the light the Hoarhound burst, teeth snapping, swinging its jaws back and forth. Frost-laden wind whipped apart the flames.

The two fought: The Hoarhound with its clanking jaws and hammerlike snout. The man with charms of root and bone, powerful talismans of glass and stone. Finally, when his charms were exhausted, the man leaped upon the beast in a frenzied impact: fire meeting ice, fur and flesh, man and hound.

Ray knew—the man knew—that he would not defeat the beast. He had to escape. Mustering all his strength, all his power, the man changed. He transformed. At that moment, as he was disappearing from the swamp, transporting himself a great distance, the jaws of the beast closed over his hand, teeth sinking into bone.

The two locked together and vanished.

Ray woke with something heavy shaking his shoulder. A pair of full-moon eyes peered out of the dark. "You okay, Ray?" Conker asked.

Ray sat up, trembling with the nightmare vision and struggling to regain his senses.

"I heard you from the hallway. Thought you might be catching fever again—"

"No. I did it!" Ray opened his damp palm to show the lodestone.

"You have that same nightmare again?" Conker asked, squeezing into the shallow space on the floor by Ray's bed.

"I saw what happened after that monstrous hound found the man. It's called a Hoarhound, and it's mechanical. The man knew that, the man who I was in the dream. He had this pouch with all these charms and objects inside. He was so powerful."

"A Rambler!" Conker gasped.

Ray mashed his fist to his temple, thinking. "Has Buck left the medicine show recently?"

"He's always leaving unexpectedly. Disappears for a few days or a few weeks, then comes back."

"When was the last time?" Ray asked.

"Left maybe a month ago. Got back"—Conker paused, his eyes widening—"around the same time Nel bought that car."

"A month ago, Conker," Ray said. "That was about the same time I started dreaming of the Hound. The same time the lodestone began guiding me here."

They were quiet a moment before Conker asked, "Why's the lodestone showing you that man?"

"I don't know, but I know who does," Ray said.

"Buck?" Conker's eyes bulged.

"I don't mean Buck," Ray said. "I mean the girl."

"The girl from the dream?"

"What if Buck brought her here after they escaped from that Hoarhound? She could be the one who was singing in that locked car." Ray tapped a finger to his chin. "Will Si help us?"

Conker whistled a low, cautious whistle. "She won't like this. . . ."

Ray was certain she wouldn't.

WITH LITTLE JEWELS OF DEW STILL SPARKLING IN THE
grass, the busy work of preparing for the medicine show
began. Nel shouted instructions from behind the briarwood pipe clamped in his teeth. Place the stage there.
Hoist the tent. Tie the curtain a little higher on the *Ballyhoo*. Put those crates of tonics up on the stage.

Soon all the supplies from the boxcar were unloaded.
The timing was right. There wouldn't be anybody around
the locked car.

As Ray and Conker secured the ropes for the tent, their
eyes flickered toward the back of the train.

"She said she'd do it?" Ray asked as he held the peg for
Conker to hammer into the soft earth.

"Took a little convincing," Conker whispered. "I had

to tell her about your lodestone and the dream. Hope that's all right?"

Ray nodded. "Sure. When's she doing it?"

"Now. Look! Here she comes," Conker said, wrapping the rope around the peg and tightening the tension on the tent.

Si had a bundle of ribbon in her arms to rope off the performance area. She was grinding her teeth when she reached Ray and Conker. With a quick glance around to make sure nobody was listening, she growled, "Okay, I unlocked the door. I hope you two know what you're doing."

"Thanks, Si," Ray said. "I really appreciate—"

Si snatched Ray by the collar of his shirt, pulling him down until they were nearly nose to nose. "If you get us into any kind of trouble doing this, you won't have to worry about what Buck does to you . . . 'cause you'll have me to deal with. You understand?"

"Y-yes," Ray stammered. "I . . . just want to find out why the lodestone led me here. That's all."

Still holding Ray's collar tightly, Si shook her head in confusion. Conker reached in to gently pull Si back. "Don't worry, Si. You can trust him. Ray's a good guy."

Si let go of Ray's shirt and began untangling the ribbon.

Conker looked around. "Okay, Ray. Buck's over there talking to Mister Everett. Looks like everyone's out here working. Get on over there and be back quick, before someone notices."

Ray gave one sly glance around the lot as he adjusted

his cap. Trying to be as inconspicuous as possible, Ray cut through the gap in the *Ballyhoo*'s cars and turned once he was on the back side of the train.

When Ray reached the car, he walked tentatively up the steps. He decided to give a knock, rather than just barge in. "Hello," he called softly. There was no answer, and he grasped the handle.

The door opened with a click, and he slipped inside.

His eyes took a moment to adjust after the bright sunlight outside. The interior was a vast boxcar with narrow windows near the ceiling, but they did little to illuminate the dark. The first quarter of the space was an antechamber with a dresser decorated with a solitary oil lamp. This seemed ordinary enough, but what surprised Ray was that the remainder of the car was encased in glass three-quarters of the way to the ceiling and filled with water. Wax and pitch sealed the seams.

What was this? he wondered. Where was the girl? There was a dresser, but no bed, no chairs. Maybe he was wrong. Maybe Buck and Nel were not hiding the girl here. So what was so important that Nel and Buck needed to act secretive about a circus car full of water?

As he faced the tank, Ray felt a chill come over him.

Slowly he approached the glass. The tank must have extended to the other end of the car. Ray squinted but could not see that far. As the light from the narrow windows entered the water, it dwindled rapidly into deep midnight murk. Ray leaned closer and pressed his hands to the glass. Had he heard something? A splash, maybe. He listened. There was the faint ring of hammers in the distance, but the tank was silent. For an instant he thought he saw a shadow move in the watery gloom. His pulse quickened as he put his nose nearly to the glass.

A burst of bubbles struck the tank in front of him, scattering like a school of minnows. Ray yelped and jerked back from the glass. When the bubbles parted, a face appeared before him. For a moment, Ray was panic-stricken that the girl might be drowning in the tank. But then he saw her expression; it was not the face of one drowning.

The girl's face was placid with a hint of curiosity, but Ray perceived a cool malice from the storm-cloud-colored eyes. She seemed that uncertain age between a girl and a young woman, with her bracken-brown hair drifting in a tangle of twists and snares. Hovering in the water, she wore a greenish gown that clung to her bare ankles.

It was the girl. Just as he had seen in the nightmare, her pale wiry arms were crisscrossed with scars, as were her cheeks and neck. Her skin had an ashen color and dark circles rimmed her eyes.

She released another jet of bubbles from her nose, and Ray realized that she did not have to hold her breath to remain under the water. Her brow pinched defiantly. Ray was frozen and no part of his brain seemed capable of clutching to modesty or good manners. He simply stood there—eyes locked to the girl.

From inside his ears he felt a reverberation rise, the

slightest tremble of a melody. Her mouth did not seem to move, and he wondered if she was singing or if the song was inside his mind. He wanted to get closer to her, to tell her that he knew her, but his tongue felt heavy, his lips sealed shut. Stronger still was the urge to hear her song better.

Ray took a step toward the glass. The girl drifted backward, pushing herself with the barest bit of her fingertips, at the same time beckoning Ray forward. He found his hand reach for the rim and soon he was pulling himself up and over the top of the tank. When his waist rested on the glass wall, the girl lurched forward and grabbed Ray's wrist.

The door behind him burst open and strong hands clasped his ankle. The girl's eyes widened, and she released Ray's wrist. In a cloud of bubbles, she disappeared into the recesses of the tank.

Ray was pulled sharply down from the tank and dropped onto the floor with a thud. Buck leaned over him, his eyes pale but fiery. Ray felt his senses return to him as the song's enchantment passed.

"What are you doing here?" Buck shouted.

"I didn't mean to . . . I—I just wanted to meet her," Ray stammered.

Buck turned toward the tank and called, "Jolie, are you okay?" When no reply came, he turned back to Ray and hissed, "Go outside and wait."

Ray scrambled to his feet and out to the warm flood of

sunlight. What was that girl? No person could have re-mained underwater as long as she had. No person lived in a tank. Fear—not only of the girl, but of Buck—swelled in Ray's throat.

Buck came out and locked the door behind him. "You're lucky you're still breathing! She might be sick, but she could have—"

"Who is she?" Ray asked.

"That door was locked for a reason," Buck growled. "Get back with the others."

"Please, Buck. I've . . . got to understand."

"Understand what?"

"A dream!" Ray clutched his hands together. "I had a dream, and you and that girl—or whatever she is—and an-other man were in it. You were in a swamp, running from a hound. A Hoarhound, I think."

Buck's mouth parted. "How could you . . . ?"

"What is she, Buck?"

Buck shook his head, running a hand beneath his hat into his tangled silver and black hair. He hesitated a mo-ment, then bent his head toward Ray. "A siren. She's what's called a siren."

"A what? You mean a mermaid?"

"Did you see a fish tail on her?" Buck scoffed. "No, she's a siren. A daughter of the ocean. A child of the swamps. Sirens are like us in many ways, but they are not human. They sleep beneath the water. They have powers we do not. Their song—"

"I heard it! A few days ago. And just now . . ." Ray trembled.

Buck furrowed his brow. "She didn't know who you were! She thought you were with him . . . the one who is trying to capture her."

"Who's after her?"

Buck shook his head. "I've told you more than I should."

"Let me see her again," Ray said. "Let me just talk to her."

Buck turned to leave. Then he paused a moment, his back still to Ray. He turned his head, deep shadows cast over his face from his cowboy hat. "Jolie. The siren's name is Jolie." Then he walked away.

The *Ballyhoo* moved on to Spencer the following day. They were two days early, but Mister Everett decided to use the time to make some repairs to the locomotive's driving rods. Conker and Ray were placing the bottletrees around the *Ballyhoo*'s camp and talking about what had happened with the siren when Buck found them.

"I checked with Nel. He says it will be fine," Buck said in his gravelly voice. "Come by my room a little later, and I can go with you this first time. Remind me to show you where I keep the key. That way Si won't have to pick the lock again."

After Buck walked away, Conker frowned. "You told him Si unlocked the door?"

"No!" Ray said. "I swear, I didn't. How do you think he knew?"

Conker smiled as he wedged the next bottletree in the ground. "That's Buck for you."

Buck knocked as he unlocked the door to Jolie's car. "Wait here a moment," he said to Ray before going inside. Ray felt more nervous waiting on the platform than when he had jumped from the back of Mister Grevol's train, even more than when Hobnob had smashed the poison acorns.

Buck returned a minute or so later. "It's okay. Go on in."

Ray looked back at him tentatively before going into the small antechamber. As before, the light was dim and seemed absorbed and refracted strangely by the tank of water filling the back portion of the boxcar.

"Hello?" Ray called, noticing that his voice sounded small in the space. He couldn't see her. She wasn't waiting in the antechamber, and the murky green water swirled with shadows.

He slowly approached the glass tank. "Hello?" The room, maybe it was the water, sucked away the sound of his voice.

"Don't be afraid, I was just coming by to—"

Water splashed over the edge of the tank, and the siren pulled herself up on the rim, poised like some wild beast. Her face was ghostly pale, scars running along her arms, neck, and face. Her eyes were dark and threatening.

"I am not scared of you," she spat, before lunging over the side of the tank. Her bare feet smacked wet and hard on the floor. Her hair was dripping about her neck, but the dress she wore appeared dry. It was not woven of cloth, but of some sort of leaves or vegetation interlaced as tightly and subtly as silk, which kept it from absorbing water.

Ray drew back as she marched toward him. Had she not attacked him already he would not have guessed that this twig of a girl would be strong, much less a threat. Even if she was sick, she was intimidating.

"You think I am afraid?" She had a strange accent, as if English was not her native language. It was filled with trills and a heavy use of the tongue along the teeth, unlike any way of speaking he had ever heard.

"No, it's just that I called and . . . and you didn't answer. . . ."

She bent slightly at the knees, crouching like a wildcat ready to spring. Ray was not sure whether it would be at his throat or back into the tank of water. Jolie circled him, looking him over.

Through clenched teeth, she said, "You think I like being locked in here all day? You think I am hiding because I am afraid?" She jabbed a finger at him. "What do you know about me, you little sneak?"

Ray was so flustered that he didn't understand that this was a rhetorical question. "I . . . I know you're a siren."

She glared at Ray, crossing her arms and flaring her nose. "You have seen a siren before?"

"No, never."

"You probably thought I would have scales, gills, something like that?" She bit at her lip but continued to scowl, her eyes lightning-streaked.

"I . . . had no idea what a siren was like. I didn't even know there was such a thing before . . ." As soon as he said it, Ray winced and wished he could retract the word.

"*Thing?*" she growled. "You find me to be a *thing?*"

"No, you know I didn't mean it that way. You're nothing like that. You're normal."

"I am anything but that." She began circling him again. "What is your name?"

He watched her movements closely. "Ray."

"Buck explained to me that this," she gestured to the door and outside, "is part of some sort of performance. People come to see it and to buy healing potions." Her arms relaxed slightly. "And what do you do here?"

"Just help out. I'm not a performer, if that's what you're asking." In his nervousness, he blurted, "My sister would probably make a good performer. She's funny and likes to dance. . . ."

"You have a sister. Is she here, too?"

"No. We were on this train, and I left her—"

Jolie winced. "You left her? Why would you do that?"

"Our parents, they're dead. We were sent off to get adopted with the others from the orphanage, but I didn't think she'd find a good home with me tagging along."

Jolie blinked several times and fidgeted with her fingers. "What is an orphanage?"

"Oh. That's a place for children who don't have parents."

"I do not think I understand why you left your sister. Did she want you to leave her?"

"I doubt it. I didn't tell her I was going to leave. It's just that I knew she wouldn't understand. She's young and I don't think she saw the whole picture of what would happen if we tried to find a home *and* stay together."

"And you did?"

"Yes," Ray said forcefully. "She's just a child. Of course she'd want me to stay with her."

"Then you should have."

"But if I had, she might not have found a good home. Don't you see? I . . . I just thought at the time it was the right thing to do. I would like to find her again! To see if she's found a good home and all. I hope to one day. And . . . well, what do you know about it anyway?" Why did he have to justify his decision to this girl? His cheeks felt blistering hot, but Jolie met his emotion with a flat, hard gaze.

"I know that *my* sisters are not coming back for me," she said. "They are gone. They left for the open sea. But I could not follow them, since I am only part siren." Her jaw trembled a moment before she continued. "My sisters left me to fend for myself in the Terrebonne, to be hunted down and held prisoner." Her voice dropped to a cold, low register. "I will never forgive them for it."

Ray lowered his head from her defiant face. "I'm sorry. I didn't know. Why did they leave you?"

"To escape from the Gog," she said.

"What is the Gog?" Ray asked, remembering what Hobnob had mentioned about the Gog killing the Ramblers. "Is he a man?"

Jolie laughed grimly. "I have never seen him. From what they say, you could scarcely call him a man, because he has none of the compassion that the rest of us, siren and human and creatures of the earth, were born with. They say he has a clockwork heart and a mind of pistons and gears."

Ray blinked hard, trying to comprehend this. Jolie narrowed her eyes at him. "Why did you come here, anyway? Why did you sneak in like that the other day?"

Ray hesitated half a moment before producing the lodestone from his pocket. He held it up to show it to Jolie. "Have you ever seen one of these before?"

"It is just a piece of string tied to a stone." She frowned and looked up at Ray with puzzlement.

"No, it's not, see. It's a lodestone. Do you know what that is?"

"A rock that pulls to metal."

"Right. But this one not only does that, it gives me these strange dreams. I think it's been showing me things for a reason. I dreamed of you and Buck and some man trying to get away from that Hoarhound."

Jolie's eyes grew big and she dropped her hands to her sides. "You saw that? How did you get this stone?"

"From my father. He gave it to me eight years ago, before he left—"

"That is when the Gog killed most of the Ramblers," Jolie said, her eyes darkening. "In the battle after John Henry's fall. Little Bill. The man you saw in your dream. He was the last of the Ramblers." She clasped her hands together, her brow wrinkling urgently. "Did this stone show you what happened to him?"

"Yes," Ray said. "Sort of. I saw him fight that Hound. He was having trouble and then the Hoarhound bit him. . . . I think it might have killed him."

Jolie's mouth opened. Bright tears sprang to her eyes. "Little Bill . . . is dead?" She began trembling and collapsed to her knees on the floor.

"I'm sorry," Ray said, kneeling down and reaching until he almost touched her shoulder. "I didn't mean to . . . Maybe he's not. I don't know. He and the Hound just disappeared . . . after it bit into . . . ."

Jolie twisted away from him, her hands to her throat and shaking with sobs.

"Should I . . . ? I'm so sorry. Do you want me to . . . ?" But Ray didn't know what to do to console her. Jolie began crying harder, laying her face to the floor.

Ray stood and backed away. He looked down at her once more and then opened the door gently and left.

-9-

STEAM, OIL, AND FLAME

"So did she talk to you?" Conker asked as he wedged himself through Ray's doorway.

Ray sat up from the bed. "Yes."

"Didn't try to . . . you know, drown you or nothing?" Conker squeezed onto the floor.

"No," Ray said. "Nothing like that." He told Conker what little Jolie had said about the Gog and how he was after the sirens. Ray kneeled on the edge of his tick mattress. "But the man. He was a Rambler! His name's Little Bill and when—"

"Li'l Bill?" Conker jerked up, banging his head back against the wall. "I've heard of him. In those stories about my daddy. Li'l Bill helped him win that competition against the steam drill."

Ray curled his brow quizzically. "I don't think it was a

steam drill, Conker. I think that's just the story people tell about John Henry because they don't know about the Ramblers. Remember what Hobnob told me? I think your dad and Li'l Bill were trying to destroy the Gog's Machine."

"Conker!" Nel's voice called from outside the passenger car.

Conker smashed around as he stood and opened the door. "Be right there, Nel." Then Conker turned back to Ray and said, "It still don't explain why that lodestone led you here."

"Yeah, I know," Ray mumbled.

Conker paused as he squeezed through the doorway. "You going back to see that siren?"

"I'd better give her a little time. She was pretty upset when I told her about that Hoarhound getting Li'l Bill. But yeah, I'm going back."

After a while, Ray's brain was too heavy, and he left his room. Stepping out into the bright sunlight, he wandered over to where Redfeather was helping to make a repair on the *Ballyhoo*. Because of Redfeather's skills with fire, Mister Everett had asked him to fix a driving rod that had cracked. Using a piece of burning coal from the locomotive's firebox, Redfeather could increase the heat simply by palming the coal and holding his hands around the broken driving rod.

Ray was growing accustomed to seeing Redfeather's

extraordinary ability to handle heat, and he looked about as the boy worked. Si was reading a book on the vestibule above them. Marisol and Seth whispered together nearby, sitting barefoot in the grass. Seth had his sword case open by his leg, the scimitar and the other two blades sparkling in the late day sun. He had begun carrying it around more and more, wearing his turban and caftan even when it wasn't showtime.

"Here comes Eddie," Redfeather whispered. Eddie strolled down the side of the train from the caboose.

"So? What's wrong?" Ray asked.

"He's been pestering me for my copper."

"Yeah, I remember Eddie mentioning your copper."

"I bet he did." Redfeather shook his head.

"What is it anyway?"

Redfeather motioned with his wrist to a thin, wedge-shaped piece of copper hanging from a necklace. "It was my great-uncle's. He got it years ago during a potlatch in my village—it's like a party where if you're hosting it you give lots of stuff away. Anyway, this copper is how I learned how to handle fire. Protects you from being burned. I've learned the magic now. Don't really need it."

Ray eyed Eddie coming closer. "He just wants it 'cause he's always getting burned shoveling the coal up in the locomotive."

"I know," Redfeather sighed. "It's just that Seth . . ." But his voice trailed off as Eddie reached them.

"Hey, Ray. Hey, Redfeather. Fixed that rod?" Eddie asked. Eddie seemed to have made a valiant attempt to scrub the soot off his face and hands. But even the starched white shirt and crisply creased derby could not hide the greasy film on his skin from the coal fire.

"Not yet," Redfeather answered dryly.

"Oh. Hey, Redfeather, I was wondering if you'd thought some more about what I asked you, about—"

"Cindereddie!" Seth laughed from Marisol's side. Eddie winced sharply but didn't turn. Seth stood and swaggered over with a cocksure glee. Marisol followed him, smiling a little tentatively.

Seth asked, "You think that Kwakiutl copper's going to keep you clean?"

"It's the burns," Eddie said, looking at Redfeather pleadingly, trying to ignore Seth. "Sparks get me when I open the firebox. I get a hundred burns every time we drive the train."

"I don't know why you bother to wash," Seth said, plucking the derby from Eddie's head. "Just let the grime build up. Maybe a little protective layer of dirt is what you need—"

"Why don't you shut up?" Eddie said, snatching back his hat. His voice shook and his eyes glowed with anger.

Marisol grabbed Seth's elbow as he lurched toward Eddie, his shoulders reared back. "What did you say, Cindereddie?" Seth threatened.

Redfeather was concentrating hard on the burning rod in his hands. "I'm trying to work here!" he shouted.

"You—you're always—putting me down. I—I keep this train going. I can't help that I'm—I'm covered in this—coal dust. I'm tired of you talking to me like that." Eddie was shaking visibly and took a step back.

Seth kept coming until he was nearly chest to chest with Eddie. Ray pushed his hands between them. Seth lunged forward again, and Ray shouted, "Enough, Seth! You're always tearing everybody down all the time."

Seth looked back and forth between Ray and Eddie, his eyes narrow and steady. Redfeather refused to look up, his concentration seemingly fixed on mending the rod. Si walked slowly down the steps from the platform, her eyes trained on Seth. Seth watched her for a moment and then let Marisol lead him away.

Before he left, he glared back at Ray, saying, "You grunts are just jealous. We get the limelight and you have to watch them applaud for us—for me! You're nothing. You've got no talents. You're nothing but dirty grunts."

When Seth and Marisol had disappeared into the passenger car, Ray put his hand on Eddie's shoulder. "Don't listen to him," he whispered.

Redfeather opened his hands from around the rod. The skin glowed white-hot for a moment before returning to a normal pink color. The driving rod had a slight bubble, like an old wound. "Well, I suppose it's fixed, strong enough at least to get the *Ballyhoo* back on the tracks after tomorrow's show." Redfeather looked up at Eddie, his eyes blinking. "Come see me before we leave. You can borrow the copper for a bit."

Eddie pulled his shoulder sharply out from Ray's grasp and rushed off.

Redfeather stood as he watched Eddie leave. "Try to offer a fellow a favor . . ." He frowned in Eddie's direction before carrying the rod back to the locomotive.

Left alone in the setting sun with Si, Ray looked at her. Si nodded slowly to him and then went back to her book.

The medicine show performed in Spencer. The show did not meet Nel's expectations, and he hoped their luck would be better in Georgia and Alabama. After packing up that night, Ray decided to visit Jolie again.

"I was sure you would not come back," Jolie said, after Ray had closed the door behind him. She sat on the floor with her back against the dresser and her chin resting on her knees.

"I wasn't sure you'd want me to," Ray said, sitting down tentatively across from her. "I'm sorry about Li'l Bill. He was important to you?"

"Yes." Jolie jutted her jaw and nodded. "Like a father."

"You said Li'l Bill was the last Rambler?" Ray asked.

"After Ferrol and Sanderson died," Jolie said. "They protected me, along with Little Bill. But they were not around as often. Buck would come and visit, too."

"But Buck's not a Rambler, is he?" Ray asked.

"No," Jolie said. "A Rambler draws his power from the wild. They are skilled in hoodoo magic. They can speak to animals and call upon the elements. Buck has powers, the way he can see even though he is blind. But he does not have powers like Little Bill or Ferrol or Sanderson. Little Bill said once that Buck could have been one, except he lives by his guns. The Rambler has no need for guns."

Ray thought about that a moment before asking, "What happened to the other two? Ferrol and Sanderson? Did the Hoarhound kill them?"

"No," Jolie said. "The Gog has many agents. Men who serve the Gog tracked them down and killed them." Jolie hunched forward, pulling her legs tighter to her chest and letting a dripping tangle of hair fall across her face.

Ray peered through the veil of hair covering Jolie's expression. He could see the gaunt look about her eyes, as if she had not slept for several days.

"Are you feeling any better?" Ray asked. "Buck said you were sick."

Jolie pushed back the hair and dropped her knees to the floor. "A little better. Mister Nel is giving me his potions."

Ray stammered as he asked, "D-do you sleep . . . in the water? Do you have to be . . . in there?"

Jolie smiled slightly. "A true siren must always sleep in water. She can never be from it for more than a few hours. Since I am not a full siren, I do not have to always be near water. I can go longer. I do not know how much longer. I have never really tried."

Ray felt his shoulders relax, glad he had not offended her. "Jolie, I'm not just asking about the Ramblers because I want to know. My friend Conker, his father was John Henry. Have you ever heard of—?"

"The son of John Henry is here!" Jolie gasped. "On this train?"

"Yeah," Ray smiled. "So you have heard of him?"

"Little Bill talked about him all the time. He was there when John Henry died. Little Bill helped lead him to the Gog's Machine."

"So John Henry did fight the Gog's Machine," Ray said. "I told Conker that. See, Conker doesn't really know what happened to his father. Nel doesn't want him to know, and he made Buck promise not to tell either."

"It is wrong that I am telling you? Will Buck be upset?"

"No," Ray waved his hands. "I think he wants you to tell us. But what I still don't understand is who this Gog is! You only said he wasn't really a man. Something about him being made of clockwork. What's he after?"

"To complete his Machine." Jolie's eyes flashed as she spoke. "I will tell you what others have told me. Little Bill and siren elders. They spoke of a time, years and years ago, when sirens lived in many of the wild places, swamps and lakes and rivers. Then the world began to change with machines. Machines running on steam and coal—such devices that a siren would never understand. As men started clearing land for farms, finding new places to settle, the sirens began to leave for the open water, out to sea, maybe even out of this world altogether. My sisters raised me in the swamps of the Terrebonne, protected, we hoped, from the changing world."

Ray was listening intently. He glanced down a moment to Jolie's crossed arms, and saw her fingernails digging against her skin as she spoke.

"Before I was born, years back, word began to spread of a man known only as the Gog, who built machines, but not just ordinary machines. There have been many ordinary machines that have brought no harm to the sirens. They have been a benefit to your kind. And there have been many ordinary machines that have led to our worsening, siren and human. But this Machine that the Gog built was for an evil purpose. It does not just kill. This is a Machine to ruin one's soul."

"I thought John Henry destroyed the Machine?" Ray asked.

"He did," she said. "With Little Bill's help, John Henry found the Gog's Machine. He broke it open with his weapon—the Nine Pound Hammer. John Henry died doing this. But the Gog was not destroyed. He has begun rebuilding his Machine. He is making a new and far more terrible Machine."

"So why is he after you?" Ray asked.

"I do not know," Jolie replied, fear twitching at her brow. "He wants a siren for some purpose, but I do not understand why." Jolie leaned forward on her hands. "Bring your friend. I want to meet John Henry's son. Will you do that?"

"Of course," Ray said.

Jolie stood and turned to go to her tank. Ray had reached the door when Jolie said, "Thank you, Ray." She was perched on the top of the glass.

"For what?" Ray asked.

She smiled before plunging into the dark waters.

As he reached the sleeper car, Ray stopped on the vestibule and looked out at the moon rising through the trees. The Gog was after Jolie. They were in danger: all of them aboard the *Ballyhoo,* all these performers in the medicine show, these children of Ramblers.

Ray took out the lodestone. His father had told him it would guide him. It had. He had discovered so much. But what was he to do? His father was dead. The Ramblers were all dead.

An image of the Hoarhound flashed in Ray's mind, its terrible jaws, the grinding of the machinery beneath its frost-armored hide. Ray shoved the lodestone back in his pocket. The train would set off in the morning, continuing the medicine show's tour of the South. And somewhere out there the Hoarhound was looking for Jolie.

* * *

The *Ballyhoo* reached the tobacco warehouses and factories on the outskirts of Atlanta the following afternoon.
Ray helped the others set up for the next show. As he was
carrying another crate from the boxcar, Si met him halfway to the tent.

She looked around to make sure nobody else could
hear her. "Conker says you're taking him with you to talk
to the siren."

Ray adjusted the heavy crate in his arms. "Yeah."

"I want to come with you." She held his gaze firmly.

"Okay," Ray said. "Tonight. After supper?"

Si's mouth twitched a moment before she muttered,
"Thanks." Then she turned, whipping the long braid
around from the top of her head and heading back to the
boxcar.

After supper, Conker and Si waited for him as Ray got
the key from Buck's room. Thunder echoed in the distance,
and a spattering of warm rain began to fall. Coming down
from the vestibule, he heard the whine of Ox Everett's fiddle, the *clunk* and *twang* of Shacks and Eddie playing
banjo and guitar. The others would be listening to the
music in the mess car.

"Come on," Ray said, and went up the steps to Jolie's
door. As he opened the door, he called inside, "Jolie?"

There was a splash and Ray heard Jolie land on the
wooden floor. "Ray," she said.

"I've brought Conker," Ray said, peering into the dark. "And Si."

Jolie lit the oil lamp as Conker and Si came in after Ray, their eyes curiously darting around the car. Jolie backed a step away from them, her chin tucked.

Ray said, "Jolie, this is Conker and Si."

Jolie smiled at Si and then up at Conker. Her eyes lingered on the giant a moment longer, and she said, "You . . . you are very large."

Conker laughed his easy laugh. "Yes, I reckon I am."

"We're glad to meet you," Si said, sitting on the floor. The others followed her lead.

"So," Jolie began. "You are performers?"

"Not Ray," Si said. "Did he tell you he was?"

"No, I didn't," Ray said.

Conker said, "Unless we count that show he put on for Marisol."

Conker and Si burst out laughing, and Ray forced a chuckle.

"What do they mean?" Jolie asked. Si quickly told her about when Ray first arrived and met Marisol on the vestibule. "You were walking around with nothing on?" Jolie asked with a smile.

"No," Ray said with chagrin. "I had my underwear on. Conker just forgot to bring my clothes back."

Jolie looked from Ray to Conker and Si. "So what do you do in the show?"

Conker and Si began telling her, going back and forth, until soon Jolie was leaning forward, eagerly hearing all about the different performances and about life in the medicine show. Soon Ray relaxed, too, settling back on his elbows as the evening got later and later.

After a while, the four grew quiet and listened to the patter of rain on the roof. Conker gave a wide yawn.

Jolie looked around at them. "I know you need to go. You are all so kind to visit me. I have seen the others out my window. The boy who makes fire, and the yellow-haired boy with the swords, and the girl with the snakes. They are all so . . . beautiful. But I am . . ."

"What are you talking about?" Si scowled.

Jolie ran her fingers over the marks across her arms, the scars on her neck and cheek. "These are ugly. I am ugly."

Conker shifted uncomfortably, shaking his head as he said, "No, you're not!"

"They're . . . just scars," Ray said. "You got them escaping from the Hound. Having scars just means you faced something terrible and difficult, but you survived. They show that you're brave—braver than any of us have ever been. You just need to get out of this car some. Then you'll feel better."

Jolie pulled her legs back up to her chest. She wrapped her arms around them, holding herself tightly.

"When we were escaping from the Hoarhound, I was scared. But if I see it again, if the Gog comes for me, I will fight. I will not let others die to protect me. If Little Bill and the Ramblers were brave enough, then I will be, too. I hate being in here, locked away."

"I'll ask Buck," Ray began, a little hesitantly. "See if you can get outside."

"Will you?" Jolie asked, her eyes wide.

"Sure," Ray said. "But don't get your hopes up."

The next day, as everyone was preparing for the first show in Atlanta, Ray spied Buck alone, resting in the shade on the stage.

The cowboy lifted his head as Ray approached. Buck was running his fingers over one of his revolvers, and giving the chamber a spin, he holstered it neatly. "How did it go with Conker and Si?"

"Fine," Ray said. "I think Jolie likes them."

A horrible look came over Buck's ragged face and, after a moment, Ray realized that this was what passed for a smile with the sharpshooter.

"Jolie . . . ," Ray began. "She wants to come outside . . . if you think that'll be okay."

"Good idea," Buck said, more easily than Ray had imagined. "I think meeting you has really helped her. I've been talking to Nel about her getting more fresh air, some sunshine."

"What about her needing to be hidden?" Ray asked. "Isn't there . . . danger?"

"The bottletrees will protect her fine."

Ray cast a glance at the cedar poles covered in colored bottles that he and Conker had been putting up at every show.

"I thought they were just for decoration."

Buck hopped down from the stage, his cowboy boots jangling as he landed. "No, they're not decoration," Buck said. "They're old magic. Hoodoo." He leaned close, whispering in his raspy voice, "They keep the Gog's servants away. If they got too close, they'd be trapped in the bottles." Then walking away from Ray, he said, "I'll tell Nel about your idea."

Ray looked over once more at a bottletree, and went to get ready with the others for the first performance.

As the *Ballyhoo* traveled from town to town over the next week, Jolie wavered between days of improvement and lapses into weariness. Finally Nel agreed that Jolie would benefit from fresh air. Although Ray had been anxious— anxious about Seth, anxious about the Gog's men or the Hoarhound storming suddenly from the forest, neither happened. Seth, along with Marisol and Redfeather, watched Jolie curiously when Ray led her outside that first day, but none of them bothered her.

As Jolie began getting outside more often, many days Conker and Si joined her and Ray on walks within the perimeter of the bottletrees, listening to stories about John Henry and his fabled Nine Pound Hammer. But Conker and Si were often busy helping with the show, and during those times, Jolie and Ray would sit in the grass by the shadow of the train and talk.

She told him stories about the Ramblers and tales she had heard from Li'l Bill and the others when they had kept watch over her. She told Ray about Jonathan Chapman, who stole a silver apple from a witch in Hudson Valley and broke it open with a rock to spread the seeds in his vast travels. She told him about Colonel Pierce and his band of Ramblers meeting the White Buffalo, who was Boss of the Western Plains, and who taught the Ramblers the power of animal speech. Ray especially enjoyed the tale of Old Tea Mat, the monstrous catfish who lived beneath the waters of Lake Pontchartrain.

Jolie was curious about the outside world and about Ray's life before he met the medicine show. She asked about Sally and about surviving on the streets of lower Manhattan.

One afternoon, when he was telling her about a time he had been caught stealing a drunken man's wallet, Jolie fainted. She stayed in her tank for several days after that, coming from the water only long enough to share a few words with Ray or Si and Conker. She looked weak and ate little of the food they took to her. Sometimes she seemed to be in a dark depression and would not come out even to say hello to Ray.

That was around the same time the lodestone began pulling again.

* * *

Ray twisted and turned sleeplessly on his straw mattress. The night was hot and all the mosquitoes in Alabama seemed to have found their way into Ray's room. He kicked off his sheets in agitation and stepped to the floor. His foot landed hard on something. Bending down, he touched the lodestone.

As his fingers met it, the stone moved. Ray sat up, watching as the lodestone began sliding across his palm. What was it doing? He closed his fingers around it, but still felt the urgent pull pressing into his palm.

Ray ran out his door and jumped down from the vestibule, heading across the grass, already wet with the muggy summer night. He had to tell Conker; maybe he was still awake. As he went under the tent, it took Ray a few moments of stumbling to find the stage in the darkness. "Conker," he whispered but got no reply.

A large dark shadow lay upon the stage, murmuring with a dream. His eyes slowly adjusting to the dark, Ray saw that Conker was twitching in his sleep, his face mashed onto a thin feather pillow.

The giant was dreaming. With the lodestone still in his hand, Ray reached out to shake Conker's shoulder.

As his fingers touched him, Ray's mind exploded with a vision.

A cavern far under the earth was illuminated with the dim glow of a kerosene lantern. A huge man, nearly the same size as Conker but older and harder-faced, was carrying a heavy long-handled hammer. He turned to a man behind him, small by comparison.

The large man had to shout to be heard over the buzzing, hissing noises that filled the tunnel. "Go back, Li'l Bill!"

The small man had a thick blond beard and long hair run through with gray. He looked as if he was going to speak, but the fierce, not unkind resolve on the large man's face stifled any argument. Li'l Bill hesitated a moment before clamping his hands affectionately to the large man's arms. Words seemed to fail to come to his lips, and he turned, receding into the dark.

Alone, the large man with the hammer held up his lantern.

Before him were a thousand clawing, churning movements, like a wall of maggots writhing in the oily light. But they were not insects. They were intricate bits of machinery. The hissing of pistons firing, the grinding of gears and rumbling chains filled the tunnel. The cold, grease-slick machinery was enormous and extended into the rock surrounding it. There was no focal point to the steel mass, no obvious function of the mechanization. It was as if this were only a small portion of some larger machine encased in the earth.

He looked back once. Li'l Bill was gone.

Then the man threw down his lantern and rushed forward with his hammer, swinging the thick iron head into the skin of rivets and rods.

As the blow sank into the machinery, the tunnel erupted with a howl of steam and oil and flame.

* * *

Ray fell back with a clatter to the wooden floor of the stage, the lodestone dropping from his hand. Conker shot up with a roar.

Ray snatched the lodestone as he backed away. For a moment, Ray saw Conker in a terrible way, for what he could be—someone frightening and powerful and dangerous.

"Conker, it's okay," Ray said. "It's just me. Ray."

The ferocious look left Conker's face as he saw Ray flinching back.

"Oh, Ray. You startled me. I was . . . dreaming and . . . you scared me." Then his eyes fell to Ray's hand. Even in the dim light, the dark shadow of the lodestone was apparent in his palm.

"What were you doing?" Conker asked.

"I . . . I was just coming to wake you . . . I didn't mean to . . ."

"Did you see my dream?" Anger rose in his voice.

"I'm sorry," Ray said. "I didn't know—"

"That ain't right, Ray! I'm your friend. You ought not to be snooping on my dreams."

"I didn't mean to," Ray said again. The realization of what he had seen overwhelmed him, and he scrambled to his feet. "I'm sorry, Conker."

As Ray jumped from the stage, Conker called, "Ray . . . where are you going? Ray!"

But Ray was out from under the tent and running. He

ran and ran until he reached the caboose and then a bottle-tree and down the track until he dropped to his knees.

Ray trembled at what he had witnessed. That had been Conker's father, John Henry, destroying the Gog's Machine so long ago. The Machine! It had been horrific. Unlike anything he had ever imagined. But that was not what disturbed Ray so greatly.

Li'l Bill. The Rambler who had helped John Henry. Ray knew him. He had recognized the man immediately. How could he not?

Li'l Bill was William Cobb. Li'l Bill was his own father.

Late in the night, maybe it was nearly dawn, Ray made his way back to his room in the sleeper car. He knew he would not sleep.

With the sun rising in the east toward the caboose, he held the lodestone, watching it draw heavily across his palm. Ray closed his fingers over it, but still felt the incessant pull. He gauged the direction against the warm sunlight spilling orange and yellow over the land.

South.

His father had been a Rambler. His father had known and fought beside John Henry. His father had not died eight years ago.

The lodestone had started pulling, started giving him the dreams of the Hound, a month before Ray joined the medicine show. That was the same time that his father had helped Jolie and Buck escape from the Hoarhound. All that time, Ray had been seeing his father but had not known it. His father had fought the Hound. His father had tried to escape, when the Hoarhound bit into his hand.

What had happened to him when they disappeared?

Eight years. Eight years his father had been away. His father had never known that Sally had been born. He had never known all the hardships that she and Ray and their poor mother had endured.

What had he been doing all that time?

Jolie.

He had been protecting Jolie.

A hatred boiled up in Ray that he could not stop. She had kept his father from his family. Ray pounded a fist into his pillow and tore the quilt from his bed.

Why hadn't his father tried to find his family again? Surely he could have. Was Jolie more important than they were?

Dawn came. And with it, the rustle and rumble of breakfast and the final preparations for the medicine show getting ready to depart.

The lodestone's pull was as powerful as he'd ever felt it.

Out his window, Ray saw Nel walk around the field where they had set up, looking around to double-check that all was safely stowed away.

Could it be that the lodestone had been leading him all along to his father? And if it was, was his father alive or dead?

Ox called from the locomotive, "Ready, Nel? All aboard!"

"Let's sally forth, Everett," Nel shouted.

A whistle shrieked. Steam and coal smoke clouded the dawn. The *Ballyhoo*'s wheels began to turn.

Ray quickly gathered his few possessions, wrapping them in his coat and tucking it under his arm. He stepped out onto the vestibule. The *Ballyhoo* was gaining speed, but not too quickly. Ray hopped down onto the smoky gravel right-of-way beside the train and dashed behind a nearby tree.

When he stepped out again, he saw the *Ballyhoo*'s caboose disappearing in the distance.

THE RABBIT'S FOOT

RAY SAT FOR A LONG TIME BY THE SIDE OF THE TRACKS. THE *Ballyhoo* was gone. Conker and Buck and Jolie and all the others were gone.

Ray took out the lodestone and began following it.

He walked all morning and into the afternoon, passing ruined plantations and poor farmhouses. An old black man driving a Nissen wagon with a mule carried Ray for a stretch along dusty clay roads. Soon Ray left the roads and followed a lazy, meandering stream. The fields, ripe with midsummer, gave way to stretches of forest, and with the sun setting through the trees, Ray was again in the wilderness.

As he journeyed, Ray thought about Jolie and Conker. Ray still burned with resentment toward Jolie, but he regretted not having made up with Conker before leaving. He hated that Conker might be sore with him, and Ray wished he could apologize to his friend. In fact, he wished Conker were with him now, out here in the woods, on some adventure.

He also wished he had taken food from the mess car. But unlike before, when he was in the Lost Wood, Ray was now able to recognize some plants in the forest that were edible. He dug up Indian cucumber and Jerusalem artichoke with the silver dagger and gathered some wild cherries from a tree. He found a cool, bubbling spring and made a camp for the night on a bed of pine needles. It was not his straw-tick bed in the *Ballyhoo,* but it was not so bad either.

Looking up at the stars through the swaying boughs high overhead, he thought of his father. A mix of emotions, from anger that his father abandoned his family to elation that he might still be alive, filled Ray's chest.

If he was alive, Ray would find him. He wondered if he would have to travel as far as the Terrebonne swamp. If it would reunite him with his father, he was willing to go that far and beyond.

On the following day, Ray continued to follow the pull of the lodestone. The intensity was increasing, and Ray felt hopeful his father might be close. On and on he walked, excitement lifting his spirits. He continued through the sunlight-speckled woods, kicking at the ferns and humming a tune that Mister Everett liked to play.

As he walked along, Ray took the lodestone from his pocket to check that he was still going the right direction.

The lodestone jerked so suddenly it slipped from his fingers. While he was pulling it up with the twine from where it had fallen in the dense bracken ferns, the lodestone jumped again. Taking it with a better hold, he let it guide his steps, quicker and quicker. Then the stone's pull stopped.

Ray looked around and found himself in a circular copse of pines. He turned around a few times wondering why the lodestone had stopped him here. His father wasn't here; nobody was here. Ray touched his fingers to the handle of the dagger in his belt.

Something flickered from beneath the willowy ferns. It was a rabbit lying on its side. Ray inched closer, careful not to scare it away. As he neared, he realized how unlikely it would be that a rabbit would lie down. Its eyes were open, showing white pulses of fear at the edges.

Pulling back the ferns, Ray saw the reason for the rabbit's strange position. It was caught in a rusted spring trap. The teeth had closed on one of the rabbit's front paws, and from the black caking of dried blood, it seemed the rabbit had lain trapped for some time. Ray bent next to the rabbit.

"Why would somebody want to catch you way out here, little guy?" Ray whispered. He touched a hand to the rabbit's ears, and it didn't flinch. Running his fingers soothingly across the hazel fur, he touched the crusted spot where the teeth of the trap met. The paw was crushed, probably through the bone, but the rabbit had not been able to get free.

Ray's chest pained for the poor animal; he hated to see it suffering.

"I know it hurts," Ray said. "I'll get you out, but I don't think you're going to keep that paw."

He put the lodestone on the ground and felt along the steel trap, following the teeth to the hinge.

"Just a moment," he whispered. He gripped both jaws of the trap and pulled. The springs were so rusted that they wouldn't open. Ray adjusted his grasp and gave another pull, groaning with the effort. The tiniest squeal began and flecks of rust broke off in a powder across his knuckles.

"Come on!" he growled.

The rabbit's eyes widened, but it remained still and calm. The squeal grew louder and louder with the breaking of the trap's bite. Swirling whines and high-pitched shrieks deepened until the noise exploded into a howl. The trap broke open all at once, and the noise gave way to a blast of bluish light and force that threw Ray back across the forest floor.

It was as if a stick of dynamite had gone off, but with no fire or heat. The air, however, was full of smoke and the smell of sulfur. Ray pulled up on his elbows and looked for the rabbit, but the gap in the ferns was now empty.

The twine that held the lodestone had snapped at his belt from the blast. Ray saw the frayed end next to his boots, the length of twine trailing away until it disappeared beneath the ferns. Ray sat up and pulled the twine back. As the weight on the end of the twine dragged across the ground, he saw a sparkle of gold.

He stopped pulling and got to his knees, crawling toward whatever it was that was shining. He reached out and touched it. There on the other end of the twine, the lodestone was gone. In its place was the rabbit's foot. The fur and skin had turned to a hardened, glistening metal—a buttery gold, which became coppery-red at the claws.

The foot seemed to have consumed the lodestone, as the twine now disappeared into the end. He held it in his palms, speechless. Jumping up, Ray dashed around the copse, tearing back the ferns, but there was no sign of the rabbit and no sign of the steel spring trap.

What was going on? What had just happened? Ray held the golden rabbit's foot. But no matter how long he held it, the talisman didn't move. The lodestone was gone. How would he find his father now?

For the remainder of the day, Ray sat in the copse of pines. There was no escaping the terrible truth: he had lost his father's lodestone. Without it he never would have found out who his father really was. And now . . .

Where should I go? Ray thought. The lodestone had been leading him, so he could try continuing in the same direction—whatever that was? Maybe he could still find his father. But before he stood to leave, a rustle sounded behind him and he turned, half expecting to see a three-legged rabbit.

But it was no rabbit. It was a small old woman, bent over nearly in half as she walked. She wore a patchwork dress. Her skin was gnarled and hardened into the color and texture of tree bark, and her cloud-white hair hung soft and thin around her shoulders.

She walked with a knotted root for a cane and approached Ray in the clearing of pines. With her deep hunch, her eyes faced the ground as she walked, and Ray was not even certain she had seen him yet. He slipped the rabbit's foot back in his pocket cautiously.

He called to her, "Hello," but the old woman did not reply.

She wandered a moment around the clearing, poking at the ferns as she went. After searching, she reached Ray's side and cocked her head slightly, looking up at him with one black-button eye. The old woman asked in a grunting voice, "Who took my coney?"

"What?" Ray asked.

The old woman hit the ground sharply with her stick. "Yonder coney, did ye spy who took it? Didn't get free from that snare on its own."

"The rabbit?" Ray answered. "I got it out from the trap."

The old woman grunted and went back to continue searching under the ferns. Ray came up behind her and asked, "Did you set that trap?"

"Reckon it weren't!" she exclaimed as if Ray had insulted her in some manner. "Was the doing of something far worse than me, lad. What's ye name?"

"Ray Fleming," Ray said reflexively. "And what do you mean, something worse than you?"

"Weren't no poacher's snare, and sure weren't no ordinary coney," the old woman grunted. She stopped her search and peered up at Ray with her dark eye. "Ye say ye set it loose? I say you're a-lying."

Ray was startled by the old woman's bluntness. "I'm not lying."

"You're a liar. I can spy it in ye."

Ray frowned, but before he could argue further, the old woman reached out quickly and grabbed his hand. She felt around his palm with her coarse fingers, holding Ray in a firm grip until he pulled his hand away from her grasp.

"Hum." She pondered a moment. "You're a liar, least about your name, but you're not a-lying about the coney. How'd ye set it free?"

"I just opened the trap," Ray said.

"Ye hear what I said," the old woman spat. "Weren't no ordinary trap. Lad like you wouldn't a been able to open it, and yet ye say ye did. I couldn't open it. Don't know another who could. Ye know what I am?"

"No," Ray replied.

"I'm a seer. Somes would call me Mother Salagi. Come from the Clingman's Dome, far up in yonder mountains." She motioned again with her stick.

Ray realized she must have come a long way, because there were no mountains nearby and the Appalachians must be hundreds of miles to the northeast.

"Come all this way, 'cause I scatter some bones and I sees something—something I need to inspect. I come here. I find that coney in the trap. I work all manner of hoodoo on it, but can't get them jaws a-opened. Something wicked keeping them shut. I been a-watching over that coney, trying to figure some way to get it out, trying to figure out why something wicked would have that coney trapped. And ye, ye opened it. Who are ye?"

"I'm Ray," Ray answered, wondering if Mother Salagi had forgotten.

"Ye said that already," she grunted. "But who are ye; that's what I wants to know."

Ray was not sure how to answer, and Mother Salagi motioned with her stick. "Come. Got a camp set just yonder. I'll get ye fed, and ye'll tell me who ye are."

Mother Salagi led Ray to a spot not more than a few minutes' walk through the woods, on the edge of a creek, where she had dug a fire pit and built a rough shelter out of branches and bark. She stoked up a fire and cut up wild tubers and watercress into a cast-iron pot.

As she prepared the meal, Ray began telling her his story, including his discovery that his father was the Rambler Li'l Bill who helped John Henry, and how he set the rabbit free.

"Rambler, eh . . . ," Mother Salagi mumbled as she stirred the simmering pot of stew. "Ye got that foot? Let me see it."

Ray took the golden foot from his pocket and handed

it to the old seer. Mother Salagi held the foot close to her eye and inspected it by the light of the fire for a long time. She coiled up the twine still dangling from the end and then touched the foot to the side of her iron pot.

"Aye. Your lodestone's still setting in that coney's foot. Just a-buried beneath." She handed it back to Ray and said, "Ye know what that coney was?"

"No, what do you mean?" Ray asked.

"That coney ye freed"—Mother Salagi pointed a crooked finger at Ray—"was your very own pappy, it was."

Ray was on his feet in an instant. "What! How can that be?"

"Settle down, lad." Mother Salagi brushed her hand at Ray. "Set. Set. And I'll explain ye."

When Ray was sitting again, she squinted an eye at him. "Ye say your pappy was a Rambler. I ain't met Li'l Bill, but ye can be sure I heard of him. He's a might powerful one, and thems like that can take the form of an animal. Li'l Bill ain't the first. But a coney must have been the form he took to cross. Ye don't know what crossing is, do ye?"

Ray shook his head.

"Crossing is to pass to the Gloaming. It's a might different world than this one." She slapped a hand to the ground. "When John Henry had to destroy the Gog's Machine, he needed to get to the Gloaming. Powerful as John Henry was, he couldn't a-cross. Needed Li'l Bill to cross him to the Gloaming, where the Gog's a-hidden his Machine."

"I still don't understand what the Gloaming is," Ray said.

"Few that do. It's a fair mystery even to me. What I comprehend is that it ain't truly a physical world like where we a-setting. It's a-connected more to our spirits and such. And it's beyond and beneath and yet being sewn into the fabric of this world." The old seer flexed her fingers and then clapped. She frowned as she looked at Ray. "I see ye ain't exactly wrapping your head around what I'm a-saying. Well, don't fret ye. It's a piece of work to understand."

"But what about my father?" Ray asked. "If he was the rabbit, and the rabbit is gone, then where is he?"

"I can't say, I'm afeared. Ye say he was fighting a Hoarhound when he disappeared?"

Ray nodded.

"He might've tried to take the coney form to escape. Being able to cross and all, he must've expected to pass through the Gloaming to get away. Then that Hoarhound bit him first. Two of them pulled into the Gloaming locked together—"

"The steel trap!" Ray interrupted. "It was the Hoarhound."

Mother Salagi nodded, scratching a fingernail to her chin. "I expect it were. As one of the Gog's infernal devices, it would twist into something else when yanked into the Gloaming. Into its essential being—that of a vicious mechanism. Fact is, that ye was able to open that Hoarhound's jaws at all is something to be marveled. Ain't no explaining I got for that, lad."

Ray felt a peculiar pride. How had he been able to open it then? He looked down at the golden rabbit's foot. He had found his father after all. His father had said the lodestone would not only guide Ray, but guide him, too, back home.

Ray looked up. "The Hoarhound severed my father's hand . . . so why did it turn to gold?"

Mother Salagi considered this for a moment as she crushed a handful of herbs into the stew. "All I can figure is that your pappy was a-casting some spell, a-working some hoodoo, to protect himself. Must've been thinking the Hoarhound's bite might kill him. Sent that spell to the hand. It has all the makings of a hoodoo charm. But something altogether more powerful than I can cipher."

Mother Salagi ladled Ray some stew in a wooden bowl and handed it to him. Ray held the bowl without eating.

"Do you think he's still alive?" Ray asked.

"I'd a-reckon he is."

"Can I find him?"

"Does ye coney foot still pull like the lodestone done?"

"No. It's not moving anymore."

Mother Salagi spread her gnarled hands. "I don't know what to tell ye, lad."

Ray pushed the foot deep into his pocket. The rabbit had been his father. He had rescued his father from the Hoarhound. But now his father was taken from him again, and Ray had no idea how he would ever find him.

"Mother Salagi," Ray began. "Who is the Gog?"

"Now that's a question, a right confounding one even for me," Mother Salagi said, nodding over and over. "A devil, maybe. Something worse. There's been men a-fearing and a-speaking of the Gog and the Magog right on back into the Bible."

"The Magog?" Ray gasped. "What's that?"

"The Gog's Machine!" Mother Salagi jabbed a finger at Ray. "Which be the Gog's very own soul—exchanged for whatever natural soul he once possessed. How he come to survive John Henry destroying his first Machine. Evil like that, it can just build a new soul. Evil like that ain't easy to kill."

Ray looked down at the bowl of stew in his hands, his hunger escaping him. "What's the Gog want?" Ray asked at last.

"What all the wicked want," Mother Salagi grunted. "To rule. To steal the destiny right away from men. To possess what never should be possessed. When I come down from the Clingman's Dome, ye know what I seen in my travels?"

"No," Ray replied.

"Roads, train tracks, and them poles strung up with wire."

"Telegraphs," Ray said.

Mother Salagi snorted. "Aye. Ye seen them. To some, they's bridges. They's a-making the world connected. Progress they says. But they's walls, lad. They's nothing but walls. It's a grid that we all going to get shackled to. That's what the Gog wants. That's how the Gog's going to rule.

"But for a person to grow to greatness, they need vast spaces. Wide openness. It's there the heart and the mind and the spirit can expand to greatness, not a-shackled to the Gog's grid. Aye, the precept of the Rambler. Ye see?"

"I think so," Ray answered, not at all certain.

Mother Salagi was about to ladle more stew into Ray's bowl, when she stopped. "Ye ain't eat hardly a bite. Ain't it good?"

Ray shook his head to clear the cacophony of thoughts.

"Yes. Yes, ma'am, it is." Ray smiled as he began eating. When he finished the bowl, he accepted another.

Ray slept on the ground by the fire, and when he woke, Mother Salagi had already packed up her camp. She was busy putting the final stitches in a small bag of red flannel.

"What's that?" Ray asked as he stood and stretched.

"A toby. What a proper Rambler carries his hoodoo charms in. It's for ye, for that coney foot." She knotted off the last corner and handed it to Ray.

"Thank you," Ray said, examining the simple bag.

"I stitched a fair piece of protective charms in that toby. It'll keep your coney foot safe if ye keep it in there."

Ray took out the silver dagger from his belt and cut the twine from the end of the rabbit's foot. Then he placed the golden foot in the toby and stuck the toby in his pocket.

"What should I do, Mother Salagi?" Ray asked. "Should I keep looking for my father?"

Mother Salagi winced, her ancient wrinkled face drawing up tightly. "Ye can't cross into the Gloaming. I don't know as there's much ye can do except a-wait until Li'l Bill gets his own way out and comes a-looking for ye. Be patient. Have hope."

She saw the disappointment in Ray's expression and tapped a hand to his arm. "I been a-thinking on ye this past night, Ray," the old seer said warmly. "Thinking on all ye told me about yourself. Seems to most you're naught but an ordinary boy. But ye opened the Gog's steel trap. Took something more than the strength of John Henry to do that.

"Ye ain't a Rambler like your pappy yet. But ye could be. Ye've got his very hand therein your coney foot of gold. Ye've been a-carrying his lodestone. But ye've powers all your own. Ye will uncover them in time." She collected Ray's hands in her crooked fingers and shook them gently. "Time ye took up his path."

Ray narrowed his eyes. "What do you mean?"

She squeezed his hands. "The Gog's been a-kidnapping

folk, taking people away that nobody misses. I seen it casting bones. Can't see who, but he's been taking the weak, the unwanted." Her button eye narrowed. "Their spirits he's a-wanting. He's a-going to use their spirits to fuel his Machine. That's why he's seeking that siren your medicine show's a-hiding."

"Jolie?" Ray asked. "Why is he after her?"

"I tried to figure it, and way I'm a-seeing: sirens have songs of power to control others. The Gog needs a means to capture those spirits to feed his Machine. Aye, siren could do it. Even if he's a-capable of finding yours, he ain't going to convince or even force a siren to do his wickedness. Sirens ain't a race to give toward threats and such. So he's a-searching for a way to control the siren."

The old seer let go of Ray's hands. "Said your pappy was protecting that siren when he died? Then ye must follow his path. Ye must keep that siren safe from the Gog, as best ye can."

"So I should go back to the *Ballyhoo*?" Ray asked.

"I ain't telling ye what to do. Just a little steering is all."

She handed him a bowl of the warmed stew. As Ray ate, Mother Salagi doused the fire and stowed the final few items in her pack.

"Keep the foot hid. Keep it safe in the toby."

She gave a grunt and turned to leave. "Ye ever want to learn to work some hoodoo, come find me up on the Clingman's Dome. I'll teach ye to do a job of work."

"Thank you." Ray watched the old seer leave, beginning the long journey back to her mountain.

After she disappeared into the forest, Ray realized what she had said. To work hoodoo magic was called doing a "job of work." That's what his father had said when he left years and years ago. He was going south for a "job of work."

Ray smiled and shook his head.

How was he possibly going to find the *Ballyhoo* again? They must be hundreds of miles away now. He vaguely remembered that they were going to play the next show in Tupelo, wherever that was.

He decided his best course of action was to get to a town and ask for directions. He might be able to catch up with them in Tupelo or at least ask around to find out where the medicine show was going after that.

Ray headed west, the direction he guessed the medicine show was now traveling. As he walked on through the gray, dreary day, he was no longer certain which way was west, no longer certain where he was even going.

Ray considered whether he should try to find his father despite Mother Salagi's advice. Maybe the rabbit's foot could help him cross into the Gloaming.

He took the golden foot from the red flannel toby. It did not move. He had no idea how he could get the strange talisman to do anything. Discouraged, he put it away but paused to admire the simple toby. A Rambler's charm. He remembered how his father had carried one back when Ray was just a child in Maine. The same one he had used to fight the Hoarhound. It had been full of herbs and roots and magical objects. Would his one day, if Ray learned to be a Rambler?

That was ridiculous. How could he become a Rambler? He needed his father. Tears burned at the corners of Ray's eyes, and he ran his knuckles angrily across his eyes.

Jolie. He still felt bitterness toward the siren. But he had to help, even if he wouldn't be her friend.

Breaking through the brush, Ray found himself before a large, snaking river. The black water was too wide to cross, and he turned to his left to follow its bank. The ground grew softer as he traveled, and by late afternoon, he reached a marsh. The river broke into a hundred traipsing creeks. His pants were muddy up to his knees, and his brogans and socks were soaked.

He was not going to reach a town going this way. All he wanted was to find a dry embankment to rest for the night, but rain began to fall and the bog only worsened. Then he noticed in the marsh a trail made from the broken reeds of grass. The path must have been made recently, he thought, as he saw the broken ends of the grass still floating in the water below.

Someone must have just passed this way.

Maybe they had a boat, he hoped. Maybe they could row him to a nearby town.

As he slogged his way through the marsh, trying to follow the rough path, the wind carried the murmur of voices in the distance. Ray cocked his head to determine the direction. Thank goodness, he thought. He had to hurry to get to them before they left.

He splashed along urgently now. In the muggy film of rain falling among the marsh grass, Ray saw a shadowy figure. He was waist-deep and facing the other direction. "Hey!" Ray shouted.

The man ducked suddenly into the reeds and disappeared.

"Hey! Can you help me?" Ray called, pushing his way into the grass. Twenty yards away, the grasses rustled. Ray headed toward the movement, but it stopped. Tearing his way ahead, Ray knew he was nearing the man. As he snapped aside the gray-green reeds, the man leaped on him.

Ray fell beneath the water, the man's arms clasped about his shoulders. Ray struggled up for a gasp of air, unable to break from the man's crushing hold. He was thrown about for several moments, before the man pulled Ray up by his sleeves.

"Ray!" he shouted with surprise. Ray coughed up lungfuls of marsh water, and wiped his hair out of his eyes. Grabbing the man's overalls to hold himself up, Ray saw who had attacked him.

"Conker?" He felt dizzy with relief. The giant grabbed Ray in a series of hugs.

"Ray! Ray! We've been looking for you. . . ." Conker laughed until he nearly sobbed.

"In the middle of this marsh? What are you doing out here?"

Conker fished Ray's apple cap out of the water and handed it to him, never taking his eyes off Ray, as if he feared that if he looked away Ray might disappear. His expression went from giddy excitement to wide-eyed terror.

"They got her, Ray." Conker's lip trembled as he spoke. "They took Si."

"Who?" Ray asked.

"Pirates, Ray! Them pirates got her."

"I THOUGHT THE *BALLYHOO* WAS OFF FOR A SHOW IN Tupelo," Ray said, still baffled that Conker was standing before him.

"We were, but the driving rod broke again. Nel decided to let me and Si go out to look for you," Conker explained. "We didn't know where you got to. Thought maybe we accidentally left you behind. What happened, Ray?"

Ray shook his head. "There's so much . . . That night when I saw your dream, I saw Li'l Bill helping your father destroy the Gog's Machine." Ray took a deep breath. "Li'l Bill, he's my father, Conker."

"What!" Conker gasped.

"There's more, and I'll tell you later," Ray said. "But we've got to help Si. What happened to her?"

Beyond the rain, a choir of insects began trembling and buzzing.

With worry twitching his chin, Conker said, "Si was leading us using her hand. We'd been following the river a day or so when we ran into this marsh. She thought you were nearby, and she's so much faster than me. Si went ahead"—Conker gestured toward the way Ray had just come—"to search for you. Weren't long. Just half hour ago. And Si weren't far, but that's when I heard them, voices shouting. I ran as fast as I could manage, but this bog! They already got her in their pirogue. I got lost here coming back to the river." Conker put his face in his coal-shovel-sized hands.

"What we going to do?" Conker cried.

"We're going to find her," Ray said.

"How's that?"

As if in answer, the twilight breeze again carried the sound of voices. Conker raised his head to listen.

"They can't be too far away. Ship must be nearby in the river. We've got to get moving."

They made their way through the marsh toward a peninsula of trees and mud. Ray and Conker climbed onto the roots. The purple, leaden sky swirled ominously, occasionally split by a trembling skeleton of lightning.

From the murky marshes a boat glowed. It was a motley paddle-wheel steamer illuminated by swaying lanterns along the railings circling the hull. Ray had seen plenty of fancy steamers in the harbors of the cities. But this was no showboat, nor was it a working barge. The steamer was not very large, compact enough to be maneuverable in inlets and shallow portions of the river. The hull was battered and spotted with rust. Ray was certain that several of the small speckles were bullet holes. This may not have been *The Queen Anne's Revenge* flying a Jolly Roger, but there was no doubt that it was a pirate vessel.

Above the ash-gray hull was a long single cabin punctuated by grimy windows. A pair of smokestacks extended above the bow and a raised pilothouse was at the stern. At the rear was a wide paddle wheel, the only portion of the vessel actually in open water. The rest of the steamer pitched up onto a bank of reeds.

Figures were running about the quarterdeck shouting to one another. "Put about, damn you!" "Hoist another outboard, you mangy rats! And heave!" Grappling cables were being thrown from the stern beside the paddle and grunting groups of men from the deck pulled and cursed and moaned.

Ray asked, "You remember that fellow I told you about? Peter Hobnob. The one who could fly?"

"Yeah," Conker said.

"Well, he told me about this Pirate Queen who ran a ship called the *Snapdragon*."

"Yeah, I remember that. You think this is her?"

"I hope not," Ray said, remembering all the horrible things Hobnob had told him about the Pirate Queen. He was glad he hadn't told them to Conker, because the giant looked like he was about to lose his nerve.

"I think they're stuck," Conker whispered.

"Yeah, looks like they've run aground. May be the right time to get on board."

"Wh-what?" Conker stammered. "There's got to be two dozen pirates on that ship!"

Ray pointed into the growing dark. "But they're at the rear. If we can get on the front—"

"How?"

"Well, I'm not sure yet. I can't see well enough, but it's too dark for them to see either. They'll be too busy to notice us anyway, and if we can get to the front maybe there's a ladder or something we can use to get on board."

"What then?" Conker asked, clearly disliking the plan more and more.

"I don't know! Find Si. Remember when we were talking about your father? You said you weren't brave enough. But you are, Conker. Now's the chance to prove it—for Si."

Conker drew in a deep breath, his chest expanding as he nodded. "Yes, we got to help Si. Can't imagine that they could keep her anyway. Can't no lock or shackle hold her."

Some gruesome images came to Ray's mind, Si's dead body among them, but he kept quiet. "Well, even so, we'll get her out."

"Ray," Conker said softly.

"Yeah?"

Conker jabbed a finger toward the dark channel. "We better not find no snakes."

"We won't see any snakes," Ray promised. He looked around. They were in the middle of a vast marsh that had to be full of thousands of snakes. He could only hope that it would be too dark for Conker to see any of them.

Ray led Conker out to the end of the peninsula. It was the farthest point from the pirates. As they began to wade out, Ray asked, "Think it's deep?"

"Why?" Conker asked.

" 'Cause I can't swim," Ray replied.

Conker went first, as he was head and shoulders taller than Ray. He took a few steps and then descended with a splash beneath the water. Fishing himself out with a jumble of flaying arms, Conker climbed back onto solid ground and spat a fountain of water from his lips.

"Yeah, it's deep," he said.

Ray waded back to shore and found a broken log. The two of them dragged it into the water and pushed it before them as a raft. "Can you swim?" Ray asked.

"Good enough," Conker said, kicking with his feet.

"All right, quieter this time."

They paddled out into the channel toward the bank of reeds where the steamer was grounded. The engine barked and sent a shower of sparks from the smokestack as the pirates tried to reverse the engine. The steamer shook violently but didn't come loose. As the din of the engine receded, Ray blinked in surprise at the creative string of swears the pirates shouted at one another.

Conker suddenly stopped paddling. "What?" Ray whispered.

Conker's eyes were frozen on a stick coming out from the dark water.

"It's just a—" Ray said, but Conker exploded in a frenzy of swinging arms and kicking feet. The log rolled beneath him and threw Ray into the water. He sank. All movement seemed to slow as the quiet blanket of water shut off any sense of direction or escape. He looked about but all he saw were the bubbles jetting from his mouth and the black syrup of water that surrounded him.

A hand caught him at the collar and jerked him to the surface, planting him back on their raft. Ray sputtered and lay stunned across the bobbing log. Conker clasped an arm across Ray's shoulder.

"Sorry, Ray," he muttered.

Ray was too winded to reply.

"Ray," Conker said again. "I'm really sorry."

"It's okay—"

"No, I'm really sorry." Ray nearly turned to sock Conker in the arm, but then he saw why Conker was apologizing.

A woman was moving toward them, silhouetted in the light of the steamer. At first Ray thought she was standing on the water, somehow suspended at the surface. She wore a knee-length moleskin coat strapped across with bandoliers heavy with an assortment of firearms and swords. A silk sash was tightened across her brow, flattening a billowing mane. Hip boots extended up her legs with the cuff folded over her knees. With one hand she removed a cigar from her curling lips. In the other, she clasped a pair of reins.

Ray followed the reins down to the water and realized what she was standing on. It was an ancient, gnarled alligator. Conker saw it, too, and that's when he fainted across the log.

Within a minute, the rusty ache of a winch sounded from the hull of the *Snapdragon*. Ray and a semiconscious Conker were attached to the end of a cable and hoisted from the water by a davit. As they were dropped to the slick deck, a leering mob of men, boys, and even one hard-faced girl surrounded Ray and Conker.

If one had to sum up the crew of the *Snapdragon,* many words would come to mind, but *ugly* would be the most ready response. Their soiled clothes, rotten teeth, and the general stench that hovered about the deck like a swarm of flies could be blamed purely on bad hygiene. However, Ray would have bet that no matter how much you scrubbed and groomed this bunch, not one could keep a baby from crying.

"Two more!" a fish-eyed man laughed from the rabble. He wore a bicorne and poked at Ray and Conker with the butt end of a matchlock rifle. "Tie 'em with the China girl."

At the mention of Si, Conker came fully to life and sprang to his feet. As he reached his full eight feet, the pirates gasped and scuttled back, crablike. "Where is she, you scummy bandits?" Hammers clicked back as dozens of pistols, scatterguns, and rifles all leveled in a semicircle around Conker and Ray.

A growl sounded from the midst of the group and several pirates were knocked to the side as a grotesquely oversized man pushed his way to the front. Conker was gigantic, but he was proportioned as any normal man would be. This man had heavy gorilla-like arms and shoulders so inflated with muscle that they consumed his neck.

Although he had to look up to face Conker, the pirate outweighed him by at least a hundred pounds. His lipless mouth twisted into a grin as he marched up to Conker. Conker kept a calm expression, but Ray saw that he was clenching his fists, ready for a long fight.

"You know how to fight?" Ray asked skeptically.

Conker turned and said, "This is for Si! You best just stay out of this—"

Before Conker could finish or even turn around, the pirate plowed his fist into Conker's chin, spinning the boy giant across the deck. Just like that, the fight was over.

"Tie 'em tight!" the fish-eyed pirate howled, and the rabble rushed forward with coarse ropes. It took eight of them to get Conker to his feet. Conker's eyes rotated around in his sockets, and he could barely keep his knees from collapsing.

"Best not to mess with Big Jimmie," the girl pirate said.

"Gets right cranky when he's tired, and he en't got a nap in all day."

As the crew began to lead Ray and Conker, arms tied against their sides, across the deck, Ray turned to the girl to ask, "What will she do with us?"

The girl was wiry and gaunt, with strings of braids dangling from her head. She began eagerly, "Seeing as we lost five of the crew a week or more back—we's raiding on this town and how's we to know the marshal and his men was waiting in ambush—suspect she'll break you in and make you full with the crew."

"Pirates!" Ray coughed. "She wants us to be pirates?"

"Right fair life if you don't mouth off around—" but she clamped her lips shut as the winch started up below deck and the pulleys on the davit whirled the cable in again.

The cable had been wound around the belly of the alligator. The Pirate Queen was still riding upon its back. As the davit swung around to place them on board, the Pirate Queen leaped to the deck, taking a last draw from her cigar before flicking it into the dark.

The crew responded immediately to her presence. Cowering like cockroaches in the light, they gave her a wide berth. Eyes were pitched down toward their toes sticking from the holes in their boots, and Ray heard a distinct whimpering from several in the crew. Even Big Jimmie laced his fingers together at his front, meek as a choirboy. The fish-eyed pirate alone managed the courage to pass by his queen as he hurried to untie her alligator.

"Excellent catch, my lady. Right successful evening, I'd reckon," he mumbled.

The Pirate Queen took slow, heel-thumping steps around the deck, her eyes surveying her crew. In the light aboard the ship, Ray could now see that the Pirate Queen was fair-skinned, deeply spotted with coppery freckles, and had hair of flame red to match. About her neck was a tangle of necklaces, some with jewels, others with the claws of beasts. Ray saw hidden among them the small black bullet that Hobnob had told him about. The Pirate Queen cast a glance back at the fish-eyed pirate at her side, and he groveled away under her gaze.

"Successful evening?" she snarled. "Are we off the shoal yet, Mister Lamprey?"

"No, my lady."

"How did I wind up with a crew that's got the collective wit of a barnacle?"

"I couldn't say, ma'am," Mister Lamprey replied.

"Well, have you located our position on a map?"

"Not yet, my lady, but . . ."

"How are we going to find our way out of the maze?" She batted Mister Lamprey angrily but stopped as her eyes fell on Ray and Conker.

Mister Lamprey scurried forward, holding his hands over his head. "The big one, he's feisty. If I might recommend, we ought to keep them tied, too. The China girl ain't

going to slip her ropes no more now that we got her hand"—
he shivered as he mentioned Si's hand—"locked up."

"Why are you clucking around like a gaggle of geese?"
she shouted at the pirates. "Avast! I want a draw beneath
this ship and I want it now! All hands—outboard—now!"

The crew snapped into a frenzy of action, pushing and
shoving their way to the rear of the ship. Mister Lamprey
squeezed his hands together as he approached the Pirate
Queen's side. "What of the . . . prisoners, my lady?"

Looking over her shoulder to Ray and Conker as if
they were a nuisance she had tried to forget, she said,
"Joshua, Piglet, tie them with the girl."

Joshua turned out to be the most elderly of the pirate
crew, a rheumy-eyed old man, seemingly too old to help
pull the cables. Piglet, the girl who had spoken to Ray, was
surely the youngest, maybe only a year older than Sally.

She and Joshua pulled Ray and Conker along by their
bound hands to the quarterdeck. Si was tied to a crane extending from the center of the quarterdeck. Like Ray and
Conker she was tied about the waist, but the pirates, having discovered her tattooed hand, had placed it inside a
five-sided lead box and bolted it over her head. As the Pirate Queen passed her, Si's eyes remained fixed upon the
woman, hatred brimming at their edges.

The pirates tied Ray and Conker on either side of her,
each of their backs to the crane, and ran to join the others
with their grappling irons, desperately attempting to get
the *Snapdragon* back into open water.

As the Pirate Queen moved away, Si said, "How did you idiots get caught?"

"Well, I found Ray and we . . . arrgg!" Conker howled as the ancient alligator lumbered up the deck past them.

Even Si drew in her feet, pulling back from the beast. The alligator turned slightly as it passed, its gaze seeming to linger on Ray. It reached its mistress's side, and the Pirate Queen knelt to rub its jumble-toothed snout. "That's a good Rosie," she cooed. "Good girl." In between the love talk with her alligator, the Pirate Queen barked orders and curses at the crew.

"Snakes, gators, even snappers," Conker moaned. "I hate anything with scales."

"Turtles don't have scales," Si argued, but Conker, not in a state to argue about the distinction between snakes and snappers, only whimpered.

Ray cocked his head in a whisper. "Si, can you reach your hand to my back?"

"Oh, sure," she said wryly. "Where's it itch? We'll give each other back rubs."

"No, I've got a knife on my belt."

Si squirmed for a second and then replied, "No, can't get my hand over there."

Keeping an eye on Rosie the alligator, Conker tried. "I think I got it, Ray."

"Stop!" Si hissed. The Pirate Queen peered around at the three.

Si growled in an undertone, "I was sure that copper nob

was going to kill me. Now at least I won't go alone. . . . Conk, what's the matter?"

Ray turned his head sharply to peer around at Conker. The giant had an odd expression on his face, and Ray could not tell if it was pain or fear or something else.

"I . . . feel strange," Conker murmured.

"You sick?" Ray asked.

"No, not like that." Conker shook his head and seemed clearer again. "I can't describe it, but I feel like . . . I don't know."

As Ray was trying to puzzle this out, his gaze caught something bright nailed to the side of the galley. It was a yellow hat, made of dandelion petals.

Si said to Conker, "Maybe you feel your brain finally starting to work—"

"Hush," Ray said. "I'm working on a plan."

"What?" Si said. "Going to cut our ropes? Sure. The three of us will fight off a ship full of pirates armed to the teeth and drive the boat back to Nel. Great plan! Keep that knife hidden, before she sees it and guts us for her gator's supper."

"Hey!" Ray shouted to the Pirate Queen. Some of the pirates nearby cast anxious glances at Ray.

"What are you doing, Ray?" Conker whispered.

"Hey!" Ray called again. The Pirate Queen ignored him and unleashed a string of profanity upon the pirates to work faster.

"The ship's stuck, right?" Ray asked. Her fingers went

to the handle of a particularly large-barreled pistol and tapped the hammer with agitation.

"Well, we can help," he said. "We can get you free."

She tossed her fiery hair about her shoulder and gave Ray an icy stare. "You're about one breath away from your last. Why don't you save it?"

"You don't understand who we are," Ray said. Her hand withdrew the pistol, and several of the pirates nearby scattered as the hammer cocked back.

"We're Ramblers," Ray added firmly.

With the pistol leveled at Ray's mouth, she said, "You're not Ramblers. Do you think I'm an idiot? The Ramblers are gone. Heard the last died not two months back, at the mouth of the Gog's Hound."

"We'll prove it," Ray said. "I can give you what you most want."

The deck had grown quiet. The pirates no longer heaved and shouted and pulled upon the grappling cables. They all listened, some chuckling at what Ray could only credit to their anticipation at seeing a good murder, but most genuinely fearful at the way the stupid boy was provoking their captain.

"Kid, when you lay down your cards, you're going to come up short. You have no idea what I most—"

"But I do," Ray said, with a jut of his chin. "And I'll give it to you. Then we'll get your boat back into the water. We can lead you out of this swamp, too. But I want you to promise that you'll set us free."

The Pirate Queen's face was hard as granite, and several taut moments passed. Rosie nestled up against the queen's leg.

"Then let's see your hoodoo," she said at last.

Ray closed his eyes. He wasn't sure what he should look like if he was supposed to be conjuring, but he decided to take the least dramatic route. After mumbling to himself, he opened his eyes. "Cut my ropes."

The Pirate Queen, her pistol still outstretched toward Ray, motioned to Piglet. The girl's bare feet slapped across the deck as she ran over to the crane and cut Ray's rope with a rusty knife.

Ray stood slowly, one hand still behind his back. The Pirate Queen never lowered her pistol, but her face betrayed a curious anticipation.

Ray held up the Pirate Queen's silver dagger. The deck exploded in gasps, cries, and dumbfounded exclamations. The Pirate Queen's eyes popped as she reached out to snatch back her lost dagger.

"W-where . . . h-how . . . you got it?" she stammered. Turning to Piglet, "Did you check their pockets before they were tied?"

"Of course. Aye, my lady," Piglet lied nervously. "Hadn't a thing on them but some food."

The Pirate Queen holstered the pistol and lovingly ran her fingers along the knife's blade. Without another moment's hesitation, she jerked a fresh cigar from her breast pocket and sliced the tip with sigh of relief. Mister

Lamprey rushed up with a match and held it cupped in his hand as the Pirate Queen took several deep puffs to draw the flame to the pungent tobacco. Her mouth relaxed in a smile, smoke drifting in thick summertime clouds from her lips.

"I'll need my friends untied," Ray said, "so we can get your boat off the shoal and out of this marsh."

The tall Pirate Queen looked down at Ray, her expression coarse and poisonous again. "Cut the prisoners loose!" she shouted. "Let's see if these Ramblers can get us back to open water."

THE PIRATES CLEARED IN A SEMICIRCLE AROUND THE STERN.
Ray huddled with Conker and Si, discussing his plan.
"Conker, all you have to do is pull the boat off the shoal,"
Ray urged.

"You gone squirrelly! You know I can't do that!"
Conker exclaimed.

"You're John Henry's son!" Ray smiled. "Of course
you can."

"Ray, you saw that big fellow. How you expect that I
could if he can't?"

Ray argued in a low voice, "He can't be as strong as
you, Conker. I know it. I've seen what you can lift. That
Big Jimmie just got a lucky punch in on you is all."

"You've got to learn how to take a punch better," Si
agreed. But then she turned to Ray. "Conker's right. They

had twenty men pulling those cables before you all came," she said. "And they couldn't budge it a foot. When we can't get it free, she's going to slit our throats!"

"But he will—" Before Ray could continue, Piglet and the old pirate Joshua came over.

"You ready?" she asked.

Conker looked anxiously at Ray.

"Even if you get the boat off," Piglet said, "we en't going to find our way back to the river. Near true a maze out here. Shallow and full of shoals at every turn. Can't believe we got this far deep."

"Why'd you come up here?" Ray asked.

"We's chased," Piglet said. Joshua nodded wordlessly and chewed at something in his toothless mouth. "Met one of the Gog's ships in the river and they fired on us. Thought we'd lose 'em up in this marsh."

Ray exchanged a wide-eyed look with Conker and Si.

"Quit stalling," Mister Lamprey called from the Pirate Queen's side. They stood in the center of the pirates, who were all watching impatiently. "Joshua, Piglet, get back over here."

Ray turned to Conker. "Just try."

Conker sighed as he wrapped strips of burlap around his wrists to keep the cables from cutting him. As Si walked back with Joshua and Piglet, Ray paused, looking at the odd expression that was coming over Conker's face. "Is it that feeling again?" Ray asked.

Conker nodded, wincing slightly. "Strangest thing . . ."

Ray cocked a brow curiously. "Good! Pull that boat, Conker." He slipped back to the others.

The pirates had thrown six grappling irons off the stern, each attached with a hard cable to cypress knees and roots. Conker twisted the cables together and looped them around the base of the crane to use its heavy foundation as a pulley. Then he wound the mass of cables around his wrists over the burlap strips.

He pulled back slowly, letting the cables tighten. His feet were braced against wooden slats nailed to the deck. He took a step back and the cables grew taut from his hands to the crane and from the crane back over the transom, to where the grappling irons were sunk in the mud fifty feet off the stern. The sky had begun to clear, and a thin witchy moon danced in the fast-moving clouds overhead.

Conker took another step and a groan emerged from somewhere deep in the belly of the *Snapdragon*. He leaned back and all watching from the deck felt the tension as a hundred tons of hull sucked against marshy shoal. Conker's neck swelled with veins and strings of muscles. His shirt grew dark and wet as every pore burst with perspiration. A grunt began at his gritted teeth, and his body visibly trembled under the tremendous strain.

Conker suddenly howled, beastlike, and the *Snapdragon* lurched, throwing several pirates to the deck. The braces at his feet began to splinter, and Big Jimmie ran forward. Throwing his arms around Conker's waist, the pirate kept the giant from sliding. Others ran forward, and soon there was a mass of stinking pirates all holding Conker steady. Conker worked his hands one over the other, inching the cable in as if reeling in a whale. The *Snapdragon* whined and tilted as it slid across the shoal. Conker and the crew fell back in a heap as the pirate steamer finally broke free and settled into the channel.

Shouts and cheers rang out as they got to their feet. A few pirates fired off pistols in celebration. Ray and Si ran to Conker, who was flat on his back, gasping for breath. Si fell at his side, kissing his brow and cheeks and wiping the sweat from his face.

"Conker!" she cried. "Are you alive? Say something!"

He smiled weakly. "I must be dead if you're kissing on me."

"You scared me!" She gave him a light slug in the arm, and he winced, laughing.

"I can't believe I did it," Conker panted. "I was *stronger* somehow, but where the strength came from I can't figure."

The pirates that were gathered about Conker parted. The Pirate Queen's clanking boots announced her arrival. From around her back the fish-eyed Mister Lamprey whispered, "You think he is, my lady?"

"No time to find out now." She looked from Conker to Ray. "You promised you could lead us out of this morass. Does that still hold true? I don't think you realize where we are. This steamer's meant for open water, not this shallow swamp. It was ill luck that got us this far from the river's free flow in the first place."

Ray rose to his feet. "I can't, but she can," he said, pulling Si up by the elbow.

Si turned to glare at Ray, her expression full of venom.

"Come with me," the Pirate Queen ordered, turning sharply to climb the steps to the pilothouse.

Si pushed Ray ahead of her. "You're not leaving me alone up there with her." Ray cast one look back at Conker, who was now able to sit up and drink from the bucket of water that Big Jimmie held. The pirate crew surrounded Conker admiringly. Reaching the top step to the pilothouse, Ray was amazed to see Rosie the alligator climbing the steps behind him.

The pilothouse was the highest cabin in the steamer. Only the smokestacks and the davits rose higher. From that moonlit vantage, Ray could see the full extent of where they were. The marsh around them extended like a prairie, cut through with only the narrowest network of waterways. There were a thousand choices of where to go, and surely nine hundred ninety-nine of them would prove too shallow to pass.

The Pirate Queen began adjusting levers and valves, revving the steam engine to life. There was a large wooden wheel mounted at the helm, like in an old-fashioned clipper ship. To its side was the binnacle, the glass surface of the compass illuminated by an oil lamp fixed into the casing. It would do little good in this situation.

"Well?" the Pirate Queen snapped to Si. Si scowled and ground her teeth. "You speak English, I assume."

"Course I do!" Si said.

"Then where to? Does that tattooed hand of yours get you out of more than just knots and brigs?"

Si held up her hand. Ray watched from the back wall of the pilothouse. Against the black of the window, it looked for a moment as if she had no hand at all, the color so perfectly matched the night. But then shapes began to glow on the surface of her skin. It took Ray a closer look to the sky beyond and then back at Si's hand to realize that the designs upon her skin mirrored the positions of the stars in the sky. Within the celestial points of illuminated ink, other shapes arranged themselves as well. Ray could not tell what these were or what they meant, but Si seemed to be able to read them and pointed to the starboard side of the *Snapdragon*.

"That way. The channel that makes an S shape. Follow it."

"I wouldn't call these channels," the Pirate Queen grumbled. "More like ditches." The Pirate Queen rolled the wheel and pushed a lever slowly. The steamer answered from deep in its belly, unleashing a gasp of black smoke and silver puffs of steam. The *Snapdragon* cautiously maneuvered through the marsh.

"Now turn left," Si said.

"Port at the first bend?" the Pirate Queen asked.

"No, not that one, the bigger channel," Si answered, her voice a little shaky.

Ray watched with fixed anticipation. If Si made one mistake, if the *Snapdragon* again grounded . . .

Ray hardly noticed as Rosie rubbed her snout against his leg. As he'd done a hundred times with friendly dogs, Ray stuck his hand down to pat her nose. It was not until he saw the Pirate Queen's mouth agape that he realized what he was doing.

"Watch the marsh!" Si cried, and the Pirate Queen's attention jerked back to the window as she whirled the wheel to the right.

Behind them Mister Lamprey lumbered into the pilothouse, breathing heavily. "My lady?" he murmured.

Not taking her eyes from the course, she blurted, "What is it, Lamprey?"

"If I may mention, the Gog might still be out there waiting for us in the main channel. What then? We en't got the armaments to fend them off again."

She chewed nervously on her now-extinguished cigar. "Not much we can do about that, Lamprey."

"But, my lady," he said tentatively. "There might be . . . someone who can go . . . scout out where they are."

She bit down hard enough to burst the seams of the cigar, spilling strands of tobacco onto her chin.

"That thief in the brig is scheduled for execution!"

"But . . . my lady. I don't mean to be insubordinate,

but . . . wouldn't it seem that he didn't commit the crime for which we got him locked up? After all, the boy here found your silver dagger. En't that proof he didn't steal it?"

"We all know he stole it!" she growled. "But you're right, he could prove useful one last time. Unlock him and send him out to scout for the Gog's ship."

"Aye, my lady," Mister Lamprey said before skipping down the steps.

The Pirate Queen called to him, "And, Lamprey, bring me the music box."

"But, my lady . . ."

"Get it!" she shouted, sending Lamprey stumbling down the stairs.

As Si continued to guide the Pirate Queen, she spat the remnants of her cigar onto the helm and spoke from the corner of her mouth. "I know you three can't be Ramblers, but somehow you've managed to do everything you've said."

"You're going to let us go, aren't you?" Ray asked, adding, "You promised."

"Yes, of course. Rambler or not, you know some hoodoo. What I want to know is where you got my silver dagger."

Ray tried to suppress the smile on his face. "The Lost Wood, ma'am."

The Pirate Queen's eyes narrowed but then relaxed with acceptance. Their attention was drawn to the deck below, where a perplexed Peter Hobnob peered about as if he hadn't had fresh air for some time. Mister Lamprey seemed to be explaining the situation, and as he spoke, old Joshua came forward with the dandelion hat. Lamprey grabbed Hobnob by the collar of his shirt, and Ray guessed he was explaining what would happen to him if he didn't return. From Hobnob's expression, it seemed he understood completely.

Placing the hat upon his head, he scattered as he'd done before, into a million tiny seedpods. Si, who had not seen this before, dropped her hand and pressed her nose to the glass, trying to find where the prisoner had gone.

"Keep guiding—er, what's your name, girl?"

"Si," she said, raising her hand again.

The Pirate Queen glanced at Ray. "And you, *Rambler*?"

"Ray." As if in greeting, Rosie snapped her jaws open in a whining yawn and lowered to her belly at Ray's feet.

It was not long before Hobnob materialized on the stern of the *Snapdragon*. The small yellow-haired man ran around the pirates gathered on the deck and up the steps to the pilothouse. As he came in the door, he started suddenly at seeing Ray, but Ray gave a quick shake of his head.

"Uh, my lady. Allow me to first express my gratitude at your eternal wisdom and compassion for releasing—"

"Shut up and tell me what you found out!"

"The Gog's vessel is near three miles north-northwest of us, waiting at the edge of the marsh where we entered."

"Can we veer south?" the Pirate Queen asked Si.

"I'll try," she answered.

"Hobnob, on the half hour I want you airborne and scouting the Gog's position."

"Yes, my lady," he replied. Before he left, he gave Ray a perplexed glance and a quick smile.

Lamprey returned shortly with a small trunk brightly painted with nautical images. "Leave it!" she barked.

Lamprey placed the trunk on the floor and scurried away.

Ray looked curiously at the trunk and finally asked, "What is it, ma'am?"

The Pirate Queen focused on her course but answered, "A music box that plays a mermaid's song. The Gog wants it, but why, I don't know."

Ray knew. Fear constricted his throat.

Mother Salagi had told him the Gog needed a way to control a siren. This music box must be how he planned on controlling Jolie. His heart raced with the realization. "Are you going to give it—?"

"Stop pestering me, boy!"

Ray bit at his lip. He couldn't let the Pirate Queen give it to the Gog.

As Ray fretted, it was slow going for the *Snapdragon*. A few times, Ray felt the bilge of the steamer brush against a shallow portion, but Si never ran them aground. She did grow tired, and the Pirate Queen sent for plates of food and mugs of steaming bitter coffee.

At his midnight report, Hobnob arrived noticeably windblown and looking ragged.

"What happened?" the Pirate Queen shouted.

"They spotted me, my lady. Opened fire on me with that repeating gun mounted on their deck."

"Are you hurt?"

Hobnob gave himself a quick inspection before saying, "No. But they're moving south and just entered the marsh. They're coming our way."

The Pirate Queen maneuvered the *Snapdragon* deeper and deeper through the marsh, following Si's directions. As they crossed a wide stream, Mister Lamprey shouted from the deck, "My lady, they're on our—!"

A crack echoed across the marsh, followed by an eruption of water about a hundred feet from the front of the *Snapdragon.*

"Cannons!" the pirates shouted from the deck. Mister Lamprey began issuing orders as the pirates rushed to position for combat. Ray looked out the side window and saw a low vessel covered with metal plates approaching from the north. It looked like an enormous shadowy alligator breaking through the shallow marsh. It wound its way until it was in the channel behind the *Snapdragon.*

"What is that?" Ray asked.

"A genuine ironclad," the Pirate Queen said. "Si, get us out of here quickly!"

Another cannon fired from the top of the ironclad, this

time splashing water onto the starboard side of the deck. Si frantically inspected her hand.

"Take that channel, to the left!"

"But it's wider where we are," the Pirate Queen argued. "That one's nothing but marsh grass. We'll run aground."

"It'll get us through," Si said. "Trust me."

The Pirate Queen twirled the wheel, throwing pirates around on the deck. The ironclad approached them faster. A cannon shot whirled just past the window of the pilot-house, making the glass tremble. Mud and grass exploded on the port side. But just when Ray thought they'd been lucky, a cannonball struck part of the stern, dashing a spray of wood and metal.

"Damn! That's it!" the Pirate Queen roared. "Lamprey!"

Lamprey shoved his face in through the pilothouse door. "My lady?"

"Signal the ironclad. We're turning over the music box."

"No! Please!" Ray shouted.

The Pirate Queen wheeled around, her eyes wide and terrible.

"Please," Ray said. "Trust Si. She'll get us out of here."

The Pirate Queen peered at Si and then back at Ray, a suspicious expression boring into him.

"Which way, girl?" the Pirate Queen growled.

"Straight!" Si shouted. "Keep following the channel."

"It's too narrow!" the Pirate Queen shouted back. "It turns to nothing but grass ahead."

"We'll make it," Si urged.

The Pirate Queen cursed, her knuckles turning bony white on the wheel. Ray, barely able to watch, gripped the golden rabbit's foot in his pocket anxiously. He wondered if Si was making a mistake. The marsh looked impossible to cross. It seemed far too shallow for the *Snapdragon*.

Si turned her head slightly, not taking her eyes off her hand. "Did they take the bait?" she asked Ray.

"What?" he said.

"Are they following us?"

Ray saw the ironclad had turned into a wider channel in the thick marsh behind them.

"No," he gasped. "They're taking a shortcut."

"Good." She smiled, weariness pulling at her face.

The cannon fire continued for several tense minutes, but as abruptly as a summer storm that has come and gone, the firing stopped. Ray turned to see that the ironclad was getting farther behind. Mister Lamprey burst into the pilothouse.

"My lady, they're stuck! The Gog's ironclad ran aground."

The Pirate Queen handed Lamprey the music box. "Put it back."

"Yes, my lady."

The Pirate Queen struck a match and lit the end of a fresh cigar. She looked back with ember-glowing eyes and gave Si a wide smile. "Well done, Si," she said. "Well done."

—13—

THE NINE POUND HAMMER

A̲N̲ H̲O̲U̲R̲ A̲F̲T̲E̲R̲ T̲H̲E̲ G̲O̲G̲'S̲ I̲R̲O̲N̲C̲L̲A̲D̲ W̲A̲S̲ L̲E̲F̲T̲ M̲I̲R̲E̲D̲ in the marsh, the *Snapdragon* entered the wide, flowing course of the river. The pirates howled about the deck, cheering for Si, and then, remembering their manners, cheering Conker and Ray. With the excitement of the chase over, Ray felt exhausted. He wanted a bed; even a dry spot on the deck would work fine. But there was no chance for sleep yet. The Pirate Queen continued farther down the river until she found a hidden, tree-lined creek to dock the *Snapdragon,* then she shouted for Etienne Beauvais, the ship's cook, to prepare a late-night feast in celebration of their escape.

Ray followed Si and the Pirate Queen from the pilothouse. The laughing pirates had already led Conker into the galley. Tables and chairs littered the cozy room where the pirates took their meals. The room filled quickly, and the pirates pressed to the sides to allow their queen to cross to her seat. It was a velvet-cushioned bench built into the wall that ran along the back of the galley. She gestured with her cigar for Ray, Si, and Conker to join her on the bench.

Etienne had no time to cook a proper feast, but he carried in platters of pungent cheese, tropical fruits, cold slabs of smoked cod, and vol-au-vents. The Pirate Queen opened several casks of her favorite claret, but most of the pirates opted for the rum. During the noisy, lip-smacking feast, the crew toasted the three over and over before settling into roaring conversations, belching, and other gastronomical noises.

"Your promise is fulfilled, and so is mine," the Pirate Queen announced, giving Ray a nod. "If you're in need of work, we could use three such as yourselves on the *Snapdragon*."

Conker licked the fruit from his fingers. "No thank you, ma'am. We best get on in the morning. Nel will be wanting us to get back."

"Nel?" she asked. "Would that be Peg Leg Nel?"

Conker swallowed hard with surprise, and looked guiltily at Ray and Si. "Uh, yes, ma'am. You know Mister Nel?"

"Know of him. *Ramblers,* huh? I knew you weren't Ramblers. You three are nothing more than scruffs in his medicine show."

None of the three could muster a reply, and the Pirate Queen unleashed a loud laugh. She tossed back her claret and sucked on her cigar as Mister Lamprey refilled her outstretched glass.

"Medicine show scruffs. Well, if I'm not mistaken, there is a cowboy among you. Eustace Buckthorn?"

Ray smiled, remembering the rumor that Conker and Eddie had shared: that Buck had once been in love with the Pirate Queen.

"Sure. We know Buck."

Mister Lamprey scowled, splattering rum from his lips. "He was once with the crew of the *Snapdragon,* and a right terrifying outlaw. That was back before he turned yellow and joined up with them Ramblers. And now you telling us he ain't nothing more than a carnival attraction?"

The Pirate Queen laughed. "Eustace is a good man. Too good for our ilk." She added almost wistfully, "And with much more goodness than he himself is willing to recognize."

Ray imagined that the wine must be softening the Pirate Queen's mood. Either that or the memory of Buck.

"Why do you say that?" Ray asked.

"You know Eustace killed his own brother?"

Ray remembered Eddie telling him this, but now that he knew Buck, he thought it must just be a twisted rumor.

"Buck ain't a murderer, ma'am," Conker said. "I heard others tell it, but never from Buck. It can't be true."

"It is," she said. "But it's hardly the circumstances you'd think. Eustace's tough, and I've seen him get downright mean, but he ain't so mean as to kill his own brother in cold blood. It's a long tale and this night's for celebrating, but I'll tell you a bit of how it happened. Sometime you might get him to tell it right.

"Eustace loved his brother more than any brother loved another in this world. They grew up in the Wyoming Territory back before the Sioux were tamed, back when that country was still a wild place. His brother, Baldree, was the golden one, the eldest and full of greatness. The clear opposite of Eustace. Being blind since birth, Eustace's parents always saw him as an invalid.

"But over time Eustace figured how to overcome his blindness. He learned other ways of seeing, using his other senses. Mostly by smell, but there's more factors involved: instinct, guts, luck. With this talent, he secretly learned to shoot a pistol—the very thing in the West that marks a man as a man. He figured if he could shoot like a man, he'd win his father's respect."

The Pirate Queen continued, "It was on Christmas Day, his father was holding a big celebration with the other rancher families. Eustace announced that he had a special surprise. As everybody gathered in the snowy yard, he pulled his pistols and began showing off his secret gift. He had people call out things for him to shoot: a post or a horseshoe nailed to the barn. That kind of thing. Naturally they were all amazed.

"As someone called out 'mistletoe,' Eustace fired. What Eustace didn't know was that his brother, Baldree, had a sprig of mistletoe in the breast pocket of his coat because he intended to corner the daughter of a local rancher he fancied. Before anyone could stop him, Eustace shot his brother through the heart."

Ray gasped. A quiet settled over the room. Not a pirate dared let his plate rattle.

"It wasn't his fault," Si said.

"I know," said the Pirate Queen. "But Eustace never saw it that way. What he didn't realize until then was that his emotions could get the better of his senses. He felt pride, pride that he was finally impressing his father. It betrayed him that day. No, he was never the same after that. Always blamed himself for what happened. It's what led him to becoming an outlaw, what led him to us, until the Ramblers saved him from his own ruination."

The Pirate Queen shifted her eyes across the room to her sullen pirates. "Quit this moping. We need music."

"Aye," Mister Lamprey said, clambering drunkenly to his feet. "No rue and repining tonight." Kicking a pirate from his chair, the fish-eyed Lamprey bellowed, "You heard the lady, you sour cretins. Strike up the band!" Movement and warmth returned suddenly to the galley.

Mister Lamprey produced a button accordion from a shelf, and other pirates traded their plates and knives for whatever musical instrument was at hand: spoons, a triangle, a washboard. A trio of pirates played bass by blowing on empty crockery jugs. The music forced Buck's dark tale from Ray's mind. A strange, jangling song began with a melody he could hardly follow. But the pirates seemed to know it or at least its chorus, and all shouted the refrain in baritone unison—except for Piglet, who gave a piercing squeak—as it came around each time.

A romping dance began as the three heroes were pulled to their feet. Conker danced with Si. Piglet threw Ray around in a series of twirls, and as there was little choice in female dance partners—and none dared ask their queen to dance—every pirate not playing an instrument simply grabbed whoever was nearest. Hobnob's crime seemed to be forgotten as he danced with Big Jimmie.

After several songs, Ray was able to escape and follow Si and Conker back to the velvet cushion by the Pirate Queen.

The Pirate Queen sat as no other woman Ray had ever seen. She slouched off to one side with an elbow on the cushion and kicked one of her high-booted feet out upon the table. Despite her volatile temper, Ray knew he liked her immensely and felt he understood why Buck had fallen in love with her.

The Pirate Queen let her gaze shift from Conker to Si and then to Ray, curiosity or maybe suspicion filling the dark-rimmed eyes with a stormy light.

"I was ready to get rid of that music box," she growled at Ray. "But you stopped me. Why?"

The ruckus in the galley was enormous, and Si and Conker leaned in anxiously to hear.

"I knew Si could guide you to safety," Ray said. "I trusted her."

A wicked, playful smile curled at the corners of the Pirate Queen's lips.

Conker, who had not been in the pilothouse with them, asked, "What's the music box?"

The Pirate Queen gulped the last of her claret before pouring another.

"I'll tell you children, there are strange things in this world. Mermaids even. Do you believe that?" Her eyes fogged a moment with the effects of the wine, but she continued. "I bought that music box years ago from a sea captain in Havana. Said it played their song, which is known to charm many a sailor to his death. But he told me the real value was that if you ever encountered a mermaid, it could charm them back. You could have a mermaid ready to do your bidding.

"That sea captain didn't really believe this, however. He thought it was nothing more than a child's amusement, but he had never seen a mermaid for real. I have. They're a rarity, mind you, but sometimes on a remote key or swimming along the reefs . . . I knew a music box that played a mermaid's chantey could be real handy if the time ever came that the *Snapdragon* ran into a brood of siren sisters."

Ray's heart was racing.

The Pirate Queen dropped her foot from the table. Her

eyes narrowed as she looked hard at Ray. "I know what you're hiding, *Ramblers*. I suspect even a pea-brain like Big Jimmie over there could figure it out. You're taken up with Eustace Buckthorn, a certified friend of the Ramblers. And here I am, listening out for things as I do. Little time back, I hear how the Ramblers are all killed, hunted down by the Gog and murdered. Why? The way I hear it, the Ramblers are protecting a siren.

"And here you are, a couple of scruffs working in Peg Leg Nel's medicine show, where Eustace's working, too. And you tell me not to give the Gog the music box! Nel's harboring that siren, ain't he?"

Ray looked down at his shifting hands.

"Get up, you scruffs." The Pirate Queen extinguished her cigar in a half-finished glass of wine and rose to her feet. "Come with me."

Ray got up nervously. Si gave Conker an anxious glance, but Ray motioned for them to follow. What choice did they have?

The Pirate Queen led the three through the boisterous destruction that had once been the galley. Shoving aside drunken dancers, she grabbed Mister Lamprey by the hair of his beard. "Where did you put the box?"

Lamprey's eyes watered as he said, "Down . . . down in the vault, my lady."

She pushed him toward the fray of dancers and curled her finger back at Ray, Si, and Conker to follow. They went down a companionway to a lower deck. At the end of a hall, she produced a set of keys and unlocked a door.

As she lit an oil lamp on the wall, Ray realized that this was the booty room. Treasure from hundreds of pillaging missions all up the waterways of the Mississippi River basin lay before them. It was just as Ray imagined Blackbeard's hoard would look were he still marauding in this age. There were gilded mirrors, jewel-encrusted necklaces, and scores of gold and silver objects, but there were also stacks of now-worthless Confederate money, bellows folding cameras, a nickelodeon, and even a taffy-pulling machine.

The Pirate Queen waded her way through the room, tossing lavish items about as if they were nothing more than salvage-yard scraps. The others looked about with slack-jawed amazement. This was better than any mercantile, better than any museum.

"Come here," she ordered. "I have one last demand if I'm to set you free."

On the table was the painted trunk. The Pirate Queen opened the lid and removed a crank box with a tiny curved horn. Then she pulled out a wax cylinder. After fastening it together, she turned the handle. Conker froze as the music began. It was just as Ray remembered Jolie's singing, but in a sweeter, sharper voice. As he listened closely, he noted that there were many voices singing together in unison. He felt again the uncontrollable desire to hear the music better, to do whatever the singer asked, if only the song would continue.

"Sounds wretched," Si said, hands over her ears.

Conker swayed and his eyes fluttered. "It . . . it . . . it's the prettiest thing I ever heard," Conker sighed.

The Pirate Queen stopped it abruptly. "Can't stand it either," she said to Si. She disassembled the music box and returned it to the brightly painted trunk. As she handed it to Ray, she said, "The Gog will keep hunting for me until he gets this. I'll not risk my ship another day with this menace on board. Take it, before I toss it in the river."

Ray picked it up hesitantly. "Thank you. I appreciate—"

The Pirate Queen snarled off his gratitude, saying, "I suppose I don't need to remind you that you should take special care with this. Keep it secret. Keep it hidden. I'm not sure why the Gog wants a siren, but the fact that he's returned, after we've heard nothing of him for so long, worries me."

"Somebody has to stop the Gog," Ray said. "Won't you help?"

A strange smile, full of sadness and admiration, tensed on the Pirate Queen's face. "I have no desire to see whatever evil the Gog is building come to completion, Ray. But if it comes to fighting, I'll not put my neck out for him to lop off." She paused, a smirk coming to her face. "But help? I might have something that will help. Just maybe . . ."

The Pirate Queen fixed Conker in a penetrating gaze. "I've got my suspicions about something."

Conker looked at her curiously.

She went to a chifforobe at the far wall. Opening the

cabinet, she removed something long and wrapped in a black shroud of waxed cerecloth. She carried it back and set it down before Conker.

The Pirate Queen spoke low and solemnly to Conker. "If my instinct is right—and I'll know in a moment if it is—then this is meant for you."

Pulling back the coarse cloth, she exposed the corner of an octagonal block of iron and then tugged off the entire cloth to reveal a long-handled hammer. It could have been any hammer used by thousands of workmen to break rocks or drive railroad spikes. But by the fragile trembling of emotion that came to Conker's face, Ray knew it was no ordinary hammer.

"It can't be possible. . . ." He touched his fingers to the raw weathered wood of the handle.

"Yes," the Pirate Queen said. "I thought as much. When you pulled my steamer off that shoal tonight, I thought there was only one person who could do such a feat, only one other with that kind of strength. This hammer gave you the strength to do it, Conker. There is no denying the resemblance. You're John Henry's son."

Si asked, "But what . . . Conker, what is it?"

Not taking his eyes from the hammer, he whispered, "My father's weapon. The Nine Pound Hammer."

"RAY."

He heard his name in his sleep, and when it dawned on him that it wasn't part of his dream, Ray opened his eyes.

The yellow explosion of Hobnob's hair gave Ray a start.

"You awake?" Hobnob smiled.

Ray looked around and saw he was the last one still sleeping in the galley. He could hear the pirates' voices bouncing cheerfully around the decks up above. The disaster that had been the galley was now back to relative order, although how Ray had slept through it all remained a mystery.

"Is it still morning?" Ray's voice croaked with sleep.

"Not yet even midmorning. Been wanting to talk to you when the others weren't about."

Ray sat up on the velvet cushion, wiping the crust from his eyes.

"You en't told her, have you?" Hobnob squatted at Ray's side, his dandelion hat on his knee.

"What?" Ray asked.

"That you was the one that set me free in the Lost Wood."

"Oh. No."

"That's good. Don't tell her. Best not. She'll have our thumbs if she knows the long and short of it all. But this is twice you done me a good turn." Hobnob poked a friendly finger against Ray's chest.

"That's okay—"

"I've got a mind to pay you back, Ray. Set things square, if you see."

Before Ray could argue, Hobnob plucked a dandelion from the hat.

"You take this. Ever you get in a fix just give three claps of your hands, call my name three times, and blow three breaths on the petals. Got that?"

"Sure," Ray said, taking the flower.

"I'll come, anywhere. None's the difference where you might be."

Since Hobnob could fly, this gave Ray an idea. "Actually, I do have something you could do."

"That right?" Hobnob asked enthusiastically.

"I've got a sister; her name's Sally. Before I met you, she was heading south on an orphan train and has probably been adopted by now. The only thing is, my father is still alive."

"He is! Congratulations." Hobnob smiled.

"But see, I don't know where he is. It's too much to explain, but if he does come back, he'd want to meet my sister. And I've got no idea where she is."

"Ah, you want to find her? I see. I see. Wanting to keep kin with kin; that's it, en't it? My poor old ma. Left her back in the old country—"

"Right. Can you help?"

"I'll do my best, Ray. You know what towns that train was heading to?"

"No."

"Rail line, any such like that?"

"Sorry, no."

"None's the difference. I'll do my best—"

"Oh. The woman who was arranging the adoptions is Miss Corey, Constance Corey, I think. And this rich man named Grevol owned the train. It was a beautiful train. Really fancy. That might help."

"Sure. I'll poke around, ask some questions, and drop by your medicine show to let you know what I find."

"Thanks," Ray said. "And of course, if I can ever help you—"

"No, no." Hobnob waved his hands. "Least I can do."

Ray got to his feet and followed Hobnob out into the bright sun of the deck.

* * *

"I'm sorry I can't persuade you three," the Pirate Queen said. "I've been known from time to time to keep a promise, and I suppose you've earned your freedom."

The Pirate Queen's arms were locked behind her coat as she walked to the stern. The crew was busy readying the steamer while the Pirate Queen spoke with Ray, Si, and Conker.

"We're taking the *Snapdragon* south, out into the Gulf. The Gog will be looking for us, and it's best we put some distance between us and him."

She produced an envelope sealed with drops of black wax and handed it to Ray. "For Eustace. Can I trust that he'll get it?"

"Yes, ma'am," Ray said, placing it in his pocket next to the toby containing the dandelion and the rabbit's foot.

She escorted the three to the gangplank that led to a grassy bank by the mouth of the creek. Ray held the siren-song music box, secured in a gunnysack. Conker had the cerecloth-covered Nine Pound Hammer over his shoulder.

"I do hope we meet again." The Pirate Queen smiled briefly and shook each of their hands. "You'll find your way back to Peg Leg Nel's train?"

Si lifted her tattooed hand. "Four days' travel northeast."

"Well, be careful and stay to the woods if you can."

"We will," Ray assured her. He waved to the crew, who had stopped their work to watch the three depart. The ragtag pirates pressed around the bulwarks and waved heartily. The Pirate Queen drew her pistol and shot it several times over their heads, cursing and roaring until they scuttled back to their posts.

The adventure aboard the *Snapdragon* had deepened the friendship between Ray, Si, and Conker. As they traveled across the wooded lowlands, they laughed and retold stories of the feats they had each performed, over and over. By campfire at night, Si especially enjoyed mimicking Conker's reaction to Rosie and the way Conker had tried to fight Big Jimmie. Conker retaliated with his own version of Si tied to the crane and desperate to murder the Pirate Queen, but even Conker had to agree it wasn't nearly as funny.

As they traveled toward the medicine show, their conversations returned to everyday life on the *Ballyhoo*. Ray was not sure why, but Conker began acting strange. A glum mood descended over him as they got closer to home.

"Conker, think you'll change your act after what happened on the *Snapdragon*?" Ray asked one afternoon in an effort to lift his spirits. "With the Nine Pound Hammer you could pull the whole *Ballyhoo*—"

"I'm not changing nothing, Ray," Conker said quickly, drawing the Nine Pound Hammer close against his side. "I don't want you telling Nel about that."

"Why not?" Ray asked.

"Just don't."

They were quiet for some time after that. When they

stopped for the night, Si and Ray went off to gather fire-wood.

"What's going on with Conker?" Ray asked her. "Why's he want to keep what happened from Nel?"

She picked up a broken branch and stuck it beneath her arm.

"You have to understand, Ray, Nel took us in, all of us in the medicine show. Conker never knew John Henry. His mother, Polly Ann, died not long after John Henry did. Conker was just a baby then. Nel is the closest thing he's ever had to a father. Conker would never want to do anything to upset Nel. And Nel would never want us to run off and try to stop the Gog, not that we'd stand a chance at stopping him anyway. But now Conker's been given his father's hammer!"

Ray said, "The Nine Pound Hammer. Looks like about ninety pounds!"

Si agreed with a nod. "Conker must see a new path before him, and it's not Nel's path or that of the medicine show. It's the path of taking up his father's hammer and destroying the Gog. Carrying on his father's work."

Ray picked up some more branches as he thought about what Si had said. "Were your parents Ramblers, Si?"

Si continued collecting sticks. After a few moments Ray thought she was ignoring him, but then she said, "I'm not sure."

Si cast a glance at Ray, adjusted the sticks, and continued, "My parents came with their families across the

Pacific to California, my father and his brothers all wanting to get rich working on the railroad. I was the youngest of four sisters. Having all girls was bad enough, but being the fourth was . . . an unlucky omen, as my uncles and aunts saw it. My name means *four,* a number that's associated with death in China. But the worst of all was how I was born with a black hand."

Si's gaze lingered a moment on her hand, holding the bundle of firewood. "My parents left. Maybe to help John Henry fight the Gog. My uncle, who was taking care of me, thought I was cursed, some sort of demon. When my parents never returned and relatives of ours started dying mysteriously, my uncle took me on a trip into town. At least that's what he said we were doing. He tied me up and left me in the woods."

Ray saw the pain in her expression and knew that bringing up the memory was not easy. Si heaved her chest in a sigh, but then scowled as her ferocity returned.

"I got loose. At the time it seemed so simple. I didn't realize that those knots would have been impossible for any other little girl to untie. It was also simple for me to find my way back home. It was my hand. The markings came up on it for the first time. They showed me the way.

"When I returned, my uncle was horrified. But my aunt must have felt some sympathy for me. She knew Mister Everett. He worked on the same railroad as my family at the time. Mister Everett told her about a man he knew who could take me in—a man who understood about such things as the strange markings on my hand. Without so much as a hug or a goodbye, she gave me to Mister Everett. And he took me to Nel." She shrugged and bent once more to collect another branch.

Ray felt sad for Si. That her own family could be so heartless and superstitious filled Ray with disgust.

They started walking back toward the campsite. After a few moments Ray said, "I found out something before I left, Si. Do you know who Li'l Bill is?"

"Sure," Si said. "He and John Henry were thick."

"He was my father."

Si's eyes widened. "You're . . . Li'l Bill's son?"

Ray nodded. "And, like you said about Conker, there's a new path for me; it's just that I can't see where it leads."

Si hoisted the load of branches in her arms. "I don't know much about Ramblers, Ray, but it seems to me you're on the way to being a good one."

"How about you?" Ray asked.

Si cocked an eyebrow. "How about me what?"

"Do you want to be a Rambler?"

They were nearly to the campsite now. "Wherever Conker goes," Si said, almost in an undertone, "I'll go."

When the pair returned, Conker was bent over the smoking kindling. Ray's eyes pulled to the Nine Pound Hammer lying on the ground, wrapped in the cerecloth. Here was the weapon that had destroyed the Gog's Machine.

As Ray stood watching Conker blowing a blaze up

from the circle of stones, he wondered if his friend might be the hero who would finally defeat the Gog. And Ray felt, like Si, that if he did, that he would be there at Conker's side.

That night as the fire burned down to embers, Ray sat up. He gave up on falling asleep. Too many thoughts swirled about his head. Ray turned and was surprised to see Conker awake and sitting with his back against a log, gazing into the dying fire.

"Can't sleep?" Ray whispered.

Conker gave a thin smile and shook his head. Ray got up and sat at Conker's side.

"I'm sorry, Conker."

"Why's that?" Conker's eyes widened curiously.

"For using the lodestone to see your dream."

"Oh, that weren't nothing."

"But I'm also glad I did," Ray said. "If I hadn't, I never would have figured out who my father was."

"So where'd you go anyway, Ray? You didn't need to run off. I didn't mean to get so mad, but you know I wouldn't have held it against you."

"No, it wasn't that," Ray said, prodding a stick to stir up the fire. "I was mad at Jolie."

"Jolie? How come?"

"Because, all that time she was the reason my father wasn't around."

"That ain't true," Conker said. "It weren't Jolie's fault.

You want to blame someone, blame the Gog, or blame the goodness in your pa's heart, 'cause he was only doing what none other could."

Ray told Conker about finding his father as a rabbit and showed him the golden foot. Conker listened intently to all Ray had learned from Mother Salagi.

When he finished, he and Conker sat for a time before Ray asked, "What are you going to do, Conker? Now that you have the Nine Pound Hammer?"

Conker sighed. "Why you think I can't sleep? I don't know. When I pulled the *Snapdragon* off that shoal, I've never had no strength like that. It's the hammer, Ray. That's what I was feeling as soon as we got on that pirate steamer. I think just being near to it started to change me. But I'm afraid, afraid of the Gog, and worse, I'm afraid of my father's hammer."

"But the hammer can help you," Ray said.

"That hammer led to my father dying," he said solemnly. In the fire's glow, Conker's eyes appeared illuminated, dancing with phantom flames. "And I'm scared it'll be my death, too. But if my father weren't scared, maybe I need to quit hiding under Nel's skirt."

Ray sat quietly a moment and then said, "I'll help you, whatever you decide to do."

"I don't know what that'll be," Conker said.

"What would Li'l Bill and John Henry do? I think we need to protect Jolie. If the Gog is after her, the best thing we can do is keep her as far away from him as possible."

"Just because you two can't sleep," Si grumbled from across the low coals of the fire, "doesn't mean you have to keep me up with your yapping." Ray and Conker turned to see her sitting up. She gave one of her rare smiles and then rolled over.

Ray and Conker sat in silence for a long while, watching the sparks pop from the fire and drift into the dark.

The following day Si led them to the *Ballyhoo* in the dusty hill country of eastern Mississippi. The show was nearly set up and there were hours until it was to start. Seth was practicing with his swords as they walked into camp.

"You again," was all Seth said in a flat voice to Ray before returning to his routine.

"Like to see what would happen if he'd been on the *Snapdragon*," Si said out of the corner of her mouth. "Try using those swords for real for once."

Eddie, as soot-covered as ever, stepped from the locomotive and broke into a big grin. "Ma, they're back. And Ray's back, too!" he called. Ma Everett poked her head from the kitchen car and ran out to greet them, giving each a big kiss on the cheek.

Marisol's face peered curiously from the window at the sleeper car. Several windows down from her, Redfeather called out a hello. Buck sat in the shade of the locomotive, his head cocked. As Ma Everett hustled the three to the mess car for a meal, Peg Leg Nel strolled out in his bandy-legged fashion. His smile went to surprise and faded to a curious scowl as he saw the black roll of cerecloth in Conker's arms. He turned without a word of greeting and went back into his car.

Conker gave Ray an anxious look. "It'll be okay," Ray said. "I'll be there in a second. Save me a bite."

Ray turned to jog up to the locomotive.

"I met someone you used to know," Ray said before handing the envelope to Buck.

The cowboy ran his fingers over the wax before breaking the seal. He lifted the envelope to his nose and inhaled its scent. A vague smile twitched on his thin lips.

"How is Lorene?" Buck asked.

Ray assumed this must be the Pirate Queen's name. He wanted to laugh. The sudden realization that she had once been a girl with a normal name before becoming a feared outlaw caught Ray off guard.

"Good, I suppose," Ray replied.

Buck shook his head and chuckled. "You never cease to surprise me, Ray."

"I do my best. I have something else, too, but I can't show you here."

"Come with me." Buck led Ray to the cowboy's sparse room, where Ray took out the siren-song music box from the small painted case.

Buck ran his fingers over it. "What is it?"

"A music box. It's got a wax cylinder," Ray said as he assembled it and turned the crank. Buck tilted his head as the sweet, eerie singing began.

"You got this from Lorene?"

"Yes. The Gog attacked her ship trying to get it. He could use the music box to control Jolie . . . if he captures her."

Buck stopped the turning cylinder. "He won't. We'll put it somewhere safe."

The cowboy took the box and slid it under his bed.

"Buck, I have something else to tell you. . . ."

Buck sat at the table, his hands folded in front of him as he listened to Ray. Ray told him everything—about the lodestone and about seeing Li'l Bill in Conker's dream, about the rabbit's foot and the Nine Pound Hammer. As Ray spoke, Buck's craggy face remained placid and expressionless. When he finished, Buck muttered, "He ain't going to like this."

Ray was about to ask what he meant, when the cowboy stood. "Come on. Let's get Conker. It's time we talked to Nel. It's time you knew."

—15—

CHILDREN OF THE RAMBLERS

PUZZLED, RAY FOLLOWED BUCK TO THE MESS CAR.
Conker was halfway through a plate of grits, fried wild
tubers, and jelly-slathered biscuits. "Come with us,"
Buck said.

Conker looked up anxiously, his spoon perched before
his open mouth. "What's going on?" he asked, looking
to Ray.

Ray said, "We're going to talk to Nel."

"Now?" The giant's eyes widened. Picking up the Nine
Pound Hammer as he stood, Conker said, "Just one moment, Buck. Need to go to my room first . . ."

"Bring it with you," Buck growled.

Conker gulped and joined Ray behind Buck. As they
entered Nel's car, the pitchman was chewing anxiously on

the end of his briarwood pipe and gazing out the window. When he saw the boys enter behind Buck, his eyes fell immediately to the bundle of cerecloth in Conker's hands.

"Sit down," Buck said to Ray and Conker.

As the four sat around the table, Buck began, "Nel, we've got some talking and it ain't going to be quick. First, you need to know what these boys have been up to. And then, I think it's time we told them a few things."

Nel shifted in his seat, his elbows cocked awkwardly as he squeezed the arms of the chair. Nel looked first at Conker. "Where did you get it?"

"What?" Conker asked.

The deep folds and wrinkles around Nel's eyes relaxed until Nel looked both patient and sad.

Conker took a deep breath. "From the Pirate Queen."

Nel looked at Buck, and Buck said, "I gave the Nine Pound Hammer to her to keep years back. You wanted it off the train, remember? You worried that it put the children at risk. Her steamer was the safest place I knew."

Buck then cocked his head toward Ray. "Go ahead, Ray. Tell Nel who you are."

Nel frowned, "What do you mean?"

Ray picked at the edge of the table nervously. "I'm not Ray Fleming, sir."

"You're not?"

"No, my real name is Ray Cobb."

Nel's eyes were bright and wild as Ray began telling

him about the lodestone and how he had found his father and gotten the rabbit's foot. ". . . the lodestone disappeared, too. Well, not exactly. I still have it but it's buried inside my father's hand."

"His hand?" Nel gasped. "Severed by the Hoarhound! Ray, is it made of silver? Can I see it?"

"It's not silver," Ray said as he took out the toby and removed the rabbit's foot. "It's gold." He handed it to Nel.

Nel looked down at the rabbit's foot for a long time, before saying, "This is troubling to an old man, boys. There are many things I hoped to protect all of you from. But those wicked hounds won't get off my trail." He gave a dry snort. "Metaphorically and literally, I suppose." Still gazing down at the golden foot, turning it over and over in his hands, Nel added, "It would seem the Hoarhound's jaws have taken another."

Conker and Ray exchanged a puzzled look. "What do you mean, Nel?" Conker asked.

Nel placed the rabbit's foot on the table. He removed the tasseled fez from his head and loosened the cravat to unbutton the top buttons of his shirt. His fingers located a cord of rawhide around his neck and pulled up what seemed at first to be a pendant. It was large and heavy and fashioned of silver. As Nel held the object up for the boys to see, Ray realized it was a foot—an animal's paw.

"This old fox paw"—Nel nodded to the silver paw—"was once here." And he tapped his peg leg with a knuckle.

Ray snapped his eyes to Conker to see if Conker had known this, but the giant's mouth opened and closed a few times before he was able to speak. "You were a Rambler?" Conker whispered.

Nel nodded as he returned the paw back inside his shirt. "Long ago. Until a Hoarhound took my leg off."

Nel sighed and Ray could see the struggle in the pitchman's face before he continued. "It happened not long after your father died, Conker. The Machine was destroyed, but not the Gog. I was part of a band of Ramblers—along with your father, Ray—who hunted him down. There was a battle against the Gog's army: men and beasts of clockwork and frost. Many Ramblers were killed. I was attacked by a Hoarhound. I was fortunate to only lose part of my leg. In the end, the Gog's army was defeated. But the Gog escaped.

"The battle broke me. To see so many of my friends die, it destroyed a part of me, in a way I can never explain. And my Rambler powers, too; once my leg was severed, I lost them. I don't know why.

"If it had not been for your mother, Conker . . . I loved Polly Ann very much. She was like a daughter to me. She was fearful that agents of the Gog might come for her. There were Ramblers disappearing, being killed . . . their families, too. The Gog knew who she was. He might find her.

"Fortunately the Gog thought I had died in the battle. You see, Ray, you are not the only one who has had to take on a pseudonym in order to hide from the Gog's agents. Cornelius Carter is not my real name. I'm Joe Nelson. Not so flashy, is it?" He chuckled. "No, the Rambler Joe Nelson was dead. And the pitchman Peg Leg Nel Carter was born. I took you in, Conker. I took in other children who were in danger from the Gog. I was a Rambler no longer—in both name and ability. But I knew how to do root work. I could make tonics. That is how the medicine show began."

Ray stumbled for words, but the revelation that Nel had once been a Rambler left him speechless.

Conker's jaw tightened as he asked, "Did the Gog . . . did he kill my mother?"

Nel's expression saddened again. "She tried to hide. She moved around, keeping to the wilderness—for what you don't realize, Conker, is that Polly Ann was a Rambler, too."

Conker's eyes widened and then narrowed. "But the Gog tracked her down?"

Nel nodded. "His agents. Yes. Those were hard times. With John Henry's sacrifice, the Ramblers had struck a terrible blow to the Gog. He was weakened. He needed to rebuild his Machine. The Gog still had his servants. And one by one the Ramblers were hunted down and killed."

Nel paused to light his briarwood pipe. After drawing on it, he motioned with the pipe to Ray. "I wasn't the only one who left the Ramblers. Your father, Ray . . . he had met a wonderful woman, your mother, and fell in love. He had seen so much death and destruction at the hands of the Gog. He no longer wanted to wander the fringes of the world as a warden. He wanted more than ever to be a part of *this* world.

"He left the Ramblers, left the wild. But years later, when you must have been just a youngster, word got to him that the Gog was building a new machine, one far worse than the first. And for reasons the Ramblers didn't know at the time, the sirens were threatened."

"How did you know all this?" Ray asked. "If you were no longer a Rambler. Who told you?"

"I did," Buck answered, crossing his arms on the table. "Nel and I became friends after I left the *Snapdragon*. But I was also helping the Ramblers, and they sent me to find your father. It took several visits to convince him."

"You?" Ray asked.

Buck nodded. "Li'l Bill was afraid that your mother might be threatened, that the Gog might come for his family if they found out about you. So she moved around and changed her name.

"Ray, your father"—Buck put his hands together as he continued—"he wanted to return to you, to his family. All those years, he didn't even know that your mother had given birth to a daughter. It was hard on him, Ray. Hard to be away from those he loved. But it was a sacrifice he had to make."

Ray could not help but feel the jealous anger toward Jolie well up in him. Jolie had said his father had loved her as a daughter. Had he loved Jolie more than his own family?

Ray asked, "What will happen to Jolie?"

Buck cocked his head. "What do you mean?"

"Mother Salagi said the Gog needs Jolie—her siren voice—to capture people for his Machine. What will happen to her? You can't hide her on this train forever!"

Buck frowned as Nel said, "The truth is, we don't know what we are going to do with her. We're just worried about getting her healthy and strong again. Then we will look for a place—not on the train, I assure you—where she can live safely."

"But the Gog might find her," Ray said. "You think he doesn't know about you, Mister Nel, but he knew that the Pirate Queen had a siren-song music box. He will find her eventually."

"And what are you proposing?" Nel answered, his brow darkening.

"We need to stop the Gog!" Ray frowned.

Nel spread his hands wide on the table, looking from Conker to Ray several times. "Don't you understand all that I just told you? Weren't you listening? The Gog is more powerful than you imagine. Do you think that because Conker now has the Nine Pound Hammer and you have your father's hand, that you are going to be able to defeat the Gog?"

Conker leaned forward, his jaw trembling as he spoke. "But Nel . . . if we had your help and Buck's and Si's . . . she's awful tough!"

"Three children and a couple of old men aren't going

to defeat the Gog!" Nel shouted. He winced, closing his eyes and trying to calm himself. "Don't you see, Conker? I promised your mother I'd protect you. I have the lives of all these children aboard our train to think about. Get it out of your heads, boys! We stand no chance against the Gog."

A long silence followed. Finally, Nel pushed back his chair. "Go eat, boys. You've had a long journey. You probably need rest. But please think about what I've said. Promise me you won't do anything foolish."

Ray looked at Conker, but the giant's eyes were downturned. Nel looked sharply at Ray. "Promise me."

Ray nodded. "Okay, Mister Nel. We won't do anything foolish."

When they had stepped back into the blazing sunlight, Conker turned to Ray. "What are we going to do?"

"Figure a way to stop the Gog," Ray said.

"I thought you promised we wouldn't do anything foolish?"

"Foolish would be pretending that the Gog isn't going to find us, isn't going to track down Jolie, isn't going to rebuild his Machine!"

Conker waved a hand to shush Ray.

Ray frowned at him. "Remember what you said, about not hiding under Nel's skirt anymore?"

"Yeah," Conker mumbled, as he headed up the steps to their sleeping car to hide the Nine Pound Hammer in his room. "But it ain't that simple, Ray."

* * *

Redfeather was bobbing for flaming apples as he finished his performance. The crowd was roaring. Sitting at the back of the stage, Ray was frustrated. Frustrated with Conker. Frustrated with Nel. Frustrated with his father. But mostly, he was frustrated with himself. He had been holding the rabbit's foot when he slept, talking to it, rubbing it, trying to figure out some way to make the rabbit's foot do something, anything!

He had no idea what he was supposed to do. How could they stop the Gog?

After he helped Nel sell the tonics to the last of the crowd, Ray took his cap from his head, wiped his sweaty hair, and plopped on the edge of the stage to rest his feet. A few people from the audience remained, as they often did, to talk to the performers.

Ray watched Marisol as she let a trio of children pet Javier. She smiled and spoke encouragingly to the kids. Ray raised an eyebrow. This was not a side of Marisol he saw very often. She could be kind, when she wasn't ingratiating herself to Seth.

Looking around, Ray saw Seth at the far end of the tent, speaking to a man. With his stiff bowler hat, somber dark suit, and serious expression, the man did not look like one of the usual types of people who attended the medicine show. Seth said something, and the man gave a sour smile, a gold tooth flashing from his mouth.

"Ray."

Ray turned as Buck approached. "Oh, hey, Buck."

"Jolie says you haven't visited her since you got back," the cowboy said in his low, crackling voice.

"Yeah, I will," Ray sighed.

"Something wrong?" Buck asked, his eyelids parting a moment to reveal the pale orbs beneath.

"No," Ray said. "I've been meaning to."

"How about now?" Buck said. He held out the key.

Ray grimaced and took it. "Thanks."

He hopped from the stage and walked slowly down the train until he reached Jolie's car. He knocked at the door as he unlocked the latch. "Jolie," he called, turning the handle.

There was a splash of water and then the smack of wet feet on the floor. Ray blinked as he came in, letting his eyes adjust to the dimness. Jolie stood before the tank, smiling at Ray.

"Hey," Ray said. He tried hard not to think of those eight years his father had been away.

"Hello." Her smile faded as she looked at Ray curiously.

He propped his hands in his pockets. "How have you been?"

She shrugged. Ray looked at her face. Her complexion looked worse, even more ashen, with darker circles hanging beneath her eyes.

"Buck said you left," she said.

"Yeah."

"Where did you go?"

"Away."

"Oh," Jolie said softly. "Has something upset you?"

"No." Ray glowered at the floor.

"Oh," Jolie repeated. Awkward silence lingered as Jolie stared at Ray and Ray stared at his brogans. Finally, Jolie said, "Why did you come here, Ray?"

"Because Buck wanted me to," Ray said.

"Is that the only reason you have been visiting me all these times?"

Ray clinched his jaw. A hurt look welled up on Jolie's face, and she turned away, her wet, tangled hair slapping across her bare arms. Then she spun back to face Ray fiercely. "I thought you were my friend, Ray. At least, I thought we were becoming friends. I did not realize this was just out of pity for the poor siren. Well, I will give you permission. I will let Buck know. You do not have to come here anymore."

"Fine," Ray said.

"Fine!" Jolie snapped back, but Ray saw bright tears flash to her eyes.

Ray got as far as the door when he stopped. She doesn't deserve this, he thought. He walked back to Jolie, who was about to climb over the glass into the tank.

"What?" she said, a dark tangle of hair veiling part of her face. "Why are you being so terrible?"

"I know I am," Ray said. "It's not your fault. It's not even my father's fault. Conker tried to tell me all that."

Jolie dropped from the glass back to the floor. "What are you talking about?"

"Jolie, I left because I found out my father is Li'l Bill." Ray took out the rabbit's foot and showed it to her. As Ray sat on the wooden floor, Jolie knelt beside him, listening intently. Ray explained about everything that he had discovered. He also laid out all the anger and resentment that he had felt toward Jolie. She nodded sympathetically as he spoke, but did not interrupt.

"I know I was wrong, but I couldn't help it," Ray said, feeling much better when he finished.

"Ray, I am sorry," Jolie said, resting her chin on her knees. "I know it does not make up for all that you have had to go through, but Little Bill did speak often about his family. He did miss you and your mother. Of course, he never knew about your sister, but I am sure he would be sad to know that he had missed her birth and her childhood." Then Jolie winced, a sad expression falling over her face. "I have caused so much trouble."

Ray shifted uncomfortably. "Jolie—"

"You were right to be angry with me. All the others must hate me for the danger I am bringing. I would not blame them. I wonder if it would be better if I just ran away." She shook a long lock of hair over her eyes.

"You know that's not true!" Ray said.

Jolie shrugged, running her fingers through a puddle on the floor.

Ray watched her a moment before saying, "We're going to find a safe place for you. Nel and Buck are trying. Don't worry."

"I just wish I could understand why the Gog is after me . . . ," Jolie murmured.

"I think I know."

Jolie looked up at Ray, her eyes wide. Ray sighed and then said, "It's your song. He wants to use it to control people. To lead them to his Machine."

"I would never do that!" Jolie growled. "I would never help him."

Ray nodded. "You used your song on me . . . that time you thought I was after you. What does it do? Can you just make people do whatever you want?"

"In a way," Jolie said. "I have never used it much. I have never had a need, except when hunting. The sirens tell of sisters who rescue drowning sailors and use the song to make husbands of them. A siren born this way is a full siren. My father gave his love freely to my mother. That is why I am only part siren."

She seemed to struggle a moment to take a breath. Her complexion looked pale, paler than usual. She continued, "Love given freely like that means it can be taken away again. My father left my mother and she died because of it."

Ray waited before asking, "But if the Gog's agents

came for you, couldn't you just use your song to stop them?"

Jolie shook her head and for a moment seemed dizzy. "My powers are not the same as my sisters'. Their song could stop a great number. It is why the sirens have escaped captivity and notice . . . for so long. I do not think"—she was breathing heavily now, long slow gulps— "my song could control more than one at a time."

"Are you okay?" Ray asked, coming closer to Jolie.

"I do not feel well." Jolie staggered as she stood, and Ray grabbed her elbow. "I . . . just need to get into . . . the water." She fell, and Ray dropped quickly to one knee to catch her.

"Jolie?" he asked. Her eyes were swimming and she did not answer.

"Help!" Ray called. "Buck! Anyone!" He turned back to Jolie, trying to place her gently to the floor.

Conker was through the door first, followed by Buck and a gaggle of faces on the vestibule beyond.

"Get her into the tank!" Buck ordered.

Conker lifted Jolie effortlessly, and she opened her eyes to look at him and then over at Buck. "You're going to be okay. . . . You'll be fine once I get you in here . . . ," Conker said soothingly as he placed her over the glass into the water.

Jolie sank a moment, but then a cloud of bubbles burst from her nose and she waved her arms to swim. She brought her head back to the surface and said, "I am . . . fine. Thank you."

But Ray could see that she still looked washed out, her eyes ringed in dark circles.

"Everyone out!" Buck growled. "Jolie, I'll get Nel to bring you a tonic."

"Thank you," she mumbled, her eyes blinking heavily. "I just need to rest."

Ray followed Conker out to the crowd parting around the train. "She going to be all right?" Conker asked.

"I don't know," Ray said. He looked back once more at her car.

The following day, Si found Conker and Ray trying to escape the afternoon heat in the shade of the train.

"How's Jolie?" she asked.

"Better," Ray said. "Not great, but better."

"Well enough to get out?"

"I guess," Ray replied. "Why?"

"I have an idea," Si said. "Let's go into Ray's room so I can tell you."

It was cramped with Conker filling most of the space. Si sat by Ray on his narrow bed while Conker squeezed onto the floor.

"What are you thinking?" Ray asked Si.

"Jolie's not used to living on a train, eating our food, being cooped up indoors. But not only that. She *can't* do it. She's a siren. She needs to live like a siren, not like a person."

"But we can't do nothing about that," Conker said.

"Conker's right," Ray agreed. "With the Gog search-ing for her, she's got to—"

Si held up a hand. "I saw a pond in the woods a little ways away. Not more than five minutes' walk from here. We need to take Jolie to it."

"Buck ain't going to let us do that," Conker said.

"Buck's not going to know, now is he?" Si said.

"It's too dangerous," Conker argued. "Nel said we shouldn't do anything foolish."

"Quit being such a petticoat!" Si sneered. "If we—"

Before she could continue her argument, Ray stopped her. "Let's do it tonight."

"So you think it might help?" Si asked, looking re-lieved.

Ray nodded. "It's worth a shot." But what worried him more than running into danger from the Gog, more than getting caught by Buck or Nel, was whether they could trust Jolie not to run away once she returned to the wild again.

"YOU'RE LATE," SI WHISPERED FROM THE DARK OUTSIDE the sleeper car.

The night was thick and muggy, and Ray's shirt was damp with sweat despite the late hour. Haze clung to the bone-white midnight moon. There was a tinkle of glass, and as Ray peered in the dark, he saw that Conker had brought three bottletrees, as well as the Nine Pound Hammer.

"I nodded off," Ray said as they headed for Jolie's car.

The door opened to Jolie's car and she descended the steps. "Si said you have a surprise for me?"

"Follow us," Conker whispered. "Quietly. We don't want Buck catching us."

As they followed the side of the train to where the tracks led into the dark woods, Conker handed a bottle-tree each to Si and Ray. Jolie curiously eyed the stripped cedar branches, each with a dozen or so colored bottles placed where the limbs were broken off.

"What are those?" she whispered.

"Bottletrees," Ray said.

"What do they do?"

Conker answered, "The empty bottles trap evil. Least that's what Buck says. I ain't sure otherwise, but they've got to be stuck in the earth to work and they ain't doing us much help here, so let's keep moving."

"But where?" Jolie asked.

"You'll see," Si replied.

She led them a short distance down the track. Holding her hand up to the sky, she consulted the glowing patterns and then nodded into the trees. "Down here."

They stepped through the bracken and low vegetation to where the land sloped down. Had they not been so close together, Ray was sure he'd be lost in the woods at night. Soon the dark jumble of shrubs opened into what at first seemed a clearing. With the moonlight reflecting off the surface, Jolie gasped as she saw it was a pond not much farther across than the length of three train cars.

"Why are we here?" she asked.

"Si had the idea," Ray said. "We've been worried about you, about how you've been so sick. Si thought that maybe if you could swim in a real body of water, it might do some good."

"I . . . I do not know what to say," Jolie said. "You did not ask Buck? He will be angry?"

"If he finds out," Si answered. "We're going to keep a good watch. That's why we brought the bottletrees. We'll scatter around the edge of the pond, but if anything happens, you should get to Conker as quickly as possible. He'll protect you."

Jolie looked down to see the heavy hammer wedged in Conker's belt.

"We can't be out here too long," Conker warned. "I'll give a whistle when it's time. Go on."

Jolie nodded, smiling at each of her friends in turn. "Thank you." She ran to the water's edge and with a soft splash disappeared into the inky water.

"I'll stick here," Conker said, planting his bottletree in the moist earth by the pond. "You two spread out."

Si went to his left and Ray followed the curve of the pond to the right. He made his way until he thought he was about halfway around the pond. Even in the thin moonlight, he could see Conker's shirt, ghostly against the dark across the water. Gripping the cedar pole with both hands, Ray worked it into the ground until it stayed upright. He felt a mild reassurance at having it there and hoped it worked as Buck had said.

An old tree had fallen long ago and settled out into the pond, its far end sinking beneath the surface. Ray pulled himself up onto its roots and walked on its trunk until he was several yards out over the pond. He peered around for Jolie but could not find her. A sick knot formed. Please don't run away, he thought.

Trying not to dwell on that concern, Ray dangled his feet over the water. The night was hot and thick, and Ray thought how nice the pond must feel. He looked again for Jolie. The surface of the water was still, and he could only hope she was simply swimming somewhere in the depths of the pond.

Ray dug the red flannel toby out of his pocket and held the rabbit's foot in his hand. It seemed silly, but he thought that it might somehow keep Jolie from leaving. He nervously ran his fingers over the edge of the smooth metal surface. Why was it so warm? Dim speckles of light formed on the golden skin. Startled, Ray jerked and the foot slipped from his fingers. The rabbit's foot hit the log and bounced toward the water. Ray leaned forward quickly to catch the foot, but it was too late. It fell into the pond with a plop.

Ray began frantically untying the laces of his brogans. Maybe it wasn't so deep.

Just as he was about to jump into the pond, the dark surface broke. Jolie smiled up at him. "I thought you could not swim?"

Ray's voice came out in panicked chokes. "I can't. . . . The lodestone! I dropped it."

"I know." Jolie held up her hand, the golden foot sparkling in the moonlight. "I was watching you."

Ray took the rabbit's foot back gratefully, tucking it safely into the toby. "You were watching me? Where?"

"Here. Just below the surface," she said, waving her arms as she floated. "You looked worried."

"I was!" Ray said, stuffing the toby in his pocket.

"Why?"

Ray looked down at her, blinking up at him from the water.

Jolie whispered, "Did you think I was going to run away?"

Ray shrugged. "I just knew you felt guilty . . . it's so silly."

Si broke through the underbrush and leaped onto the log. "Come on," she said. "Conker just whistled for us to go."

Jolie clambered up onto the muddy bank as Ray tied his shoes and took the bottletree from the ground. The three hurried around the edge of the pond until they met Conker, who was peering into the dark up by the tracks.

"I heard voices," he said urgently.

"Voices?" Ray asked. "From where?"

"Over there. Let's get out of here."

The four moved quietly through the forest, away from the pond. They ascended the hill up toward the track, but before they broke from the tree line, Conker motioned for them to wait. He stepped out onto the gravel and crossties of metal and wood and looked in both directions. Conker gave a sudden yelp, jumping back off the track.

"What's the matter?" Ray asked.

"Snake." Conker pointed to the track. Even in the thin light of the moon, they saw the dark shadow of a snake wriggle off away from them.

Si groaned. "You're such a baby sometimes. Come on. Let's go."

The four jogged quietly back toward the *Ballyhoo*. As they did, Ray whispered to the others, "Don't you think it's strange to see a snake at night?"

"Naw. Not with hot weather like this," Conker said. But Si stopped them with her hand. She bent forward and strained to see into the forest at their left.

"What is it?" Jolie asked.

"Something . . . I'm not sure. Thought I saw—"

A rustle sounded from the dark foliage. Ray pushed Jolie behind him. Conker drew the hammer from his belt and raised it defensively, but Si was already going forward. "Don't—" Conker began.

"Seth?" Si asked, pulling back the underbrush. "It's Seth."

Seth sat up, his eyes wild. "They took her!"

Si sneered, "What do you mean? They took who?"

Seth put a hand to his head and closed his eyes.

"Seth? You all right?" Conker asked.

His eyes fluttered. "They hit me in the head. I was . . . knocked out."

"What are you talking about?" Ray asked, squinting at Seth's head. He saw blood in the boy's blond hair by his temple. "Who did they take?"

"Marisol!"

"The snake," Ray said. "That was Marisol's snake we saw back there."

Seth cupped his hand to his temple. "Marisol and I were coming to look for . . ." He grew tentative, and Ray knew that Seth and Marisol had been snooping on them.

Ray asked, "Do you know which way?"

Seth shook his head.

"What did they look like?" Conker asked.

"I don't know!" Seth snapped. "Just regular men—two of them. Suits, hats. I think they had guns."

Si helped Seth to his feet. "We might be able to follow them. Come on." She and Conker began running down the track.

Seth picked up his sword case but stumbled dizzily a moment. "I . . . I better go back," Seth said. "I'll warn Nel and Buck."

Ray frowned, but turned to Jolie. "You should go back, too."

"I am not afraid," she said.

"That's not the point. What if it's the Gog?"

"The Gog?" Seth scoffed. "It's not the Gog. He's not real."

Ray ignored him. "I don't know why they took Marisol, but they want you, Jolie. You have to go back. We've got to hurry and I'm not going to stand here arguing with you!"

"Then don't," she said, and ran after Si and Conker.

Seth rolled his eyes at Ray and said, "Hurry, Ray. I'll send Buck and Nel as soon as I can." Ray gritted his teeth and turned to rush after Jolie. Soon they caught up with Conker and Si.

"Hey!" Ray said, stopping the others. He pointed to the edge of the forest. Some young pine saplings were snapped over. "I think they cut into the forest."

"We must split up," Jolie said.

Ray pointed at Conker and Si. "Keep following the track." They nodded and ran off.

Jolie and Ray entered the forest. Ray looked around but every direction looked the same. "Do you see a broken branch?" Ray asked. "Some sign of where they passed? A snake, even!"

He and Jolie scanned the dark forest. "Here is something," Jolie said.

Ray spotted a small shrub, broken over at the base. "Good!"

They continued past it, and then Ray saw where the leaves had been turned up by recent footsteps. Soon after that, Jolie saw where a limb had been dragged a short distance. They ran on. Even in the dim half-light, Ray quickly realized the two of them had an eye for spotting a path of broken shrubs and snagged sprigs. They went deeper and deeper into the forest.

"I'm not sure we're still going the right way," Ray mumbled. But then Jolie pointed to a fat viper winding its way through the low briars. They rushed again, leaping through bushes and passing first a fallen hat and then a hissing adder.

A voice called ahead, "Mister McDevitt! You here? We got her!"

It came from an illuminated clearing, and as Ray and Jolie reached it, they crouched behind a downed oak log at the edge. They heard Marisol trying to shout but a hand seemed to be muffling her mouth. "What did you say, Mister Horne?" a man asked.

Ray laid the bottletree gently on the ground and looked over the log. From the low vantage he could see two men in simple black suits, one wearing a round bowler hat, trying to contain the kicking and struggling Marisol. They had lanterns set on the ground, which spread a thin orange light around the clearing.

A third man, dressed as the others, entered the clearing on the far side. As he approached them, he waved his hands irritably. "Take that stuffing from your ears. You got the wrong girl!"

One of the men holding Marisol managed to pluck something out of his ears while keeping Marisol's writhing legs in the crook of his elbow. His hat had been lost, and his bald skull-like head glistened in the night's heat. The other man, holding Marisol's shoulders, had a short-barreled rifle slung over his shoulder.

There was nothing particularly out of the ordinary about their appearance. They were plain-faced, indistinct in many ways. But Ray knew these were the Gog's men. Only they would be after a siren. And the fact that they looked so ordinary chilled Ray most of all.

"What'd you say, Mister McDevitt?" the bald man who had just pulled the wad from his ears said.

"That isn't the siren, you idiot!" McDevitt snarled. "You were supposed to meet us here with . . ."

As the men argued, Ray turned to Jolie.

"I'll go around—" But as he said this, a dry branch snapped beneath his knee.

The man with the rifle dropped Marisol with an ungracious thump and swung the carbine rifle to his shoulder, scanning the surrounding forest. Ray scrambled to get to his feet, but before he could, Jolie grabbed a stone and hurled it at the man.

The rock caught him in the temple, and he stumbled back, the carbine firing into the trees overhead. He dropped to his knees, his hands to his bleeding head.

McDevitt pulled a pistol from under his coat as Ray charged from the underbrush, catching the man in his lower back and knocking him to the ground. The pistol tumbled a few feet away. Ray pressed his weight onto McDevitt's head, mashing his face into the dirt and trying to hold him down as the man scrambled flat on his stomach.

The bald-headed man grasped Marisol from the ground, holding her around the shoulders and keeping her arms pinned tightly against her sides. She kicked back with her heel, but was unable to find the man's shins. Jolie stopped a few feet before the bald-headed man, her head bent forward in a frightening stare.

The man seemed to realize that with her strange gown and wild-eyed ferocity, this was the real siren.

"Hello there, missy," he said as he let go of Marisol and drew a pistol from his belt. Before he could grab Jolie, she relaxed her jaw and began a thin, piercing note. The man's arms dropped limply to his side, and he stared at Jolie with a slack-eyed stupor. The pistol fell to the ground, and Jolie kicked it away.

The man who had been struck by Jolie's rock seemed to regain his senses. Trying to wipe the blood from his eyes, he searched the ground for his rifle.

Scrambling to keep McDevitt pinned, Ray saw him. McDevitt used the moment to throw his elbow hard into Ray's chin. Ray rolled to the ground. McDevitt stood, spitting dirt from his mouth, and kicked Ray in the ribs. Electric waves of pain shot through Ray's body.

McDevitt pulled a tarnished whistle from his pocket. As he blew it, he gave Ray a slimy smile, flashing a gold tooth from his mouth.

That tooth. That terrible smile. Hadn't McDevitt been talking to Seth after a show?

Something roared from the depths of the forest, bringing a pregnant silence over the scene of the fight. Marisol had scrambled to get away from the men but now froze with fear as another roar echoed across the night forest.

McDevitt backed away several steps, still smiling. Ray had heard this roar before, in his dream.

The Hoarhound.

The forest crackled as a deep cold enveloped it. The leaves around Ray shriveled with the frigid air filling the clearing. Ray felt his clothes, damp with perspiration, stiffen with ice. The glass on the lanterns cracked, but they stayed lit, still casting a dull glow onto the Gog's men.

"You might just want to leave the siren with us and get out of here," McDevitt advised.

McDevitt looked over to Jolie. She had stopped singing and was looking fearfully toward the far side of the clearing. The bald-headed man blinked heavily from the passing effects of the song.

The bleeding man got up and aimed the carbine at Marisol as he pulled stuffing from his ears. McDevitt said, "Make one little note, my dear siren, and Mister Horne here will turn this soiree into a tragedy. I don't think your snake-charming friend would want that now, would she?"

Jolie looked between Marisol and Mister Horne's rifle barrel. McDevitt bent to pick his pistol off the ground. He narrowed his eyes at Ray and said, "Don't even scratch your nose, boy."

McDevitt held his hand out toward Jolie and motioned with his fingers for her to come to him. "Time to go, siren," McDevitt whispered. "Say your goodbyes before the Hound breaks this party up."

Jolie backed a step away. McDevitt frowned and began walking toward Jolie. "If I have to ask again, Mister Horne will—"

Before he could finish, Conker leaped into the clearing

behind McDevitt and Horne, his large hands grabbing their heads and clapping them together. The two struck one another with a loud *thunk* and tumbled into a heap. The bald-headed man scrambled around, looking for the pistol Jolie had kicked away.

Si emerged holding a bottletree in each of her hands. "Let's go!" she called.

Ray jumped to his feet, and as he did, an earth-splitting roar filled the clearing. The air swirled with ice and rimy mist.

He turned to see the Hoarhound.

Breaking from the forest, the monster was more terrifying than Ray remembered from his dream. Larger than a bull, the Hound bristled with frost-hardened spikes of fur. Long, terrible fangs crowded its mouth, and as it swung its head, the deathly, bitter cold breath whipped out from its snout. Ray felt his legs grow weak, and feared that neither he nor any of the others would be able to escape the beast.

Conker was closest. With a kick of its powerful legs, the Hoarhound lunged. Conker drew the Nine Pound Hammer from his belt and began to swing it, but the Hound reached him first, knocking him across the clearing onto his back.

"No!" Si yelled.

The Hound rounded on her next, baring its teeth.

Si dropped one of the bottletrees and took the other with both her hands. As she tried to spear it into the ground, the Hound charged. Si somersaulted backward, out of the way, and the Hound struck the bottletree, spinning it in a clatter across the clearing.

"Drive the other in the ground!" Conker cried, getting to his feet. The bald-headed man had found his pistol, and as he lifted it to cock the hammer, Conker leaped over and slugged him in the jaw, sending the man reeling.

From his pocket, Ray felt something warm against his leg. The rabbit's foot!

The Hound turned to glare at Ray and then charged. Ray backed up a step, starting to run, but his feet tangled as he turned. Falling flat, he felt the cold emanating from the Hound's jaws. As Ray cast a fearful glance back, he saw those fangs and then, beside the Hound, Conker crashing down with the Nine Pound Hammer. The steel of the hammer's head made a high-pitched *ping* as it struck the metal beneath the Hoarhound's frosty hide. The Hound tumbled sideways, rolling until it landed back on its feet.

Stunned by how close he had come to the Hound's jaws, Ray struggled to stand.

McDevitt and Horne were getting up dizzily to gather their firearms. But Conker reached them first, the Nine Pound Hammer clattering against the barrels, jarring them from their hands. The men scrambled backward on the ground to get away from him, backing almost into Si.

In a fury, the Hoarhound rushed at Si. She took the other bottletree with both hands and thrust it into the icy crust of earth. Si dropped to her knees by the bottletree and covered her head against the Hound's attack. But the Hoarhound pulled away just before reaching the bottletree.

McDevitt and Horne, closer to the bottletree than the Hound, vanished into a phantom mist, which was drawn into the mouths of the bottles. Conker turned to confront the bald-headed man, who was getting dizzily to his feet and reaching for Mister Horne's rifle.

Growling, the Hound circled the bottletree but seemed unable to get any closer to the protective charm. Si was safe for the moment, but ultimately trapped.

Si called to Jolie and Marisol, "Run! Before it's too late."

The two girls hesitated, shivering against the paralyzing cold. Ray nodded for the two of them to run. The rabbit's foot in his pocket was growing hotter. What was it doing? As he took it from the toby, he saw it glowing a bright gold-white, nearly too hot to hold.

As soon as he did, the Hound snapped its terrifying head around and looked at Ray. Its nostrils flared and the beast took several steps back from him. It's afraid, Ray thought. Why was the Hound afraid of the foot?

Marisol took Jolie's hand and began running. Immediately the Hound turned from Ray and ran in a wide arc around the bottletree. They would never get more than a few more steps!

In helpless desperation, Ray leaped after the Hound. The vast jaws of the Hoarhound opened, exposing the rows of jagged teeth. Marisol looked back to see the jaws about to catch Jolie. Stumbling, she shoved Jolie out of the way, but Marisol's head was thrust into the path of those icicle-silver teeth.

Ray cried aloud and felt his hand reach the cold hind leg of the Hoarhound.

Still clutching the Hound, Ray fell, half-dragged over the hard frozen earth. He closed his eyes against the horrible fate about to take Marisol.

There was a tense grinding of machinery locking up, metal tearing and whining in the resistance of gears frozen shut. Then the forest was oddly quiet. Ray lay outstretched in the bracken, one hand over his head, holding the hard iron encased in the brittle, cold fur of the Hound's leg. His other hand squeezed the rabbit's foot, the metal nearly searing Ray's palm.

He looked up to see the bald-headed man who had been defending himself against Conker. Both he and Conker had stopped. The Gog's agent stammered in dumbstruck amazement. Then with a shuffle, the man was gone, running as fast as he could into the shadows of the forest.

Fearing what he would see, Ray looked up.

The Hoarhound was statue-still, hunched up like a climbing wave suddenly frozen to ice in the surf. Within its jaws, inches from the teeth, Marisol stood trembling.

Jolie got to her feet. She took Marisol's hands, and whispered to her, "Come with me."

Marisol responded by squeezing her eyes shut and unleashing a gush of wetness on her cheeks. Jolie led her from the frozen jaws and looked down at Ray still lying on the ground.

Conker stared in disbelief at the silent Hound. As he took a step closer, the Hound's jaws snapped shut. Ray felt the machinery beneath the Hound's hide fighting against its paralysis.

"Let's go, Ray!" Conker shouted.

"No!" Ray said, still holding the Hound. "If I let go, it might come back to life."

"It's already coming back to life," Si said.

"The bottletrees," Conker said, turning to her. "Get those bottletrees."

Si pulled up one bottletree and the limp, unconscious forms of Horne and McDevitt appeared, dropping to the hard earth. She drove the bottletree into the ground by the Hound. As she went back for the other, she said, "Where's the third?"

Ray struggled to remember. "I dropped it somewhere. Over there. Behind that log."

Si placed the three bottletrees in a triangle surrounding the Hound. She then came over to Jolie and Marisol. "Run. Follow me and just keep running no matter what."

Conker knelt next to Ray and said, "When I count to three, let go of that Hound."

Ray nodded.

"One."

Ray got to his knees, still holding the Hound's leg.

"Two."

Ray stood. Conker began backing away into the dark of the forest.

"Three."

Ray let go and began running after Conker. In a terrifying eruption of coils and machinery coming back to life, the Hound roared. Ray looked over his shoulder and saw the beast writhing and howling and snapping, its form struggling between matter and mist, trapped within the barrier of bottletrees.

They ran and ran, all the way back to the tracks and all the way back to the *Ballyhoo*.

—17—

BOTTLETREES

Fire heated water. Water made steam. Steam thrust
the pistons back and forth. Rods and cranks chugged re-
lentlessly as the pistons moved the wheels across the tracks
in the Mississippi night.

In the locomotive, sooty-faced Eddie was shoveling
coal from the tender into the firebox. Ox held down the
throttle, leveling the *Ballyhoo* to a steady fleeing speed.
The engineer wiped his slick forehead and tapped the glass
of the pressure gauges to make sure there was adequate
water in the boiler. "Stoke it! Get them coals pretty and
even," he barked at his son as he released the steam whistle with a wildcat howl. The first dim blues of dawn filled
the sky.

* * *

Ma Everett fretted about the kitchen. Her hands shook, and she seemed to have no capacity—nor would anybody expect it of her—to cook a hot meal. They ate what was left over from dinner, and few did more than pick at their plates as Marisol told them about the encounter in the forest.

Seth narrowed his eyes at Marisol's retelling of the events. Nel paced the middle of the kitchen car, his hard mahogany leg thumping throughout the telling. The others listened while they sat upon sacks of beans and flour or in chairs. When Marisol described how Ray had stopped the monstrous Hoarhound simply by touching it, she got up and came over to him.

"*Te agradezco,*" Marisol said as she held Ray in an embrace. Then she kissed him on the cheek. "You saved me, Ray."

Ray did not know what to say and tried to keep his eyes on the floor, but Seth's gaze was burning a hole into him.

"But how?" Nel asked, almost rhetorically. His pounding peg leg stopped, causing Ray to look up.

"I don't know," Ray said.

"It's . . . inexplicable!" Nel said. "I've never heard of such—"

Ma Everett asked, "What was the beast?"

"The Gog's Hoarhound," Ray said.

Buck asked, "Was the Gog there? Did you see him?"

"There were the three men Marisol described. I don't think any of them were the Gog. They seemed . . . ordinary in many respects, just hired men following orders."

"Stinking Pinkerton agents," Buck snarled.

Nel's peg leg barked on the wooden floor as he turned. He swayed a moment with the motion of the train, his hand clutching the silver fox paw through his shirt. "The rabbit's foot," he said. "How he's done it, I can't divine, but, Ray, your father has worked some hoodoo into that foot."

"They'll be after us," Buck said.

"And soon." Nel nodded. "Ox is looking for a place for us to hide."

Ray thought again about the battle, about the Gog's agents. "I recognized one of the men. I've seen him before." As Ray's eyes fell on Seth, the boy shifted uncomfortably. Ray hesitated before saying, "He was talking to Seth after one of the shows."

Nel pivoted sharply toward Seth. "Is this true? Did one of the Gog's men approach you?"

"I—I didn't know who he was," Seth stammered. "He said he worked for another show. He was asking if I wanted to be hired on. I told him no, of course!"

"What else did he say?" Buck snarled, his pale eyes emerging from his trembling brow.

Seth was shaking as he spoke, wringing his hands together. "He was asking about the siren. I didn't tell him anything. I swear!"

Nel leaned heavily against the back of a chair. "The Gog's agents had already found us when he spoke to you, Seth. I'm sure you didn't do anything to give us away." Ray saw that Buck did not look so certain and was trying to contain his fury. "But somehow they discerned she was here."

"Or were told," Buck said.

"Leave the boy alone, Buck," Nel said. "Seth's been through enough as it is. We don't need to turn on one another. Our attention needs to be firmly placed on keeping Jolie safe and finding somewhere to hide."

Ray looked to Jolie, her expression a tangle of guilt and fear.

"Until what?" Ray asked.

Nel frowned. "Until we figure out what's the best course of action. We can't afford to be impetuous. There are lives at stake here, son! But there's no denying it. Our performing days are over. We are a medicine show no longer."

The *Ballyhoo* rushed on into the night.

A few hours later, while sitting with Jolie, Si, and Conker in the jumbled hallway of the sleeper car, Ray felt the train slow and heard the sharp whine of brakes. As the four stepped out onto the vestibule, the *Ballyhoo* was stopping. Marisol peered out the window of her room. Nel and Buck came out from their car.

Eddie ran down the side of the train shouting, "Pa's found a track! Everyone up to the locomotive."

Ox had located a new trestle that had been built over a shallow river. As he had hoped, the old track split off just before the crossing. With no other trains using it and with a dense forest all around, he hoped it would make a sufficient hiding place.

There was some brush on the old track, which everyone frantically worked to clear off. After the *Ballyhoo* made its way slowly down the unused line, Conker toppled a stout poplar over the track behind them for good measure.

Soon they found a spot to stop in the thickest part of the forest. Ray heard the whistle of a train in the distance passing over the new trestle and hoped the *Ballyhoo* was far enough away to remain unnoticed.

"I want those bottletrees set up," Nel ordered. "No one is to take one step outside their perimeter. We'll take turns keeping watch. For now, two down past the caboose. Ray, you and Conker take that first. Two down past the locomotive. How about you, Si and Marisol? And Seth, Redfeather, Eddie, and Shacks scattered in the forest along the sides. Jolie, to your car. Buck, why don't you keep watch outside her door? We must be vigilant! No need to be heroes. If you see anything, run back to the train immediately and let us know. Hopefully we won't be here long. Mister Everett and I will figure out what to do."

Ray followed Conker to his room, where the giant took out the Nine Pound Hammer from under his mattress and unwrapped it from the black cerecloth. As they stepped onto the vestibule, they heard Seth and Redfeather walking down the side of the train. "You believe that about that Hound?" Seth scoffed. "They're delusional. Crazy as Nel!"

"You think they're lying?" Redfeather asked in a quiet voice. "Marisol too?"

"Course I do! She fancies Ray now. And that jealous rube just wants to play Rambler because he's sore he can't be on stage. The worst is Nel believes them! Now there's no more shows! Nel probably . . ." The boys' voices disappeared into the forest.

Ray irritably swung a pair of bottletrees around to hand to Conker.

Conker said, "I don't think so."

"What?" Ray asked, picking up two more bottletrees.

"I know what you're thinking. You reckon Seth told that agent about Jolie. He's got a little meanness to him, but he wouldn't do that."

Ray shook his head. "I'm thinking worse than that, Conker."

They walked down the track, past the caboose, until they saw a good spot to plant the first bottletrees, marking the boundary of safety. They turned and walked farther into the forest to a lichen-speckled boulder, where they planted the next bottletree.

"I'll walk a little ways," Conker said. "Get an idea of the land. Put out the others."

Ray nodded. The silence of the trees was welcome after the terrifying night. He settled his back against the cool stone and closed his eyes against the thoughts storming his head.

What kind of plan was Nel devising? To run away. To hide. Jolie needed to be kept safe, but ultimately, the Gog had to be stopped. How could he be? Ray squeezed a fist to his temple.

The cackle of crows broke his thoughts. A pair of the large black birds fluttered around one another in a small tornado before swooping up to separate branches nearby.

Ray watched them, trying to find a way to calm his raging thoughts. Their caws sounded almost like laughter, as if they were mocking Ray's frustration. "Yeah, go ahead," Ray mumbled. "What do you know? You're just a couple of ugly crows."

But they weren't ugly, he realized. Ray had never given much thought to how a crow looked. As he saw the light reflecting off the smooth folds of their backs and wings, the way their colors ran from black to purple to blue, he decided these were beautiful animals. He had never appreciated them, maybe because they were not colorful like cardinals or bluebirds.

The crows cocked their heads and turned their oil-spot eyes to look down at Ray. They called back and forth to one another, and Ray noticed the subtlety of the sounds they made: sometimes sharp barks, sometimes low, drawn-out croaks and caws.

Ray closed his eyes and focused his thoughts fully on

the crows. Suddenly it was as if a voice whispered inside his head, "He's coming."

Ray's eyes popped open. The crows were looking at something, bobbing their heads and shifting on their branches. Ray turned.

Nel was walking into the woods ten feet away. "Whatever they said," Nel called, "their advice should be taken with a grain of salt."

"What?" Ray asked with a perplexed turn of his voice.

"You were listening to them, or trying to at least. I was watching you."

Nel reached the boulder and settled himself down next to Ray by steadying a hand on his knee above the wooden leg. He then looked around. "Where's Conker?"

Ray nodded to the left. "Just over there. Putting out the bottletrees. He'll be back." Ray sat up, leaning toward Nel. "Could you teach me to hear them, to better understand what they're saying?"

"I'm afraid not," Nel sighed. "If I've once understood how to discern the speech of animals, it's been lost to me. Besides, understanding animals isn't something anyone can teach. It comes from being in the wild. You grew up in the city, Ray. You didn't have the same exposure from a young age that your father had or I had. It would be hard for you to learn, but not too late."

Ray wondered how different things might have been if his father had never left.

"When you're a baby, nobody actually teaches you to talk," Nel said. "You need a reason for communicating, and in time as a baby you learn to speak by listening. Keep listening to them, Ray, and you just might pick up something."

"Is that how you learned, Mister Nel? Listening to animals?"

"I spent my formative years around many woods."

"But how did you become a Rambler?"

Nel took his briarwood pipe from his jacket and lit it before speaking. "I was born a slave down on the Santee River in South Carolina. My people were Gullah, and, like generations before them, they worked the rice plantations down in that marshy country. I knew slaves that ran off, heading up north. And when I was a little younger than you, I escaped as well. But there were times before my eventual escape, when I was still on the farm, that I was sent out in the woods to collect wood or herbs. The wild had a particular power that I felt. It wasn't until I followed that group of runaways, hiding by day and heading up through the woods by night, that I really discovered what I could do."

"What was that?"

"Understand the speech of animals, for one," Nel said. "And live off the land. Not just survive, but really experience the feeling of being alive for the first time."

"Was that when you learned how to change, to become a fox?" Ray asked.

"No, that came later," Nel said, making circles in the air with his pipe. "I helped those of us that ran away reach Ohio. Up there I met a family of abolitionists, Reverend Mason and his sister, who took me in. They had been helping runaways get jobs and settle into new lives, as well as secretly funding groups down south that helped others escape. The Reverend and Missus Mason housed me, educated me, and in return, I helped with the abolitionist cause. I went back south and led others to safety. I had skills that only the wild could teach: tracking both men and animals, foraging for berries and tubers and tender shoots, finding shelter, reading the signs of winterberry and clouds, knowing the ways of the forest. There were other gifts, too, now forgotten. It was during that time that I met up with a Rambler named Porter Wallace. He was a great man, Ray. He showed me that I was a Rambler and didn't even know it. He's the one who taught me about making tonics and root working.

"And in time, I learned to change into the fox. They were rare moments and hard now to recall. But when I was thinking a certain way—when my thoughts were able to extend beyond myself to something vaster and wilder—I was able to become a fox. I was able to cross into the Gloaming."

"I want to learn, Mister Nel. I want to be a Rambler," Ray said.

"You're already doing it, Ray. It's just a matter of finding the right path and listening to yourself."

This didn't make Ray feel better. In fact, it worried him. How would he know the right path?

"If I listen to myself, then it's telling me to find my father. If he's still alive, Mister Nel, maybe he can help us stop the Gog, to stop him from building his Machine."

Nel drew on his briarwood pipe before answering. "I don't want you to have false hopes. I don't know whether your father survived."

"I have to find out."

"Would you leave us? Leave Jolie?" Nel replied.

"Can we go on running and hiding forever?" Ray asked. "Maybe my path is to face the Gog."

"I don't think you're ready for that, son." The heavy lids darkened Nel's eyes. "Jolie must be kept safe. I need to figure things out for the medicine show, figure out how I can keep us all safe. I need you here, now. I'm depending on you. I need you to do something."

"What's that?"

"From what you said, the rabbit's foot seems to indicate when the Hound is near. I need you to be on guard. Watch the foot."

"I can do that," Ray said.

"But it's not that easy." Nel nodded back toward the train. "I saw you and Conker listening to Seth. I heard what he said, too."

"He's a jerk, Mister Nel! How can he really think that?"

"He's angry and is letting his disappointment cloud his reason. I somehow failed that boy along the way. . . ." Nel grew quiet for a moment before continuing. "Seth doesn't seem to grasp the peril we're all in. I need you to stay away from him. You need to be vigilant. Stay out here with Conker near the edge of the bottletrees. I trust you two enormously, as you must know. But trust me to work out a plan that's in our . . . in Jolie's best interest."

Ray nodded. Nel's careworn face relaxed into a smile. He put a hand on Ray's shoulder as he stood up. "I know I can count on you, Ray. And in time, you'll make a fine Rambler."

Those were strange, quiet days for the former medicine show. To Ma Everett's displeasure, they no longer ate together around the makeshift table. Keeping everyone on duty at all times was impossible, but each took a turn, alone or in pairs, and came back to the train to eat and briefly sleep.

Buck seemed to always be on Jolie's vestibule, armed with his rifle and cautious to every scent and breath of wind. Ray shifted to different posts, sharing duties with Si, Marisol, Eddie, Shacks, and once, Redfeather, but never Seth, who remained in a particular spot in the woods just off from Nel and Buck's car.

When Ray returned for a bite of dinner, he saw Nel discussing possible plans with Ox Everett, who was additionally anxious because their coal supply was running low. The increasing tedium of the watching and waiting left everyone jittery.

Ray noticed that Marisol had transformed. After what had happened with the Hoarhound, she was a different person. She had even visited Jolie in her car. Ray also noticed that she was not speaking to Seth. It made little difference; Seth no longer spoke to her either.

The rabbit's foot had not shown any signs of the Hound's presence. Although the pair of crows had returned sporadically, Ray had not yet grasped their speech. As he sat on the boulder pinching off pieces of biscuit to throw on the forest floor, a blue jay hopped around the leaves, grabbing at the bits and keeping an eye on Ray. A few times, Ray thought he almost heard beyond its birdcalls to another voice, one that wanted to enter his thoughts, but he was not quite able to catch what the bird was saying.

Just as he was trying to mimic the blue jay's call, the bird took flight and disappeared into the trees. Ray turned and saw Marisol approaching.

"*Oye!* My turn to watch. Thought you might be thirsty," she said, holding out a skin of water.

"Oh, thanks. I've got some," Ray said, nodding to the fat skin at his feet. A flash of disappointment came to her face.

"But I'll take more," Ray said. "It's warm out here."

She handed him the skin. It was unusual to see her without a snake encircling her shoulders. Even in her bright red and violet spangled dress, she seemed less mysterious and somewhat vulnerable without her snakes. Ray found Marisol much more approachable without them, without the haughty smile she used to wear, without Seth hanging on her arm.

"How are you?" Ray asked.

"Bored," she said. "Do you think we'll be here much longer?"

"I hope not."

They sat in silence for a few minutes. Then Marisol said, "I saw you talking to those birds." She smirked.

Ray knew he must look a little crazy doing it. He chuckled. "Not having much luck."

"You know I can speak to snakes."

"Yeah," Ray said. "How did you learn?"

"From my parents," she said, brushing her curling black hair over her shoulders. "They were Ramblers. My father was from the deserts of Mexico. My mom was a Hopi. Her people have powers with snakes."

Ray hesitated. "Were they . . . killed by the Gog's men?"

"No. In the battle fighting the Gog. Not long after John Henry fell. I was raised by my father's parents, in a village down in Mexico. On the San Miguel River." She smiled, holding the memory a moment before frowning. "A Rambler came one day and told us what happened to them and that we were in danger."

"And Nel took you in?"

She nodded. "You've been out here a long time. Why don't you go back? Get a bite to eat. Get a little sleep. I'll be okay."

"Sure," Ray said, feeling weary.

Thinking of what Marisol had told him, he reached the train and saw he was not the only one exhausted from the constant watch. Buck was sitting on a chair on Jolie's vestibule with a rifle across his lap, his chin fallen to his chest.

"Buck," Ray said.

The gunslinger lifted his head. He grunted and said, "Ray. I just . . . nodded off."

"When was the last time you slept?"

"I'm doing fine," Buck growled, sitting more upright. "Just need a little coffee."

"Can I see Jolie?" Ray asked.

Buck shook his head. "There'll be time for visiting later. If you're not on guard duty, you need to sleep, too."

Ray supposed Buck was right. "I'll get Ma to brew you some coffee."

"Much appreciated," Buck said, standing and stretching.

Ray woke a few hours later and sat up from his bed; the light was fading and turning the long shadows in the forest outside his window from bright green-gold to blue-gray. He stepped down onto the right-of-way and was surprised to see black puffs of smoke coming from the locomotive. He heard the churning of the engine being stoked. Ox Everett was inspecting the driving rods and touching a spout of oil to the joints in the metal. He stood as Ray approached.

"Are we leaving?" Ray asked.

Mister Everett scratched at his walrus mustache. "Soon as we can."

Down on the other end of the train, Nel was talking to Buck, and Ray ran down to them. As he neared, Nel was saying, ". . . Shuckstack's too far. The springs are our best bet."

"What are we doing?" Ray interrupted.

Nel turned from Buck. "Crossing the Mississippi. It's a bit of a journey, but there's a series of springs in a great wilderness south of the Ozarks where the sirens used to frequent. Should be a safe place for Jolie to hide, and they might help heal her as well."

"But the Gog will keep looking—"

"Of course he will, Ray!" Nel snapped. And then waving a hand to apologize, he added, "We've just got to get there safely. We've risked enough, lingering here. Go. Help round up the others."

"Sure," Ray said.

Ray found Conker and Eddie at their post beyond the caboose. As they returned, they saw the others standing around the train. Buck tripped as he hurried down the vestibule, nearly toppling into Ray.

"Have you seen Jolie?" he asked.

"She's not in her car?" Ray asked.

"Must have . . . stepped out when I fell asleep." His pale eyes widened fearfully. "Where would she have gone?"

Si ran down the train toward them, Nel loping behind her. "What's the matter, Buck?" Si asked.

"She's gone," Buck said. "Jolie's missing!"

As Si held up her hand, Ray watched the pattern of stars arrange and rearrange across the surface of her skin.

Si cursed. "Nothing! I can't seem to find her."

"Why not?" Ray asked.

"I don't know. Something's . . . blocking her."

Nel quickly said to Ray, Conker, and Si, "Spread out! Start looking for her."

Ox Everett called, "We ready to go, Nel?"

"No!" Nel hollered. "Hold the train. . . ."

Ray was already running, splitting off from Conker and Si as they went into the woods, calling Jolie's name. A quarter of an hour later, they had found nothing to indicate where Jolie had gone. They made their way back to Nel's car, hoping she had been located.

Buck was roaring, "Who knows how far she's gotten? How could I have been so stupid! That's been hours now, and she could have gone in any direction."

"I'm still having trouble seeing her," Si said. "I'd have trouble if she's gone too far, or if there's lead blocking her. . . ."

"Why would there be lead?" Redfeather asked tentatively.

Buck slammed a fist to the table. "The Gog!" He pulled a pistol from his belt and opened the cylinder to touch a finger to each of the bullets.

"What are you doing?" Nel asked.

"Going to hunt for her," Buck said, turning to leave.

"Wait," Nel said. "If Si can't find her, then continuing the search will surely be fruitless."

Buck snarled as he headed out the door. "I'm loading the guns anyway."

After Buck was gone, Nel sank his face in his hands. "There's got to be another way. . . ."

"I know," Ray said, remembering suddenly. He reached into his pocket and removed the dandelion from his toby. It was still yellow and fresh, despite its days of being carried around in Ray's pocket.

The others looked curiously at the flower.

Conker exclaimed, "Peter Hobnob!"

"Who's that?" Nel asked.

"Someone who can help," Ray replied. He clapped three claps, said Peter Hobnob's name three times, and blew three breaths on the petals. The yellow rapidly faded to gray, and the petals became wispy before scattering on the breeze into the night.

EVERYONE SAT AROUND THE TABLE, PICKING WITH LITTLE appetite at some food Ma Everett had brought. Every minute that passed Ray felt Jolie was getting farther from the *Ballyhoo*.

Something tickled Ray's cheek. In the light of the table's oil lamps, Ray saw a white seedpod float past like a lost flake of snow. He sat up from his chair as a small cloud of seedpods fell around. Others noticed, too, and looked about curiously.

Nel stood and looked to Ray. "Is it . . . ?"

The pods swirled around more and more quickly until they coalesced into a shape, gaining color and form. Peter Hobnob appeared. He looked around as if unsure of his location until spotting Ray's face in the awestruck crowd.

"Ray, I know I promised about your sister," Hobnob chirped. "Been planning on looking, I swear to you. But between robbing this town and—"

"It worked!" Ray leaped to his feet to greet his friend. Hobnob pulled the dandelion hat from his tousled mop of yellow hair. The others stood around the table in stunned silence, mouths gaping.

Just then Buck came back into the car, carrying several rifles. "I know that voice," he growled. "It couldn't be. . . . What's that scalawag doing here?"

A smile grew on Hobnob's face as he eyed the cowboy. "Ah, Eustace. En't you charming as always."

"I called Hobnob to help us find Jolie," Ray said, surprised that the two were acquainted. But of course, Ray realized, they knew each other from the *Snapdragon*.

"You call *him* help?" Buck growled at Ray.

"He can help," Ray insisted. Turning to Hobnob, he added, "Can't you?"

"Well, I'll be needing specifics if you want my aid. What's the trouble?"

"Wait!" Nel said. "Are you sure he can be trusted?"

"No!" Buck shouted.

"He'll have to be," Ray said.

"Maybe I ought to come back when Eustace—" Hobnob began.

"Don't leave," Ray said to Hobnob, and then turned to Buck. "Buck, you know what Hobnob can do."

Buck scowled before giving a reluctant nod.

Ray began to explain to Hobnob. "We've been hiding a siren—"

"H-here?" Hobnob stammered. "A siren? On this train?"

"She's gone. Earlier this afternoon, she disappeared."

"Kidnapped?" Hobnob asked.

"We can't be sure." Ray gulped. "But something's preventing Si from locating her, and with the Gog's Hoarhound after her . . . She's a girl with dark hair. Really pale. A strange green dress. Barefoot. Can you look?"

"Not much to go on . . ." Then Hobnob looked from Ray to Buck. "Do you know what direction she went?"

"No, but I thought since you could fly—"

"None's the difference. I'll leave straight away." Hobnob lifted his dandelion hat, but Ray stopped him.

"Take this," Ray said, placing the golden rabbit's foot in Hobnob's hand. "This will tell you if the Gog's Hoarhound is near. If he is, then the Gog might have caught her."

"How's it work?" Hobnob asked hurriedly.

"It glows if it's near the Hound. I don't know if it will work for you, but I thought it might help."

Hobnob nodded, taking the foot with a quick, curious inspection.

Ray looked at the rabbit's foot hesitantly. "I need you to be careful with it."

"Like it were my dear old mother's."

"Just don't drop it," Ray said. Hobnob gave a look

of hurt and made a swishing cross over his heart. Situating the hat with a tight pull over his yellow locks, Hobnob quickly faded, dandelion pods scattering into the wind.

Buck shook his head. "If I'd known you were mixed up with that one . . ."

"Can we trust him?" Nel asked Buck in a low voice.

Through gritted teeth, Buck said, "What choice do we have?"

Ready for a quick departure, Mister Everett moved the train to the end of the abandoned track and telegraphed the switch operators on the main line to find out what other trains were expected. Conker pulled the toppled poplar off the track. As night settled fully, he and Ray sat on the vestibule, waiting anxiously for Hobnob's return.

Si sprinted down the side of the train. "Ray! He's back!" They jumped from the vestibule and followed Si in a run toward the locomotive.

Mister Everett had a rail map unrolled on the grass with a lamp holding the corner. Nel and Hobnob squatted as Everett traced his finger over the bramble of rail lines. Buck stood behind the three, listening.

"What happened?" Ray asked Buck.

"The rabbit's foot glowed as he passed over a train that was stopped several miles to the southeast of here," Buck said.

"Saw men loading a girl into a boxcar," Hobnob explained. "Didn't get a close look, but she must be your siren. And that train. I've seen it once before, and heard rumors aplenty about it. They call it *The Pitch Dark Train*."

"Is it—?" Ray began.

"Yes," Buck growled. "The Gog."

Terror struck at Ray's heart. "We're going after her, right?"

Buck nodded and continued listening to Mister Everett explain. "This rail line we're going to get on will meet up with the westbound one the Gog's using. Heads toward the Mississippi River. Hopefully we won't be too far behind their train."

"But will we be able to catch up to them?" Nel asked.

"Don't know," Mister Everett grunted. "I'll give her all we can. . . ."

Hobnob stood as Mister Everett began quickly rolling up the map and shouting instructions to Shacks and Eddie.

Nel turned to Hobnob. "We'll be crossing the Mississippi. You said the *Snapdragon*'s coming up that way. Return and tell your queen to head for the trestle. If we don't catch the Gog's train before then, we'll need her—"

Hobnob shook his head. "I don't think you understand the Pirate Queen. She's no friend to the Gog, but she en't exactly the type to rush into battle for nobody or nothing but her beloved steamer. She's going to have my ears when she finds out I'm missing!"

Buck held out an envelope, the one Ray had delivered to Buck from the Pirate Queen.

"What's that?" Hobnob asked.

"Never mind," Buck replied. "Just give it to Lorene . . . your queen. She'll understand, and she'll help. Hurry!"

"All aboard!" Mister Everett motioned everyone to the *Ballyhoo*. The others clambered up into the cars.

Nel caught Hobnob's shoulder. "After you tell the *Snapdragon* what's happening, can you come back? We might need you again."

Hobnob tucked the envelope in his pocket. "I'll try." He nodded and then handed the rabbit's foot back to Ray. "Good luck," he added before disappearing.

The *Ballyhoo* raced on as they waited for Hobnob to come back and tell them the *Snapdragon*'s position. Ray had never felt the train go this fast before. He had his doubts nevertheless whether it would be fast enough to catch *The Pitch Dark Train*.

Nel was explaining why the Gog was after Jolie. While Ma Everett, nervously scrubbing pots and pans that already shone like copper mirrors, gasped audibly from time to time, Seth kept rolling his eyes. As Nel finished, the train began slowing down. Conker hurried to the window.

"Brushfires or something up yonder," he said in his deep voice.

Nel got up to join him at the window. Ray felt the train slowing and could smell a hint of smoke seeping into the car.

"Shut them windows," Ma Everett ordered.

Ray shut the one nearest him; through it he saw the land in flames. Fire lapped at the edges of the raised tracks.

"How'd a fire like that spread?" Ray asked.

"Some farmer clearing some land," Nel answered. "Must have allowed it to get out of his restraint."

"Or it's the Gog's doing," Buck said darkly.

Nel turned with a tight brow, but before he could reply, the door to the vestibule opened and Hobnob quickly entered. "Could hardly find you. Smoke's a pinch thick out there."

"Did you reach her? Did you tell the queen?" Ray asked.

"Yes. Don't know what you had in that envelope, Buck, but she's heading north. The *Snapdragon* will be ready. Also spotted the Gog's train. They were farther south than I thought. This old bucket reached the track first."

"We're ahead of them?" Nel asked, running his thumb along his jaw.

"By near ten miles," Hobnob said.

Buck got to his feet. "We could let them get up close behind us and stop them."

Nel shook his head. "I'm going over it. Let me think. . . . We don't have the guns to take the Gog on. He'll have his men, those Pinkerton mercenaries. They're a vicious lot."

Buck hit a fist to the wall. "Damnit! We've got to, Nel."

Conker turned to face the two men. "Reckon we could tear up the track?"

"What?" Buck snarled, but Nel raised a hand.

"What are you thinking, Conker?" Nel asked, his eyes narrowing sharply.

"We stop just long enough to tear up a little bit of the track—"

"They'll crash! Jolie might be killed!" Buck shouted.

"But the smoke's pretty thick," Conker continued. "See how Mister Everett's had to slow the *Ballyhoo* to near a crawl. They'll slow, too. Can't go fast with all this smoke. You won't know what's ahead. So when they hit the torn-up track, the locomotive will get stuck, but I don't suspect they'll wreck, not bad anyways."

"That's a big risk," Ray said.

Nel nodded. "But I think Conker's right. They wouldn't go fast enough for a real wreck. And when they stop, we wait until they're out trying to get the locomotive back running and sneak in for Jolie. It's a good plan, Conker. It might just work. Don't you think, Buck?"

Buck thought for a moment. "The Gog will suspect an ambush, so we'll have to stay one step ahead. It might work. Redfeather, get up to the locomotive and tell Everett."

As Redfeather ran out the door, Nel turned to Si. "Go to the boxcar. Get out the crowbars and hammers—"

"Won't need them," Conker said, and touched a hand to the Nine Pound Hammer.

"Good," Nel said. Drumming a finger on the table, he mumbled, "Need something. Just the right potion to even the odds . . . Do I have enough frankincense? . . . Where are those skullcap flowers?"

Amid the frantic energy of preparation, Ray watched as Nel dashed here and there though his root doctor supplies—pulling down a coil of dried snakeskin and crushing it into a powder, burning coltsfoot, mixing various herbs and powders, and mashing them all into a vat of vinegar.

"Yes, this will manage nicely," the old pitchman muttered with a smile. "This will manage quite nicely."

As the *Ballyhoo* was coming to a stop, Nel gave Ray a set of phials, small bottles made from thinner glass than he used to hold the tonics sold during the medicine shows. A cork was wedged into the top of each. Nel explained that the phials held a soporific, something that would cause an immediate sleep to overcome anyone who smelled them. With the supplies he had, he managed to make a dozen phials.

Nel said that it would be best if they were thrown so that the phial broke, as the vapors would be spread wider. On the chance that Ray or the others should accidentally inhale the tonic, Nel gave them each a small pinch of bitter leaves to eat that would guard against the soporific's effects, as well as some extra leaves for Jolie if—or when, hopefully—they were able to reach her.

The *Ballyhoo* stopped between two low hills where the fire was not as close to the track. As Ray stepped down he could see that, ahead and behind, a sea of flames nearly overtook the rail line. Conker propped the Nine Pound Hammer on his shoulder. Si took a bottletree with her and followed Redfeather and Seth, who carried his sword case. Buck came out last, armed with rifles. The air was dense with acrid smoke, and all but Redfeather quickly tied wet bandannas around their noses to keep from coughing.

Mister Everett moved the *Ballyhoo* ahead to wait. He wouldn't risk being seen as the Gog's train approached, but had to be near enough that they could leave quickly after Jolie was rescued. When the lights of the caboose disappeared, the six were left in an unnatural twilight. The smoky sky overhead glowed crimson-orange with the fires.

Conker gave a kick to the wooden crossties. "I'll handle this." He rolled back his sleeves and spit once into his hands before gripping the Nine Pound Hammer's stout handle.

"Where'd you get that?" Seth asked as he eyed the hammer curiously.

Before Conker could answer, Buck shouted, "Don't just stand around. There's not much time. We need to scout out a place to hide when they arrive."

"There's a hill just off the south end of the track," Si said quickly. "It looks wooded. The fires haven't gotten up there—"

"Go! You and Ray, check it out," Buck said.

Seth said, "Redfeather and I'll go watch for the Gog's train."

Buck nodded. "Be quick and hurry back." The two jogged down the track and disappeared into the smoke.

Ray followed Si up the hill, searching for a good position to watch the track secretly. Looking down, Ray saw Conker destroying the track with his hammer. Sections of rail ripped from the crossties like wheat under a thresher's blade. In little time, a thirty-foot portion of track was broken apart, and Conker and Buck scattered the pieces down the far side of the right-of-way.

Conker shouldered the Nine Pound Hammer and led Buck up the hill toward Ray and Si. Ray hoped Conker was right, that the Gog's train would not be going too fast. If it hit that section at full speed, it would be a devastating wreck. Their gamble was a risky one.

As Si set the bottletree in the ground for protection, Conker and Buck reached the top of the hill, slipped the bandannas from their noses, and settled to their knees on the pine-straw-littered ground next to Ray. In the trees of the high ground, it was darker than down below, where the smoke and nearby fires bathed the railroad tracks in an eerie glow.

"What will we do when the Gog gets here?" Ray whispered to Conker.

"Go get her."

Si added, "We'll have to be quick and quiet and sneaky."

"Where are those boys?" Buck grumbled.

At that moment a figure came stumbling out of the smoke from along the track. "Over here!" Si called, and then said to Buck, "It's Redfeather, but he's alone."

"What!" Buck said, getting back to his feet.

When Redfeather reached them, Buck shouted, "Where's Seth?"

Redfeather had a red mark on his cheek that was beginning to swell. He looked around fearfully. "He's . . . gone. We had a fight. He kept saying the other show would treat him better. That now that Nel had canceled the medicine show we wouldn't—"

"What are you talking about?" Buck snarled. "Where's Seth gone?"

Redfeather gave a hesitant glance at Buck and then looked down at his rifle. He mumbled, "To . . . *The Pitch Dark Train.*"

"HE'S—HE'S JUST BEEN SO WORKED UP OVER THE SHOW stopping," Redfeather stammered. "He convinced himself that this man pursuing us is from another show. . . ." Redfeather trailed off as his eyes followed Buck's angry pacing steps.

"That's not some other pitchman out there!" Buck shouted, jabbing a finger toward the track.

"I know," Redfeather mumbled.

"It's the Gog!"

"There's something else," Redfeather said. "The man . . . the Gog's agent, he told Seth they were looking for a mermaid act. He asked Seth to look for something for them. Something hidden on our train. Before, when we were all keeping watch, Seth took something from your room, Buck. I don't know what, but—"

"The music box!" Ray gasped.

"Did he bring it with him?" Buck exploded.

"I don't know. Would it fit in his sword case—?"

"Yes!" Ray said.

"I'll kill him!" Buck shouted.

"He doesn't believe these men are agents of the Gog!" Redfeather urged.

"What does that matter? He's flagging down the Gog's train. Now they won't wreck on the track. We'll be found out!"

Conker said, "The Gog will back up for certain now. And we've cut the track off, so we can't follow."

"Jolie's lost . . . ," Ray said.

"Not yet," Buck said, grinding his teeth. "There's not another track for miles for them to turn their locomotive."

"So we should go after them on foot—" Si began.

"The fire. We can't reach them," Buck said.

"What if we followed the track?" Ray offered. "The fire doesn't get all the way to it and we might be able to use it as a path."

As he said this Ray felt the rabbit's foot grow warm in his pocket. Ray said, "Too late. They're coming!"

He looked down the hill. The Gog's train—*The Pitch Dark Train,* as Hobnob had called it—was a looming shadow against the glowing fires. It chugged to a stop and a dozen men dismounted and passed the front of the locomotive. In the smoke and half-dark, it was hard to discern what the men looked like except for round-topped bowler hats on their heads. Ray was certain that not all the long objects they carried were tools for repairing the track.

"What are they doing?" Buck asked.

"They're going to fix the track," Conker whispered.

"At least they're not backing up," Si said. She whipped her long ponytail around as she turned to grab the satchel from Ray. "The phials from Nel! If we knock them out now, we can—"

Buck shook his head. "We need to save the phials for rescuing Jolie from the train."

Conker looked over at Buck. "But how can we get down to the train? We need some sort of cover. What about you, Buck? Could you get them from here? With your rifle?"

Buck took several deep breaths, holding the air in his lungs each time. "Maybe. It'd be tricky with all this smoke. And it might force them into a retreat. We don't want a gunfight. We need to keep the train where it is until we get Jolie back."

Shadows moved about the broken track as the Gog's men set to work. One man's voice called orders, and Ray wondered if it belonged to one of the three they had fought in the clearing. As several men picked up the disassembled pieces of rail, more than half spread out with rifles to keep watch. The locomotive reversed and began to slink away in the dark like a viper curling back into its den.

"Oh, no!" Si said. "They're pulling the train back." She held up her hand and examined the swirling designs.

After a few moments, she said, "They're stopping about a quarter of a mile back."

Buck cursed sharply.

"What?" Conker asked.

"They know we can't get to Jolie with the train back there," Buck said. "They're using the fire as a shield."

Ray said, "Even if we could sneak past those men and follow the track, they'd expect us to come that way. We'd be too obvious. We're stuck!"

"No, we're not. I can go through the flames," Redfeather said.

"By yourself?" Buck said.

"No. I can take others."

"What! How's that possible?" Ray asked.

Redfeather bent his head forward and pulled a necklace over his long braids. "You'll hold this."

Ray looked at the copper that Eddie had been pestering Redfeather to loan him.

"What is it?" Buck asked, cocking his head to the side.

"A charm from my great-uncle. It can protect whoever wears it from fire."

"You don't need it?" Ray asked.

Redfeather shook his head. "Fire doesn't affect me anymore."

"Who should go?" Ray asked.

"I'll go," Conker said, heaving the Nine Pound Hammer up on his shoulder.

Redfeather hesitated before saying, "You're pretty big,

Conker. I'm not sure it would work for you and Jolie . . . and Seth."

"Seth!" Buck barked. "We're not risking Jolie to take that backstabber back."

Redfeather cringed. "I'm still worried Conker's too big."

"I can go," Si said. "You might need my hand."

"What about me?" Ray asked.

"Yes, you go, too," Buck ordered. "Especially if the Hoarhound is around. Will the copper cover both of them?"

"Yes," Redfeather said.

"Good." Buck motioned toward Conker. "There's a lot of smoke. I'll need you to keep an eye to those men at the track. If they start to finish the repair too soon, we might need to slow them down."

Redfeather handed Si the copper. "Just wrap the necklace around your wrist and Ray's."

"Take the bottletree," Conker said, pulling it from the soft earth. "You'll need it more than us."

Redfeather nodded as Conker handed him the staff covered with a dozen securely fastened colored bottles. Ray picked up the satchel holding the phials and followed Si and Redfeather down the back of the hill. As they made their way into the field, the smoke began to grow thick. Ray pulled the dampened handkerchief from around his neck and slid it up over his nose. Even so, the smoke caused him to cough.

"Go ahead and use the copper," Redfeather said. "It'll help you breathe."

Si helped Ray take the copper and wrap the cord in several loops around his wrist. It was awkward for them to walk so close together and find the right rhythm for their steps, but when Si took Ray's hand in hers, they were able to maneuver better.

"Here's the fire," Redfeather said as they neared the field. It was so consumed by lapping flames and thick smoke that they could see nothing beyond. "Can you tell which way, Si?"

She spent a moment observing the movements on her hand in the orange illumination. As she found the route, she turned to Redfeather. "Are you sure this copper will work?"

"Of course. Just walk like you would normally. Trust me."

She and Ray exchanged nervous glances. Several feet ahead chest-high flames licked the dried grass of the field. Redfeather went first. The flames danced against his legs and clothes but didn't even blacken his pants. It was as if he were doing nothing more than walking through tall grass.

"Come on," Redfeather encouraged. It was scary to see him standing in the fire.

Ray had to work against every natural impulse of survival to take those first steps toward the heat and flames. He squeezed Si's hand once and began; she jumbled her steps to catch up with him. As they approached the edge of the fire, the flames damped beneath their feet as if a heavy wet blanket had been extended before them. The embers crinkled and popped as they continued forward, the flames extinguishing in a circle around them, rising up again after they had passed. Not even the heat from the cindered ground passed through the worn soles of Ray's brogans.

"See," Redfeather said. "You're fine. Keep going."

Ray and Si looked again at one another and laughed at the impossibility of what they were doing. Ray could not get over the sensation of being completely encased in fire but feeling no scorching heat, much less the quick roasting that should have occurred.

Within several minutes they came to an area that the flames had not yet reached. Looking across, they saw the long black wall of the Gog's train. Enveloped in smoke, *The Pitch Dark Train* waited on the rise of the tracks, its locomotive puffing and heaving. Ray slipped the copper from around his and Si's wrists. He could feel the dull warmth of the rabbit's foot in his pocket. The three knelt in the unburned grass and surveyed the length of train, dark against the glow of the surrounding fire.

"Looks like we've got a leg up on them," Si said.

"How's that?" Redfeather asked as he laid the bottle-tree at his side.

"They're expecting us to come from the front along the track," she answered, pointing to the locomotive. "See how they've got most of their guards stationed up there? They don't know we've got you, Redfeather."

Ray smiled. Si was right; it was hard to see in the dim

light and smoke, but it looked as if a dozen or more guards were positioned down at the locomotive, rifles ready, scanning the smoky railroad track between the Gog's train and the section of rail beyond where the others were repairing.

"So let's head straight to the train and start searching for—" Ray began.

"Not that easy," Redfeather said. "See that car about four from the caboose? Look close."

Ray spied them. "There's guards on both ends of the car. Which is bad and good," Ray said. "Bad 'cause we've got to get past those guards, but good—"

Si picked up on his thought: "—because we now know where Jolie's being held. And I think I know how we can get to her."

"How?" Redfeather and Ray asked together.

Si knitted her brow as she thought out her plan. "They'll certainly spot us coming across this field if we head straight there. So let's circle back through the flames to the caboose. Ray, you and I will sneak down the side of the train. When we reach the agents, you'll hide under the car behind the one they're guarding. I think if I go along the roof of the car where they're keeping Jolie, they won't see me, and I can be plenty quiet. When you hear me give a low whistle, I'll hit the ones in the front vestibule with one of Nel's bottles, and you hit the ones in the back. They're clustered together, so one phial each should get them."

"What should I do?" Redfeather asked.

"You come with us but stick back a ways. If we run

into trouble, you use the bottletree. And if something goes really wrong and those guards up at the locomotive come for us, you distract them while we get Jolie away. The bottletree should protect you. If we get separated, at least you won't need the copper to escape into the flames."

Ray and Redfeather thought over Si's plan. Ray could think of a million ways it could go wrong, but it seemed better than any plan he could come up with. Finally Ray nodded. "Let's do it. First, eat the leaves." They took the herbs that would protect them from the soporifics and popped them in their mouths, wincing at the horrible taste.

The three went back into the flames until they reached the track by the caboose. As they got closer, they saw a single guard standing on the platform at the end of the caboose. He was dressed in the same type of black suit and bowler hat that they all wore. A rifle rested over his shoulder. Sipping a cup of coffee, he had a slightly bored look on his face, as if he didn't expect to see much trouble at his post tonight.

In the shadows, Si reached for a phial in Ray's satchel. Ray put his hand to her arm and whispered, "I got him. Played loads of stickball back in the city. I know how to throw it."

Ray nestled his fingers around the small phial, getting the proper grip. With a quick flick, he fired the phial toward the guard. As the phial flew harmlessly over the caboose like a grouse taking flight, the guard's gaze followed it curiously.

With a growl, Si shoved her hand into the satchel and took a new phial. The guard peered out in the dark and set down his cup of coffee. Cocking his rifle, he swung it up. Si threw the phial square into his forehead, knocking the guard backward with a shattering of glass.

"Stickball!" Si scoffed.

Ray mouthed a few incoherent utterances as Redfeather ran up onto the caboose to check the guard. "He's out cold, but I'm not sure if it's from Nel's sleeping potion or from getting knocked out by Si's throw."

Ray looked at Si. She shook her head at him and began trotting forward.

"Okay, we'll keep close to the side of the train," Si whispered to the boys. "When we get down to that car just before the one they're guarding, Ray, you crawl underneath and get into position. Redfeather, you stay back with the bottletree. Got it?"

Redfeather clutched the bottletree and nodded.

"Ray, listen for my whistle," Si said. "Then throw the phial, but *hit* them this time."

They moved down the train cars slowly and cautiously, stepping into the shadows between the cars to check that no guards were coming. Just as they reached the car behind the one where Jolie was imprisoned, a guard stepped down from her car. Fortunately, he looked toward the locomotive and not back to where Ray, Si, and Redfeather were standing.

Quickly Ray, Si, and Redfeather dropped under the car,

Redfeather holding the bottletree to his chest to keep the glass from clanking. Ray held his breath as the guard walked past. After a moment, the guard turned back and returned to Jolie's car.

"That was close," Redfeather whispered, little more than moving his lips.

Si grabbed a pair of phials from the satchel, slipped out from under the car, and climbed up the ladder. Ray crawled on all fours toward the end of the car. When he reached the gap between the cars, he peeked up at the vestibule.

From his low vantage, Ray saw four guards standing together, all holding rifles. They didn't speak to one another, and Ray felt a grudging respect for the discipline of the Gog's agents. A quick shadow flickered over their heads. Not a single guard noticed. These were disciplined guards, but not sharp enough to catch Si quietly moving above them.

Ray held a phial and waited. The tense seconds felt like hours, but then he heard a low, quick whistle. The guards looked at one another curiously just as Ray flicked the phial up into the vestibule. It hit a guard in the chest and fell to the iron platform at his feet with a tinkle of breaking glass. The guards swung their rifles toward Ray, but all collapsed into a heap before firing a shot.

Ray exhaled sharply and listened to determine if Si was as successful. There was a collection of groans and then the clatter of tumbling bodies from the front of the car.

Ray crawled out from under the train car, peering cautiously for other guards.

Si leaped down from the train and ran back to join Ray. "Got them."

A guard stepped out of the doorway on Jolie's car, looking down at the heap of men on the vestibule. "What the—?"

Si threw the other phial and shattered it on the man's temple. He fell forward stiffly onto the others. "Oops. Guess I missed one," she murmured.

"Check if there's others!" Ray whispered, shoving another pair of phials in her hand. Si leaped onto the vestibule and peeked around the doorway before heading into the car. She came out a moment later. "All clear. Think anyone heard us?"

Redfeather shook his head firmly. "Nobody heard that."

"I'll go get Jolie," Si said. "You two keep an eye out for any others."

Redfeather slipped between the train cars to watch on the other side. Putting his hand in the satchel, Ray counted the remaining phials. Seven left, including the pair Si had.

Coming up onto the vestibule, Ray took Redfeather's copper necklace from his wrist and slipped it into his pocket, noticing the heat intensifying from the rabbit's foot. A shiver coursed down Ray. The Hoarhound was near.

And with the Hound surely was its master. The Gog was here, somewhere aboard this dark train. Although part of him was curious to know what the Gog looked like, Ray hoped they would get away without finding out.

Ray poked his head into the hallway and whispered, "Did you find her?"

Si answered from about halfway down, "This door's plated with lead! She's here but the door's locked. I'm trying to get it open."

Ray was getting more nervous. As he stepped down from the vestibule to look up and down the train, a gunshot erupted; out of the corner of his eye Ray saw the bullet spark off the side of the train just inches from where he stood. A bowler-capped man came down from a car just a few in front of Jolie's. He ran toward Ray, shouting. Ray quickly pulled a phial out and threw it just as the guard reached him. It hit the man square in the nose and shattered. The man dropped instantly.

Carrying the tinkling bottletree, Redfeather came between the cars and looked from Ray to the man lying on the ground. "They heard that." Redfeather's voice trembled.

"Redfeather—" Ray began.

But Redfeather finished the thought. "I'll distract them." He grabbed the bowler hat off a slumbering guard's head and began to run.

"Hey, Redfeather!" Ray called.

He turned.

There were a lot of things Ray wanted to say, but he settled on, "See you back at the hill."

Redfeather gave a grim smile. "You too." With the

bottletree, Redfeather ran out from the side of the train into the smoky field, where a wide gap remained between the train and the surrounding fire.

Ray jumped up the steps and went into the hallway. "Can't you get it open?"

"It's a tough lock!" Si growled, working her knife into the keyhole with one hand, and holding up the tattooed hand for guidance. "Some sort of complicated mechanism . . ."

"Want me to look for the key?" Ray said, looking around at the unconscious guards littering the vestibule. Ray began digging around a guard's pockets for a key but found nothing. Exasperated, Ray called down the hallway to Si, "I can't find it."

"Keep looking," Si said.

A moment later, Ray said, "Got it!" and held up a key triumphantly.

A sharp click sounded, and Si turned the handle and opened the door. "Never mind."

Jolie was waiting behind the lead-plated door as it opened; she rushed out into the hallway, a bundle in her hands. Si held her hand over Jolie's nose and said, "Wait. Hold your breath. Ray, give Jolie some of the herbs." Ray ran down the hallway, digging them out of the satchel before handing them to Jolie. As she ate, he noticed how ornately decorated the dark hallway was: the detailed paneling on the walls, the unlit brass lamps lining the corridor.

"Eat them quickly," Si said to Jolie. Her eyes fell to the bundle in Jolie's hands. "What's that?"

"A book," Jolie mumbled as she chewed the leaves. But before explaining further, she asked, "Ray? What is it?"

Ray frowned. "Something about this train . . ."

Giving Ray a shove, Si took Jolie's hand and pulled her along. "No time for admiring the sights. Let's move!"

The three of them ran down the hallway and jumped from the vestibule. Si pushed them back into the gap between the cars. "Agents!" she hissed.

Ray took a quick peek around the car. From the front of *The Pitch Dark Train,* a group of men was charging through the smoke down the gravel right-of-way.

"We've got to get out of here," Ray said.

Ray looked for Redfeather. He was standing out in the field between the Gog's train and the edge of the fire. Silhouetted against the flames and wearing the bowler hat, Redfeather looked just like one of the Gog's mercenaries. Ray could not see the bottletree and figured Redfeather had it hidden in the tall, unburned grass.

Redfeather waved at the running guards. "Over here!" he bellowed through the smoky air. The guards looked over at Redfeather and turned his way. As they were nearing him, Redfeather knelt to pick up the bottletree.

One of the guards shouted, "That's not—" and aimed his pistol. Ray nearly cried out. A shot erupted.

Redfeather had just driven the bottletree in the earth

when the bullet flipped him sideways and threw him to the ground.

Light flashed from the bottletree, and the guards were sucked in a vaporous swirl into the colored glass.

Ray began to scramble from between the cars toward Redfeather when Si grabbed his arm.

"What are you doing?" she said, terror breaking in her voice.

"I've got to help him." Ray pulled the copper from his pocket and handed it to Si. "Take it. You and Jolie get away."

Si pushed the copper back to Ray. "No, you keep it. I'll get Jolie to the front of the train. We can follow the track to get through the flames."

"How will you get past the guards?" Ray asked.

Jolie tucked the bundled book under her arm and said, "I can use my song."

"Only on one—!" Ray started.

"Let us worry about that!" Si took another phial from Ray's satchel. "Go help Redfeather. You'll need the copper if you're going to get him back to the *Ballyhoo*."

"Okay," Ray said, and sprinted toward Redfeather, his legs ripping through the tall grass. Ray looked over his shoulder. A breeze parted the smoke momentarily, and he saw more guards coming from the locomotive. Ray also saw the train more clearly. The locomotive was elegantly painted—a powerful, sleek ten-wheeler.

He reached the bottletree and found Redfeather lying

facedown. Ray turned him over and his hand grew wet and hot from blood covering Redfeather's shirt.

"Redfeather!" Ray cried.

Redfeather's eyes flickered, and he uttered a moan. He was barely conscious, but he was alive.

"I'll get you out of here," Ray said. He hoisted Redfeather onto his shoulder. He was heavy, and Ray stumbled as he stood. With his free hand, Ray pulled the bottletree from the ground. Nearly a dozen unconscious men materialized on the ground around him as they were released from the bottletree's spell.

Ray could not run, but he trudged as fast as he could toward the edge of the fire.

Shouting voices sounded nearer to him and several rifles fired. Although none hit him, Ray fell to the ground under Redfeather's weight.

"Redfeather, you still with me?" Ray asked, touching Redfeather's face.

Redfeather answered with a painful groan.

Lying in the grass with the waves of smoke rolling all around Ray and Redfeather made it hard for the Gog's men to see them. The way their shots scattered all over the field, Ray knew they were not certain of his location.

Through the smoke, he caught glimpses of other guards running in his direction and several more men in bowler hats coming from other train cars, searching the field. With grim satisfaction, Ray thought that at least this was providing the distraction Si and Jolie needed.

Then Ray saw another figure among the mercenaries.

He was not wearing a bowler hat, nor was he carrying a rifle. He was tall and wore a stovepipe hat and a long flowing coat. While the others ran, this man walked with a deliberate stride, punctuating his steps with a short walking stick.

Setting eyes on the tall man froze Ray deep into the marrow of his bones. The shadowy man sucked the hope and will to escape out of him, until all he wanted to do was lie on the ground and never get up. There was no doubt in Ray's mind: this was the Gog. And what terrified and confused Ray the most was that the man looked strangely familiar. But from where?

As the first group of guards neared Ray, he fought against the terrible urge to quit, to surrender. He had to get Redfeather to safety. Ray fingered one of Nel's potions.

"There he is!" one of the guards shouted. It was Mister Horne. Ray sat up and aimed the phial at him. Horne shot the phial in midflight, and it sprayed the soporific over all the guards. They tumbled en masse.

"Hold your fire," the man in the stovepipe hat—the Gog—called. "Don't kill the siren."

Ray was afraid he could guess what they would do when they discovered the siren was not with him.

The other guards began to close in on Ray, rifles all leveled on their target. The Gog followed behind, his features still shadowy.

Ray threw another phial at a pair of guards nearing

him. They dropped, one after the other. Then, growing brave with the hope that these men would follow orders and not shoot him, Ray stood up with the bottletree. Several of the men—possibly Mister McDevitt among them—seemed to understand what the bottletree could do. They turned to run, but Ray drove the cedar pole in the ground. He watched as nearly half a dozen were sucked into the colored bottles.

But there were still more coming, along with the Gog.

Ray took the copper necklace from his pocket and dropped it over his neck. He bent to pick up Redfeather. It was not more than forty feet to the edge of the fire. The bottletree had bought them some time, but Ray was not sure if it would be enough. Mustering all the strength he had, Ray pumped his legs. Twenty more feet.

Just as he neared the fire, Ray stumbled and fell. He grabbed his ankle. It had twisted painfully. Feeling at it with his fingers, he hoped he could still walk on it.

Ray looked back at his pursuers. The bowler-capped men were afraid to go near the bottletree and scattered in a wide path around the charm. But one among them was not afraid of it: the Gog.

The tails of his coat sweeping out around his legs, the Gog walked up to the bottletree and knocked it over with his walking stick. The guards trapped in the bottles spilled around him. The Gog stepped over the unconscious men, marching toward Ray. His agents joined him as he came nearer.

Ray had only one of Nel's phials left. The Gog was still pretty far, but Ray thought he could make the throw. Winding his arm around and throwing his weight into the pitch, Ray sent the phial straight at the Gog. It was a perfect throw.

The Gog held up a gloved hand to keep the phial from striking him in the face. The phial shattered as it hit his finger, spraying a fine sparkle of glass and potion over his coat and stovepipe hat. Four men at the Gog's side tumbled to the ground. The Gog kept striding toward Ray, his even, deliberate steps unbroken.

Ray's heart sank. He squatted to pull Redfeather over his shoulder. He was so exhausted and sore and terrified that he could barely lift him. A wave of pain shot from his ankle as he stood. There were only a few more feet until he reached the fire.

After he had gotten several yards into the fire, Ray turned to see if the Gog would follow him. The elegantly dressed man had not been affected by the bottletree, nor by Nel's soporific. Would the Gog be able to enter the fire as well?

The Gog stopped just as he reached the fire's edge. Half a dozen guards spread out behind him. They shielded their faces from the blistering heat and smoke and waited for orders.

The Gog's features were illuminated by the swirling orange flames. He gazed in Ray's direction with a ferocious iciness. The light danced off the Gog's dark coat and reptilian-green and black striped suit beneath it. His nostrils flared above his curly silver mustache.

Ray felt a wave of horror. He knew the Gog.

"He doesn't have the siren," the Gog said. "It's a trick. She's escaped in another direction."

With a swirl of his long coat, the Gog turned and pointed back to his pitch-dark train with his walking stick.

Redfeather groaned, and Ray's attention returned to his friend. He had to get him back to the *Ballyhoo*. Ray hurried, staying at the edge of the field fire nearest to the tracks.

But Ray could not tear his thoughts away from what he now realized. He had met the Gog before.

The pieces came together in his mind. The train, that elegant pitch-dark train. Ray had hardly noticed its exterior when he and Sally boarded the wonderful train that was leading them from the city.

The finely dressed man in that green and black striped suit. The Gog. It seemed so obvious now. It was not just a name. They were the initials of G. Octavius Grevol. The man who had been so generous, who had brought Sally and all those other orphans to new homes. Mister Grevol was the Gog.

RAY LEFT THE FIRE. FOR A MOMENT HE WAS DISORIENTED and worried that he had come out in the wrong place. But he heard the clang and shouts of the Gog's men working on the broken track. Through the swirling orange and black smoke, he managed to spot the dark rise of the hill where Buck and Conker waited.

"Redfeather, can you hear me?" Ray asked.

Redfeather did not respond, but Ray could hear his breathing and hurried toward the hill.

Within a few minutes, he reached the tree-crowned hilltop. Buck had his pistol leveled on Ray, but he lifted it as he realized who it was. Startled, Conker said, "Ray, you're back—" And then seeing Redfeather, he stammered, "Is he—is Redfeather . . ."

"Blood!" Buck barked. "What's happened?"

"He's shot," Ray panted. "But he's still alive."

Ray lowered Redfeather to the ground. Conker pulled open Redfeather's dark, wet shirt. Searching with his hands across the film of blood, he found the wound on Redfeather's stomach. The bleeding seemed to have slowed, but he needed help fast.

"I'm getting him back to Nel," Conker said. He slid the Nine Pound Hammer into his belt and lifted Redfeather easily in his arms. "Where's the others?"

"Jolie?" Buck urged. "Did you rescue her?"

"We were separated," Ray began. "They were coming down the track. They're trapped down there by the men working—"

"Redfeather can't wait," Conker said. Ray took off the copper necklace and put it around Conker's neck.

"Keep it for him," Ray said. Conker nodded and left, running swiftly down from the hill toward the *Ballyhoo*.

"Can you see them down there?" Buck asked after Conker was gone.

"I don't know." Ray squinted hard. "There's so much smoke."

Buck turned toward the sound of the hammers coming from below. "If they're trapped, we've got to draw those men's attention."

As he said this, the rhythmic trill of the hammers stopped. One of the men—Ray recognized him as Mister McDevitt—was waving his hands at the other agents, motioning them over.

"What's happening?" Buck growled.

"I . . . I can't tell . . . ," Ray mumbled.

He looked closer and saw Jolie and Si moving from the smoke and shadows behind Mister McDevitt. Jolie's mouth was moving—she was singing. The other men were looking curiously at the girls and seemed confused by McDevitt's odd behavior.

Before the agents could react, Si smashed a pair of phials at their feet. There was a clatter of falling hammers, tools, and rifles. McDevitt turned, smiling placidly at Jolie, as Si smashed a phial on his forehead. He toppled backward.

"They're coming!" Ray shouted.

Jolie and Si ran from the smoky tracks up the hill. Buck holstered his revolver and threw the rifles over his shoulder. As soon as Si and Jolie reached the crest of the hill, Buck ordered, "Let's go! Down the other side. We'll follow the track and make for the *Ballyhoo*."

Jolie and Si gasped at the blood covering Ray's shirt. "Where's Conker? Where's Redfeather?" Si asked.

"No time to explain," Buck barked. The four began running through the thick smoke, Si clutching Buck's arm to lead him more quickly.

Ray looked back as they reached the track heading toward the *Ballyhoo*. Other agents had arrived. Just before the smoke and darkness obscured the men, Ray saw them throw aside their rifles, pick up the fallen men's hammers, and begin working furiously.

Ray, Jolie, Si, and Buck ran and ran, the field fires quickly giving way to true night darkness and a pine forest. Ray looked over at Jolie. In the dim light, she looked as frail as before.

"What happened to you?" Ray asked.

Jolie was silent a moment, breathing heavily. She adjusted the bundle under her arm. "I am sorry. I thought it would help if . . ."

"Jolie," Ray panted. "You shouldn't have run away."

"I know. But I did not want to bring more danger to you."

"Are you okay?" Ray asked. "Did they hurt you?"

"No," she replied. "They caught me in the forest and locked me on their train—"

"Hallo?" Shacks's voice called from ahead. The lights from the caboose appeared around a bend in the tracks, and Si gave a call in return. Shacks blew a high whistle to his father in the locomotive, and the *Ballyhoo* roared to life.

"Conker's already aboard with Redfeather," Shacks said. "Get on quickly!" The train began trudging slowly forward as Ray and the others reached the ladder to the caboose and climbed aboard.

They were out of breath and collapsed on the wooden floor of the caboose. Ray quickly told them what had happened as Jolie, Si, and Shacks listened in horror.

Only Buck remained focused on what lay ahead. He ran his fingers through his pockets, scattering out cartridges to count. The train chugged faster and faster.

As Ray finished telling about the events at *The Pitch Dark Train,* he said, "I saw the Gog, and I've met him before! I've got to tell Nel."

The train rattled, nearly reaching full speed, as Ray headed through the caboose.

"I need ammunition!" Buck hollered. "The Gog's train won't be held up for long, and this junker ain't fast enough to get away. We'll need to be ready with guns."

"I'll get them, Buck," Si said, standing up to go after Ray. Jolie followed, and the three scrambled up the ladder and crossed the top of the train.

In Nel's car, they found Marisol and Peter Hobnob standing around anxiously as Nel bent over Redfeather, who was lying on the table. Ma Everett was tearing old sheets and clothing into strips.

Conker rushed forward and hugged Jolie. "You're okay."

"Yes. How is Redfeather?"

Nel answered as he worked on Redfeather's wounds. "He's lost a fair amount of blood, but the bullet isn't deep. I got it out already. Once we clean him up and I can put together some tonics, he should pull through fine."

"I'd better go," Conker said.

"Hurry," Nel called over his shoulder. "Tell Shacks: take only what can't be spared. Leave everything else on the caboose. What's most important is to be quick! They'll be here before long."

Si rushed into Buck's room. She returned a moment

later, her arms filled with cases of bullet cartridges. There were more than she could carry back to the caboose, so Marisol took some, as well as a pair of Spencer rifles Buck used occasionally in shows. Then the two girls were out the door.

"What's happened?" Hobnob asked Ray. His yellow explosion of hair looked as if he'd been pulling on it apprehensively.

Nel and Ma Everett continued to work on Redfeather but listened intently as Ray explained how Conker had broken the track and they had rescued Jolie.

"But the Gog," Ray said. "I saw his face. Do you remember how I left my sister on that orphan train? I thought she was taken in by a family somewhere . . . that Miss Corey was going to get all those orphans to homes. Mister Grevol, the man who owned the train, *he's* the Gog! The orphans were kidnapped!"

"What?" Nel demanded, looking over his shoulder.

"I heard voices when I was locked up," Jolie said. "If they were the children, I think they moved them toward the back of the train. And, Ray, look at this." Jolie began unwrapping the bundle she had been carrying: a woolen scarf covering what seemed to be a book. "Some of their belongings were in my room. I found this."

As Jolie tore the scarf away, Ray saw it—the blue linen binding, the title etched in silver. *The Incunabula of Wandering.*

"Ray, this book belonged to your father," Jolie said. "Little Bill told me about it."

"It can't be . . . ," Ray murmured, a white-hot heat blazing behind his ribs. "If you found this on the train, then Sally must still be . . ."

"What?" Jolie asked.

Ray frantically tried to explain. "Mother Salagi told me the Gog was stealing people to use their souls, their spirits, to feed his Machine!"

"Ray, slow down," Nel said, trying to follow Ray's words and tend to Redfeather.

"My sister is on that train back there! We've got to save her!"

Nel's eyes grew wide, his voice trembling as he spoke. "Ray, you've got to hurry and stop Conker. We needed a way to stop the Gog, and I told him . . . He's going to release the caboose!"

"No!" Ray shouted. He looked once at Jolie, her storm-cloud eyes filled with terror, and then Ray flew to the door and out onto the vestibule.

As he climbed onto the top of the train, he felt the first lurch of the *Ballyhoo* as Conker tried to remove the pin holding the caboose to the rest of the train.

If his sister and the other orphans had not been on *The Pitch Dark Train*, it would be a perfect plan. The released caboose would smash into the locomotive of the Gog's train, certainly causing it to wreck, and the *Ballyhoo* might easily escape. But if Conker got that pin out before Ray stopped him, Sally might be lost forever.

Ray could not waste time crawling on hands and knees across the top of the train. He stood and sprinted. The cyclone-force wind pushed against him, but Ray steadied his steps and leaped from one car to the next until he reached the caboose.

Ray jumped over the gap between the boxcar and the caboose, landing on the edge of the caboose in a tumble. He fell to the deck of the vestibule, nearly knocking Shacks and Si off their feet.

Conker had his feet across the gap in the cars, the Nine Pound Hammer perched in the air as he readied to strike the pin loose.

"NO!" Ray screamed.

Conker looked up in fright. "What? What's the matter, Ray?"

"Don't pull that pin! My sister's on *The Pitch Dark Train.*"

Conker got up onto the vestibule and helped Ray to his feet. Buck and Marisol were in the doorway to the boxcar, where they had been moving supplies from the caboose.

"If we don't release the caboose," Buck said, "the Gog will catch us."

"But if you do, my sister will be killed," Ray answered. "We've got no choice."

Buck turned to go back into the boxcar with Marisol. "Shacks," he said. "Let's get these rifles loaded."

Ray, Conker, and Si looked at one another as they stood on the vestibule, the fear of what was going to happen sinking in. *The Pitch Dark Train* would catch them now, and the Gog's agents would attack. They would fight their way onto the *Ballyhoo* to get Jolie. The Gog had too many men even for Buck to hold off for long.

Ray asked, "I wonder how long those soporifics we used to knock the Gog's men out will work?"

"Not long," Conker answered. "Nel said he didn't have much of the herbs left, so he made a mild version. That way he could spread it into more phials."

"So he can't make any more?" Si asked.

Conker shook his head.

"What about the bottletrees?" Ray asked. "Couldn't we use them to keep the Gog from getting onto the *Ballyhoo*?"

Buck called from the doorway of the boxcar, "They won't work on the train. They have to be placed in the earth. That's where they draw their power from."

"The *Snapdragon*'s going to meet us at the Mississippi," Ray said, struggling to find some faint spark of optimism. "We'll have to hope the Gog won't reach us before then. . . ." He trailed off as he touched his hand to the toby. The rabbit's foot was growing warm.

At that moment, the train buckled heavily and a terrifying screech wailed as the wheels tore against the track. Ray found himself thrown, flying through the air along with Si and Conker. The three tumbled together through the doorway into the boxcar where Buck and Marisol and

Shacks had been flung into a storm of flying crates and loose supplies.

The caboose pushed against the groaning vestibule, nearly crushing into the boxcar. But the wheels settled again into motion, and although they were moving slower, the *Ballyhoo* was still going.

"What just happened?" Ray shouted as he rolled over.

"*The Pitch Dark Train,*" Buck said, getting to his feet stiffly. "It caught up with us."

Ray could see the blaze of *The Pitch Dark Train*'s headlamp illuminating the back of the *Ballyhoo*'s caboose in harsh yellow light. The two trains were ominously close to one another. Gunfire blasted over the caboose, scattering glass down from the cupola onto the floor below; Ray and the others ducked back into the boxcar.

After the gunfire receded, Buck and Shacks rushed out onto the vestibule. The back half of the caboose had been crushed by the collision, and although they could not get through it to return gunfire, neither could the Gog's men get through the damaged car. They would have to go over the top of the caboose.

As Buck and Shacks climbed up the ladder to the top of the caboose, bullets whizzed and sparked around them. The two lay flat against the roof and began returning fire, round after round.

"Give me another rifle!" Buck shouted. Marisol grabbed one and rushed up to exchange it with Buck's empty rifle.

Shacks dropped back down from the top of the caboose. "Do you know how to load a rifle?"

As he explained, Marisol picked up one of the Spencers and began loading. Ray, Conker, and Si brought the extra rifles and boxes of cartridges out onto the vestibule so they could keep handing reloaded rifles to Buck and Shacks.

Si leaned out around the side of the train to survey *The Pitch Dark Train*. She pulled back as a bullet buzzed past her face. "The Gog's men are all over their locomotive. If they ram us again, they can hold their train against ours while their men storm the *Ballyhoo*."

"What should we do to help?" Ray asked.

Shacks pushed past Conker and Si to climb back up with one of the Spencer rifles. "Just keep down so you don't get shot!"

The Pitch Dark Train collided once more with the back of the *Ballyhoo*. Buck and Shacks took cover at the top of the caboose, crouching side by side on the ladders as the gunfire thickened. As it slowed momentarily, they popped back up to return fire around the cupola.

"Nearly got me!" Shacks snarled, and wheeled back up to fire over and over.

Nel stepped out onto the vestibule carrying a broken-off broom handle, its splintered end wrapped in damp, vaporous rags. He handed it to Conker along with a box of stove matches. "Get this lit," he said. Nel slowly climbed the ladder to Buck, pulling himself up by his arms.

He stayed low, keeping his head beneath the top of the train car.

"Our caboose seems to be the worse for wear," Nel said.

Buck grunted and fired the Spencer. "Rear brakes are certainly ruined. Going to have a hard time stopping the *Ballyhoo*."

"How are you faring?" Nel asked.

Buck steadied the Spencer and fired, hitting one of the Gog's men as he sprang around the cupola. The agent tumbled from the side of the caboose.

"Been in worse spots," Buck said. "Nevertheless it's hard to sniff them out with this wind."

Ray took a quick peek around the side of the caboose. *The Pitch Dark Train* had crushed its way into the back of the caboose. The two trains were now joined, allowing the Gog's men to crawl across their own locomotive and leap onto the back of the *Ballyhoo*. Many of the Gog's men held positions on the broken balcony of the *Ballyhoo*'s caboose and some seemed to have made their way up behind the cupola, firing across the top of the caboose at Buck and Shacks. So far, Buck and Shacks had managed to pick off any of the Gog's men who came around the cupola.

"They'll be preparing to come across the roof at us soon," Buck said.

"And then?" Nel asked, reaching back to take a reloaded rifle from Marisol.

"I'm a realist, Nel. We'll take quite a few with us, but not all of them."

Nel nodded. Buck discharged the last bullet in the Spencer and dropped it down to Marisol. Nel placed the reloaded rifle in Buck's hand. An eruption of gunfire came from the Gog's men, scattering sparks across the top of the caboose.

"I've prepared something. It just might meliorate our injurious standing," Nel said.

"English, if you don't mind," Buck said. He took aim and fired at one of the Gog's agents. His shot missed, but the man was forced to take cover behind the cupola.

"I made something that might help," Nel said.

Shacks glanced over at Buck and Nel, and then leaned around the side of the caboose and shot one of the Gog's men. Ray listened anxiously with Conker and Si.

"More potions?" Buck asked.

"I had no time for root work, but given the urgency of the situation, I was able to put something together that might be just as effective."

Shacks took a new rifle. "There's nearly ten of them on the back side of the cupola. They're readying to storm us."

From a satchel twisted over his shoulder, Nel pulled out a bottle with a bit of cloth snaking from the mouth. Ray looked at it curiously.

Buck sniffed and then gave a grim smile. "Kerosene." The whine of a bullet passed Buck's ear.

Nel called down the ladder. "Conker, have you got that torch lit?"

"They're about to charge!" Shacks shouted.

Conker lifted the broom, its flames whipping in the fierce wind of the moving train. "Hold her steady," Nel said as he dipped the bottle's fuse into the flame. When the flame caught, Nel pulled himself up over the top of the caboose. Ray leaned out cautiously to see what was going to happen.

"Here they come!" Shacks called.

Four of the Gog's men fired rapidly from the back of the caboose. Other agents charged forward around the cupola. Shacks cried out as a bullet grazed his neck. He dropped the Spencer and tumbled backward, landing on the vestibule between the train cars. The rifle clattered and disappeared onto the track below.

Nel threw the lit kerosene bottle; it smashed on the cupola's roof, encasing the dome in flames. Burning liquid spread, splashing onto the charging men. Several screamed and dropped back onto the smashed balcony. Others beat at their burning clothes helplessly and fell from the sides of the train.

Ray turned to Conker. "We've got to do something. My sister's back there. It's not just a matter of fighting off the Gog's men. We've got to get her and those orphans."

Shacks called over to Nel as he climbed back up. "I remember this stretch of track. There's a tunnel coming up, if I'm right."

"What good is that?" Nel asked.

"Hold your fire a moment, Buck," Shacks said. "Nel's flames are already dying back. They'll try again to get through. Let the Gog's men come up a ways. Then, Nel, you throw another one of those bombs."

· "Yes," Nel said. "The flames will be concentrated by the tunnel. . . ."

"I've got a plan, too," Conker mumbled to Ray and Si. He looked at Ray with hard, dark eyes as he thought. At that moment, Conker looked terrifying. Ray had seen him this way once before: the night that he had woken Conker from the dream about his father fighting the Machine.

The whistle blew from the *Ballyhoo*'s locomotive. Conker turned at the sound.

"That's the tunnel," Shacks said. "Throw it, Nel!"

The top of the caboose erupted in flame.

"Come on, quick!" Conker said.

"What?" Ray asked.

"Before we reach that tunnel. Quick, up the ladder. Si, you too."

Si looked to Marisol, who was loading the next rifle to pass up to Buck and Shacks. "I can handle this," Marisol assured her.

The gunfire had stopped as the Gog's men fought to escape the flames and got down before the tunnel.

Conker, Si, and Ray climbed to the top of the boxcar. Ray could see the dark form of a hill coming toward the front of the train. Conker stood, balancing himself atop the swaying train. He slid the hammer into his belt and pulled Ray and Si to their feet.

"Grab ahold of my back. Real tight," he added.

Ray looked ahead in terror as he saw the front of the *Ballyhoo* enter the tunnel. Any second, the masonry face above the tunnel was going to crush them from the top of the train.

"Conker?" Ray cried.

"Hold on!" Conker roared. Si reached her hands around Conker's neck, and Ray hurried to cling on behind her. Just before they met the tunnel, Conker jumped.

The impact would have smashed any ordinary man like an insect. But carrying the Nine Pound Hammer, Conker was no ordinary man. When he hit, his enormous body absorbed the blow. Ray felt rattled as his chin struck Si on her shoulder blade, but he held on tightly.

Conker's fingers dug into the mortar. Ray felt dizzy as he watched the trains speeding by below them. He could now see that Si had been right. Clinging to the sides of *The Pitch Dark Train*'s locomotive and its tender were men clutching rifles, ready to board the *Ballyhoo* to recapture Jolie.

Ray could not tell how many men there were as the train passed quickly beneath him, but there were many—too many. He could see other men rushing from car to car across the vestibules, all running toward the locomotive for the battle.

"Ready?" Conker grunted over his shoulder. And

before Ray could get ready, Conker pushed off with one powerful arm, flipping around to land on his stomach on the top of *The Pitch Dark Train*. As Ray rolled off his back, he felt Conker's hand pin his shoulders to the car as they entered the tunnel, its ceiling whirling past, several feet overhead. Within a moment they were out the other side, and Conker let go.

"Y'all okay?" he asked. Ray sat up, grabbed a guardrail, and looked around. They were midway down the length of *The Pitch Dark Train,* far behind the shouting voices and gunfire.

Si grunted and gasped for breath. Apparently, he had been holding her down, too. Conker helped her sit up, and Si held a hand to her chest. "Knocked . . . the wind . . . out of me," she managed to say.

"Sorry," Conker said.

"Big . . . oaf," she wheezed.

Getting to his knees, Ray held the guardrails tightly to keep steady against the sway of the train and the tremendous gale-force wind. Conker pulled the Nine Pound Hammer from his belt and clutched it with one hand.

"Do you know where the children are?" Conker called over the howling wind.

"Jolie said they were toward the back of the train," Ray shouted. "But they could be in more than one car."

"We'll check the others," Conker said. He nodded toward the middle of the boxcar's top they were on. Ray and Si followed him.

Conker crouched over the handle for a hatch in the roof of the boxcar. He stuck his head down into it. "Not here," he said. "Get on and try the next one."

It was slow moving across the top of the train car, and only Ray's eagerness to find his sister kept him brave against the fear of being flung over the side. They jumped across the gap between the train cars and checked the next hatch. The boxcar had an assortment of crates and food-stuffs, but no children.

"Just a few more," Si said, closing the hatch and leading them to the next car. As she opened it, she turned her head curiously. "Something's in there."

The rabbit's foot was blazing through the toby.

A roar exploded from the opening and a heavy smash rocked the ceiling, nearly knocking the three from the top of the boxcar. Ray swung around onto his back, holding on with one hand to the guardrail.

"Hoarhound!" Conker shouted. They were toppled again as the beast leaped into the ceiling, this time crack-ing the joints of the boxcar's frame beneath their feet. The three scrambled to the end and leaped onto the next car, the one where Jolie had been prisoner. The Hound contin-ued to shake the train ferociously.

They kept going, to the next one. Squealing voices of terror issued from inside the boxcar—children's voices. "In here!" Ray said. Before he could reach the hatch, a man climbed up the ladder on the far end of the car. His bowler hat flipped away in the wind as he reached the top.

He pulled out a pistol and tried to aim it as he swayed on the top of the train. Conker charged across the car. The man's eyes widened in terror as he fired.

Conker pulled back slightly as the bullet thudded into his shoulder. The man's next shot went wild, and Conker swept him from the top of the train with his hammer. The man shouted as he disappeared into the dark.

"You okay?" Ray called.

Conker held his hand to his shoulder and nodded. Ray turned back and tore open the hatch, calling into the dark, "Sally!"

Some of the children were crying, others murmuring and whimpering in terror. But a small, shaking voice rose above them, "Ray? Is that you?"

"Sally," he said again, and slid his feet in through the opening of the hatch. The children moved aside as Ray dropped in among them. There was no light except for the dim glow from the square of starry night at the hatch above. The children surged forward from the benches all at once to grab on to Ray. There were many more than those who had traveled with him from Miss Corey's orphanage, but those who knew Ray called out his name and clutched his arms.

"It's okay," he assured the group. "We're getting you out of here. Where's Sally?"

"I'm here!" Ray heard her voice in the dark but could not see her. Trying to be gentle with the scared children that clung to his arms, Ray pushed toward Sally's voice.

"Sally!" he cried. He could not see her, but when he felt the arms go around his neck, smelled her hair, and heard her voice in his ear as he lifted her, he knew it was her. "I found you," he choked.

"Ray—Ray—Ray," she said over and over.

Conker's face darkened the hatch above. "Ray, Si's opening the door on the caboose side. Get them down there."

Ray felt the train rock once more and knew the Hoarhound was working its way out of its cage. When he led the children—there must have been thirty or more—toward the door, he heard the lock click. Si opened the door onto the vestibule.

The Pitch Dark Train shook again. Si led them into Grevol's parlor and then down the hallway of his ornate sleeper car until they reached the door for the caboose. "Come on," she said, waving her hand to hurry the children. "Get in quick."

"Is the Hound out?" Ray called up to Conker.

From above, Conker leaned over. "He's near through, Ray."

"What are we going to do?" Ray asked.

Conker came down the ladder, his sleeve wet and dark with blood. "Got to get these children to safety."

"How?"

Conker nodded down beneath their feet to the pin that held the caboose to the rest of the train. "Going to bust that pin out and set the caboose loose."

The Hoarhound roared, its voice loud now in the open air. "It's free!" Ray said.

"I got to have time to work the pin loose," Conker said. Ray understood and began climbing up the ladder toward the top of the train and the Hoarhound. He would have to hold off the Hound to give Conker time to save the children.

Si herded all the children into the caboose, but Sally was pushing her way back through the mass of children. "Ray!" she cried.

"Stay there," Ray said over his shoulder. "Stay with Si."

"Ray!" Sally called. Ray gritted his teeth and reached the top of the car. He crouched down, one hand holding the guardrail, the other hand slipping into his pocket for the rabbit's foot. The Hoarhound had broken an opening in the top of its boxcar and was wrestling itself out of the hole and onto the top of the train. The Hoarhound brought its metallic eyes around to meet Ray. It growled and hunched low as it crossed the cars.

Conker's hammer struck the pin. "Hang on, Ray!" he called.

Loosening the toby's string, Ray walked toward the Hoarhound; the clockwork beast bared its steely teeth. The Hoarhound was ridiculously large on the top of the train but kept its balance by digging its metal claws into the roof. Its eyes never strayed from Ray. The Hound readied itself to pounce.

Ray held up the hot, glowing rabbit's foot. "Remember

this? You remember me?" he shouted, mustering all his bravery.

The Hound eyed the rabbit's foot warily, but then leaped, landing on the car not ten feet from Ray. It took every ounce of Ray's courage not to flee. He steeled himself: the rabbit's foot had protected him once from the Hound, but if the Hound charged and snapped its jaws quick enough . . .

The hammer struck again. "Nearly there!" Conker shouted.

As the Hoarhound took a step forward, Ray stepped forward as well. The Hound growled but stopped, its eyes flickering from Ray to the golden foot.

Ray felt the train shake a moment. "I got it, Ray. They're free."

"Ray!" Sally's voice wailed, drifting away behind him as the caboose parted from the train. Ray desperately wanted to look back. To find Sally and lose her again so quickly caused an unbearable ache in his chest. But if he turned, if he tried to jump for the caboose to stay with Sally, the Hound would follow.

Ray heard Conker climb up behind him. The Hoarhound snarled when it saw Conker but stayed back. "Keep it right there," Conker whispered. "Keep it back till they're gone."

Ray felt a tremble in his lip; his courage wavered. The Hound, sensing this, swung its jaw open and lunged into the air. Ray fell back, holding out the blazing rabbit's foot.

He saw the dark shadow of Conker rise up over him, the iridescent blur of the hammer swinging through the air. The hammer met the Hound with a burst of breaking metal and grinding gears.

Ray rolled over to watch the Hound topple onto the edge of the train beyond Conker. The beast flipped and then fell over the side of the car into the dark.

—21—

THE PITCH DARK TRAIN

RAY SEARCHED THE DARK TRACK BEHIND THEM, BUT THE caboose was too far away now. Sally was gone, but at least she was safe. He and Conker were not.

Helping stanch Conker's bleeding, Ray turned to look toward the locomotive as another burst of flames appeared from the collision of the two trains. He redoubled the pressure on Conker's bullet wound, and the giant grunted. After a few more moments, Ray took Conker's shirt and bundled it into a bandage to wrap the bleeding shoulder.

Conker pulled back his shoulder. "Enough. Ain't going to get no better now."

Ray placed his hands on his folded knees and bent his head. "How are we going to get back to the *Ballyhoo*?" he mumbled. "And Sally . . . ?"

Conker reached for the hammer and got up on one knee. He wavered dizzily for a moment and had to place one hand down to hold himself up. Ray touched Conker's side, knowing he would not be able to support the giant if he fell over.

"Sit back," Ray said. "You've lost a lot of blood."

"I feel I seen him, Ray."

"What are you talking about?"

"My father. All this time, my whole life, I been wanting nothing more than a chance to see my father. But just lately, I been remembering I seen him."

Ray shook his head, unsure if Conker was delirious. "He died when you were just a baby. I thought you never knew your father."

"Not back then. He's been coming to me—coming in the night, in my dreams. Only I couldn't recollect it at the time."

Ray remembered the night he had awakened Conker from his dream. He had seen Conker's vision of John Henry destroying the Gog's Machine with the very hammer that Conker now held in his hand.

"You remember your dreams about him?" Ray asked.

Conker nodded. "My father, he died fighting the Gog, fighting his evil Machine. And now my father's hammer, it belongs to me. I'm taking it up again, Ray. I got to carry on the work."

"You're dizzy, Conker. You've got to rest."

"No! Ain't no time for faltering now. I've got to destroy him." Conker pushed up on one knee and slowly stretched to his full height. He cocked his head to one side, as if taking the measure of his growing strength.

Ray stood, too, spreading his stance to brace against the train's sway and the wild, whipping wind.

"You sure you're—" Ray began.

Conker turned toward the front of *The Pitch Dark Train,* gripping the handle of the hammer across his chest. Conker broke into a full run, leaped from car to car. Ray rushed after him.

The agents of the Gog clung to the locomotive like a swarm of insects, scuttling across the sloped cowcatcher and onto the *Ballyhoo*'s caboose, which shimmered with the dying flames of the last of Nel's crude bombs.

Conker charged the Gog's men from behind, bursting from the coal smoke and shadows just beyond the bright blast of the headlamp. He leaped onto the roof of the engineer's cab, sweeping his hammer, scattering men off the sides of the locomotive. Conker struck into the cab. The impact of his hammer blew out the glass and hurtled the engineer through the side door.

The Gog's agents at the *Ballyhoo*'s caboose shielded their eyes against the headlamp's glare, hardly knowing what they were witnessing. The shadowy giant braced himself against the smokestack, hurtling his hammer about in great arcs. Conker was no mere man, nor even a giant. With the Nine Pound Hammer, he had become an unstoppable force.

By the time the Gog's agents opened fire, Conker had

jumped down the cowcatcher, delivering a fury of heavy blows from both the hammer and his injured arm. Men fell in clumps from the sides of the train.

Conker took several shots from their rifles at close range. Roaring with fury, he pummeled his hammer into the last of the gunmen and rid them from the back of the *Ballyhoo*.

With one foot on the cowcatcher of *The Pitch Dark Train* and the other on the back of the *Ballyhoo*'s caboose, Conker struck his hammer against the twisted metal that held the trains together.

"Ray!" Conker shouted. "Hurry!"

Crouched on the last car before the tender, Ray looked at the locomotive and realized that with no engineer, *The Pitch Dark Train* was now being pulled by the *Ballyhoo*. Conker broke through final clinging strands of metal and grabbed the grille of the cowcatcher before the trains separated. He swung the hammer into the balcony of the caboose. The force of the two trains pulled Conker in opposite directions, and he issued a fierce roar. Thick bands of muscles across his bleeding shoulders, chest, and arms rippled under the enormous weight of the opposing trains. He couldn't hold on for long.

Nel and Buck had already moved to the cupola, where the flames had died down, ready to hoist Conker and Ray up onto the caboose.

Ray raced through the thick smoke belching from the locomotive. He leaped from the passenger car down onto the smooth roof of the tender car. A hand caught his ankle midflight and threw him down in a tumble.

"Wait, Ray," a voice said. "Don't leave me."

Ray flipped over to see Seth clutching his ankle from the passenger car's vestibule. Ray snapped his foot back to kick Seth away but was stopped when he saw the anguish welling in the boy's eyes.

"I was wrong," Seth said, voice trembling. "Terribly wrong."

Seth climbed up onto the tender after Ray but turned as the door from the passenger car opened. The Gog stepped out onto the vestibule.

"You've reconsidered taking employ with my . . . carnival?" he said to Seth.

Seth stood over Ray and raised his cutlass over his head as the Gog approached the tender.

"Seth, put it down, son!" Nel cried through the smoke and rumble.

Seth ignored the pitchman, saying in a low voice to the Gog, "Don't come any closer! Or I swear, I'll kill you!"

Nel's voice pitched with alarm, "No, Buck!"

A shot fired. The cutlass dropped with a clatter on the top of the tender. Seth stumbled and turned. Ray could see a dark stain spreading across Seth's shirt. Ray looked back through the smoke toward the *Ballyhoo,* where Buck was crouched, his revolver still leveled.

"No!" Ray cried.

Seth's eyes turned upward, and he dropped with a slap

to the tender's roof. Ray crawled over to him, touching Seth's neck. "No, Seth. No," he whispered. But he could see clearly that he was dead.

From the corner of his eye, Ray saw something moving along the side of the train. A pale, ghostly form rushed along in the dark, equal to the speed of *The Pitch Dark Train*. It galloped, its white bristling haunches moving up and down as it ran.

The Hoarhound.

"Give my thanks to your gunslinger," the Gog said to Ray. He blew a sharp whistle, and the Hoarhound jumped, its front paws tearing into the metal of the tender. Ray rolled away, and Seth's body was knocked from the train as the Hound pulled itself aboard. Its shoulder was crushed like a rotting melon where Conker had struck it with his hammer, and its head hung gruesomely to one side. But when the Hound bared its teeth, Ray knew it was still deadly.

The Gog climbed the steps of the ladder and walked to the Hoarhound with one hand on his walking stick. When he reached the Hound—the mechanical beast towering beside him—the Gog rubbed his fingers up into its frosty fur.

"There was a time when I would have considered him my greatest construction." The Gog smiled at the beast. "But I have been working on another, one that will soon reshape this sad world into something truly great and useful. I am missing but a few final . . . necessities."

Buck fired from the back of the *Ballyhoo,* unloading the chambers of his revolver in quick succession. Shots sparked off the Hound's hide. The Gog did not move or take his eyes from the Hoarhound. He simply held up his ebony walking stick, and the bullets scattered harmlessly around him.

The Gog looked at Buck and shouted, "Pity, it's not so simple, cowboy!" The Gog took a step toward Ray, who was still lying on his back. The metal beneath him was growing painfully cold. Shards of ice formed across the top of the tender and on his clothing. The Hound might have been injured, but his powers were little diminished.

Ray pulled the rabbit's foot from his pocket and held the shining talisman out before him for protection.

"No need for that either." The Gog swatted with his walking stick. The golden foot flew from Ray's hand and tumbled off the side of the train.

"No!" Ray cried.

"Now, if we can get down to business," the Gog said, standing over Ray, one hand reaching up to massage the Hoarhound's broken shoulder, the other making small, theatrical motions in the air with his stick. Grevol called out to the *Ballyhoo,* "Old Joe Nelson. Or is it Mister Cornelius Carter? I assume you are back there as well."

Nel called from the back of the caboose, "You can have me. I'll turn myself over to you. Just let the boy go."

The Gog laughed. "I have no more use for a crippled old man than a foolish young brat. You were a great Rambler once, Mister Nelson, but what are you now? Don't play the fool. It insults us both. You know what I want."

From the Gog's feet, Ray called out, "Conker, let go!"

Conker could issue little more than a strained groan.

Ray looked up at the Gog, "We don't have Jolie," he lied. "She's on your caboose, gone with the rest of the children you kidnapped."

"Jolie? Is that what the mermaid's called?" The Gog smiled, the corners of his mouth curling beyond his silver mustache. "What a lovely name. No, the orphans are disposable. I can get more to feed my Machine. But the siren—this Jolie, who I know is still on your train—she is a rare thing indeed."

"She can't help you," Ray said. "Her song is not as powerful as other sirens'."

The Gog raised his crooked eyebrows, flashing black, oily eyes. "A valiant attempt. Oh, I suspect her voice will work just fine."

The Gog patted the Hoarhound. "Mankind is a pitiful lot. Weak and superstitious. I want to raise them out of the muck of savagery that they've lived in for thousands of years. They are crude and they will need to be remolded, reshaped. But alas, they won't come willingly. Your Jolie—more specifically, her siren song—will help me influence them, to lead them to a new destiny by way of my Machine. She can come willingly . . . or I can use the music box your swordsman so generously delivered."

"If I come, you will let him go?" a voice called.

Ray turned to look over his shoulder. Jolie was standing on the caboose, on the other side of the cupola from

Buck and Nel. They turned in surprise, but Jolie rushed past them before they could stop her. She jumped from the *Ballyhoo* onto *The Pitch Dark Train*'s cowcatcher, where Conker was holding the trains together.

"Stop, Jolie!" Nel yelled.

Jolie grasped the headlamp of *The Pitch Dark Train* and was pulling herself up when her fingers gave out. She slipped.

Conker jerked the hammer from the caboose and swung around to catch Jolie, pinning her to the front of the cowcatcher. One fraction of a second more, and she would have fallen to the track beneath *The Pitch Dark Train*'s wheels. As Conker held Jolie, the two trains parted. The *Ballyhoo* quickly moved ahead on the track; *The Pitch Dark Train* began its slow deceleration. Nel and Buck's shouting voices faded as it departed.

Dawn had begun to break. In a thin blue glow, the forests surrounding the tracks gave way to the low marshes and creeks that fed the Mississippi River. Dark birds swooped over the cypresses and grasses.

The Gog smirked at Ray. Ray pressed one foot against the guardrail and reached back with one hand to pull away from the Gog. As Ray moved to the edge, he saw a golden glow on the side of the tender.

"What a fine morning." The Gog waved a hand out to the silver sky. "Fine indeed. I see why you are so fond of her, your Jolie. She has initiative. So rare a quality in these times. And you, young Ray, you have admirable qualities as well . . . the very reason I couldn't keep you aboard my train back when we first met."

Ray's eyes flickered again over the edge. The rabbit's foot clung magnetically to the tender's iron frame, just four feet down.

The Gog backed away a step, allowing the Hoarhound to inch forward. The beast pressed close to its master, its gleaming jaws slack and eager.

The Gog sighed. "Your willingness to leave your sister on the pale hope that she would have a better life without you . . . well, it's striking. Pity that after all this, I have no real need for you. There's plenty of fuel for my Machine. You are not necessary . . . not anymore."

The Gog took another step back.

"No!" Jolie shouted. She slipped from Conker's grasp, climbing up onto the top of the locomotive, just as the Gog released the Hoarhound.

The Hound lunged, jaws snapping.

Ray kicked his foot against the guardrail, propelling himself over the side of the train. With one hand, Ray held tightly to the guardrail, swung down along the side of the train, and reached for the rabbit's foot. With a sharp click, it came loose from the black metal of the train.

The Hoarhound's teeth flashed as it snapped at Ray. Jolie screamed and rushed toward the Hound and its master, who was pressed against its side.

Ray got his foot to the lip above the wheel well and pushed himself up onto the tender. When the Hound saw the rabbit's foot, the beast reared back into the Gog. Ray landed on the top of the tender, rolled once, and grabbed the Hoarhound's icy leg.

The Hoarhound's mechanical insides ground to a sudden halt, setting the beast into an eerie stillness. With the jarring motion of the train, the Hound toppled to one side.

The Gog's eyes widened as his clockwork monster fell toward him. He shouted once and then disappeared beneath the mass of its body, pinned to the roof of the tender. The train shuddered beneath the immense weight of the toppled Hound.

With one hand, Ray clutched the golden foot. With the other, he clung to the Hound's frosty fur. Jolie grasped Ray about the shoulders, quaking at what had almost been Ray's end. From beneath the Hound, the Gog issued an angry, bubbling grunt. A gloved hand extended toward the ebony walking stick that lay inches away.

Conker crossed from the locomotive onto the flat top of the tender.

"Ray!" Conker said. "His stick!"

Ray turned to see the Gog's finger touch the walking stick and pull it into his grasp. Ray had time only to let go of the Hoarhound's leg and push Jolie down against the surface of the tender car before the Hoarhound's body exploded away from the Gog, smashing into Conker. The blow sent Conker across the locomotive; the Hoarhound tumbled and disappeared off the side of *The Pitch Dark*

Train. Clutching his hammer, Conker slumped down the front of the train, toward the cowcatcher.

"Conker!" Ray cried.

The Gog rose. His suit was smeared with oil and grime from the Hoarhound. His face was horribly gashed. The Gog brushed a gloved hand across his sleeve and glared down at Ray and Jolie. His eyes flamed; his lips curled into a snarl.

"You are becoming quite a nuisance," the Gog spat. "Let me make myself clear. I am taking the siren."

The Gog reached out and snatched Jolie by the arm, hurtling her to his side. Ray jumped up, but the Gog swung his ebony walking stick. An invisible force flipped Ray sideways and threw him against the rear of the locomotive.

Jolie struggled against the Gog's clutches, pulling and kicking. "Yes, we will go in just a moment," the Gog patiently explained. "But your friend hasn't yet departed."

Jolie stopped pulling against the Gog and locked his eyes in her fierce gaze. Her lips trembled, and she began to sing her siren melody.

A pleasant smile settled on the Gog's mouth as he listened to Jolie. Then his gloved hand swatted her across the mouth.

"I have no interest in hearing that now," he said. "Soon, I'll have you singing it for others, and we'll build quite a following. But save your tongue. Your charm has no effect on me."

The Gog extended the ebony walking stick toward Ray. Ray squeezed his eyes shut. With a terrifying roar, Conker sprang at the Gog. A flash burst from the Gog's stick, but Conker was between Ray and the blast. The Gog's spell broke on the Nine Pound Hammer's head, deflected, and crushed into the engineer's cab, just to Ray's side.

Conker rose before the Gog and swung the Nine Pound Hammer. The Gog released Jolie to wield his walking stick with both hands. The hammer and the stick met with a thunderous clap.

Conker and the Gog faced one another, all of their strength directed into the locked weapons. Conker roared and pushed his weight into the hammer. Despite his appearance as an older man, the Gog was equal to Conker's might. The Gog stepped back and pulled the ebony stick away. The Nine Pound Hammer struck, bursting the metal of the tender's roof and released a cloud of black dust from the coal within.

Jolie had scrambled away from the battle and was calling to Ray. Ray reached from the back of the locomotive to take Jolie's outstretched hands.

The Gog danced around Conker and swung his ebony stick; its blast threw Conker off balance. Conker managed to spring forward, swinging the hammer with one hand.

The two weapons met again in a sizzle of force.

"We've got to get off the train!" Jolie shouted.

The Pitch Dark Train moved slowly now over the tracks. Marsh gave way to water, and the tracks continued onto a trestle of wood and steel, high over the Mississippi River. It was time to jump.

"We can't leave Conker!" Ray cried.

Despite Conker's immense size and strength, and despite the Nine Pound Hammer, his friend was struggling. The gunshot wounds were bleeding freely, and Conker seemed to be faltering before the Gog's terrible power. The hammer and the Gog's ebony stick met again and again; Conker staggered, while the Gog smiled grimly, stoic and fierce.

Conker hooked the Gog's stick with the iron head of his hammer and pulled up, trying to wrestle the ebony stick from the Gog. The Gog kicked, catching Conker's knee and hobbling the giant. With a burst of force from the walking stick, the Gog sent Conker flying through the air. He flipped and landed on top of the locomotive. One hand caught the smokestack, the other grasped the hammer.

But the blow had also snapped the walking stick from the Gog's hands—where it spun to the end of the tender—and the Gog fell from the side of the train. His gloved fingers gripped the metal edge as the Gog dangled against the side of the tender.

"Ray! Jolie!" Conker cried from the nose of the locomotive. "Quick, you got to jump. Get off the train!"

Ray looked down at the dark river below. Even if he survived the impact of the fall, he could not swim. Jolie tightened her grip on his hand.

"We'll jump together," she assured him.

Ray turned back to Conker. "Go before he reaches his stick!"

Conker shook his head. "No! It's got to be finished, Ray. That's what I got to do. We may not have destroyed the Machine, but I'm going to destroy its maker."

"No!" Ray cried. "Just jump!"

The Gog pulled himself onto one elbow and swung a knee up onto the tender.

Balanced upon the top of the locomotive, Conker lifted the Nine Pound Hammer high above his head. "Ray! Jolie! Go now!"

The Gog reached the top of the tender. Crawling and scuttling, he moved toward the stick.

Jolie squeezed Ray's hand and jumped, jerking Ray off the train. Ray and Jolie tumbled from the side and into the air.

Conker howled and brought the hammer down, piercing the locomotive's metal skin and exposing the fiery boiler.

The engine erupted in a great explosion of fire and twisted shards of metal, consuming Conker and the Gog. The front of the train buckled, tumbling and blurring into a kaleidoscope of whipping flames and rocketing debris.

Ray fell with Jolie's hand clinging to his, the two spinning over and over, until her fingers slipped. Ray and Jolie tumbled apart. Ray reached for her, letting go of the rabbit's foot. But it was too late. He hit the hard surface of the river. And then all became black.

Ray sank into the dark universe of water. It was quiet and still. He was alone, and he was conscious of nothing and nobody. Many forces worked upon him, holding him suspended between the hard pull of the living and the gentle dissolve of death.

Ray drifted down toward the bottom of the river, the swirling and twisting murk storming around his body. Bubbles and mud and bits of flotsam rushed past. But a river is not just a track of water. It is a place of change, a place where decaying matter settles, and a place where tiny organisms are born. Over time, rivers shape the world. They destroy it. They renew it.

Ray descended into the darkest depths of the river.

A shadowy creature kicked its way toward Ray. Writhing back and forth as it swam, it drew closer and closer. When it found him, it circled and opened its scaly mouth. The jagged arrangement of teeth bit down, taking the collar of Ray's shirt. It jerked its head, pulling Ray from the darkness.

Hanging from the reptile's mouth, Ray dangled limply as the alligator swam with powerful strokes of its tail. It broke the surface of the water, and nudged its nose beneath Ray's chest, flipping him up onto its back.

When Ray woke again, he was lying on velvet cushions in the *Snapdragon*'s galley. A heavy, soft blanket covered him. Dust motes swirled in a crack of afternoon sunlight slipping from between the heavy drawn curtains over the window. How long had he been asleep?

Despite the warmth and comfort of the bed, a chill descended over Ray. He shook as his memories returned.

What had happened to Jolie? He remembered her holding him as they fell into the river, but after that, Ray could not recall anything until waking on Rosie's back. Had Jolie been hurt in the fall? Had the swift water of the river pulled them apart so that she could not find him?

And Conker.

Ray tried to think of some way his friend could have escaped. He wanted so badly to believe that somehow Conker had survived. He was a giant. He was John Henry's son. But Ray knew it was impossible. Conker was dead. The explosion of the train had killed him.

A wave of anger forced hot tears out of Ray's eyes, into

his hands. He had trouble seeing the glory in his friend's triumph over the Gog. Given the choice, he would rather have Conker here by his side, even if it meant not stopping the Gog.

But that was foolish. That's not what Conker would have wanted, he thought. Nor was it what his father would have wanted.

Ray thought of the rabbit's foot. He had been holding it when he fell . . . but then he had let go of it as he reached for Jolie. Rising from the cushions, Ray found his damp clothes draped over the back of a chair. He dug through his pockets, searching desperately. He pulled out the red flannel toby, but it was empty. The golden rabbit's foot—his father's hand and his mysterious guide for so long now—was gone. It must have disappeared to the bottom of the river with his fall.

Compared to losing Conker, this loss was inconsequential, but Ray was disappointed nonetheless. Drained of emotion and wanting nothing more than to forget the horrible memories pounding in his skull, Ray crawled back into the bed.

The door cracked, and the Pirate Queen peered in. A pitying expression flickered for a moment on her face, and then she forced a smile, turning back behind the door. "He's awake. You can go see him," she whispered to someone in the hall.

The door swung open, and Sally entered, running to Ray's side. Sally's look of pure joy and relief warmed him from his chill. He held her and then clasped her hands within his.

"Are you hurt?" she asked. "Is that why they have you in here?"

"No, I'm not hurt. I don't think so, anyway. I'm just tired." He leaned back to look at her. "Where are the others?"

Sally sat up. "Si, your friend, she led us to the river. We walked and walked. Then she found this boat. The other children are up above on the deck, getting fed."

Ray almost asked her if Jolie was upstairs as well, but he was afraid of the answer. "What time is it?" Ray asked.

"Late. Nearly sundown. There are men in boats looking all over the river. Are they pirates? That's what Si told us. They look mean enough, but they're really nice, fixing us whatever we want to eat and playing songs for us." Sally took a deep breath before continuing. "I was so scared, Ray. I thought I'd never see you again. That man, Mister Grevol, he kept us for so long."

"What happened?" Ray asked anxiously.

"At first he was kind," Sally said, pushing back her blond curls and twisting her mouth as she thought. "He told me you had gone on a special errand for him, but that you were coming back with surprises for us all. He told us we didn't have to go to new families after all and that he was taking us to a wonderful place. At first we were happy. It sounded so fun. But he took us to a big building surrounded by all these factories and workshops.

"We were all kept in this sort of orphanage, but we couldn't even go outside. And the women looking over us were terrible. They wouldn't tell us what happened to Miss Corey or when you were coming back."

Sally laced her fingers in Ray's as she continued. "More kids showed up all the time, other orphans. Some of them tried to run away, but they were always caught. Then one day Mister Grevol showed up, and he put us all back on his train, locked up in a boxcar. We were in there for so long. I thought that something bad had happened to you. But it didn't. Something good happened. You met Si and the pirates and those others. You saved us."

"Sally, I'm sorry I left you," Ray said.

"You left on purpose?" Sally frowned quizzically, pulling her hand from his.

"I thought it was the right thing to do," Ray said, squeezing his fists tightly. "I thought I was helping you, but instead . . ."

Sally blinked several times before asking, "Who was Mister Grevol? Si said he was a bad man. What did he want us for?"

Ray couldn't tell her. He never wanted Sally to know the truth of Grevol's plans.

Ray shook his head. "I don't know, Sally. When somebody gets so twisted up like him, they forget what it's like to be a kid. I guess he thought that if he had a bunch of kids around him, he could forget how bad he was."

The door opened behind them, and Sally turned around quickly.

"Come on, lass," the Pirate Queen said from the doorway. "Your brother needs to rest."

Ray sat up. "I'm feeling better. I'm ready to—"

The Pirate Queen shook her head. "Rest awhile longer, Ray."

Sally got up reluctantly and passed under the Pirate Queen's arm. "See you soon, Ray."

When he woke again, the room was dark. He smelled food and saw a shadow bent over him.

"Ray," the voice whispered. A match crackled brightly and a lamp on the table was lit. Peter Hobnob turned back to him, holding a tin plate piled with food.

"Hobnob?" Ray mumbled, blinking against the harsh light.

"You ready for your dinner?"

"Sure," he said, pulling back the covers. "Can we go up to eat?"

"Best have it here," Hobnob said. "Eat first. Then we'll go up on deck."

Ray ate quickly and without enjoyment. Hobnob said nothing; he looked tired. The mass of golden hair on his head was windblown and tousled. When Ray finished, Hobnob led him up the steps. The stars were out and the air was warm. Small, sleeping bodies of rescued children were scattered around the deck, and Hobnob guided Ray to the foredeck, where Nel and Buck stood talking to the Pirate Queen. Marisol was leaning against the railing, peering out across the river.

Ray saw Si kneeling on the deck, her back shaking and her face in her hands. She was weeping quietly. In front of her lay the broken handle of the Nine Pound Hammer. The iron head was gone.

Hobnob put a hand to Ray's shoulder. "We searched all day. It's all we found."

Ray spoke with Nel and Buck for some time, but he hardly could recall what he said. Something about Grevol. Something about their final battle aboard *The Pitch Dark Train*. Something about how Conker had died. His eyes lingered on the broken handle and on Si.

Buck's hand clamped onto Ray's shoulder. Ray flinched as he saw the expression on Buck's face, terror welling in his pale eyes. Buck said in a low voice, "Ray, I've got to know. Seth was attacking you. I thought he was going to kill you. I wasn't trying to . . . but there was so much smoke . . . and I was enraged. Just tell me. Did I kill him?"

Ray knew that it had been an accident—a horrible, unfortunate accident—but there had been so much tragedy already; he couldn't bear for Buck to take on the burden of Seth's death.

"No, Buck," Ray said. "The Gog's Hound killed Seth. Not you."

Buck turned, relief struggling in his expression. As he walked away, he passed Sally approaching Ray.

When she reached her brother, she smiled and took his hand in hers.

"Did they find her?" she asked sleepily.

"Who?"

"The mermaid. They've been looking for her, but I heard them say she'd left. Was she a friend of yours?"

"Yes. She was."

"Then why did she leave?"

Ray thought about this before answering. Had she been hurt? No, they surely would have found her. She had left. But why had she gone without saying goodbye? Why hadn't she helped him when he fell into the river? Ray pushed these nagging thoughts away.

He was grateful to Jolie. He concentrated on his gratitude; a wave of understanding came over him. Jolie's separation from her siren sisters. Her illness. Her confinement to the tank aboard the *Ballyhoo*. It was all because the Gog had been hunting her. But now he was dead. Jolie was free.

"She wasn't meant to live on a train or on a boat or in a house," Ray said to himself as much as to Sally. "She was wild. She was too much a part of the wild to stay."

Something nudged Ray's leg. Rosie, dripping from the river, had left a trail of water across the deck. Sally hid behind Ray, shaking with fear and clutching his sleeve tightly.

"It's okay," Ray said. "She's a friend."

Rosie opened her mouth and dropped something

golden onto the wooden planks. Ray kneeled and picked up the rabbit's foot.

"You found it!" Ray smiled and gave Rosie a rub around her scaly snout.

He showed the golden foot to Sally. She took it in her hands and examined it.

"What is it?" Sally asked, glancing warily at the enormous alligator.

"It belonged to Father," Ray explained.

"Like my book." Sally smiled.

The book. *The Incunabula of Wandering*. Ray thought about the strange book he had read many times to Sally. Ray had never understood it before. But now he saw: his father had been a Rambler, and this book, whether a source of inspiration or a philosophical guide for his kind, contained his father's handwritten notes scrawled in the margins. It could be a teacher, at least until he found out whether his father was still alive.

"Is it for good luck?" Sally asked, handing the foot back to Ray.

He held the foot a moment, half expecting it to move as it had when it was the lodestone, or to glow and grow warm. But it did neither of these things. The metal surface was cold. The Gog was dead—and luck had nothing to do with that.

Ray said, "It will help Father find us." He slid the rabbit's foot into the red flannel toby and put it in his pocket.

* * *

Conker's funeral was held the following morning on the western bank of the Mississippi. While no hole was dug, Buck had fashioned a marker out of an iron plate from the damaged caboose of the *Ballyhoo*. Etched into the metal was the name *John Conker Henry*.

In the gauzy light of the glade, a large group gathered around Nel, who presided over the ceremony: Ray and Sally. Si and Marisol. The Everett family. Redfeather, recovering from his injury. Buck. The Pirate Queen and Peter Hobnob. The crew of the *Snapdragon*, all but Mister Lamprey, who stayed with the rescued children on the steamer.

The ceremony did not lend any sense of relief or peaceful closure. Nel mentioned the Gog briefly; his destruction was the only comfort the mourners could take in the sad loss of their friend.

"What now, Nel? Will you continue with your medicine show?" the Pirate Queen asked later that day, after the funeral.

Nel rested his elbows on the rail of the steamer, looking out at the swift currents of the Mississippi River. "I don't believe I have the appetite for root doctoring anymore, at least not commercially. We'll need to get these children to homes of one sort or another. Mister Everett left to make arrangements in a town just upriver. I've given each of the children a choice, and some are staying on with us."

"Why do you want a herd of brats if you're not doing the medicine show any longer?"

"I have my reasons," Nel said.

The Pirate Queen's eyes flickered to Ray, who was eavesdropping nearby. "What of him?"

Nel turned, smiling as he realized Ray had been listening. "It would seem that not an utterance I make misses young Ray's ears. I believe Ray will have to make up his own mind about where he will go."

"You're welcome on board with us," the Pirate Queen said to Ray.

"Thank you, but I have my sister to consider," he said without hesitation. "I don't know where Sally and I will wind up, but I don't think the *Snapdragon* would be best for her."

The Pirate Queen laughed and lit a cigar. "Didn't think you would. You don't strike me as one who's cut out for thieving and pillaging. Just thought I'd offer." She walked away, chuckling.

Ray turned to Nel. "I'd like to stay with you, Mister Nel. I know you're not sure of your own plans, but Sally needs a home. And you're all the home I've got."

Nel smiled and draped his arm over Ray's shoulder.

The Everetts returned late in the afternoon. They had taken most of the orphans into town, making arrangements with a local parson. The children would be housed in his church until they could be carefully placed with good families.

Ray stood with Redfeather, gazing out on the swirling

river. The Kwakiutl boy was still weak from his injury, but Nel's tonics had nearly restored him to health.

"Poor Seth . . ." Redfeather brushed at his eyes.

Ray clapped a hand to Redfeather's shoulder. "Seth realized that he was wrong. He didn't understand who the Gog really was until it was too late. But he tried to protect me . . . in the end."

After a few moments, he nodded up to the pilothouse, where Buck and the Pirate Queen stood together talking. The Pirate Queen had a strange, gentle smile on her face.

"That's an odd pair," Redfeather chuckled, wiping his knuckles across his nose. "I could never imagine Buck being in love with anybody."

"Or anyone in love with him," Ray laughed. It was peculiar to see the two of them together—the gruff cowboy and the surly pirate.

"I wish I could go with them," Redfeather said.

"Who?" Ray asked.

"The pirates," Redfeather said. "Now that looks like a fun life."

"You don't know the Pirate Queen." Ray smirked, looking back over his shoulder at her and Buck.

"Well then, what are we going to do?" Redfeather asked.

"What do you mean?"

"Cornelius T. Carter's Mystifying Medicine Show and Tabernacle of Tachycardial Talent," Redfeather mimicked in his best Nel roar before returning to his own voice. "The medicine show's over. So what now?"

Ray shrugged. He had never quite felt a part of the show, but he would miss watching the performances. He'd miss the excitement of preparing for another extravaganza when they pulled into a new town. He'd miss the tired but cheerful sense of contentment as the *Ballyhoo* packed up to leave. He'd miss . . . Conker and Jolie.

"And then there's these kids." Redfeather nodded to the children. Sally was deep in a game of pirates and marshals with the group of orphans. "Mister Nel tell you why he's taking them with us?"

Ray shook his head. He had an idea, a hope, but he wanted to hear it from Nel first.

After a few moments, Redfeather's voice broke Ray from his reverie. "Hey, Ray, do you still have my uncle's copper?" he asked.

Ray looked at him curiously. "Didn't you . . . ? I gave it to . . . to Conker, before we were attacked."

"Oh," Redfeather said. "It's okay. I don't really need it. It's just . . ."

"Something from your home," Ray finished for him.

They grew quiet and watched the river.

"Ray." He turned to see Si walking across the deck toward him. Her eyes had dark circles under them, but she managed a smile.

As Si and Ray watched, Redfeather went over to the

children. They stopped their battle to gather around Red-feather. Sally led them in a pleading chorus until he took down a gasoline lamp, dipped his fingers inside, and formed a ball of flames around his hand. The children squealed and cheered.

Si looked up at Ray. "What about the Machine?"

"What do you mean?" Ray asked.

"I've been talking to Buck." Si traced a finger across her tattooed knuckles. "Conker . . . killed the Gog. But the Machine is still out there. Maybe if we could find it—"

"The Machine is hidden in the Gloaming. Even with your hand, we could never enter in there unless we knew how to cross."

"You mean like how your father and Nel took animal forms?"

Ray nodded. "And even then, how would we destroy it? Without the Nine Pound Hammer . . . without Conker."

Ray sighed, but Si linked her arm through his and nodded. "You'll learn how to cross, Ray. You'll find a way to do it. And then, somehow, we'll destroy that wicked Machine." She pulled him gently. "Come on."

They walked together until they reached the stairs down to the *Snapdragon*'s galley. Music wafted from below, along with the smells of one of Etienne Beauvais's famous feasts. Ray's thoughts lingered on the future as they descended belowdecks. There would be time for figuring out what lay ahead another day. Tonight, they would enjoy one last meal with the rowdy pirates.

The following morning, Ray stood on the riverbank with the orphans and the remainder of the medicine show, to wave goodbye to the *Snapdragon*. Piglet waved next to Big Jimmie. Hobnob's glowing hair rustled in the morning air while he shouted promises to visit Ray one day.

As the Pirate Queen climbed the stairs to the pilot-house, she scanned the riverbank until she found Ray. With only the quickest flicker of a smile, she headed to the wheel, barking orders for Lamprey to get everyone to work. Mister Lamprey's salty curses floated over the river as the *Snapdragon* chugged its way south.

Mister Everett had the *Ballyhoo* turned around to set off at dawn. Its locomotive faced the rising sun as it blew the whistle and set off. Rumbling across the countryside east of the Mississippi, deep green forests gave way to golden, rolling farmland. The orphan children who had come on board the train found rooms to share. Sally and a girl named Renny took Conker's room to be close to Ray. Ray thought that Conker would like that.

Ray stuck his head into Nel's car. Redfeather was helping Nel tie herbs into bundles for drying. The old pitchman puffed on his briarwood pipe as he worked and hummed a fiddle tune. Marisol played with a copperhead that Redfeather had found for her. She looked content, at peace. Si and Buck had a hand of cards spread on the table.

"You wanted to see me?" Ray asked as he entered.

Nel looked over his shoulder, his dark, worn hands finishing a final knot. He motioned for Ray to sit down.

"I wanted to speak to you all together," Nel began as he leaned back in his chair. "We haven't had much of a chance to talk."

Peg Leg Nel looked around at each of their faces soberly. He sighed before continuing. "You know I'm not planning on recommencing with the medicine show. Redfeather, Si, and Marisol, you are all sterling performers. You love the stage. I just want you to know that if you want to follow that ambition, well, you certainly don't need my permission to—"

"We don't want to," Redfeather said.

"We've been talking," Marisol said, looking from Redfeather to Nel. "We're staying with you, Nel. We don't want to leave."

"Can't pass us off that easily," Si joked.

Buck chuckled, and Nel relaxed into a careworn smile. The pitchman said, "I'm glad. I'm glad, if that's what you really desire."

"We do," Redfeather said.

"Well, then I have an idea," Nel said. "One that I know Buck shares. For a long time, I've tried to protect you all from the Gog, from the outside world, to hide you away, in a manner of speaking. But now with these recent events, I think it's time I return to an old path I never thought I'd travel again. Just because the Gog is gone doesn't mean the Ramblers are no longer needed. I want to restore the order in what limited way I can. I want to see that the ways of the Ramblers are not forgotten.

"I've lost many of my own powers, but that may not matter. One cannot really train to be a Rambler. There is no school, if you see? It is a path one walks in life and requires little more than a deep attention to the world around you. Many have walked this path without ever calling themselves a Rambler."

Excitement swelled in Ray's chest, and he could see that Si, Marisol, and Redfeather were having the same reaction. They sat forward in their chairs, eager smiles lighting their faces.

"You four have extraordinary gifts," Nel said. "And with these other children accompanying us now, the Ramblers have a future. I can't make you Ramblers. That's a path only you can choose. I could guide you, of course. Help you find those who can pass on hoodoo lore. But any countenance is nothing without the wilderness. It is there that you will find how to enter the . . . oh, well, it's all too much to explain just now, and I'm getting ahead of myself." Nel rubbed his callused hands together. "What do you think?"

"Where would we go?" Marisol asked.

"We'll have to give up the train life," Nel answered. "The Everetts are going to move on, which I think Ox has been eager to do for some time. There is a place I visited once long ago in the southern highlands, deep within the

Appalachians. Shuckstack Mountain. It's a special place, a protected wilderness. I've longed to return to those ancient mountains. The six of us and the other children will make a new home."

Si and Redfeather and Marisol burst into excited conversation with one another. But Nel seemed to sense Ray's hesitation, and he narrowed his eyes curiously. "What is it, Ray?"

The others quieted and turned to him.

Ray said, "It's just . . . what about my father? I know that I've got to take care of Sally, but I've been considering going to look for him. To see if I can discover what happened to him."

This was only partially true. Ray did want to find his father, but he also wanted to find Jolie. He had to know what had happened to her. He wanted to know that she was all right.

"He was a Rambler," Buck said, his gravelly voice low and comforting. "If Li'l Bill's still alive, he'll find you."

Ray thought about this. He did not understand why his father had not found him yet. But maybe there were reasons. Maybe there had not been enough time. Ray would have to trust that he would see him again.

Nel stood. "Well, we've got lots to do, lots to prepare. But not tonight. You need your rest."

The four consented and headed for their sleeping car.

"Good night," Si, Redfeather, and Marisol whispered as they went into their separate rooms.

The familiar hallway was cluttered with Nel's boxes. Ray stepped around them to reach Sally's room. Ray found Sally asleep next to Renny, with a book open on her stomach. Her lamp was still lit, swaying overhead with the movement of the train.

Ray gingerly took the book from Sally's hands. *The Incunabula of Wandering*.

With a smile, Ray closed the book and placed it on the top of a stack of Si's books by Sally's bedside. He bent back over Sally and kissed her cheek.

As he stood over her, he tried to imagine the new home, Shuckstack, where he and Sally and the others would soon live. They would learn to be Ramblers. They were learning to be Ramblers.

Ray turned out the lamp and gently closed Sally's door.

The Nine Pound Hammer grew out of a song. I'm a musician from the South, and you don't play music there for very long without hearing the song "John Henry." Nobody knows who wrote it, but versions have been performed for more than a century.

The song's hero, John Henry, is an ex-slave who works on the railroad, a "steel-drivin' man" who lays tracks and digs tunnels through the mountains. One day, a steam drill is brought in to replace the men digging the tunnels. In an attempt to save the men's jobs, John Henry challenges the steam drill to see who is faster: man or machine. With Li'l Bill, his shaker (the man who holds the drill bit for the steel driver to hit with his hammer), John Henry carves out more rock than the steam drill. But as everyone cheers, he collapses with his nine-pound hammer still in his hands. The mighty steel driver's huge heart bursts from the exertion. Whether or not John Henry really existed, he is a powerful symbol of our humanity: the self-sacrificing hero who fights the soulless machine until his heart bursts.

I was playing the song "John Henry" when the idea struck me to turn America's legends and myths into epic fantasy. Most fantasies focus on Europe's mythic golden age: medieval times, with castles and kings, and chivalrous knights fighting dragons. The Clockwork Dark trilogy takes place in the late nineteenth century, America's golden age of steam trains, cowboys, and medicine shows.

I started mining our country's folklore, in particular customs from the South such as hoodoo. Still practiced in some places and not to be confused with voodoo, hoodoo is a folk magic that blends African, Native American, and European lore. It often involves making a toby or mojo, which is a small red flannel pouch containing roots, herbs, lucky coins, rabbit paws, and other charms. Drive some Southern backroads today and you can still see bottletrees— another example of hoodoo lore—in people's yards, warding off evil spirits.

The *Ballyhoo*'s medicine show comes straight from American history. Traveling medicine shows, which were performed all across the country beginning in the nineteenth century, featured musicians and performers who sold bottles of supposed cure-alls. These "medicines" were usually little more than cheap alcohol and had none of the magic of Peg Leg Nel's concoctions. With the dawn of radio, television, and movies, medicine shows died out.

Fortunately, America's myths and legends live on in stories and in songs. And the adventures of Ray and Jolie and the heroes of the *Ballyoo* continue in the next book in the Clockwork Dark trilogy, *The Wolf Tree*.

John Claude Bemis

ACKNOWLEDGMENTS

My deepest gratitude goes out to my wife, Amy, whose un-wavering belief and support propelled me through this jour-ney. My daughter, Rose, was too young to help type but shared many walks in the woods with me. My parents, Bill and Claudia, have always encouraged me to pursue what I love. Enormous thanks go out to my critique group—Jennifer Harrod, Stephen Messer, and Jen Wichman—talented writers who helped shape this book in so many ways. For their insightful advice, I am happily indebted to David Andrews, Mike Bauldree, Greg Hanson, Noah Hoff-man, Karen Morse, and Jason Walker. Special thanks to Pe-ter Kramer and Susan Gladin for providing me with an in-spiring space to write on their farm. I've been fortunate to work with an extraordinary team: Josh and Tracey Adams of Adams Literary, who put their energy and skill behind the novel, and Jim Thomas, whose thoughtful and eagle-eyed editing brought out the real magic of *The Nine Pound Hammer*.

TURN THE PAGE TO FIND OUT
WHAT HAPPENS NEXT IN . . .

THE WOLF TREE

BOOK TWO OF THE CLOCKWORK DARK

From

THE WOLF TREE

Marisol's attention caught on something over Ray's shoulder. A man with a dark beard mounted the last step up to the porch. He shook the snow from his wide-brimmed hat.

"This Joe Nelson's place?"

Ray looked out in the dark and saw a horse tied up to a sapling in the yard. He had been so intent on his conversation with Marisol that he had not heard the horse's footsteps in the snow.

"Can we help you?" Ray asked.

"I sure hope so. Name's Herman Bradshaw. I come all the way from Kansas to find a Mister Joe Nelson. If he's the Rambler that Water Spider says, he's the only one who can help me."

Bradshaw broke into a fit of coughing such that he doubled over. Marisol went inside and soon Nel stepped out onto the porch after Buck and Si.

"Mister Bradshaw," Nel said, talking over the music and laughter flooding from the lodge. "Won't you come inside? You've traversed a fair distance, and we've got food and a warm fire."

Bradshaw twisted his hat in his hands and said, "I appreciate it, but I didn't come here to interrupt your party."

"We realize that it's not your intent, but you're here and it's late so why don't you come in?"

"Frankly, what I've got to speak of ain't fit for the joy of that room in yonder."

Nel turned to Si. "Will you get Mister Bradshaw a plate and some warm cider to drink? Bring it down to my room." Nel turned back to the man. "Let's go downstairs. There's a stove you can warm yourself by, and we can talk."

Nel led them down the stairs to an outside door to his room in the cellar. Ray followed with Buck and Marisol. Nel lit the stove and offered Bradshaw a chair. In the yellow glow of the room, Ray noticed how strangely discolored Bradshaw was. Ray had never seen anyone the unnatural shade of Mister Bradshaw. His white skin had an odd gray tint like paper turned to ash.

Nel asked, "Why have you come so far to find me, Mister Bradshaw?"

"If I were to tell it proper, it would take us all night, Mister Nelson. And I feel sore that I've taken you from your party, so I'll tell you as briefly as I can. I know you're friends with Water Spider of the Oklahoma Cherokee. I live up in Kansas, but he and I have become acquainted over the years. He says you're the only one who can help me."

"With what?"

"The Darkness." At these words, Bradshaw broke again into a terrible, hacking wet cough.

Something about the way he said the word drenched Ray in iciness.

Before Nel could continue, Si came down the stairs with the food and cider. Mister Bradshaw, released from the fit, wiped at his mouth and nodded his thanks to Si as he took the plate and mug. For a moment a curious expression passed over his brow as he seemed for the first time to notice the strange group of people all listening expectantly to his story.

Nel leaned forward from his stool. "What do you mean, the darkness?"

Mister Bradshaw set the plate on his lap, already forgotten as he collected his thoughts. "Where to begin? I come from Omphalosa, Kansas. Smack in the middle of the state. Came out there with my brothers when it was still just a territory. We made a good life for ourselves. Good, honest people there. Built a respectable town.

"I reckon we first noticed it around New Year, just over a year ago. With the passing of the winter solstice, days should have been lengthening. On the prairie, you count on the land and the weather for survival. You notice that kind of thing. Each day the sun set a little earlier, when it should have been later. And dawn just extended more and more into the morning."

Mister Bradshaw rubbed his clenched fist in his other hand as he continued, "By summer, we knew something was powerful wrong. The sun wouldn't rise until nearly eleven o'clock. Just pass in a low arc across the horizon and then drop again by two. By October, the Darkness set in for good."

Mister Bradshaw gauged the faces around him. Nel chewed on the end of his unlit pipe. Buck cocked his head. Ray, Marisol, and Si frowned.

"I suspect you take me for a fool or a madman, mayhaps. I ain't, but I've no way to assure you of that except through my words. Some from our town traveled out from time to time, visiting acquaintances, trading goods. They found the same. It weren't near the same complete darkness that had covered Omphalosa, but it settled in bit by bit. A darkness spreading over the towns of the prairies! You head out for a hundred miles any direction of Omphalosa and you'll see the growing dark.

"Can you imagine eternal Darkness, sir?" Mister Bradshaw asked, looking at Nel. "And cold. It's turned our flesh this fearsome shade. I had to leave. Fever took me after I left. No doctor can cure it. It's a slow, lingering killer. I'm afraid I've got it."

Nel's eyes widened with apprehension, and Mister Bradshaw waved a hand. "Don't worry, sir. It's not contagious. It comes from being in contact with the Darkness. Your people are safe.

"As I was saying, Omphalosa ain't the same town I helped settle years back. People are scared, powerful scared. Preacher says the Darkness and the discoloration to our skins are plagues. A curse laid upon us by God for our wickedness. We are good people, as good as you'll ever meet. But something about the Darkness, sir, it's turned us. Family against family. Brother on brother. Fingers pointing. Accusations swirling about what others done to bring the Darkness on us.

"My brother got shot 'cause some folks said his black dog was seen wandering around the churchyard by his house. A dog! What kind of foolishness is this, I ask?" He spread his hands with the question; then, shaking his head, dropped his arms to his knees.

"Superstitious idiots. I knew it had to be something else, but I weren't going to stick around to find it out."

"You said you knew Water Spider?" Nel asked.

Bradshaw sat up straighter. "Right. Water Spider. I met him trading horses. We hit it off, you could say. Like to play cards and such whenever I'm over his way. I rode out to consult him. The Darkness didn't reach as far as the Indian country, but he was already aware of it. Got an Indian boy with him said you raised."

"Redfeather." Nel nodded.

"The boy was about to come back here, he says, to tell you about it. I told them I had enough. I'm heading back with my people in Virginia, but I needed to find you and deliver the news. Redfeather says you can help."

Mister Bradshaw coughed deeply, finally seeming to remember the mug of cider cooling in his hand. He drained it in a long gulp.

"That's a strange story, Mister Bradshaw," Nel said. "I know you've come far out of your journey to relay it to us. But . . . I'm not sure what we can do for you—"

"You ain't doing it for me," Mister Bradshaw answered quickly, wiping his mouth with a handkerchief. "I'm finished with Omphalosa. I feel the effects of the Darkness. It pulls on me. I've got this terrible urge to return, and many days in my travels I had to force myself not to turn back west. It works on you. The Darkness draws until I feel like some reverse moth—not longing for the flame but for the dark beyond.

"I had to leave before . . . Going to start me a farm and hope the Darkness don't reach the East. But it's the people in Omphalosa. There's still good people there. It's them you'd be helping. They ain't all like the ones that shot my brother. And if somebody don't help them, there's to be a lot more burying before it's all done."

Nel turned to Buck, whose silver-streaked locks nearly hid his closed eyes.

"Sir," Ray began tentatively. "Were there any strangers in your town back when the Darkness started?"

"Strangers? There's workers for the mill, and I guess there's always the rare traveler passing through."

"Men wearing bowler hats?"

Mister Bradshaw snorted. "I don't keep track of the fashion of everyone who sets foot in Omphalosa."

"Ray," Nel said, frowning.

"You know what I'm asking, Nel," Ray said, his voice respectful and calm.

"There could be another explanation for all this," Nel said.

Then Buck said to Mister Bradshaw in his gravelly voice, "I think what young Ray is asking is, are there agents who ever work in Omphalosa?"

"Agents? Like Pinkerton detectives?" asked Mister Bradshaw.

Buck nodded.

"Well, there's a man who built a mill a decade or so back. That's why them foreign workers been coming in. He had a few detectives overseeing the construction to make sure there weren't no local trouble with the business being started."

Nel gripped his knees, glaring at Buck, but he refused to look at Ray.

"Come to think of it," Mister Bradshaw began, but broke into a wracking cough. "Those Pinkertons . . ." His coughing got louder and his face turned a darker gray.

"Those agents . . ," he tried again but could not get the words out.

"They . . . they . . ." Bradshaw slipped from his chair, but not before Ray caught him. Bradshaw's horrible cough grew deeper and wetter.

"Marisol!" Nel barked, getting to his feet and clapping his hand against Bradshaw's back. "Get that jug of water."

Marisol rushed to grab the crock and filled Bradshaw's mug. But Bradshaw could not drink the water, his coughing grew so fierce.

"The agents . . ." He choked again. Before he brought his handkerchief over his mouth, a splattering of blood hit Ray on the back of his hand. Bradshaw looked up at Ray and choked, "They . . . wore . . . bowlers."

Bradshaw's eyes rolled, and he passed out.

"Ray, Buck," Nel ordered. "Get him on that cot. Bring me damp rags."

Ray stared at the speckle of blood on his hand.

"Ray!" Nel barked.

Ray touched his finger to the blood.

"What is it?" Nel asked.

Ray looked at Nel in shock, dabbing his finger across the blood. He sniffed it and held his finger up. The smear was not red, but dark, inky black. "His blood . . . it's oil!"